Dopey Women
Laura Barnard

Published in 2015 by FeedARead.com Publishing

Copyright © Laura Barnard

First Edition

The author has asserted their moral right under the Copyright, Designs and Patents Act, 1988, to be identified as the author of this work.

All Rights reserved. No part of this publication may be reproduced, copied, stored in a retrieval system, or transmitted, in any form or by any means, without the prior written consent of the copyright holder, nor be otherwise circulated in any form of binding or cover other than that in which it is published and without a similar condition being imposed on the subsequent purchaser.

This book is a work of fiction. Names, characters, businesses, organizations, places and events other than those clearly in the public domain, are either the product of the author's imagination or are used fictitiously. Any resemblance to actual persons, living or dead, events or locales in entirely coincidental.

A CIP catalogue record for this title is available from the British Library.

This book is dedicated to my Step-Dad Mick. Taken too soon, I'll always remember you as the cute, hilarious, cheeky and full of life guy that you were. The world is missing my favourite Gemini.

Chapter 1

'Sadie,' my boss's PA calls to me. 'Reuben wants to see you.'

He wants to see me? Oh my God, this must be about the raise I asked for. That was only last week. I assumed with the way he'd shrugged me off that I had no chance of getting it. And I know it's more Reuben's style to ignore my requests. Maybe he's had a change of heart. I could be getting more money!

I nod, standing up and following her tight pencil-skirted arse into the office. She must do one hundred squats before bed every night. God, who could be bothered? She knocks on the door for me, her gold bracelets jingling.

'Enter,' Reuben calls from the inside.

I place my shaky hand on the gold doorknob and push forward the stiff, creaky door. Reuben is sitting back in his chair, his grey hair seeming wirier than usual. He doesn't even look slightly sorry to be putting me through this. The suspense is killing me! He must know I'm wondering what this is about.

Seated next to him is Pam, head of Human Resources. Why is *she* here? Surely she doesn't have to be present when talking about raises and promotions? She wasn't here when I got promoted to manager all those years ago. Okay, now I'm starting to get worried.

I force a smile as my shaky legs take me over to the chair.

'I'll cut right to the chase,' he says, frowning thoughtfully. He leans forward, his face no friendlier.

Wow. He's just gonna hit me with it. I remind myself to look gracious if it's a raise. To not shout *'yeah, motherfucker, yeah'* while punching the air. It might look common.

'I'm afraid your department, along with others, is to be made redundant with immediate effect.'

I stare back at him, motionless. My stomach feels like I've swallowed lead, so heavy it almost drops out of my knickers. Shit. This is absolutely *nothing* to do with a raise. My hopes of continuing to grow within the company now feel ridiculous and far-fetched. I was still clinging onto some absurd hope that this was a promotion. But redundant? They're *firing* me?

'That will be all,' he adds coldly, already looking at some other documents on his desk.

He's already dismissing me? I look helplessly over at Pam. She grimaces apologetically.

I feel sick. That's it? That's what I get for ten years with the company? Ten years of working my arse off? For working late with unpaid overtime, and worrying before I go to sleep at night. Why the hell have I cared so bloody much when I'm only just a number to them?

I stand on my jelly legs, eager to get out before the dam of emotions break. From the tightening of my chest it's pretty clear my body wants to erupt into angry tears, but I'll be damned if I let it. I don't want to show them my weakness. I won't give the bastards the satisfaction.

'Thanks,' I mutter as I leave.

Why the fuck am I thanking them? My damn politeness is taking over. I *have* to get out of here. The room feels like its closing in on me. More tears are filling my eyes, and I seem to be unable to control my shaking breath.

I walk into our open plan office. Will this be my last time here? I look around at the cold light blue walls and silver filing cabinets. I suddenly feel nostalgic, sad to never see them again.

I walk over to my desk, but don't sit down. I'm still reeling, my body is going into shock. What the hell am I going to do? This is the only job I've ever had. I don't have any real qualifications. I look up to see my team staring at me with intrigue.

Mags scrunches her dark brown eyes at me, for once looking like the sixty-two year old she is. 'Something wrong, dear?' she asks.

I stare back at her, unable to move any facial muscles. I should react. Try to tell her something. Reassure her. Or warn her that she's also out on her ear. He did say this was for the whole department.

'I…we're…' I take a deep breath trying to pull myself together. I owe it to them. 'We're being made redundant.'

Lexi and Steph's eyes widen at my words.

'Sorry?' Steph asks, her small voice quivering. She flicks her long strawberry blonde tousled waves behind her shoulder. 'Did you just say what I think?' Her eyes fill up with tears immediately.

Bless her heart; she's been a bit more emotional since returning from maternity leave. Her baby, Ruby, is only six months old, but apparently she needed the money. This has screwed that over for her.

'Yeah, what the fuck?' Lexi shouts. She's never been one to blend into the crowd. I'm always having to pick her up on her swearing, especially when she's trying to beat the fax machine to death. She's easily recognisable with her bright pink hair too, so her excuse of 'it must have been someone else' doesn't really fly.

Now that I've had a chance to think about it from their point of view, I'm angry. *Really* fucking angry. Call it the good manager in me, but I want to fight for them. Fight for *us.* All we've ever done is work fucking hard. We don't deserve this. I feel the rage boiling my blood until I'm sure steam is coming out of my ears.

With a pounding heart and adrenaline coursing through my veins, I walk towards Reuben's office, my fists balled by my sides. I just want to talk to him, maybe reason with him.

I push his door open and barge in, ready to fight for us. But I stop when I find Pam from HR on the desk with Reuben on top of her. Her blouse is off, exposing a shockingly awful greying bra, and they're snogging passionately.

What the *actual* fuck?

I freeze, my mouth dropping open in horror. Here I am wondering what the fuck I'm going to do with my life now, what my team is going to do, and these two are trying to screw each other's brains out.

'Nice to see you're still so worried about my future,' I snarl, outrage clear in my tone.

Reuben straightens up, frowning. 'Sadie, I thought you'd have left by now,' he says, clearly inconvenienced. He obviously thought he was about to get his dick wet.

I can't help it. I feel the surge of red hot hatred rise within me. I grab his stapler and stamp down his tie to the desk. They both look up at me, eyes wide in surprised horror. But I'm not finished. Oh no, sir. I've flipped the crazy switch and there's no going back. My shaky hands grab a picture of him and his family on a yacht from the wall and throw it at them. It narrowly misses their heads, the glass smashing against the wall.

'Sadie!' he yells. 'Have you lost your fucking mind?'

'Maybe I have!' I scream, grabbing his potted plant and throwing it out of the open window. I hear someone yelp from below. Whoops. I didn't mean to kill anyone.

'You selfish bastard!' I shriek. 'Too busy trying to fuck her than giving me and my team a second thought. If I'd been sleeping with you would things have been different? Huh?' I demand, my eyes wide and crazed.

They both look back, clearly terrified.

'ANSWER ME!'

Arms are suddenly around my waist. I look up to see Steph trying to pull me out. Mags gets a hold of my hand, interlinking her fingers with mine. I look down at the sweet gesture, the simple act of solidarity, and burst into tears. Lexi stands in front of me.

'Fuck you guys!' she snarls. 'We are *SO* out of here.'

I'm turned and led out of their office and back to my desk. I ignore the curious faces of everyone else. They're clearly in shock that the sensible bird, Sadie, has lost it.

'Let's get our things,' Mags says to all of us, trying to smile reassuringly. 'Before security arrives.'

They scuttle off to their desks like scared little ants. I look down at mine through the blur of my tears and try to think of what's mine. A box of tissues, a stapler and a picture of me and Samuel. That's it? That's the only personal bits I have after ten years? How pathetic.

It doesn't matter. I just need to get out of here. Go home and drown under a sea of snotty tissues and watch Flash Dance. That'll perk me up. I mean, they weren't even allowed to *dance*. At least I can still enjoy dancing. Unless I get so poor I end up dancing for money at a seedy club. I shudder at the thought.

I pick up my things, smiling shyly at the girls who also seem ready and then head towards the exit.

I'm almost at the door when I see Fat Farah getting up from her desk. She's gotten on my tits from the day I started here when she reminded me that I wasn't to steal any of the stationary. Whatever bitch, I took one envelope. There was really no need to start such a fuss.

I have no choice but to pass her, but I *really* wish I didn't have to. I look down even though I can feel her smirking and pretending to be concerned.

'Oh, Sadie?' she calls. I stop dead in my tracks and swivel to face her. Better to get her snide comment over and done with. I force a smile. '*Really* sorry to do this,' she says, though she doesn't sound sorry at all, 'but I don't think that's your stapler.'

I look down at the stapler in my hand, totally confused. Is she seriously asking me to leave behind this stapler? This stapler has been with me since I started here as an office junior. If it's *anybody's* its mine. I look back at her fake apologetic face and feel it happening again. I'm turning into the hulk. Have I been exposed to some extreme radiation that I'm not aware of?

My hands start to shake uncontrollably as blind rage fills my entire being. I drop the tissues and picture to the floor and open up the stapler so that I'm holding it like a gun.

'You want *this* stapler?' I ask cutely. 'Come and get it, *bitch*.'

I start walking towards her, firing staples out as if I am firing a gun. I wish. They shoot all over the office. Nowhere near her, but it's enough to scare her a little bit. That's all I want to do. Scare the shit out of her. I stop when my face is so close to hers I can smell her disgusting coffee breath. Has she not heard of mints?

'You want it,' I snarl, 'come and get it.'

She smiles at me, faking sympathy. 'Don't worry. If it really means that much to you, you can keep it.'

Well, now I feel pathetic. How does she do that? Who the fuck is *she* to dictate what I can and can't take?

Before I have time to reason with myself, my hands are out and I shove her backwards. She stumbles, complete shock apparent on her face. I'm shocked too. Who knew I was even that strong? It doesn't stop me from revelling in her fear though. Adrenaline is rushing so fast through my veins that I'm pretty sure I want a fight. I could take her. What's she going to do? Sit on me?

'There's no need for mindless violence,' she chastises, making me feel even more petty.

She turns to walk away, and it's as if something bursts inside of me. Every pent up emotion I've ever repressed in this place comes firing up, spilling out, and wanting to hurt someone.

I lunge for her back, the sheer force of my rage knocking her to the floor. I start pulling her frizzy hair and screaming obscenities at her. I'm not even sure what I'm saying at this point. All I can do is feel and let my body take out its fury on this little bitch.

She rolls over to face me; her fat podgy cheeks flushed and scrunched up in fear. I slap her round the face mindlessly with both hands, so mindlessly that they're not even strong slaps. It's more like pathetic little bitch slaps. It still does the job. She shields her hands in front of her face, shrieking for help.

I feel the same hands as before around my waist as I'm pulled back. Steph sure is strong for someone with such tiny hands.

'Just leave her,' Steph shouts.

'Yeah, she's not worth it,' Lexi adds, walking in front of me and spitting on her.

I look back at her in absolute horror. Did she really just *spit* on her? It's enough to break me free from the rage. I mean, I might have attacked her, but spitting's a bit much, right?

I turn around to see the old man security guard, Ronnie, waiting for me. He's got soil in his hair. Ah, so he's who I dropped the plant on. Whoops.

'Time to go, love,' he tries to reason, looking pretty worried that I'm going to fight him. God knows I could take him with his dodgy heart and all. Poor bloke.

As I'm led outside, I start to calm down substantially. In hindsight, stapling Reuben's tie to his desk and throwing the potted plant out of the window was slight overkill. And maybe Fat Farah didn't deserve that. Except she totally did. I still think Ronnie dragging me out of here is dramatic. Especially as everyone is staring at me. They must think I'm having a nervous breakdown. Maybe I am.

What the fuck am I going to do with no job? It's not like getting a reference will be easy now. Why am I so stupid? And what about the women in my department? I look at them following me. They must be crushed too. If I wasn't so dramatic I could stay to console them, but I'm too upset and selfish. What a bad manager I am. No wonder they got rid of me.

No. I shake myself. Buck your ideas up, Sadie. You can do this. You just have to update your CV, sign up with all of the agencies and apply for everything. You can do this. You've got yourself out of bigger holes than this before.

Chapter 2

Two months later - Friday 7th August

As I queue up in the job centre two months later, my resolve is slightly weaker. My redundancy pay has dwindled considerably, almost down to zero. It didn't help that my car broke down and I needed it fixed. And that I bought that dress from that shop in a moment of depressed despair. When the hell am I going to wear something that fancy again? Probably never.

The first few times I came here to sign on I was still positive. I wore my lucky navy pencil skirt with my white blouse and approached it like a job interview. Now I'm wearing jeans. That's right, jeans! I *never* wear jeans. I always pride myself on looking tailored and put together. I *live* to recreate Paris chic. But even though I have on a smart tailored coat, suede flats and a loose white shirt, I still miss the days where I could wear heels and dresses. Is it shallow that it was my favourite reason for working?

My self-respect has hit such an all-time low that I want to look as bad as I feel. Worthless. I've not even bothered with any makeup today. I almost put on tracksuit bottoms this morning. *Tracksuit bottoms.* Yet as I look around all I see are tracksuit bottoms. Some are even still in their pyjama bottoms. Apparently getting dressed was too much effort for them. They'll still probably get a job before me. With Reuben refusing to give me a reference it's pretty impossible to even get an interview.

'Sadie?'

I feel my shoulders clench and raise, curling up like a snake. Shit. Who the hell is going to notice me here? Why oh why did I ever think it okay to not wear makeup? This is my own damn fault.

'Sadie?' the voice comes again. Shit. I know that soft voice. It's Mags.

I turn round to face her warm brown eyes behind her spectacles. She's forcing an enthusiastic smile from her thin lips. Her shoulder length brown hair is still as neat as ever, although her wispy fringe always looks a mess. She's still looking as perfect as ever, wearing pearl earrings and a necklace with a twin set. Yet she seems down, her shoulders slumped as if she's defeated. Of course she is. She's jobless because of me.

'Hi, Mags, how are you?' I ask, genuinely interested.

Her chin begins to tremble. Shit, I didn't mean to make her cry. I look around, desperate for her not to cause a scene. Not that any of these pyjama wearing layabouts would give a shit. I spot pink hair sticking out in a place like this. I know immediately its Lexi. The normal clientele seem to favour bleach blonde. She's got her hands in her leather jacket pockets and is looking around, her eyes covered by her ray bans, seeming completely uninterested.

'Lexi!' I call out. It's the perfect kind of distraction away from Mags' sad eyes. She visibly shrinks and tries to pretend she hasn't seen me. 'I've seen you, Lexi! Get your arse over here.' Sometimes I can't stop being a manager.

She skulks over like a moody teenager, which I suppose she is. She's only just turned nineteen, but she's got the sass of a much older lady. I can't see her eyes behind the dark ray bans, but I just know that she's rolling them at me.

'Hey,' she grunts, seeming no friendlier. She looks closer at Mags. I imagine her eyes narrowing in concern. 'You okay, Mags? You look like you're about to lose it.'

I shoot her a warning look. She has *zero* tact. How on earth did I ever think she could help me with her?

Mags looks down at the floor, twiddling her pearls between her fingers.

'Bill died,' she says on a whisper.

My stomach hits the floor. Crap, I wasn't expecting that. I just assumed she was down about having no job. Not her husband of forty years dropping down dead.

'Shit,' Lexi gasps. I shoot her another evil eye.

'I'm so sorry, Mags.' I touch her arm and realise she seems skinnier than normal. Before she had a well-rounded figure, but now she's almost gaunt in the face, her cheekbones protruding.

Her eyes water over. 'Sudden heart attack. Went just a week after we left work.'

Jesus, how can life be so cruel? There I am so wrapped up in my own tragic life that I've forgotten to think of anyone else. I'm whinging about wearing jeans and Mags has lost her husband forever.

'Why don't we go for a coffee or something?' I suggest. Not that I have any bloody money, but I've got my credit card. It's already been bounced around. I might as well add some more to it. It's the least I can do.

'There's a Costa across the street,' she smiles, taking a tissue from her bag and dabbing at her eyes.

'Make mine a mocha latte and I'm in,' Lexi grins. It's probably the most enthusiastic I've seen her. Ever.

We're interrupted by someone screeching across the room. God, these damn chavs are always causing drama. My second week here I had to break up a fight between two women because one allegedly *'looked at her baby funny.'*

'But I have a BABY!' they scream. 'Don't you understand that I can't afford to feed her? My breast milk is drying up because I can't afford to eat!'

We look at each other and roll our eyes. It's so typical of this place. I follow the voice, intrigued to see who's causing such a ruckus. This place is like my own soap opera. It's probably the highlight of my week which is tragic. I see a job centre staff member trying to calm a lady down.

'God, the people here!' I whisper. 'They're actually scary.'

They both nod and look back over at the screeching woman. It's only when the staff member moves out of the way that I see a long mane of strawberry blonde hair. She turns, a baby in her sling crying hysterically. It's Steph from work.

Bloody hell. I've never seen her raise her voice, let alone shout at anybody.

She seems to realise everyone is staring at her, her cheeks burning red. She drops her head to the floor, walking towards the door, while trying and failing to calm down baby Ruby, who's red in the face from screaming.

'Steph!' I shout out. The poor girl. My heart twists for her.

She looks up and spots us. Her face is a mix between pleased to see us and mortified that we witnessed her shouting fit.

'Hi!' she says, trying to fake brightness in her voice. In reality it sounds small and wobbly. 'What are you guys doing here?'

'The same as you,' Lexi snaps, leaning on one hip. *'Obviously.'* God, she can be cruel.

She's never really cared for Steph. She's always found her too weak, which I know Lexi, being the hard ass bitch she is, hates in a woman.

Her face falls in a flash of embarrassment. I have to save her from it.

'We were actually just going for a coffee. Fancy it?' I say loudly over Ruby's cries.

'Erm.' She shuffles on her feet, trying to rock Ruby into a better mood. 'I'm not sure if I can afford it to be honest.'

'My treat,' I smile, holding up my credit card.

###

We must look like a right bunch of saddos as we settle down with our coffees, our faces glum and our bodies sagged.

'So what was all that about back there?' I ask Steph when Ruby's in the calm arms of Mags and she's got a bit more colour in her cheeks.

Her emerald green eyes sadden again. I've never seen her so low. She's normally always so chipper.

'It's a long story,' she sighs, looking down at the floor.

Lexi laughs cruelly. 'I don't know if you've noticed, but none of us have any jobs to run off to.'

I shoot her a warning look. She's still got her sunglasses on so we can't even see if she's joking. I hate that. I always feel like you can see so much of a person's soul through their eyes.

She sighs, looking down at her tea, obviously resigned to telling us. 'Dorian left me. Done a runner.'

'What?' Mags gasps in horror.

Dorian is Steph's Greek boyfriend. She met him while on holiday in Crete. The typical story of him being her waiter, her being drunk on screwdrivers, and them shagging each other shitless on the beach every night. I've never understood the whole fascination with sex on the beach. I did it once and it was bloody awful. Sand up your butt crack, vagina, and somehow in your mouth. You're both supposed to be really turned on by it, but you know both of you would much rather go to your hotel room, yet you still go through the motions while trying to have fun.

Anyway, after declaring their love to each other before she left and skyping non-stop for three months, he came over to live with her. She got pregnant by 'surprise'. I say 'surprise' because I have my suspicions that she planned it deliberately. She'd always said she wanted a baby by the time she was thirty, and she was twenty nine when she announced she was pregnant. She was always worrying about her biological clock ticking. Some women in her family have been plagued by fertility issues, so you can kind of understand.

Apparently Dorian was all for it though. He promised to look after them both and seemed like an alright bloke at the Christmas do. Well, apart from taking off his shirt when breaking out his moves to Grease Lightening. We all did things that night we're not proud of. I wish I hadn't danced on the table and fell off, breaking my ankle. But we live and learn. Now the prick's done a runner.

'Ran,' she sniffs. 'Left a pathetic note saying he can't handle it. I literally have no idea where he is. I've rung his family in Greece, but they claim they don't know. So child support is trying to track him down to get some payments sorted. Until then, I'm screwed.'

'Can't you claim everything?' I ask. 'I mean, I can't turn on the news without seeing everyone claiming thousands in things the minute they pump out kids?'

'No,' she sniffs again. 'Because the flat is mortgaged they can't help me. If it was rented I'd get it paid. It's so unfair.'

'So sell it,' Lexi offers, inspecting her nails as if it's more interesting. Would it *kill her* to show some compassion for once?

'I can't,' she says breaking into a light sob. 'I'd only get thirty grand profit, if I'm lucky. I won't be able to get a mortgage again with no job, but I'll have too much money in the bank for the council to house me. I'm fucked.'

I balk. Steph never swears. This is bad. We all sit in an awkward silence, not sure what to say next. I mean, what do you say to that?

'I've got breast cancer,' Mags blurts out, scaring the bejesus out of me.

We all swing our heads around to face her; our mouths drop open in complete surprise. Is it not enough that her husband died? Now she has cancer?

'What?' I gasp, hitting her on the shoulder in annoyance. This is how we find out? She holds herself as if I've damaged her. Whoops. I probably shouldn't hit the lady with cancer.

'Yeah, what the fuck, Mags?' Lexi asks aggressively. 'Warn a bitch. I almost spat my hot coffee on my legs.'

Is that all she cares about?

She nods slowly. 'Yes, unfortunately. I got diagnosed soon after Bill died. Just had my first round of chemo.'

Shit the bed. And I thought I had problems. I'm starting to think I'm a self-indulging twat.

'Well, now I feel terrible,' Steph snorts. 'Whining on about my love life when you have a deadly disease.'

I cringe at the word deadly. She's having chemo. There must be hope for her. I look at Lexi, still in her aviator glasses. What the hell is she playing at?

'For fucks sakes, Alexis, take off the shades! We're inside and the girls are pouring their hearts out here,' I snap, some spit leaving my mouth in my moment of rage. I hope no one notices.

Everyone looks at her expectantly. Why the hell does she think she's such a princess? It's *beyond* irritating. She looks back at me in tense silence for a long time. I'm sure she's glaring at me from behind her shades.

'Fine,' she eventually snaps, begrudgingly taking them off.

Once thrown onto the table, I see that her hazel eyes are tired and one is clouded with purple and yellow bruising. What the hell? She's got a black eye? Where the hell did this come from? Has she been scrapping at some bar or something?

'What on earth happened?' Mags asks, jumping up and grabbing her face for a closer inspection. It squashes her cheeks out so she looks like an adorable baby. I bet she was. The idea of her in a pink frilly dress makes me smile. It's a world away from her black ripped jeans and Doc Martin boots.

'It's no big deal,' she shrugs, pushing her away. 'I fell.'

'What, onto your *face*?' Steph shrieks sarcastically. 'Who on earth did this to you?'

'Your boyfriend,' I state rather than ask.

I know it too well. See, the thing that the girls don't know is that I spent some time living on the streets when I was younger. It's kind of a long story. Anyway, I've met too many women like her from my years of seeing girls come and go. These women are forced to run away from a guy beating them, but are still too ashamed to admit it as the truth. I saw it far too often.

'It was an accident,' she spits out through gritted teeth.

Now it's my turn to roll my eyes.

'Why don't you just leave him?' Steph asks, clearly agreeing with my version of events.

'It's not as easy as that,' she snorts, putting her drained cup down.

'Oh, sweetheart,' Mags sympathises. 'Has he ruined your self-esteem?'

It's hard to imagine anyone being able to do that. Hell, anyone laying a hand on her is unimaginable. Most women in the office were terrified of her. I can't tell you the amount of complaints I had to deal with.

Alexis told me she'd rip my balls off if I looked at her again.

Alexis told me I smelt like a baby prostitute.

Alexis told me she'd kick me in the face if I ate her baby bell by mistake again.

'No, nothing like that,' she sighs. 'I asked for it. I was winding him up and I punched him right back. We're both just as bad as the other.'

I can imagine her being in a volatile relationship like that, but it doesn't make it any better. For any man to lay a hand on a woman is appalling. Don't get me wrong, I agree she shouldn't have hit him too, but I saw him at the Christmas do. He's six foot three with strapping broad shoulders. Far bigger than her. It would have been an unfair fight.

'That has nothing to do with it,' I say to her seriously. 'The fact is he laid a hand on you. He'll do it again. You have to move out.'

'And go where?' she snaps. 'I have no money and no job. And I'd rather die than go back to live with my parents.'

'You might just get your wish!' I retort back at her.

'Anyway,' Mags says, clapping her hands together. 'Let's change the subject.'

I fold my arms over my chest and lean back, still glaring at Lexi as my heart pumps violently in my chest. She's too stubborn for her own good. She's going to get herself murdered, and her ghost will be hanging around to say it was no big deal and she brought it on herself.

'Um…' Mags starts, obviously searching for something to say. 'I've been thinking about trying marijuana.'

We all stop glaring at each other and turn to her, completely astonished.

'Mags! What the hell are you talking about?' I ask, checking that no one around us heard her.

'For the chemo, you know,' she says, turning bright red. 'A woman was telling us she gets it from her grandson, and it really helps with the nausea and vomiting.'

'Really?' Steph asks, taking Ruby from her as she starts to get fussy.

'Yes, but I wouldn't know where to get it from.' She shrugs. 'A lot of the other women feel the same. We don't want to be mixing with drug dealers, and I'm too embarrassed to ask anyone to get it for me. So I guess I'll never know.'

'That's a missed market right there,' Lexi laughs.

She's right. Those poor women, too embarrassed to ask someone to get it for them. It gets me thinking. It really *is* a missed market. I wonder how many other cancer patients are out there, curious to see if weed could help them. But they're too scared dealing with big beefy men that they'd meet in a pub car park. What if they had some normal women to buy off of that they could trust? Surely it would be safer for everyone?

'You might actually be onto something, Lexi.'

'Huh?' Steph asks, looking at me as if I'm mad. She stands to rock Ruby around, her whines only getting louder.

'What if there was a group of friendly women they could buy from? I bet they'd clean up,' I grin, seeing pound signs.

I can almost imagine my credit card being paid off.

Lexi and Mags clock on straight away. Lexi smiles devilishly, while Mags frowns.

'Do you think we could?' Mags asks, pushing her glasses back up her nose as she always does when she's nervous.

'I think we could,' I smile, nodding confidently.

'What on earth are you guys talking about?' Steph asks, her face scrunches up in confusion.

My poor, little, naïve Steph.

'I think,' Lexi grins, leaning forward so that no one can hear her, 'that we just agreed to be drug dealers.'

Chapter 3

<u>Monday 10th August</u>

So on Monday morning we find ourselves in a seedy sex shop in Soho. According to a forum I found on the internet, they sell marijuana seeds here. Apparently it's completely legal to buy them, thanks to some loophole in the law. There were some available online, but I felt better getting them from a shop.

We agreed to stick together once inside, but as soon as we come in out of the rain everyone dissipates in different directions. Thanks guys! I go to shout after them, but I have to try and remember that I'm not their manager anymore. I can't boss them around and force them to listen to me.

The guy behind the counter with an emo hanging fringe covering an entire eye glances up at me suspiciously. I suppose I don't look like the normal kind of clientele with my cream trench coat over my black cigarette trousers. But then again, this *is* a sex shop. Surely everyone can be into sex. They don't have to look or act a certain way. I can't open a newspaper without reading about some posh society totty having a drug fuelled orgy.

I push my shoulders back and decide to brash it out. I raise my eyebrows at him in question. He quickly loses his nerve and glances back down to his graphic novel. Oooh, I wonder what he's reading. I *love* graphic novels.

I look around the dark dingy shop that smells of soil, wondering if marijuana seeds are something that will just be lying around to purchase or something you'll have to ask for. The girls are too busy looking at everything else. Lexi is flicking through a tantric sex book, looking completely unimpressed. Typical. Steph is in the dildo section laughing at the size of them, while Mags looks like she may seriously consider purchasing a PVC corset, sizing it up against her chest.

I decide to just ask. I mean, why should I even be embarrassed? Look where we are. I take a discreet deep breath and walk back over to Emo boy.

'Hey,' I smile, leaning against the glass counter. I place my hands awkwardly on top of each other and pretend to be looking at the ball gags in the cabinet.

'Can I help you?' he grunts, flicking his fringe from his eyes only for it to fall back over one eye immediately.

'Yes. Um…I'm…' My voice is high pitched and wobbly. Don't lose your nerve now, Sadie. I swallow down the lump in my throat and pray that my tongue will stop shaking. 'I'm looking for seeds.' I clear my throat, trying to authorise my authority. 'Marijuana seeds to be specific.'

He stares back at me for a long while, obviously considering if I'm serious. It's torture.

'We don't sell them here, I'm afraid,' he says, completely unapologetic. He goes back to his graphic novel as if I'm dismissed.

I crease my forehead in badly concealed confusion. I'm sure the website said they did. It was just a forum, but still. They're normally pretty spot on.

'Really? Because a good source told me I can get them from here,' I press, getting annoyed with his bad customer service skills. How can this guy have a job and not me?

'Look, lady,' he snaps, 'I know you're a copper. We don't sell them anymore. I'm sick of you guys bothering us. You're not getting me.'

'Huh?' I blurt. He thinks I'm a policewoman?

'You think I'm a police lady?' I ask in disbelief. 'How dare you! Have you even seen my shoes?' I throw my leg up onto the counter, years of adult ballet working in my favour. I present my black patent stilettos with a red strap. 'Do these *look* like the ugly shoes of a policewoman?' I ask, my voice rising higher than it should. Damn it, he's offended my shoes. He might as well have called me fat.

'Well…no,' he admits, his eyes wide and darting from side to side, alarmed by my outburst.

'Do these look like the kind of shoes that could run after a robber? I don't think so,' I answer for him. 'And would a boring copper know that you're reading Fox Head Return of the Rabbit?'

His one eye that isn't concealed by the fringe creases in bemusement. 'You know the Fox Head series?'

'Of course I do.' I nod arrogantly, flicking my hair behind me.

I don't tell him it's because it was the only decent thing to read when I was in a foster home. Back then it wasn't as cool or 'vintage' as it is now. It was just a comic.

'Look, I'm sorry,' he says sheepishly. 'I just thought you were a bit well dressed to be in here.'

'I *am* well dressed.' I nod proudly. 'Thank you. Now I'd like you to give me my seeds.'

He starts moving things from underneath the desk, obviously searching for these forbidden seeds. I feel a thrill of excitement go through me at the thought of it. I'm like a bond agent. What would I call myself? Pussy Galore's taken. Maybe Gorgeous Chick. No, that doesn't sound like a name. Maybe Gigi Paris. Yeah, I like that.

'We've had a copper trying to get information on who we sell to lately. It's just not worth the hassle,' he explains.

I nod and glance to my right. I freeze with what confronts me. The girls are all together. Lexi has a strap-on attached to her and has Steph bent over, pretending to shove her giant purple dildo up Steph's arse, while Steph twirls nipple tassels dramatically, having them tickle Ruby's head and making her sneeze. Lexi starts shaking her plastic penis all over the place, screaming, 'Uh! I'm gonna come! I'm gonna come!' Dear God.

Mags is the only one appearing normal. At least I can count on her. Oh wait, her face is acting strange. Is she having a stroke? It's only then that I see she has some device on her nipples and she's clearly having an orgasm. Right here in the shop.

Emo boy lifts his head, presenting a packet of seeds onto the counter. I try to look at him and ignore them, but he follows my gaze, his eyes landing on the women I call my friends.

'You're not supposed to try out the nipple teasers,' he says crossly, storming over to Mags.

The others stop immediately, but Mags can't seem to hear him. Her face is contorting, her lip is trembling. Dear God, Mags!

'I said,' emo boy shouts louder, now in her face, 'that you can't test these out.' He reaches out to unclip one.

'No!' she screams, pushing him away, completely out of breath. 'Please! Let me…please…' she pants, her cheeks red and flushed.

Oh my God. This is *so* humiliating.

'Just let her finish, dude,' Lexi snaps. 'Can't you see when a woman hasn't had some in a while?'

'Not my problem,' he snaps, completely revolted and reaching for one again.

'Hey,' Lexi growls, grabbing his arm. 'You reach for her tit one more time, and I'm telling you, I'll call the police.'

'Oh my God!' Mags screams, her face and neck getting more red and blotchy by the second.

'Call the police!' he shouts back defiantly, crossing his arms across his chest. 'I dare you.'

An ear piercing screech fills the room. I cover my ears and turn to see where it's coming from. It's from Mags. She's orgasmed. She falls to the floor, squirming all over the blue grubby carpet like a caterpillar having a seizure. Shit, maybe she *is* having a seizure.

Steph looks back at me alarmed, raising her eyebrows as if to ask what the hell we should do. Lexi is too busy shooting evils at emo boy.

I rush over to her, releasing the nipple clamp and taking her in my arms like a baby. She's white as a ghost now, her whole body trembling in shock. Jesus, should I call an ambulance? I feel her pulse and notice it's racing wildly.

'Ssh,' I try to be soothing while rocking her gently. 'It's okay, Mags, it's just an orgasm. It's done now. Come back to us.'

Slowly her body begins to still and her laboured breathing returns back to normal. She seems to enter her body again, her eyes searching around as if she's just blacked out. Jesus, maybe I should buy these.

'It's okay,' I smile reassuringly. 'Give me a hand,' I call to the others, trying to get her up to standing. Steph comes over to help, but not Lexi. I look around for her. She's probably stronger than both of us.

I find her snogging the face off emo boy against the counter. Their hands are in each other's hair, as if they haven't eaten for months. It's gross. How the hell did that even happen? She was ready to kill him a moment ago. Plus she's supposed to have a boyfriend, even if he does sound like the son of Satan. I shake my head. She never fails to shock me.

'Get off him,' Steph yells, pulling Lexi off him by her hair. Lexi spins round and glares at her.

'Always ruining my fun,' she mutters under her breath, flicking her pink hair back.

Emo boy is out of breath, while Lexi doesn't even seem to be affected.

We help Mags up and walk sheepishly back to the counter. Emo boy looks at us with a mix of amusement and annoyance.

'So…just the seeds please,' I nod, desperate to maintain *some* self-respect.

'And these,' Mags says, throwing down the nipple clamps. 'Definitely these,' she pants, still out of breath.

After an afternoon full of buying all of our supplies from the local hardware shop, planting the seeds and getting everything set up in my loft, I'm shattered. Thank God for YouTube tutorials.

But when Samuel comes home from a shit day at work, I have to try and pretend that I haven't been up to trouble all day. So when he suggests a gay bar I can't say no. Luckily it's the only place I can tolerate right now. No disgusting men hitting on me. Just topless ones dancing to Madonna. He offers to pay my way as I only really need two glasses of red wine to be shit-faced anyway.

We start off in a cool, relaxed black and gold bar, but quickly I'm drunk and begging him to take me somewhere *really* camp. It's always my mission to see as many different gay bars as possible when I'm out with him. They make me feel safe, free and exhilarated all at the same time.

He leads me into another bar which looks completely normal and boring. It doesn't even look as good as the black and gold one.

'So…did you not hear my brief?' I ask him, confused. I take in the very cosy looking red leather booths. This looks more like the place for sophisticated conversation. I want wine and gay boys.

He grins devilishly, his eyes lighting up with mischief. 'Downstairs.'

A thrill of excitement runs through me. I know he won't let me down. I follow him down a set of stairs at the back and into a basement room. Wow.

Its ceiling is filled with disco balls, sending shimmering flickers of disco lights around the room. There's a drag queen cabaret act on a small stage in the corner, pulling people up on stage and screaming that she's found a pretty lesbian. Now *this* meets my brief.

He smiles, clearly proud at my reaction, before thrusting a tenner in my hand.

'You go get the drinks. I'm going to get us a seat.'

He's gone in an instant, waving towards a guy wearing no shirt.

That's the only thing about Samuel. He *will* dump me on a night out so he can go home with a guy.

I stand at the bar, twirling my locket in my hand. It's the first piece of jewellery I ever bought myself and that means a lot. It was my way of celebrating being fully independent. After sitting on the pavement and just dreaming of a hot meal, the idea of jewellery was a luxury beyond belief.

When I got my first pay cheque I made sure to keep back a little to treat myself. Because of that it's only a cheap silver little thing. Everyone keeps telling me I should upgrade it, but it means too much to me. On one side is a picture of me and Samuel from all those years ago. On the other is an up to date one. It always reminds me of how far we've come. I just hope this weed grows quickly and we don't end up back like that.

I shift from foot to foot, trying to attract the attention of the bartender. At least here I know it's not my lack of boobs that's not getting me served. It's my lack of penis.

Something cold and wet splashes onto my shoulders, tickling its way down my back. I turn around to see a giant of a man having spilt his tray of multi-coloured shots over me. *Great.*

'What the hell, arsehole?' I shriek, grabbing a napkin from the bar and trying to dry myself off. It's sticky and it's in my hair. Gross.

'Oh my God. I am *so* sorry,' he says, his blue eyes sincere. They're probably the bluest eyes I've ever seen, even in this dark club. I smile despite myself. The gays are so nice, even when they're chucking drinks at you. It's hard to stay mad at them.

'It's okay,' I sigh, quickly realising I'm just going to have to feel sticky and icky all night.

'Are you sure? I feel terrible,' the silky voice says again, concern etched onto his beautiful features.

I look up into the gorgeous strangers face, deciding I'll treat myself with a lazy look over him. He's got jet black hair and warm golden skin. His perfect pout is surrounded by the slightest of beards. Yum. Shame he's gay. Looking around it seems all the good ones are. Before I met Samuel I just kind of assumed they all acted like Alan Carr. I've come to realise with most there's no way of knowing. If we were anywhere else I'd be fluttering my eyelashes and making a fool of myself.

'Yeah, honestly,' I nod, smiling reassuringly. Well, I think I am. I'm so in awe of his good looks I could just be dribbling right now.

'Well, sorry again.' He smiles shyly before walking off.

My eyes follow him. Wow, what a tight arse he's got. I'd pay money to bite it. Whoa. I need to get some.

I give myself a minute to compose myself. Sex on legs or what! My lady bits are tingling with excitement. *Calm down, lady, he doesn't play for our team.* In my next life I'm coming back as a gay man.

I re-join the queue and finally get served. When I make my way back to Samuel I find the sexy drink spiller in the crowd and point him out.

'He *is* fit,' he grins, shamelessly checking him out from head to toe. 'Haven't seen him around here before though. He must be new.' He sips his piña colada, the pineapple wedge poking him in the eye.

'New?'

He rolls his eyes at my innocence. 'As in just came out.'

He always says he finds my naivety into the gay life annoying, but I know he secretly loves explaining it all to me.

Such a waste of good talent.

'Or...this is just the first time he's come to this bar?' I offer reasonably. I look back and watch him closely. He's laughing at some joke a guy in his crowd told. He really is a beautiful specimen.

'Nah. I know the circuit. Everyone in here knows of each other. He's not part of the Soho gays, darling,' he jokes.

'You really are ridiculous,' I snort, taking a large glug of my red wine.

I suddenly have an overwhelming urge to rush home so I can dream filthy things about him. This is even worse than that time I saw Lee Ryan from Blue.

'Just count your lucky stars I'm a loyal friend, or I'd be over there offering myself to him naked on a plate with a rose in my teeth and a pineapple up my arse.'

'Samuel!' I shriek, collapsing over laughing.

At least if everything else goes tits up I can always count on Samuel. Even if he does ditch me for guys, he's always back and there for me when I need it. I dread to think what might have happened to me if I hadn't found him. I could be dead now, although I'd like to think I would have been strong enough to survive on my own.

If he finds out what we're doing I have no doubt he'd kick my arse. He's as vehemently against drugs as am I, normally. Plus he works for a high profile chef who has a real wholesome family image. Any bad press would probably get him fired, if not at least disciplined.

He shakes my shoulders. 'You should loosen up, Sades. Let your hair down a bit.'

Oh, if only he knew how loose on my morals I've become...

Chapter 4

<u>Monday 7th September</u>
Four weeks later and all of us are *still* unemployed. I have to admit that I was holding out some hope that while we were waiting for it to grow I'd be snapped up. I must have applied for well over two hundred jobs and I've heard nothing back. Nothing. Not a single email reply with 'thanks for applying, but…' No, they don't even have the decency for that. Especially after completing the five page application forms that they all seem to want. *Even* when I'm asking to be employed as a supermarket clerk. I mean, how much information do you need to ring up grapes through that beeper thing? It looks easy. I now realise those women are more employable than me.

But I suppose they're just not that desperate for an admin manager who went bat shit crazy and attacked everyone at her last place of work. All of this not hearing back is getting me depressed. Why the hell doesn't anyone want me? I've completed nearly ten years with a great company. I may not have an amazing reference after losing my mind, but hell, everyone makes mistakes, right? Are women writing down that they're up to giving blow jobs to get ahead? I just don't get what I can do to set me apart from everyone else.

So it's back to the drawing board. Or back to the weed growing in my loft. It's taking seriously longer to grow than I first thought. I would have thought with all of the pesticides around today they'd be grown within the week. I mean, I can't open the paper without seeing some headline about how pesticides are in all of our food; stunting our growth and making us start puberty earlier.

Meanwhile my credit card is getting used to just survive; groceries, utility bills, petrol. Its soul destroying. My job seekers allowance doesn't even cover my half of the mortgage. Samuel's helping me where he can, but I don't want him having to bail me out. I told him I've got savings. The truth is that I did have savings, but it very quickly got wasted. I have nothing to show for all of those years of scrimping and saving.

A knock at the door pulls me out of my self-destructive thoughts. I open it to find the girls. Turning up unannounced, how annoying. I hate when people don't call. They all look super excited.

'What's up, girlies?' I ask suspiciously, only opening the door halfway.

'We're here to visit our plants,' Lexi announces, pushing the door open and walking past me into the sitting room.

Just let yourself in, why don't you? What a cheeky bitch.

'Yes,' agrees Mags, looking a bit sorrier to be barging in. 'I was wondering if I'd have any in time for my next chemo treatment.'

Well, I suppose I can't deny the cancer patient.

Now that I look at her closely I can see that the cancer is taking its toll. Although her hair is still long, it's thinner than normal. Her skin is grey and sallow; she looks tired. The scary thing is that she still looks better than me right now. I haven't been sleeping well lately. Worrying about becoming a drug dealer and all keeps me up at night.

Steph skips over to the sofa, Ruby swaying scarily in her sling. 'Plus I heard if you sing to them they'll grow quicker.'

I roll my eyes. How can she seem so chipper about all of this? And is she totally over the Dorian thing now?

'And I really need the cash,' Lexi adds, leaning against the wall. 'I heard it can take months to grow.'

Shit. We could lose our houses by then.

'If that means singing to a stupid plant I'll give it a go,' she admits. It's the first time I realise how desperate she is, just like the rest of us.

'Okay, let's go check on them.' I force myself to smile brightly. 'But no bringing Ruby. She needs to stay away from the thug life as long as possible.'

Lexi laughs.

'Okay,' Steph sighs, obviously disappointed she's not going to see them.

'I'll have her,' Mags offers. She leans forward and takes Ruby from her sling.

We look at each other with concern. Is she well enough to be left alone with the baby? What if she passes out or something?

'I've got cancer, I'm not disabled,' she snaps, glaring back at us.

'We didn't say that,' Steph tries to reason. 'It's just that we know you're tired and weak and we don't want to stress you.'

'Yeah,' Lexi and I agree in unison.

'Just go see the bloody plants.' She looks down, dangling her necklace in front of Ruby's face. She starts giggling adorably. I don't even like babies, but I have to admit her laughter is probably one of the cutest sounds ever.

We go upstairs and I take the loft stairs out. We each climb up and I turn on the heavy duty fluorescent lights so we can look at them closely. They've actually grown little buds. I can't believe they've come on so well. I feel like a proud mother or something.

'They look amazing!' Steph sings, crouching down next to some as she starts to sing *You are my Sunshine*. I roll my eyes, but secretly love how optimistic and enthusiastic she is. I wish I could be more like her. I can't believe she's gotten over Dorian so quickly, not that I'm not pleased.

'Nice one,' Lexi nods approvingly. 'Finally can start making some money.'

Steph leans down to inspect one closely. 'Err...I think we have a problem here,' she says with a furrowed brow.

'Really?' I wipe my forehead, these lamps cause me to sweat like a mad woman. She nods and I look closer. The bud looks kind of….red.

'Is that…'

'It's a tomato,' she nods.

'Huh?'

'Sorry, WHAT?' Lexi blurts out. 'You must be fucking kidding me.'

'Afraid not,' she says, suddenly looking defeated. 'It looks like we've been duped by that man at the shop. He's given us tomato seeds.'

'Are you positive?' I ask in disbelief, rubbing my temples which have started to ache. 'Have you really just been singing to tomatoes?'

'My dad used to grow them.' She nods. 'I know a tomato plant when I see one.'

My shackles start to rise, fury pumping through my veins. That little prick. He knew we were new at this and he took advantage. Gave us a fucking tomato plant and didn't think we'd notice.

'That little shit,' Lexi shrieks, ripping one of the plants out with her bare hands. 'Let's go and rip him a new arsehole.'

Before we know it we're at the shop. I suppose a journey on the tube passes quickly when you're discussing how to kill someone. Lexi storms in ahead of us. He looks up from his graphic novel alarmed before she grabs a giant red sparkly dildo, drags him across the counter by the top of his t-shirt, and starts beating him on the head with it.

'What the hell?' he shrieks in a very girly manner. Who knew his voice could go that high?

'You sold us tomato plants, fuck face!' she screams, pelting him with it as hard as she can.

Me and Mags drag her off him. Well, *she* does; I just pretend to help. I want to get another one of those toys and shove it up his arse.

'Enough,' I snap at her when his eyes start crossing over. I don't want to add murder to our rap sheet. I turn back towards him. 'What, did you think we wouldn't notice?'

He snorts. 'You birds don't know the first thing about growing weed. I just thought you'd have more chances growing tomatoes.' He smiles smugly.

The sarcastic little bastard. And to be so cocky right after a beating!

I look back to Lexi. Mags releases her and she starts pelting him again.

'You fucker!' she yells. 'We needed that money and now you've fucked us over. I'm going to fuck you over with this DILDO up your ARSE!'

Wow, great minds think alike.

She throws herself onto his back like a crazed koala bear. He stumbles around the shop, trying to bump her up against walls to get rid of her. It's actually quite hilarious to watch. She doesn't even flinch as various walls smack into her back.

'Maybe I shouldn't have brought Ruby,' Steph says, grabbing a lacy eye mask and covering the baby's eyes.

'I doubt she knows what's going on,' I snort.

She's probably wondering why she's suddenly gone blind though.

'She does actually,' Mags agrees. She goes close to Ruby's face with a big grin, lifting the mask. 'You sense bad vibrations, don't you, sweetheart?' she says in a high pitched voice I hope is reserved for babies. 'Why don't I take you outside? Hmm?'

Steph begrudgingly hands her over and Mags goes out onto the street.

'Come on, Steph,' I sigh, pointing towards the drama. 'We need to break this up.'

She nods, a steely determination appearing on her delicate features. She goes for Lexi while I pull at emo boy. We *eventually* get her off him. She's bloody strong for such a little thing. Remind me to never piss her off.

'I'm fine,' she cries as Steph pushes her into a chair. 'Ah!'

She jumps up, clutching her butt. We look at the chair to see that it has a vibrator attached to it. Gross. Do people actually buy shit like this?

'Yeah, you *look* fine,' Steph smirks, staring at the dildo still in her hands.

I turn my attention back to emo boy, who is still trying to catch his breath after the attack. We've tried violence. Maybe I need to try the soft touch.

'Look,' I say lightly, smiling sweetly, 'the only reason Lexi's so upset is because she's being forced to live with a bad guy because she can't afford to leave him. This was going to be her way out. All of our ways out. Steph's a single mum and Mags has breast cancer.'

He crosses his arms over his chest and rolls his eyes. 'And what about you?' he asks suspiciously. 'What's your excuse?'

Well, I clearly don't have anything that looks good on paper.

'Just the fear of losing my home and being homeless.' I look deep into his eyes, trying to penetrate his soul. He must have one, right? I step closer and lower my voice to a whisper so the other girls can't hear me. 'I can't be that hungry again.'

I think back to that hunger. The stomach pains, the blurred vision, the weakness. The thought of experiencing it again terrifies me. Like a champ I manage to squeeze out a tear. What a good actress I am. Probably from when me and Samuel street performed Romeo & Juliet to get money for food.

'Okay,' he finally submits on a sigh. 'You've made me feel bad.'

'So...what are you going to do to make it right?' I sniff, trying to look far more upset than I am.

He looks around the shop as if to double check that we're alone. 'I can give you seeds and a few plants already grown. My own personal stash.'

'That would be marvellous,' Steph sings, attempting to high five Lexi. Lexi looks at her hand in disgust, leaving her hanging awkwardly.

Mags walks back in, bouncing Ruby to her delight. 'All sorted?' she asks casually.

'Yep,' I smile, for once feeling optimistic. I was beginning to forget what that felt like. 'We've got a few plants to tide us over.'

'Brilliant. I've got my chemo session this Wednesday afternoon, so we need to start getting a move on.' She looks scared. It's crazy when someone older than you is scared. It always makes me feel out of control.

Emo boy walks back into the room carrying two small plants. So that's what they're supposed to look like. Wait, how are we going to bring these back?

'How the hell are we going to bring these back on the tube?' I blurt out, my optimism sliding down a slope.

Steph's eyes widen in horror, as if she's just realised this.

Lexi leans on one hip, narrowing her eyes. 'Well don't look at me. They're hardly going to fit in my pockets.' She points to her super skinny black jeans. I doubt you'd get a polo in there.

Mags looks down at her tiny handbag and back to me again. It's obvious that's not going to work.

'I might have an idea,' she says, suddenly seeming brighter.

So this is how we've found ourselves on the tube with me using Steph's baby sling as a carrier for the plants. I've wrapped another blanket around the top of it so it can hopefully pass as a baby. Not that it smells like one. It stinks. People keep looking over in disgust.

'There, there, pudding,' I fake gush, patting the blanket. 'As soon as we get you home we'll change your stinky nappy.'

Lexi rolls her eyes at my dramatics. Ruby keeps trying to grab her blanket from me, obviously pissed that I'm wrapping it round a stinky plant.

'Steph, control your daughter, will you?' I hiss while smiling, but warning her with my eyes.

'If I knew how to do that I wouldn't have to be here right now,' she hisses back. 'I'd be the next bloody super nanny and be stinking rich. I'd have a programme called The Baby Whisperer, only with better hair.'

'Alright, Steph,' I sigh. 'I get it.'

This is far too stressful. All it would take is for someone to notice the plant and we'd be busted. The police would be called, and before I know it I'll be a finger puppet in some prison. Oh God. And lesbians love me. I'm constantly having to fend them off in gay bars.

A lady in her sixties gets on at the next stop. She looks so polished; all grey hair and tailored suit. I hope I'm that glamorous when I'm her age. Hell, I hope I'm a free woman! By then who knows, I could be running a heroin factory. You hear about how quickly these things progress.

The instant she sees Ruby she's cooing like a bird. What *is* it with women like this? They physically can't see a baby without making weird noises.

'Hello, my little cutie putie pie,' she says in the most ridiculous baby voice I've ever heard. 'Are you being a good girl for your mummy?'

Steph forces a smile. See, this is why I think it would be so annoying to have a baby. Random strangers trying to incite conversation from you *all the time.* Like you're not tired enough looking after an infant, you then have to talk idle chit chat with strangers and pretend to be all mother earth cooey with them. Is cooey a word? It is now.

Ruby is jumping up and down in Steph's arms, ridiculously excited by this stranger's attention. Steph will have to watch her when she's older. If this is how she reacts to strangers she'll be dating a motorcycle gang leader by the time she's fifteen.

'I bet she's a daddy's girl. Am I right?' she asks with a smile.

Uh-oh. No mention of Dorian. We all freeze, waiting for Steph's reaction. Please stay calm. PLEASE just stay calm.

'Um...no,' she says, her voice wobbly. She's way calmer than we expected. Maybe she really is starting to get over him. I smile back at Mags. Crisis over.

'Well...' she starts.

Uh-oh. Shut up, Steph!

'She *was* a daddy's girl...before...before...' her voice breaks and she's suddenly full on howling. Not just crying, *howling*. People in the carriage look over, fearful. Way to draw attention to yourself.

'Oh,' the woman says, quickly realising her mistake. She grimaces and leans away. Well, she must feel awkward.

Mags goes to comfort Steph, who is still making the most ridiculous noises. And on public transport. How classy.

The woman looks around the carriage, clearly looking for a distraction and clocks my fake baby. Her eyes light up like she's just spotted a pot of gold under a rainbow.

'And who is this little one?' she asks me, leaning in to try and see my fake baby. She recoils when she notices the smell.

What is it with this bitch? I lean away so she can't see. I realise she's looking expectantly at me. Oh, right, she wants a name.

'It's...Priscilla,' I blurt out like a fucking idiot.

Lexi side glances me, letting me know how much of a ridiculous name choice that is. Why did I pick Priscilla of all the names in the world?

'Priscilla,' she repeats. 'What a beautiful name!' She leans in again, clearly trying to take a look so she can have a proper coo. Is it not enough that she's upset Steph? Now she wants to interfere with my baby. Well, my fake baby.

I put my hand over the blanket, making sure not to reveal anything.

'She's sleeping right now,' I say, pretending to sway her.

'I'm sure she won't wake up,' she says, eyes wide and crazy, leaning in by the second. 'Just a little peek.'

The cheeky bitch goes to lift the blanket. I catch her wrist and forcibly move her hand away. She looks back at me, eyes wide, as if I'm mental. You're the mental one, lady. Obsessed and demanding to see sleeping babies? What is the saying? Let sleeping babies lie. Or was it bunnies? Oh God, something like that.

'She's not good with strangers,' I offer as a way of an excuse.

'I'm sure she'd be fine with me. Babies *adore* me.'

Well adults clearly don't. Lexi is suddenly by my side, leaning on one hip aggressively.

'I don't think so.' I try to smile apologetically. Acting like a real mum and everything.

'One little peek,' she says, going for the blanket again.

Does this bitch not learn? Do I have to break her wrist?

'No!' Lexi and I both shriek at the same time.

Her hand freezes. She looks back to us in confusion.

'The...' Lexi starts, looking around for a way out of this. 'The baby has leprosy!'

'Leprosy?' she shrieks, jumping back and wiping her hand frantically on her trousers. 'Why on earth didn't you say before? I could have caught it!'

Is she really that insensitive to my fake baby's condition? What a heartless cow.

She gestures around the whole carriage. 'We ALL could have caught it!' she shrieks, backing away further. 'Stop the train! I need to get off the train!'

Oh my God, we've released a monster. Why is she so nutty? And why did Lexi have to say leprosy?

'What's going on?' someone else on the carriage asks.

'I think she has HIV and she's cut herself,' another random one answers.

What the frig? How can that get so twisted in two seconds? Steph only howls louder, still completely incapable of speech. Poor Ruby is looking at her from Mags' arms as if she's mad while she attacks a rice cake.

The train starts to slow down for the next stop. The woman is so close to the doors that when they open her scarf gets stuck in it. She's almost trampled to death when every single person in our carriage pushes past her to get out. The doors close, leaving us completely alone.

'Well,' Lexi smiles. 'At least we don't have to worry about anyone seeing us now.'

Chapter 5

<u>Wednesday 9th September</u>

We rushed our arses off to get the plants back to my house. We googled how to cut the weed up and Mags put them into her 'legendary' brownie recipe. So on Wednesday I'm driving her to the hospital with a bag full of dope brownies. I've never been so nervous before in my entire life. Mags says we should just drop it into conversation with the ladies there, but how on earth do you drop that you have drugs into the conversation? She's crazy.

I look over at her while we are in the car. I've been so preoccupied and worried about myself that I haven't actually considered how Mags must be feeling. This is only her second session. It's still all so new to her. It hadn't actually occurred to me until now that I'm going to have to watch women and men at their lowest. Getting poison pumped into their veins to fight a deadly disease. And now I'm basically preying on them, pushing drugs. What an arsehole.

I try to assess how she's feeling as we pull into a parking space. She keeps tucking the same strand of brown hair behind her ear and twiddling her necklace. She must be nervous. Not that she'd ever voice it willingly. I think she's so used to being a mum that she's forgotten how to appear human.

'So how are you feeling, Mags?' I ask her as I take the keys out of the ignition.

'Fine, dear. You?' She smiles, appearing care free.

Typical Mags. Trying to ask how I am. The woman is ridiculous.

'You know I'm fine, Mags,' I say, waving off her question. Really I'm shitting myself, but she doesn't have to know that. 'But you must be scared about today. Was it awful that first time?' I don't even know who went with her.

'It was fine.' She nods, looking out of the window.

'Well, do you feel better now you know what to expect?' God, it's like pulling teeth.

'I suppose,' she shrugs. 'It's just an inconvenience really. With everything online and delivered to your door nowadays it's a wonder they haven't come up with a smarter solution.'

My mouth drops open in disbelief. Is she serious? Is she honestly suggesting they do a chemo delivery service?

We pay the meter and walk into the hospital. She guides me towards the chemo suites. I follow along like a lost puppy. Now that we're here and I can smell the disinfectant from the floors, I feel sick. Hospitals have always made me feel icky. It just makes me think of needles and veins. And my mum overdosing that time. Ugh. I shiver just from the thought and try my hardest to push it out.

We walk into a large bright and airy room, a bit like a glamorous doctor's waiting room. There are La-Z-Boy type chairs scattered around, some occupying people already wired up to the machines. They all look understandably miserable.

A cheery Irish nurse comes over. 'Hello there, Mrs. Abbot. How are ya today? And who's your friend? Is this one of your daughters?' She looks at me with a beaming smile.

'No, just my good friend Sadie, here to give me some moral support.' She squeezes my arm affectionately.

'Ah, lovely,' she beams. 'Don't want you going through this alone again.'

Alone *again?* I bloody knew it! She came to her first session on her own! I glare at Mags, trying to communicate a look that says *when we leave I'm kicking your arse.*

'Well, you know the drill now, my dear. If you sit down I'll get nurse Menzie to put your cannula in.'

I shiver. Cannula. Ew. This is going to be disgusting.

I pull up a normal fold up chair next to Mags and watch as a nurse in her thirties comes over and starts prepping her arm. Is it me or is it suddenly hot in here? Maybe they crank the heat up for the chemo people. It's like it's on fire in here, especially on my neck.

I look away when she gets the needle out, shuddering at the sight of it. I stare at the wall and try to calm myself down. My stomach feels weak and queasy. I count to ten, taking a deep breath on each number. I look back, assuming it will be done by now.

'Damn, missed the vein,' the nurse sighs.

I look at Mags' bleeding arm and wince. Eugh, I swear I can *smell* the blood. The room starts spinning. Hold it together. I force a smile at Mags, but she just looks back at me strangely. I must look weird.

'Let's try that again, shall we?' the cheery nurse asks.

I turn away again. Think of *anything* but the needle. Puppies and lavender and…puppy dog tails? Ew, why am I thinking about puppy dog tails? That's not a thing. Imagine if people carried them around on key rings like a rabbit foot. Gross. The minute I see someone with a rabbit's foot, even a fake one, they're dead to me. A freak. Why would you ever think carrying around a part of a dead animal was good luck?

'Aaaaah,' Mags says quietly.

The fact that she's making any noise at all shows she must be in a world of pain. She's not one to moan. I look back in time to see her pull the bloody needle out again. It's too much. I see stars, the room going fuzzy around the edges until I see the ceiling. Then everything comes thudding down hard and goes black.

#

I wake up with a jolt. I feel around me, trying to get my bearings, and find that I'm on one of the La-Z-Boy chairs, fully reclined back. I sit up too quickly, my head feeling as heavy as a brick.

'Hello, Miss Fainter.'

I close my eyes, praying my head stops banging. I look to my right hand side to see Mags on another chair, already hooked up to one of those machine things. Well, thank God they finally got it in.

It dawns on me that I must have passed out. What a wimp.

'God, sorry, Mags. Here I am trying to be moral support for you and I pass out like an absolute pansy.'

How bloody embarrassing. Lexi's going to have a field day when she hears about this.

'Don't worry, dear,' she smiles.

I look at her hooked up to the machine. My stomach turns again.

'How does it feel anyway? You know…' I point at her arm. I can't even say it.

'It just feels cold. It's a strange sensation, but it's also strange that I'm even having chemo. I don't think I'll ever get over it.'

I smile sadly. Of all people, why lovely Mags? Aren't there enough murderers and rapists out there to put through this horrendous suffering? My sweet hearted Mags would never hurt a fly.

'Anyway,' she grins, raising her eyebrows, 'I was just telling the girls here about our little cooking experiment. They're interested in trying some.'

I look behind her to see two women grinning eagerly at me. One is only in her thirties and the other looks about the same age as Mags. Cooking experiment? Oh, duh, she must mean the weed. God, did I hit my head on the way down? I try to pull myself together and talk business.

'Of course. Let me share some.' I reach into the bag and pull out the Tupperware box. Lexi put each slice into a separate sandwich bag as I asked, but she's also added a pink glittery sticker of a unicorn on each of them. What the fuck? I find a crumpled note scrawled with her biro. I pull it out to discreetly read.

So I picked up these stickers in the local newsagents. I was thinking we could call ourselves Project Unicorn. What do you think? It rocks, right? I knew it. Have fun x

Jesus Christ. We *have* to have a talk.

Within the space of a week we're getting orders left, right, and centre. Word seems to spread fast in those cancer wards. I suppose they don't have much else to talk about. It means we've all had to start growing it in any spare spaces we have. Well, not Steph obviously. We can't have that stuff growing around Ruby. We have *some* morals.

I just hope the nurses don't become suspicious. I have a lot of 'friends' I'm visiting, and for someone who can't stand needles, they must wonder why I keep coming back. I'm just on my way back from dropping off some weed brownies to two ladies at the hospital when the aroma of coffee invades my nostrils. I glance over at the coffee house, its glow lighting up the drab street. People are bustling out of it, sipping greedily on their expensive coffees.

God, I haven't had a proper coffee in *so* long. It's pathetic how much I've missed it. Home instant is *so* not the same thing. I wonder if I could afford a small cheeky latte. We haven't actually paid ourselves yet. We've been keeping all of the money together so we can take out the expenses we've put into it before splitting it between us. I just hope to God we make a good profit. It's hard to keep track of everything, but luckily Steph's keeping notes.

I wander in, letting the warmth hug at my cold bones. Has my life really become so pathetic that this is heaven to me? We haven't made a lot of money yet and my credit card is now maxed out, but I might have some loose change. I walk slowly towards the counter, getting my purse out and trying to count some out. I've got a hell of a lot of pennies in here. Shows the state of my life right now. How pathetic.

Before I register what's happening, my purse is pushed into my chest by something and a hot steaming coffee is soaking onto my shirt, burning me.

'Aaargh! HOT! So fucking hot!' I shriek, too shocked to care about shouting profanities.

I pull my shirt away from my skin in an attempt to reduce the third degree burns I'm sure are forming on my chest. What if I'm scarred for life? I could end up looking deformed. Oh God. I'll never wear a low cut top again, let alone a bikini.

I look up to see that a clumsy man has walked into me. Didn't he see me? I'm not *that* short for God's sakes.

'Oh my God, I'm so sorry,' he says apologetically, grabbing some napkins from the counter.

I grab the napkin out of his hand and start dabbing at myself. The last thing I want is for him to cop a feel.

'Don't you look where you're going?' I grunt. Just when I was enjoying a moment all to myself.

'Hey, you had your head down,' he says defensively. 'Counting your,' he looks around at the pennies scattered amongst the floor, 'money.'

Well, I sure look like a poor bitch.

I look up, my cheeks becoming hotter than my chest, and jump when I realise it's the beautiful gay guy from the other night. The one who chucked the shots at me.

'Do you make a habit of throwing drinks all over women?' I ask, sounding enraged. I meant it to sound jokey, but I suppose you can't force a good mood.

He looks back at me, his blue eyes confused. They widen, obviously recognising me.

'Sorry, you're from the other night. Shit. I dropped drinks down you then, too. Hardly a good first impression.'

He looks so sincere that my anger starts to dissipate. It's not his fault he's a big clumsy fool. It's probably because he's so tall and broad. He can't help but knock into things and people. He probably didn't even see me down here. I'm only five foot two and he looks at least six foot.

'Let me buy you a coffee to apologise?' he asks with an apologetic smile.

I look down at the pennies on the floor. I can't be seen picking them up in front of him. Then he'll know just how sad I am. And I really did want that coffee.

'Okay, whatever,' I sigh. 'I'll have a latte.'

He smiles, pleased I'm letting him make it up to me, and turns to go back to the counter. I look down at the loose change. I really can't afford to stick my nose up at it. I quickly scramble around on the floor, picking it up and shoving it into my purse. I hate how everyone looks at me, like I'm some skin flint. I've had worse looks in my life, but I still hate being made to feel inferior to everyone else. It brings back too many memories. Plus, if the whole *see a penny, pick it up* thing is true I'm due a whole load of luck. I could do with it.

I make myself comfortable at a sofa in the corner. It's so old that I immediately sink deep into the floor, my knees higher than my shoulders. He appears as I'm trying to make myself more comfortable, leaning down to put the coffee in front of me.

'Careful now,' I joke, grinning up at him. There's no point in making him feel bad. It doesn't look like I'm scarred for life after all. Call off the ambulance.

He grins and surprises me by sitting down across from me. I assumed he wouldn't stay. He sinks into his sofa just as low as me. He's wearing a suit, even if it does look a bit scruffy with the tie pulled away from his collar, so I assume he has a job he needs to rush off to. It's three in the afternoon. Doesn't he have somewhere to be?

'So…can I ask your name?' he asks, taking a sip of what I assume is a black coffee. That's what he's just thrown over me. No stain remover will get this out. Plus he strikes me as the black coffee type. No nonsense. Doesn't have time for dairy. I doubt he has *any* with those biceps bursting through his suit jacket. Why are all the good ones gay? It's so unfair.

Oh wait, he wants my name. Must concentrate, Sadie.

'Why? So you can apologise with a name next time you throw a drink at me?' I ask with a coy smile. Why am I flirting with him? My brain clearly hasn't registered he's gay.

'Maybe,' he grins. 'I'm Harry.'

'Nice to meet you, Harry,' I nod, suddenly feeling awkward. Must not flirt with the gay men. It makes them feel uncomfortable.

He smiles and takes another sip. He's clearly not leaving any time soon. What the hell should we talk about? He's not very forth coming. Most gays I've met never shut the hell up. Not that I should stereotype. Samuel's always telling me off for it.

'So my friend Samuel said that you're new,' I blurt out, not knowing what else to say.

He narrows his eyes in confusion. Oh God, way to scare the newbie!

'New? In what way? And who is Samuel? I don't think I know him.'

'Oh, sorry,' I blush. I keep forgetting he's new. Almost everyone in the gay community knows him. 'Samuel's my gay best friend.' I wince.

Samuel keeps telling me off for introducing him like that. He said I should say best friend and mention he's gay later in the conversation, if at all. Well, he made me promise to if the guy is hot, just in case. It's not that he's ashamed, but he rightly thinks I shouldn't claim him like my gay token. Especially when I get drunk and call him my big gay panda. I really need to stop doing that.

'Oh, the guy you were with the other night. I thought you were together,' he muses, his eyes creased in confusion.

'What, in a gay bar?' I laugh. 'That would be a weird date.'

'Yeah, I suppose,' he laughs, his eyes twinkling in the light.

I take my latte and sip from it. God, it's like coffee heaven. Even the smell is enough for me to orgasm. I've missed this.

'He's single, actually,' I add, remembering Samuel's reaction to him. Hell, every gay man's reaction that night.

He curls his lip up in confusion. 'Riiiight,' he nods.

His eyes suddenly widen in realisation that I know his secret. Bless him, obviously so used to hiding it. Come out of the closet, Harry!

'Oh wait, do you think...I'm gay?' he gasps in dismay.

'Huh? You're not?'

He was in a gay bar, no? But then Samuel did say he looked newly out of the closet. Maybe he's not ready to be admitting it yet. Poor, confused guy.

'Of course I'm not,' he snaps, his cheeks reddening slightly.

'It's okay,' I sympathise, leaning forward and putting my hand supportively on his arm. The sofa makes a weird creaking noise. I hope he doesn't think that was a fart. 'I know what it's like when you first come out. It can be hard to admit it to people. I mean, Samuel's parents-'

'I'm NOT gay!' he interrupts, throwing my hand off. He's clearly trying to laugh it off, but he can't hide his embarrassment from me.

'Oh *really*?' I challenge, leaning back and crossing my arms over my chest. 'So why were you in a gay bar? Huh?' I raise my eyebrows, waiting for his excuse.

'My brother's gay. A crowd of us were out for his birthday.'

My mouth pops open. Huh? He *is* straight? This delicious hunk of meat having coffee with me is straight? Wow, that puts things in a whole new perspective. I immediately straighten my spine and feel self-conscious. Not that I can look good at all with coffee all over my shirt and my body sunk into this bloody sofa.

I stupidly feel cheated. Like he lured me in as a friend or something, and I let my defences down. What if I'd befriended him and taken him bra shopping or something? The horror!

'I swear,' he says, seeming concerned.

He reaches into his pocket and produces his phone. After a few swipes through he shows me a picture of a man pretending to be done from behind by a drag queen. He's wearing a purple and pink shirt which is horrible. I'm confused. Isn't he supposed to be trying to convince me he's not gay? The guy can't be his brother. He looks nothing like him. Instead of black hair and blue eyes, this guy in the picture has blonde hair and what looks like dark eyes. Even their builds are completely different.

'My brother,' he says, as if this is an explanation.

'That could be anyone,' I tease. 'He doesn't even look like you.'

'I said he was my brother, not my son,' he deadpans, his eyes icy.

He seems so distressed, bless him. I could really have some fun with him.

'Okay, so show me a picture of a girlfriend.' This way I get to find out if he's single too.

'I don't have a girlfriend.'

Cher-Ching!

'But I must have a picture of my old one.' He flicks through the phone again and shows it to me. 'There, that was my old girlfriend, Chantelle.'

Chantelle? What kind of chavvy name is that?

There's a picture of both of them at dinner somewhere posh looking. She's got a harsh looking face, pouting away as if she's a catwalk model. Her white blonde hair is cut close to her head in a pixie cut and her clothes look sleek and designer. I hate her immediately. I'm definitely not his type. The opposite of his type actually.

'Hmm, not who I imagined you with,' I blurt out before I can stop myself.

Oh God, why don't I have more of a filter! I blame my druggie mother for not taking her vitamins when she was carrying me. And, you know, all that heroin can't have helped either.

'Excuse me? What's that supposed to mean?' He seems pissed off.

'No, don't get me wrong, I obviously imagined you with someone gorgeous. It's just…'

Digging a hole. Why must I dig this enormous hole?

'Just what?' he snarls.

Oh, what the hell. This guy is a stranger to me after all. And I'm clearly not his type. Might as well make a dick out of myself. It's not like I'll ever see him again. I'm definitely not coming back to this coffee house after today's events.

'I just would have put you with someone a bit more homely looking.'

'Homely?' he repeats in horror. 'Is that a posh word for uggers?'

'No!' I snort. 'Just someone you could have bare feet and pregnant at home, waiting to cook you dinner and sew up holes in your socks.'

He looks repelled at the idea. 'Why on earth would you say that?'

Oh, screw it.

'I just think you look a bit like a caveman. You know, me man, me knock woman up, you obey.' I giggle, finding myself hilarious. Did he put vodka in this coffee?

'I'm not like that at all, actually.' He looks genuinely hurt.

'I'm sorry, I was just joking.' Jeez, I didn't mean to hurt his feelings. Is he sure he's not gay?

'Hmm,' he hums. 'Anyway, I should probably get back to work.'

'Oh, so you do work?' I say sarcastically. 'What kind of cushy job do you have that means you can pop out for coffee at 3pm?'

'I'm a policeman,' he smiles.

My stomach drops like I've just gone down a rollercoaster.

'You've been speaking to Detective Constable McKenzie. Imagine, you could have confessed to a crime without realising.' He chuckles as if this is obviously such a ludicrous idea, when it is in fact a possibility.

Crap. I could have said something incriminating and I would have had no idea. I quickly relay the conversation in my head, but I'm sure it's not something I'd just blurt out.

'Wow.' I start sweating. I can feel the back of my neck becoming clammy. I hope he doesn't notice. 'What kind of detective are you?'

'Drugs and vice.' He nods absentmindedly.

I gulp down the terror rising in my throat wanting to escape into a piercing scream. He's a drugs detective? Shit the bed!

'Wow.'

He looks at his watch. 'Yeah, I must go. I'm following up leads on a new drug dealer in town. Some people are upset that they're affecting their sales.' He quickly realises he's said too much. 'But obviously I didn't say that.'

'Really?' I squeal, all of my breath leaving my body at once. I sound like a scared mouse. I feel like one.

Does he mean drug dealers? Are they cross with us? Have they grassed us up? Fuck. My chest starts rising and falling dramatically.

'Nothing for you to worry about,' he smiles, showing off his perfect teeth. 'You don't look like the kind of girl to have drug dealers as friends.'

Oh, how little he knows. I need him to leave.

'Well it was nice to meet you, Harry.' I need him to go. Now. I need time to process this.

'Yeah, it was nice to meet you too, Miss No Name. I'll try my hardest to keep my drinks in their containers next time.' He grins before sauntering off out of the door as graceful as a swan.

Holy fuck.

Harry's Diary

Fuck, I can't believe I bumped into bambi eyes again. The girl I'd dropped the shots all over in that gay bar Chris forced me to go to. At first, I assumed she must be a lesbian going there and then I thought maybe she was with that guy, but that didn't stop me from thinking about her constantly since. Hell, my dick has been hard for weeks. I've wanted to do some pretty fucked up things to her, but I reasoned with myself that it was because she was a random stranger I'd never bump into again. It's always hotter when you know they'll always be a mystery to you.

But then I turn round at a random coffee shop I never go in and she's there. Only what do I do? I spill my steaming hot coffee all over her. Yeah. What a fucking stud. The way her shirt basically went see through made me get a semi. It clung to her collarbone so I could make out all the places I'd like to kiss. Why do I like collarbones so much? Then I tried to almost dab it down with a napkin, clearly looking like I wanted to cop a feel. I mean, I did, but I didn't want it to look that way.

She was the same feisty little thing that she was at the gay bar. Shouting at me. As if little ole her could scare me. She'd even dropped her purse of pennies on the floor. I mean, who the hell has that many pennies with them? Was she planning to pay with them? Maybe she's poor or something. She doesn't look it though. Especially with her navy pencil skirt, stilettos and white shirt. All of it seemed to accentuate those fuck me bambi eyes.

Somehow I managed to collect myself and buy her a coffee to apologise. She was still so guarded though. She wouldn't even tell me her name. I'm not used to women playing hard to get. I don't want to be a dick about it, but I'm a fucking catch. At least the way the ladies look at me makes me believe that. I've never had to do more than crack a smile, flirt a bit and I have them eating out of my palm. Not that it's ever gotten me anywhere relationship wise. I've never met someone who's made me want to stick around longer than a few weeks. They normally turn out to be bitches.

But her...the way she was so guarded around me. Well, if I'm honest, it turned me on. I'm starting to wonder if I'm some weird pervert. But she was so fucking challenging that I just wanted to hit her over the head, drag her back to mine and fuck her until the morning. Maybe I am a caveman.

First she thought I was gay. Me! Fucking gay. I told Chris people would get the wrong idea with me going with him. Not that she bloody believed me. She made me show her a picture of Chantelle, my last girlfriend, if you could even call her that.

Her little comment 'not who I saw you with' made me wonder if she found me attractive. Then she called me a caveman. I hate how she judged me instantly, refusing to let me in and get to know her. It pissed me off so much that I decided to get back to work. This chick was already fucking with my head and I wasn't even fucking her. Yet.

When I told her I was with the police she had a strange as fuck reaction. Paled up like a ghost. It made me wonder about her. Was she involved in anything dodgy or was she just intimidated? A lot of people are. She looks so sweet though, like butter wouldn't melt. I doubt she's even had a late library card. Oh God, now I'm thinking of her as a sexy librarian that punishes me for talking. I really need to get my head out of the gutter. Well, after my next wank anyway.

I need to get her out of my head. We've been tipped off about a new ring of drug dealers in the area. They're small at the moment, but it's my job to find them and nip it in the bud before it gets to be too much of a problem. Although I doubt they need much more encouragement. I'm sure Joaquin's sent round his men to threaten them by now. No one works on his patch without him finding out. If only I could somehow get to him too. I'm just going to have to put everything into this, build up my case and get that promotion I've been waiting too long to get. Well, after my wank.

Chapter 6

<u>Thursday 17th September</u>

I can't stop thinking about that sexy guy, Harry, from yesterday, which is so unlike me. I've never been one to obsess over a man. But if that man is six feet of lean muscled perfection, I might just write his name in my diary with hearts all over it. How pathetic, I know.

I'm just chatting to Ivy, our elderly neighbour in the flat below, when I notice Lexi walking towards us down the garden path. What is she doing here?

'Hey, Lexi,' I smile, confused. 'What are you doing here?'

She's got her sunglasses on again, but at least this time there's some sunshine so she doesn't look massively anti-social. She's wearing ripped black jeans, doc martins and her trusty leather jacket. The girl needs to wear some colour.

I once made the mistake of asking her if she was a Goth. She went mental and said that just because she doesn't dress how society and mass produced fashion houses tell her to does not mean she's a Goth. I kept my mouth shut after that and haven't mentioned it since. She can get so ghetto about things.

'Hey. Just thought I'd pop by.' She shrugs, her hands in her pockets. They're such tight jeans she can only put the tips of her fingers in them.

Something's up. This isn't like her at all. She could even pass for friendly.

'Okay, come on in.'

She nods and follows me up the stairs and into the flat. I automatically make my way into the kitchen and flick the kettle on; even though I'm pretty sure we don't have any coffee in the cupboards. She takes her sunglasses off and throws them on the kitchen table. Her black eye is no longer visible, but her eyes still show a certain vulnerability I've never seen in them before. She looks down at the table, twirling the countless rings on her fingers. She has at least three on each finger, all the way up to her knuckles. If she ever punched me I'd be scarred for life.

I lean against the counter. 'So…are you going to tell me the real reason you're here?'

She shrugs off her leather jacket to reveal her white t-shirt which says 'I hate everyone' on it. Sounds about right for her.

'I had a fight with Jason. I just needed to get out of there,' she admits quietly. She's never this quiet.

I nod in understanding. 'I have tea, but no coffee.'

She blows out some held in breath. 'Of course you don't,' she snarls sarcastically. 'What else have you got?'

She gets up and opens the fridge, pouting her lips as she considers what she wants. Make yourself at home, why don't you? She decides on the carton of orange juice on the door and starts chugging straight out of it. Ugh. Does she have no respect?

No, I must remember she's in a bad situation right now and came here to talk. I put my hand on her shoulder to comfort her, but nearly jump out of my skin when she winces, throws me off and her face contorts in pain.

I look back at her, completely flummoxed.

'What the hell's wrong with you?' I blurt out. 'I was just trying to comfort you.'

'Nothing, okay!' She sits down in a hump.

It only then occurs to me that she looked like she was in real pain. Wait, has he hit her again?

'Lex, let me see your shoulder,' I demand, leaving no chance of ignoring me in my voice.

She acts like I'm the weirdo. 'Err…okay. Show me *your* shoulder,' she laughs, trying to deflect from the question by treating me like a randomer.

I sigh. 'Show me your shoulder, Lexi. It's not a request.'

'Ooh, what you going to do if I don't? I'm trembling in my boots right now.' She puts them up on the table in defiance.

On my fucking kitchen table, the dirty bitch! She smiles back at me, so cocky and full of it. Full of hot air that is. She doesn't know that I can be tough when I want to be. I have a background of being tough.

She leans back in her chair triumphantly. I question myself for a split second before kicking the chair back. She falls back onto the floor with a hard thump. I tower over her with a bitch glare on my face. She looks up at me with her mouth agape, complete surprise evident on her face.

'What the fuck, Sadie?'

I offer my hand to her with a smirk. I just love that I was able to get that reaction from her.

She takes my hand, but when she's standing I grab her t-shirt and yank it down so I can see her affected shoulder. Fuck! I'm not prepared for the huge angry looking purple and grey bruise on it. It must be two inches thick on both sides.

'Shit,' I mutter. That's probably not helpful. 'He hit you again?'

She pushes me away from her and goes to stand by the sink. 'He didn't hit me. He just…well, he kind of pushed me.'

I roll my eyes. 'You don't get that kind of bruise from a push.'

'Okay, so it was more of a throw.'

My mouth drops open. 'He *threw* you against a wall?'

'Yeah, just like *you* threw me on the floor just now,' she snaps. 'Should I never see you again too?' she asks sarcastically.

'Don't be ridiculous,' I retort sharply.

'Why? It's the same.'

'No it's fucking not and you know it. The guys' built like a brick shit house.'

She rolls her eyes. 'Why do people even say that? Brick shit house. It's such a weird expression.'

'I know,' I nod, getting side tracked for a second. I can't help but agree. I shake my head, trying to focus. 'Look, Lexi, you came here. You must be looking for someone to talk to about this.'

'Well…okay, if I'm honest…it does hurt like a mother fucker and….well, I mean I didn't even start this fight. He just kind of picked one with me over nothing. He was apologetic this morning, but I just can't even look at him.'

'So surely now you see that you have to get out?' I ask desperately. No victim ever knows when it'll be the time it goes too far and kills them.

'The thing is…well, I haven't told you guys this before, but…he has a daughter.'

'Sorry…what?'

Lexi and children *do not* mix. She refuses to even hold Ruby.

'He has a daughter,' she repeats. 'She's eight and…well...I kind of fucking love her,' she admits, blurting it out.

My heart warms. She loves this little girl? There *is* hope for her still.

'He only has her every second weekend, but when she's around he's such a different guy. All loving and sweet. It makes me wonder if I should maybe have a baby with him.'

I spit out my tea. All over the table.

'You better be fucking kidding me right now?' I shout. 'Because for a strong, feisty, intelligent woman you're acting like a fucking dickhead.'

'That's not what I think now. She was over this weekend and he still fucking lost it with me. Right in front of her. The poor thing was scared shitless. I can't leave her with that mad man. Who's to say that if I'm not there that he won't hit her?'

'You *just* said he's all sweetness and light with her? Lexi, you need to get out of there. Before he does knock you up and you're tied to him forever.'

She rakes her hand through her pink hair. 'It's not as easy as that. I've got nowhere to go.'

I wonder how true that is.

'I know you say you don't get on with your parents, but surely it can't be that bad?'

'It is,' she snaps, offering no further explanation.

'Okay, Jesus!' I say, throwing my hands up in defeat. 'Don't you have any friends you could stay with?'

She glares at me. 'Are you accusing me of having no friends?'

'No, I just meant-'

'Because I have friends, okay? They're just still living with parents and, well, to be honest, I've kind of neglected them. I've always kind of been with a boyfriend.'

I can see that about her. She clearly did not get the hoes before bros talk. There's a knock on the door.

'You could always move in here. We don't have a spare room, but...we have a sofa?'

'Thanks, but no thanks,' she snaps, as if that's worse than being beaten. 'I just need to wait until we've made enough money so that I can move into my own place. Now do you see why I'm so desperate for this to work?'

'I did think you were an eager drug dealer,' I grin.

At that moment the front door slams and Ivy comes running into the kitchen looking terrified. Did she just let herself in here?

'Ivy?' I blurt out loud. 'That key is for emergencies.'

'This is an emergency!' she screams so loudly I have to stand back from her. She's still in her flowery night dress. 'The war has started again!'

War? What the hell is she talking about? I go to roll my eyes at Lexi, but she jumps up to standing.

'What war? Oh my God, have the terrorists declared war again? Has there been a warning?' she sounds frantic, the poor thing.

She clearly doesn't understand that Ivy's mind has been declining lately. Before now it's only been her getting things mixed up and confused. Not actually declaring there is a war when there isn't one.

'Don't be silly,' she snaps. 'It's World War Two! Quick! To the bunker.'

She opens my kitchen door, grabs both our arms, and starts dragging us down the fire escape stairs. Jesus, she's strong for an old bird.

'World War Two?' Lexi repeats, completely taken off guard.

'She's lost her mind,' I whisper. 'Just go with it.'

'Just bloody go with it?' she snarls in disbelief. 'You have to be kidding.'

We reach the bottom of the stairs and Ivy only seems to be getting more distressed. What the hell could have brought this on? She was fine only half an hour ago.

'Quickly,' she shrieks, ducking down as if she's just heard a bomb. 'The bunker! The bunker!' She runs into her shed.

Lexi looks at me completely unamused. I grab her arm. 'Come on,' I hiss. 'I read if you correct them it can make them more anxious.'

'I cannot believe I'm pretending a shed is a bunker,' she hisses, following me with crossed arms.

We walk into the shed, only I can't see Ivy. What the hell? Where did she go? Lexi looks around, just as perturbed as me.

Suddenly a hatch from the floor which I hadn't noticed opens up. Ivy is wearing a hat made from tin foil.

'Quickly, girls! The Germans are coming!'

She actually has a bomb shelter in her back garden? It's been here the whole time we've lived here and never noticed?

I don't have time to consider it as she grabs us and pulls us down into it. She turns on a little light and it shows that there's actually a substantial size room down here.

'This is crazy,' Lexi hisses.

Ivy suddenly looks confused. She looks from me to Lexi. 'What are we doing down here?' she asks.

'You've got to be kidding me,' Lexi snaps, leaning on one leg aggressively.

I must stay calm.

'You told us to come down here. Remember?'

'Um...no,' she admits, scratching her head.

Bless her. She looks like a scared little kitten. I look to Lexi for help.

We eventually get her to go back to my kitchen and have her settled down with a cup of tea.

Samuel comes in singing, 'If you want my body and you think I'm sexy, come on in and let me know.' He comes to an abrupt halt when he sees Lexi and Ivy.

'Oh, sorry, I didn't think we had company.' He looks back at me in question. He's never met Lexi before.

'Cool,' Lexi nods. 'Well...I just wanted to explain myself. Obviously got a lot more than I bargained for. Anyway, I've got to go.' She gets up and leaves without another word.

Samuel waits until the door is shut before he turns to me. 'Who was that? Did you pick her up?'

He means did I pick her up from the street. Occasionally Samuel and I go scouring the streets to find vulnerable newbies. We help them by giving them information on the council rules, local shelters, and occasionally we let them use our flat so that they can shower and apply for jobs. The only way they can get a job is if they have a permanent address. So, we offer for them to put down ours. Otherwise it's a vicious cycle.

'No. God, don't let her hear you say that. She'd rip your balls off. That's Lexi.'

'Lovely girl,' Ivy comments, sipping her tea. 'Shame about the hair.'

His eyebrows furrow. 'As in Lexi that you used to work with?'

'Do you know any other pink haired Lexi's?' I smile with raised eyebrows.

'What was she doing here? I didn't know you guys were still in contact.'

Oh, that's right. He has no idea we've started a drug ring called Project Unicorn.

I shrug. 'We bumped into each other at the job centre. And she's got an arsehole boyfriend who thinks it's okay to hit her.'

'No way!' He pulls out a chair and sits down, as if this is the best gossip ever. 'So what are we going to do about it?'

'Samuel,' I warn. Typical Samuel, trying to save everyone. 'You know there's nothing we can do. She has to decide to leave herself.'

'Bullshit. That's only because she doesn't realise she has options. Let's make a plan to bust her out of there.'

'I don't know,' I say cautiously.

'Sades, have I ever steered you wrong?' He grins when I raise my eyebrows at him. Plenty of times. 'Whatever, this is for the greater good. Now hand me my thinking hat.'

I hand him the bottle of gin.

Friday 18th September

The next day at Mags' house she's telling us about a friend of hers that ate one of her brownies and had really bad side effects. Apparently she was so paranoid she spent the entire evening hiding under her dining room table. Sounds more like mushrooms to me, but she swears she took nothing else.

'Please,' Lexi snorts, 'she's just being a drama queen.'

It does make me think though. Here we are selling it to people, just assuming its okay. We haven't tried it ourselves. Not that I bloody want to.

'Do you think...we should test it?'

Lexi's eyes light up like a kid that just saw Santa Claus. 'No way! Virginal Sadie Taylor wants to do some weed?' She holds onto her chest and lets out a hearty chuckle. It's the biggest laugh I've ever heard from her.

'Not me, you moron,' I snap. 'Obviously one of you guys.'

Steph gasps in shock. 'I can't do it. I have a-'

'Baby!' Lexi shrieks. '*Yes,* Steph, we fucking get it. You have a baby.'

She really needs to dial down her aggression with Steph.

'Don't be such a bitch,' Steph snaps, looking hurt. 'Me and Ruby are out of here.'

She starts gathering her stuff up.

'Well, I'm not sure if I should try it yet,' Mags says, wringing her hands together.

'You mean you haven't already?' I ask, confused. Surely she's been using it to help with her chemo? I just kind of assumed.

'Well...no,' she finally admits.

Lexi blows out a breath. 'Fucking hell, Mags. Right, that's it. We're doing this. Right now.'

Mags' eyes bulge, just like mine. Are they really going to do this?

'Oh, don't shit yourself, Mags,' Lexi laughs. 'We'll just have one of your brownies.'

'Oh,' she exhales, clearly relieved. 'I suppose that's not *so* bad.'

I run into the kitchen to grab one, glad to be doing something other than drugs. This way I can monitor them.

'So, Lexi, have you actually done this before?' I ask as I hand it over.

I mean she acts all badass, but for all I know she was still playing with dolls until at sixteen.

'I smoked a bit of it once when I was fifteen, but nothing really happened. I was just trying to impress a boyfriend.'

She has a serious problem with going after the wrong men.

She takes a bite and hands it over to Mags. She takes it with a shaky hand and looks at it dubiously.

'It's just a brownie, Mags,' she laughs. 'It won't kill you.'

But it might make you hide under the dining room table all afternoon.

She swallows audibly, her face now drained of all colour. Poor Mags. She looks terrified.

'Mags, if you don't want to do it you don't have to,' I reassure her.

I'm expecting Lexi to jump in and shout that yes she bloody does have to do it, but luckily she just watches Mags with an encouraging smile. She finally takes it to her mouth and has a bite.

'Mmm,' she smiles. 'You can't even taste it. Just tastes like my normal brownies.'

Lexi rolls her eyes and takes the brownie off her. In a few bites she eats the rest of it.

'So...I guess we just wait?'

Half an hour later we have two very different outcomes.

'I just...I love baking,' Mags giggles. 'And ironing. And cleaning.' She breaks into hysterical giggles over this like she's just said the funniest thing in the world.

She's adorably stoned on just a bite. Which is what I think Lexi should have done rather than scoffing down the rest of the thing. She's...well, I'm a little concerned about her. She hasn't spoken at all for twenty minutes. AT ALL. Her eyes are glazed over, her black pupils as big as saucers. She's even started dribbling. I really wish Steph would have stayed to help. She's used to dribbling babies.

'Lexi?' I attempt to shake her by the shoulders. 'Can you hear us, Lexi?'

'She's gone deaf,' Mags giggles. 'Deaf as a post. Why do they say that, eh? Deaf as a post? A post doesn't even have ears to begin with.'

Dear God, she won't stop talking bollocks. I don't know what's better; Mags talking absolute shite or not knowing if Lexi's okay. I mean, when do you get to the point of calling an ambulance?

I grab my phone out of my bag and go onto the internet. I type in *'too stoned to talk when to call ambulance.'*

Apart from hilarious videos popping up I read a few articles which all state the same thing. You can't actually digest or inhale too much marijuana. It won't cause any damage to your organs. The best thing to do is just sleep it off. Okay, phew. That makes me feel better.

I turn back to them to see Mags taking out the hoover. She turns on her stereo, Dancing in the Street by Martha and the Vandellas blasting out. Dear God. I look to Lexi, hoping the shock of the music has snapped her out of it. She still just stares ahead blankly.

Mags starts hoovering like a mad thing, dancing to the beat and singing along.

'Dancing in the streets!' she screeches. She doesn't have the best voice, bless her.

She takes off the attachment and starts hoovering the curtains. I mean, who the hell does that?

Lexi's phone starts ringing in her black patent bag decorated with diamante skulls. I should really get it for her. I look at the screen and see 'Jason' flashing up. Shit. I didn't think about him. How the hell is he going to react when he finds her in this state? He'll bloody kill her, and she won't even be able to fight back or protect herself. Crap. I have to do something. I look at my watch. 4pm. He shouldn't be home from work yet. Not that I bloody know what he does.

It stops ringing. Oh, thank fuck for that. I can breathe again.

It starts ringing again straight away. Fuck my life! Okay, think fast. I have to get Lexi back home before he arrives and hopefully into bed. Okay, I could pretend she's ill. Will he even believe me? If he's a psycho he'll want to speak to her and no one else. Shit.

I hold my nose and press answer, my fingers trembling over the buttons.

'Hello? Lexi?' he asks impatiently.

'Yep,' I say from the back of my throat, my voice completely unrecognisable, thank God.

'Lex? What's wrong with your voice?' He actually sounds concerned.

'I think I've got flu.'

'Oh no, baby. Do you need anything? Maybe turn down that music for starters. I'll be home by 5pm.'

I'm starting to see how she can still be muddled by this guy. One minute he's playing the concerned boyfriend and the next thing he's punching her in the face.

'No. I'm just gonna go to bed. If you could just let me sleep.'

'Of course, baby. I'll check on you at about eleven, before I go to bed, yeah?'

'Gweat.' I manage to breathe heavily so it sounds like I'm congested. Who knew I was such a good actress?

I hang up the phone before he can try to engage me in anymore conversation. I look at Mags who is now standing on the sofa hoovering the ceiling. Lexi's still incoherent. Right, I just have to get her home and tucked up in bed in the next hour. Easy peasy, right?

With Mags helping me we managed to get her into her car. I drove us to the nearest petrol station and bought seventeen Mars bars and three bottles of Lucozade. The cashier did look at me like I was mental, but I just smiled, wishing he'd hurry along. I've force fed her five Mars bars, and with each one she does seem to become more coherent. I just need her well enough to let us into her flat so I can put her to bed. Mags is now snoozing in the backseat of the car so I've got no helpers.

I drive to her flat, having found the address in the front of her diary. Who knew someone like Lexi was organised enough to keep a diary? She keeps surprising me. I park outside so badly that people would be convinced I was the stoned one, and walk around to her door.

'Come on, Lexi,' I say cheerfully, hoping to get some enthusiasm back.

'Uuuugh,' is all I get back. Great.

I take her arm and wrap it around my shoulders. I start leading her towards her door. I say leading, more like dragging. She's like a bloody dead weight! Every time I attempt to walk in a straight line she falls to one side, steering us into prickly bushes.

'Everything okay?' a nosy old lady calls out of her window.

'Fine,' I shout back with a forced smile. 'Just a bit unwell.'

'She looks half cut to me,' she shouts back.

Will she just piss off?

'We're fine,' I say through gritted teeth. 'Thanks.'

I somehow manage to get her to the door before she falls into a heap. I open up the door and then realise that she lives on the first floor. Fuck my life!! I check my watch. 4:40 pm. Crap. If he gets back and finds us like this we're both dead.

I look to the ceiling in despair. If I ever needed an angel or fairy godmother, now would be it. I look around. Nope, no one's coming. As per fucking usual. Have to do everything myself.

I summon all of my inner strength and grab under her arms, dragging her backwards up the stairs. I did it! I throw her inside, sweating like a beast. Whose stupid idea was this anyway? Oh right, mine. Doofus.

I find her bedroom and throw her under the covers still fully clothed. She nestles her face into the pillow as if it's the best thing in the world. I throw the covers over her and remove her boots. Then I realise that most of her clothes have some kind of spikes that could hurt her. I end up basically stripping her. When I'm happy she's safe I pull the cover around her.

    Bless her. She almost looks like a normal nineteen year old like this. Innocent to the cruel world around us. I'm interrupted by another Motown classic blaring out of the speakers from my car. I guess Mags is awake...

Chapter 7

<u>Monday 21st September</u>

We've all talked about it and decided it's time to force Lexi to leave her boyfriend. She managed to get away with the whole stoned incident unscathed, but it was too close. He can't carry on hitting her and getting away with it. I know Lexi puts on this tough act, but underneath all of that I see that she's vulnerable and scared. She reminds me of myself as a teenager. Scared but putting on a brave front.

I still remember the day I ran away from my foster home. My foster parent's biological son Marcus had been getting creepy towards me for a while. Always *accidentally* walking in on me when I was changing. He'd also been hinting heavily that once I turned sixteen I could be turned into a woman. I knew he wanted to be the one to do it, and the idea repulsed me. I wasn't so sure he could take no for an answer. I mean, he killed the cat because she pissed on his bed. Hardly a rational guy.

The night before my birthday I packed a bag and left. I knew no one would believe the foster kid over the biological son. I saw no other option. If only I'd had someone to look out for me things might have ended a lot differently.

So me, Samuel and Mags are at Lexi's flat at 4pm the following evening banging on her door. She swings it open, looking disgruntled.

'Oh,' she gasps, trying to hide some of her rage. 'What are you guys doing here?' She looks pointedly at Samuel. She hates strangers.

'We're here to bust you out, love,' Mags says, tilting her head in sympathy.

Lexi's back straightens. Way to ruin things Mags. She's taken the completely wrong approach. This girl doesn't want pity. *So* the wrong time to do a head tilt. She needs to feel empowered. We should be blasting Beyoncé from speakers right now, not doing head tilts.

'Just let us in?' I ask, smiling hopefully.

She sighs heavily, looking up to the ceiling before begrudgingly opening the door. Samuel and I drag Mags in while trying to communicate with our eyes that she's to remain quiet for the remainder of the trip.

'So come on then,' she challenges, leaning against the wall with her arms crossed over her chest. 'What the hell are you talking about? Busting me out. I live here. It's not a prison.'

'But he's basically holding you prisoner, love,' Mags says with another head tilt.

Why won't she stop the head tilts!

'He's not!' she barks defensively.

'I agree,' I insist, shooting evils at Mags. 'You're not prisoner, but...you're hardly happy here. You said yourself you're only here because you have nowhere else to go.'

She looks to Mags and Samuel, embarrassed and pissed I've told them.

'I'm fine,' she snaps. 'As soon as we start making money I can start saving or something.'

'And what if he's killed you by then?' I ask seriously, looking her dead in the eye.

'You're so dramatic,' she huffs rolling her eyes.

'It's funny,' Samuel says, pretending to inspect his watch, 'because you don't look like a victim.'

She gasps with a start. 'I'm not a fucking victim!' she screams. 'And what the fuck do you know about me? You're just Sadie's gay roommate, and unless she's been shouting her mouth off about me,' she turns to shoot me a warning eye, 'then you should know nothing about me.'

'Then stop acting like such a victim,' I snap. 'Mags has said you can stay with her until she sells the house. You can't let this guy break you down. The Lexi I know wouldn't have stood for that shit.'

'You don't understand,' she yells in frustration, her voice breaking and a tear escaping down her cheek. 'I wind him up. You know how I can be.'

Bless her. Typical; blaming herself. She never blamed herself when she broke the fax machine or was found threatening Sue in the canteen because she took the last Mars bar from the vending machine.

'I've never hit you.'

'You've never lived with me,' she counters.

I look to Samuel in dismay. She's going to be harder to break than I thought.

'For fuck's sakes, Lexi. Years from now you're going to look back on this day and you're either going to thank God that you had amazing friends who helped you out of a bad situation or you're going to kick yourself for letting a man ruin your life. It's up to you. You can be a badass like Beyoncé or you can be a wimp like...' God, why can't I think of someone wimpy? 'Like a wimpy person.'

She stares back at me intently for a long time. So long that I have to try hard not to blink and break the staring competition. But they start to water. This is torture.

'Oh fuck it, why not,' she finally says. She walks upstairs.

'That's the spirit,' Mags cheers, patting her on the back as we follow her upstairs and into the flat.

'Easy for you to say,' she snorts. 'We better hurry. He'll be home in an hour.'

She opens her wardrobe and pulls out a sports bag from the top. She unzips the bag while Mags and Samuel start opening drawers and stuffing clothes in.

Samuel nods at me, and I start helping to crush in as much stuff as I can. She hasn't actually got that much. I'm shocked to see a photo album amongst her possessions. Who would have known she'd be sentimental like that? I thought all these young ones just kept it all on Facebook.

I glance out the window, sure I can hear someone crunching on the gravel, but I can't see anyone. Then I hear it. Keys in the door. Holy. Fuck.

We all freeze and stare at each other in alarm. What the fuck are we going to do?

'Alexis! I'm home,' a male voice calls while bounding up the stairs. A *strong,* deep voice. The kind of voice that would belong to a strong man who would kick our arse's.

My heart rate accelerates, my back feeling sweaty. The main door closes behind him.

'Say something to him,' I hiss, flailing my arms about in panic.

It's the jolt she needs. 'Err, I'll be in soon,' she shouts, her voice only slightly wobbly.

'What are we going to do?' Mags whispers, her face as white as a ghost.

'I reckon I could take him,' Samuel offers, starting to stretch and crack his knuckles.

Idiot. I ignore him. 'We'll have to hide,' I suggest, immediately looking around for potential hiding spots.

I lift the sheet up from her double bed, hoping I can crawl underneath, but it's a bloody divan. Not getting under there. I open the wardrobe and there's only space for two of us. Mags looks terrified and is probably more of a liability.

'Mags, in here.' I grab her shoulder roughly and throw her in. Samuel jumps in too. I roll my eyes at him. Always one to save himself. 'Be quiet.' I re-arrange the clothes so they're over them and shut the door. I look at Lexi. 'Now where the fuck am I going to go?' I whisper to her. I don't want to panic Mags.

'Fuck knows,' she says, her eyes almost bulging out of her head in panic.

'Alexis,' he calls again, sounding pissed. 'What are you doing in there?'

She looks at me in panic. 'I was just…napping,' she lies.

What the *fuck* am I going to do? He's going to murder me. We could have said I'd just popped in, but now that she's said she was napping it'll look completely unbelievable! She looks around the room, as if a new hiding space is going to just jump out at us.

'The window!' she whispers, as if this is a great idea.

I look at it in disbelief. 'Come again?' She can't honestly be telling me to jump from the window...can she? I'll break my neck.

'There's a window sill you can stand on.' She opens the window and points to the flimsy bit of wood on the other side.

'You can't be serious?' I ask, narrowing my eyes at her.

Footsteps start coming towards the bedroom. We both turn our heads to the sound.

Fuck a duck! I'm going to be murdered!

I climb out of the window on shaky legs, my hands gripping onto the top of the ledge. Lexi slams the window shut quickly, the force making it shake unsteadily. She pulls the curtains so I can't be seen. The wind is harsh on my cheeks and I really, really don't want to look down right now. I hate heights, but I suppose who does? Those crazy window cleaner people on the gherkin, that's who. They must just be depressed people with a secret death wish. It's the only explanation.

Before I know it I glance down. The gravel greets me, warning me of how high I am. Any braveness left in my body leaves me in a whoosh through my ears. I am *not* cool with this. I force myself to look back at the window. I really wish I was better dressed for this. The pencil skirt was a mistake.

All of a sudden the curtains are pulled back by her boyfriend. I freeze, not that I can actually do anything else, but realise that he hasn't noticed me yet. He's just opened them and is looking back at Lexi. She looks close to hysterical.

I have to make myself less visible before he spots me. I try to walk along the sill so I'm more to one side of the window, rather than star fishing it, but my foot slips. I graze it along the wall, desperately trying to get any friction back. Damn these heels! It's no use. It throws my balance and I feel myself going backwards, no matter how hard I try to hold onto the top of the window.

Shit! I'm going down! I'm going to die!

I close my eyes as the strange sensation of no part of my body being on the ground surrounds me. I was never good on the trampoline. I never trusted it and now I know why. It's that same terrifying feeling, although this time there's nothing soft to greet me.

I land on my arse, pain zinging up my cocksee so forceful I lose my vision. Fuck!

I look around in shock to see that I'm alive. I can feel my fingers and toes. Yes, my arse feels raw from pain and my back is killing me, but I'm not dead. Hurrah! I attempt to stand, but my back wails in pain. Okay, so maybe I hurt myself more than I first realised.

The front door opens and the boyfriend comes walking out of it. Crap.

He notices me as I attempt to stand for a second time. No luck. I think my legs are still in shock. Wake up, you stupid legs! Can't you see you're about to be beaten to death?! He looks at me, first in disbelief, then in puzzlement.

'Err... Are you okay?' he asks, walking towards me. He actually seems genuinely concerned. I suppose that's how these men operate. Nice on the street, but beating their women at home.

'I'm fine,' I wince, attempting to stand again.

'Here, let me help you.' Before I can protest he's got his hands under my arm pits and is pulling me to my feet. Pain zings up my back.

'Thanks,' I reply, trying not to react from him touching me. His type disgusts me.

'What happened anyway?' His eyes turn suspicious. 'Wait...Do I know you?'

Shit. He probably recognises me from the Xmas do at work. What if he recognises my voice from the phone?

'No!' I shriek, putting on a French accent. 'I mean…' I try to return my voice to normal and unshaking. 'I was just…delivering leaflets when I fell.'

He looks over my outfit of a pencil skirt and navy shirt in confusion. I suppose I don't look like the normal leaflet deliverer. Idiot.

'Oh, okay,' he says suspiciously. 'Where are your leaflets?' He looks at my empty hands.

Crap. Why did I choose leaflets? I should have gone with another story. ANY other story!

'Oh…' I look down at my hands. 'I forgot them.' I force a laugh, still trying to keep it all sounding French. 'I'm so scatty, you see. This is why I don't think I'm going to be doing this job long.'

His eyes soften. 'You don't look like the normal type anyway.'

Wait a minute. Is he…flirting with me? Outside of his flat he shares with his girlfriend. Does this guy have no shame?

I'm about to retreat when I spot Mags, Samuel and Lexi behind him, attempting to sneak out of the back gate. What the fuck is wrong with them?! Why wouldn't they wait until he'd gone before attempting this? Quick, think of something to distract him.

'Well, I normally have an office job, but I'm just doing anything to make ends meet at the moment, you know,' I blabber on as Mags, Samuel and Lexi walk towards Mags's car.

'A pretty little thing like you won't be out of work long,' he smiles, his green eyes flirting with me.

Pretty little thing? I hate being called pretty and little. It's actually insulting.

I force myself to smile back and flutter my eyelashes. Anything to keep him talking.

BEEP!

Just when I think the two of them can't be anymore stupid, Mags has opened her car with the beeper. His head begins to turn to investigate. I grab it with both hands.

'Wait!' I shout desperately.

'What?' he asks, alarmed.

'Err…' Think, Sadie! Think of something!

I crush my lips to his, it being my last resort. I wave my hands around frantically to try and motion for them to hurry the hell up into the car, but he misreads it for a sign of passion and sticks his tongue past my tightly pressed lips.

 The horrifying thing is that he's not a bad kisser. He's actually pretty bloody fantastic. Oh my God, what is wrong with me? I'm enjoying a kiss from a girlfriend beater I despise? I seriously need to get some. Not being kissed in a long time is doing weird things to my brain.

'Anyway,' I say, forcing myself away. 'I should go…you know…get those leaflets.'

He smiles. He really is gorgeous. No wonder she fell for his charms. He must have reeled her in and only then shown her his anger. When she was already trapped emotionally.

'Let me get your number first,' he grins happily.

God, he has no shame. We're standing outside of the flat he shares with his girlfriend and he's not only kissing a random woman whose name he doesn't know, but now he's wanting to have some sort of torrid affair!

I take his phone and put in a fake number, along with a fake name. I go with Esmerelda. It's the only thing I can think of at such short notice. I watched the Hunchback of Notre Dame the other night.

He looks at the name and smiles curiously.

'I'll call you soon, Esmerelda.'

I force a smile before hobbling off.

'I'm telling you that I don't need to see a doctor,' I complain as Mags gives the receptionist my details in A & E.

'And I'm *telling* you that you do,' she snaps, tutting heavily.

Lexi laughs. 'Who knew Mags could be such a badass?' She chuckles, smiling at her warmly.

Mags points towards the red plastic chairs. I roll my eyes, but begrudgingly go to sit down. I wince when it stings my arse. What the hell did I do to myself? I might as well make myself comfortable. They're never quick here.

After four ridiculous hours of waiting and me bitching that this is totally unnecessary, my name is called by a doctor. We all walk behind the door and follow him to a bed, which he pulls a blue curtain around.

'What can I do for you?' he asks, all jolly. He's annoying already. He's got a big round belly and a dodgy comb over.

I sigh and roll my eyes again. This is so stupid. I could be at home icing it by now. Not embarrassing myself.

'She's hurt her bottom,' Mags says for me, as if I'm a toddler. 'Needs it seen to.'

The doctor and I turn bright red. She just said my bottom needs seeing to. How mortifying.

'Yep,' Lexi nods teasingly. 'She's been a bad, bad girl and she needs to be punished.'

Jesus, Lexi! The doctor turns puce while I whack her on the head. I'm no better than that boyfriend of hers.

'May I ask what happened to your shoulder?' he asks, trying to assess Lexi's shoulder from the t-shirt that's slipped down, making it visible.

'No, you may not,' she snaps, standing upright. 'It was an accident. We're here for my friend.' She points towards me.

'I'm well aware of that,' he reasons, 'but it's part of my duty of care to report any incidents which may have resulted from domestic violence.'

Nothing gets past this guy. He's not jolly now that he's dealing with us.

'Well, I haven't been domestically violenced!' she shrieks. 'I mean…I haven't had that done to me. I'm fine,' she shrugs, crossing her arms defensively over her chest.

'Okay,' he says, clearly still suspicious. 'Maybe I should see to Miss Taylor's injuries alone? I'm sure she'd appreciate some privacy.'

I nod shyly. Thank God. I could really do with as little people seeing my arse crack as possible.

Lexi laughs. 'That's not what she was saying at the Xmas do when she was mooning us all!' She's still hysterically laughing, tears running down her cheeks, when Mags drags her out.

'Now then,' he smiles. 'May I be as rude as to ask to see your back side?'

I feel my cheeks get so hot it feels like I'm on fire. How mortifying. I nod and shimmy out of my pencil skirt and lay face down on the bed. He pulls my knickers to the side and then coughs awkwardly.

'I'm afraid I'm going to have to lower them. Is that okay?'

I'd rather have died. So embarrassing!

'Uh-huh,' I mumble through the paper they lay on the beds.

He lowers my knickers and I cringe inwardly. And why did I have to be wearing my joke Xmas present knickers? They're bright pink with the words '*it's not going to spank itself...*' printed on the bum. He must think I'm a right slut.

'Yes,' he says, very close to my arse, 'you've got quite a few scrapes here, as well as some early bruising. Quite unusual. Do you mind if I ask how you obtained these injuries?'

Yes, I do mind, but unlike Lexi I'm too polite to decline.

'I...err...'

'It's just that you wouldn't see these kind of injuries from a normal fall. Quite severe, you see.'

'I fell off a window,' I admit, still with my face crushed into the paper on the bed.

'Fell?' he blurts out, his tone full of disbelief. 'My goodness, how on earth did that happen?'

I sigh heavily. 'It's a long story,' I admit wearily. One I'd rather be telling him when my knickers are back up.

'Okay. I can tell you don't want to go into it. I'm going to clean these cuts up and then cover some with bandages. I'll be right back.'

I look up to see him open the curtain and slip back behind it. I really wish he'd have covered my arse first. I feel so exposed.

Why is my life so ridiculous?! This would never happen to a normal person. Oh well, no point in dwelling on it. I've never been normal.

I rest my head back down and try to think of better things. Only all I can think of is how Lexi's boyfriend is going to react when he finds she's left. I've acted confident in front of her, but the truth is that I have no idea how he's going to react. Luckily he has no idea where Mags lives, otherwise I'd be seriously concerned about both of their safety.

'Coo-ee!' comes a voice as the curtain is pulled back.

I flinch and desperately try to cover myself, but it's too late. Looking at me, at my face thankfully, is Nurse Menzie, the nurse from the chemo ward. What the hell is she doing here? This isn't her department. I pull a blanket up to cover my bruised arse.

'I heard you were here so I thought I'd come down.'

How the hell would she have heard I was here?

'Sorry? You *heard* I was here?' There's no way she could have heard my voice from the chemo department. It's all the way across the other side of the building.

'Yes,' she giggles, trying to cover her mouth to muffle the sound. 'Everyone's talking about the girl who came in with the sore bum!'

My face turns beetroot. 'What?'

Just kill me now.

'Oh, don't be so offended,' she smiles. 'We get all sorts in here. Any kind of sexual injuries are always talked about.'

'Sexual? You mean…' She can't seriously mean... 'Do you think there's something stuck up my arse?' I shriek in disbelief. 'Because it's not! Look.' I throw the sheet away to reveal my scraped bottom.

'Oh, I see,' she nods, her eyes widening. She smiles devilishly. 'Boyfriend get a bit carried away with the flogger, did he? I keep telling you girls repeatedly to have a safe word, but the amount of times people forget them is *beyond* me.'

Is she *serious?*

'This isn't a flogger injury, thank you very much,' I snap. 'I fell.'

'Of course you did, dear.' She pats me on the head like a dog. 'It's all popular and normal now, isn't it? Since that book came out its all people want to do. No more missionary, or what do they call it now? Strawberry?'

'You mean vanilla,' I deadpan.

'Anyway, that's not the real reason I'm here.'

'Oh?' I turn around fully to meet her suspicious eyes. Crap. She knows something. I knew she was suspicious with me having so many friends with cancer.

'I think we both know the reason you're in my ward more than most of my patients, don't we?' She smiles knowingly.

Shit. She's totally on to me. She's going to rat me out. Call the police and send me to prison. Nosey old cow. And she had to laugh at my arse first. What a bitch.

'What do you mean?' I ask innocently. Maybe I can still wiggle out of this.

She leans down to my ear and whispers, 'I know you're dealing marijuana.'

I gulp down the panic. She knows. Oh my God. Oh my fucking God.

'Are you…' I pause to swallow down some sick trying to escape, 'are you going to tell on me?' I realise I sound like a school girl, but I'm as scared as one.

'Of course not,' she smiles brightly. 'Although we're going to have to talk about you being more discreet.'

Oh, thank baby Jesus! My body starts to unclench itself.

'Oh...okay,' I nod, sure this isn't where the conversation is going to end.

'Truth is that I get a lot of cancer patients who ask me if I have recommendations for it. They're all too scared to approach any *actual* drug dealers and they're too mortified to ask their children to help them. I was thinking I could give them your details.'

'Oh my God,' I gush in complete shock. She wants to help me? 'That's so nice of you.'

At this rate we could end up doubling our business. Amazing!

She smiles. 'I just can't bear for them to go through it. I see them come back, time and time again. They've less hair, less energy, but most of all less spirit. Sometimes they're desperate for something to ease it, and if this eases it even a little bit it will be worth it for so many people.'

She's so unbelievably sweet. Finally someone who gets what we're trying to do here.

'That's great.' I smile, trying to imagine how much more money we'll make now. Maybe we'll get really rich and I'll be able to buy a new car. Something with power steering. Oh, a girl can dream.

'And I want a five percent cut for all my recommendations.'

My mouth drops open.

'What?' I sound as flummoxed as I feel. The bitch wants commission? Well, there goes my thinking that she's Mother Theresa.

'I'd love to do it out of the kindness of my heart, but I've got a cat with a heart murmur. Vet bills coming out of my ears. I need some extra cash.'

Vet bills? Who'd have known it? A dodgy nurse.

We agree to a plan and exchange numbers just before the doctor gets back. He cleans my cuts and grazes. I have to bite into the paper as it stings so badly. Then he covers it with some big plasters.

'Now, I want you to keep an eye on your back pain. You may have damaged some lumbar discs, so if there's any intense pain go see your doctor immediately. In the meantime, I'm giving you a prescription for co-codamol. That should help with the pain.'

'Thanks, doctor.' I take the prescription and am just about to leave when I turn around again. Maybe I can try to salvage some of my reputation. 'And maybe you could help spread the rumour that this wasn't sex related?'

I don't want the whole world thinking I'm a dirty bitch with love eggs stuck up my arse.

He smiles knowingly. 'Of course. And on that note I actually have a few leaflets for you and your friend.'

He hands them over. The first one is about dealing with domestic violence and helpline numbers. The second is titled *Suicidal Thoughts*. Huh? Why the hell would he think I'm suicidal? Actually...I suppose I did tell him I fell from a window.

'Wait, you don't think...I *jumped* out of the window do you?'

He smiles sympathetically. 'I told you before, Miss Taylor. I'm not here to judge.'

Oh, Jesus fucking Christ.

Chapter 8

<u>Tuesday 22nd September</u>

The door knocks the next morning, startling me. I'm on the sofa on my stomach. It's the only position I can seem to be in that doesn't hurt my arse or my back. I grunt before peeling myself off it. I drag my tired legs towards the door since Samuel isn't going to get out of bed. His work hours are always crazy. He didn't get in until 2am last night, poor thing. Not that he'd ever get the door anyway. He treats me like a bloody assistant.

I smooth my hair down with my palms and check that I'm presentable enough in the mirror. I didn't get a chance to straighten my hair this morning, so it's wavy and sticking up at the ends. I look pale, but no paler than normal. I'll do, I suppose. I'm sure it's just Ivy informing me of another imminent war.

I swing the door open and jolt when crystal blue eyes meet mine. It's that guy, Harry. The drink spiller. What the hell? He looks back at me, just as confused, with one eyebrow raised. He almost looks comical.

'Harry?' I blurt out. I love the sound of his name on my lips.

But damn, why did I say his name? This will make him think I've been dreaming about him. When I have. A normal person wouldn't have replayed the coffee shop in their head fifteen times, each time ending with us naked and covered in coffee beans. But I never claimed to be normal.

'Hi,' he says with an odd smile. He leans back to check the door number. 'I think I've got the right address. Do you know a Sadie Taylor?'

I grin, feeling instantly giddy. He knows my name. It sounds so sexy on his lips. He must have tracked me down. It seems I'm not the only one fantasizing of coffee beans. But wait, he didn't think I was Sadie? Why not? That means he can't have tracked me down here then. Why is he here?

I'm suddenly aware of how rough I look. Maybe he doesn't even recognise me. I try again to flatten my hair down discreetly. Then I remember I'm wearing my yellow fluffy dressing gown. I must look like big bird.

'I *am* Sadie Taylor,' I state calmly. 'Were you looking for me?' I lower the gown from one shoulder, showing some of my nightdress. I lean against the door in what I hope is a sexy pose, fluttering my eyelashes. Only I must do it too aggressively because an eyelash falls into my eye, making it water like a stream. Fuck, it stings! I blink furiously in an attempt to get rid of it. I look back up to see him looking at me with a concerned expression, only his eyes show a flicker of amusement. Great way to look like an imbecile.

'Err…yes. I was. Looking for you,' he nods. 'Can I come in?'

You can do more than come in big boy.

God, why are my thoughts suddenly so filthy? I never normally react to someone like this. I must be the first person in the world to not really care for sex. It's always been mediocre, and to be frank, I'd rather do without it. I'd much prefer hot chocolate and a Twilight marathon. Not that I'd ever tell anyone that.

I nod and stand back for him to walk past me. His citrusy scent wafts into my nostrils and I almost pass out. He smells *so good!* Good enough to eat.

He looks back at me in question. I quickly try to look like I wasn't just sniffing him. I try to cover it with a cough and indicate to the sitting room. He sits down on the edge of the sofa with one leg crossed over the other.

'This is a bit awkward to be honest,' he starts, wringing his hands together. He seems stressed.

'O…kay.'

What the hell is he here for? Oh wait…he did say he was onto new drug dealers. Shit. Is he here investigating me or something? No, he can't know about us. Who on earth would suspect a little woman like me?

I'm distracted by how good he looks in his suit. It really is a mighty fine suit. Its grey pinstripe and he's wearing it with a burgundy shirt and black tie. In that suit it's hard not to notice his bulging biceps. I'm surprised it doesn't rip apart from the strain. Yum.

Just then Samuel walks into the room wearing nothing but his ridiculous smurf boxer shorts. They say 'I never kiss and smurf.' He puts his hand through his hair, clearly still not awake, and falls back into the sofa next to Harry. Harry widens his eyes in alarm. I try to bite my lip to stop me from smiling. Samuel finally looks up and notices him.

'Oh, shit,' he blurts out, jumping up to sitting. 'Hi. Sorry, I didn't realise anyone was here.' He looks at me accusingly before leaning back and having a good look of Harry, clearly appreciating the beauty. Who wouldn't? 'Did it hurt?' he asks.

Harry creases his forehead in agitation. 'Sorry?'

'When you fell from heaven?' Samuel grins, revelling in making him uncomfortable.

He is *so* inappropriate.

Harry looks like his brain might explode from bewilderment. He looks at me for help. I decide not to. It's more fun this way.

'Sorry, what were you saying?' I ask, ignoring his being uncomfortable and trying to appear serious.

'Right.' he shakes his head as if he is trying to pull himself together and gather his thoughts. 'I'm DC McKenzie. You obviously know me as Harry. We've had a tip off that there's a new gang of dealers in the market.'

Oh my fucking God. He IS asking me about the drugs. And in front of Samuel, who has no idea about any of this. Ugh! Kill me now.

'Right...?' I try to act as confused as possible.

He locks his baby blues intently with mine. His tongue sneaks out and licks his lips. God, why is everything he does so sexual?

'Someone gave us your name.'

My name? Who the fuck could have done that? One of Mags's friends? A suspicious nurse? But I've got nurse Menzie on my side now. She wouldn't tell on me, especially now she's been promised a five percent cut. Maybe I can get her to check if the others are on my trail.

'Who? And what are you saying?' I demand, trying my best to act offended and innocent, Like I'm not shitting it and worried about my future in prison.

'Are you...calling her a drug dealer?' Samuel interrupts, his face serious.

I look to him in alarm. Shit. Someone get me a bucket of wine to stick my head in.

He explodes into hilarious high squeaky giggles before I have a chance to panic further. Harry squirms uncomfortably in his seat.

I give Samuel the death stare. 'Well, are you? Calling me a drug dealer?'

He puts his palms up in defence. 'I'm here to ask you some questions regarding it. That's all.'

Shit, shit, shit.

'Do I need a lawyer?'

'Only if you've done something wrong,' he challenges with a smirk.

What a prick. Trying to trick me like this. There I was fantasizing about his cock and he's the biggest dickhead I've ever met.

'Don't worry, babe,' Samuel smiles. 'I've seen a shit load of Judge Judy. I've got this.' He turns to Harry and asks earnestly, 'What questions do you have for my client?'

Harry furrows his eyebrow at him in amusement before turning back to face me. 'Do you have any idea why your name would be mentioned in connection with drugs?'

'No! Jesus, who do you think I am?' I shout far too dramatically. My pulse is racing. I hope he doesn't notice.

'Don't say anything,' Samuel shrieks. 'Don't say *anything,* except no comment.' He winks at me. 'I told you, I've got this.'

Harry rolls his eyes, sighing loudly. He ignores Samuel and looks back to me. 'No ex-boyfriends that dealt with drugs, particularly marijuana?'

That's enough to get Samuel collapsing into fresh giggles. 'That would mean her actually having to get a boyfriend! She doesn't date.'

Shut up, Samuel! Bloody idiot!

'No,' I say to Harry, trying to keep this clear cut. 'No real exes. I mean, no bad ones.'

'You don't date?' he blurts out, sounding shocked as if I just told him I spray unicorn farts on myself as perfume. 'Why not?'

Oh Jesus, this guy wants my life story. What am I going to do? Tell him I have trust and abandonment issues that would scare the shit out of any guy? I don't think so.

'I just don't,' I shrug, praying my cheeks aren't turning pink.

'She's got issues,' Samuel whispers with an amused grin. 'I had to take this bitch's virginity.'

My eyes bulge in horror and my stomach drops to the floor.

'Oh my God, Samuel! Shut the fuck up!'

I can feel myself growing bright red from head to toe.

I look at Harry to see him staring intently at me, obviously trying to assess what the hell is wrong with me. He could be here a while.

'So…no ex-boyfriends or enemies who would put your name forward to try and get you in trouble?'

I rock on my heels awkwardly. 'Nope. Everyone loves me,' I joke, snorting nervously. Way to sound like a constipated pig.

He seems to consider this for a second. 'And can I ask what you do for a living?'

'Nothing at the moment,' I shrug, looking down at the carpet. 'I got made redundant so I'm on the dole.' It never stops being embarrassing when I have to tell people.

He doesn't seem surprised. 'Oh, I'm sorry.'

I nod. 'Me too.' I hate how people act like I just said I lost a great relative.

'So anyway,' Samuel grins, leaning forward and touching Harry's tie. 'Enough about Sadie. What do *you* do for fun?' He follows it with a wink.

He really is too much.

Harry looks at him completely bewildered, before looking back to me. 'Is there anything else that you wish to pass on to the police?'

I gulp, the panic clawing at my neck.

'No.' I shake my head, more to assure myself than anything else.

He clasps his hands together. 'Well then, I won't take any more of your time.' He stands up and walks himself to the door.

The minute it clicks shut Samuel turns to me, all evidence of a smile gone.

'So are you going to tell me what the fuck is going on?'

Harry's Diary

Fuck. Bambi eyes is a criminal. I didn't see that one coming. She looks like a little angel. Well, a little angel with the longest, sexiest legs I've ever seen. When she opened the door in her dressing gown, the hint of her sexy nightie underneath, I couldn't stop staring at her. She definitely doesn't look like someone starting a new drug ring to rival Joaquin Khoner.

I mean, how on earth did she ever get involved in this? According to her record she's had a full time job for the last ten years, but got made redundant recently. She told me the same. How do you go straight from being a responsible employee to getting mixed up with drugs? Mind you, according to the report her mother was a drug addict and she was taken into foster care when she was seven. She never stayed at one place too long and then she ran away at sixteen and was off the radar for two whole years. Maybe she got mixed up with drugs then. Who knows?

What I can tell you is that the description I read on my intelligence report and the Sadie I met today could be two completely different people. I was expecting someone messed up with greasy hair, gangly teeth and tattoos. Or the other extreme. She could have been a smooth organised criminal dripping in Prada or whatever designer shit women wear these days. But she was neither. I might have just met her properly once before, but in some ways I feel like I already know her. But she's still so confusing. I normally find women so easy to read, but this one's a fucking puzzle with six pieces eaten by the dog.

She's all bambi eyes with this almost laid back attitude to her. She wears nice clothes, but doesn't look over done or tarty. Just sexy as fuck in those tight little pencil skirts. Maybe that's the problem. I fancy her. If I'm honest with myself I've wanted to fuck her ever since I spilled those shots on her. Which causes a problem. I don't want it to interfere with the investigation. But I have a feeling she fancies me too. Of course she would, why wouldn't she? I'm a fucking catch.

I suppose I could always use my good looks to my advantage. Pretend I'm really interested in her and get her close. So close she'd confide in me. Plus, if I got to fuck her it would be an added advantage. I haven't had any in months. And I need this promotion. Every time I see Dad he's asking me when I'm going to move up in the ranks. I'm fucking sick of it.

Plus it sounds like she hasn't had any in forever. What the fuck was that whole 'I don't date' thing about? Why the hell wouldn't she? And losing her virginity to her gay best friend? What the fuck is that about? He must have been joking. But I'd be lying if I said I wasn't intrigued by her.

I'm going to get her close, break this case, bring her and her friends down and live happily ever after.

Plan. Set. Motion.

Chapter 9

Samuel was on me the minute Harry left. Luckily I sold him a big lie about knowing nothing about it. I *despise* lying to him. It actually makes me feel sick. I still don't know if he bought it, but he stopped questioning me. Well, after he reinforced to me that he can't be attached to anyone in trouble.

You see, Samuel works for THE Oliver James. That's right, the famous chef. He ran a programme years back where anyone was open to apply for a chefs training job, homeless included. We were only in a B & B back then so it was hard for us to even get a job interview. That's the vicious cycle of being homeless. You can't get a job as you don't have a permanent address, but you need a job to have a permanent address!

Anyway, he went along, knowing nothing about food except that he wished he had more to eat. Oliver saw something in him that day and took him on, along with a handful of others. They were completely trained up and taken under his wing. Samuel's now the sous chef in his restaurant Ninety Nine. Oliver's such a great guy. We've been invited to Christmas do's and family days at his house and his family is always so welcoming. That's part of the problem though. He's got such a good family man image in the media. All of his staff is warned that any involvement in illegal activity will result in them getting fired immediately. The press are always hungry to try and discredit him, and even a staff member would be used against him.

I'm really trying not to think about it. I started this thing so that we wouldn't lose our home, but if he got fired we would anyway. It's too stressful to even contemplate, so I've decided to check in on Mags today. Lexi mentioned that she was going to be out for the day and that she might need some company. It's funny how Lexi puts on such a bad ass image when really she's the sweetest thing ever.

I knock on the door and wait. And wait. Where the hell is she? I'm sure she's in. Her Ford's on the drive.

I climb over her orange roses and place my hands over her window as a shield from the sun so I can look in. Everything seems quiet in there. God, I hope she's okay. What if she's fallen or something? The cancer could have made her weak. Maybe she's crying out for help and I just can't hear her. I need to break in. What the hell, I'm already a drug dealer. I might as well add breaking and entering to the rap sheet.

I stand back to assess her house. It really is too big for just her. What woman needs a four bedroom house? But she says no one has come to view it yet. I don't know why, it's gorgeous. All white painted bricks, blue French shutters on the windows, flowers boxes full of hydrangeas. I'd love to live here. Sure, the inside needs some updating, but it's a real home.

I spot a window open upstairs. It's frosted so it must be the bathroom. I'll have to tell Mags off for leaving it open. Doesn't she know anyone could break in nowadays? Least of all me.

I climb behind her roses again, getting a thorn caught in my leg. Fuck, that stings. I pull it out and try to ignore it and instead try to climb on the window sill. The last time this happened I fell hard on my arse. I'll try everything in my power for that not to happen again. Especially with that thorn bush underneath me. I cannot go back to that hospital with another arse injury. Especially if it's covered in rose thorns.

I hold onto the guttering and try resting my body weight on it. It seems strong enough. I look up at the window. If I could climb up this guttering I'd be able to get on top of the porch. Then I could easily climb in the window. I take a deep breath. Here goes nothing.

I clutch onto the guttering and let my legs wrap around the bottom of it, using all of my upper body strength to pull myself up. It gives me flash backs to climbing the rope in gym class. It didn't matter what school I was attending at the time, that day would always end with me screaming, 'I can't fucking do it, so stop making me fucking try!' at the gym teacher. And the sensitive bastards would always make sure I was suspended over it. How dramatic. Now I wished I'd tried harder to build some upper body strength.

I'm almost within jumping distance of the porch roof when I feel the guttering give way. I feel it crumble to nothing, but I hold on and pray that the upper part is stronger. It starts to sag under the pressure of me. I'm going to fall on my arse again!

In a last minute ditch attempt to save myself, I somehow swing my body over to the porch. One hand grabs onto the felt roof just as the rest of the guttering falls away. I quickly reach my other hand out to steady myself. God, this would be easier if I wasn't so heavy. If I'd have known I was going to have to carry my own body weight I wouldn't have eaten that Crunchie last night.

I flail my legs, desperately searching for something to push myself up with. I settle on a small hanging basket. I dig my foot into it, causing it to swing wildly. I try to steady it and pull myself up. This never seemed so hard in swimming class. Now I can barely lift myself. Pathetic. Why couldn't I have strong arms like Michelle Obama? Maybe Samuel's right and I need to try one of his insanity DVD's. But I see him mop up his sweat afterwards. It's gross.

I finally manage to haul my body up onto the porch. I'm up! Thank the Lord! I lay there panting for some time. Jeez, what a workout!

The sound of vomiting fills my ear drums and I search around, checking to see if it's me. Could I be so exhausted that I'm having an out of body experience? Am I dying and my spirit is travelling up to heaven? Or maybe down to hell. God, don't think about that. I take another deep breath and look down at myself and the ground around me. I've not vomited. That's weird. I focus in on the sound and realise its coming from the open window. Mags! It has to be Mags. Shit.

I scramble up, pull the window open wider and slide my leg in. I try to get my other leg in, which I eventually manage, but only after I've damaged my vagina to a point where I'm not sure if it's now deformed. I fall into the bath with a thud. Damn, there goes my leg.

'Aargh!' Mags shrieks from her position over the toilet bowl. She focuses in on me, working out who I am. 'Sadie, what on earth are you doing here? Why didn't you just ring the doorbell like a normal person?' she demands.

'You have a doorbell?' I ask stupidly, lowering myself out of the bath. Idiot, idiot.

'Of course I do,' she snaps, flushing the loo and standing up. This isn't like Mags. 'Sorry,' she sighs. 'I'm just snappy because I'm having a bad day.'

'I figured.' I smile weakly, taking in her tired appearance.

Her face is grey and her eyes are without their usual life. Her cheeks are hollowed out, making her look gaunt. Even her collarbones are protruding. How the hell could Lexi have left her like this? Surely she must have realised what a mess she's in?

'Look at your leg,' she gasps.

What? I look down to see blood dripping down it from where I caught it on the thorn bush.

'Oh, yeah, sorry about that. I kind of had a fight with your rose bush.' I grimace apologetically. I really hope they weren't her favourite.

'Let me get the first aid kit,' she sighs, reaching into the bathroom cabinet.

'No, Mags,' I insist, pushing her down by her shoulders onto the closed toilet seat. 'Jesus, you're the one whose ill here and you're trying to look after me. What's wrong with you?' I ask rhetorically.

I stare into the bathroom cabinet and finally find the little green bag marked with a white cross. I open it up and stare dumbly inside. I literally have no idea what she planned to do. I figured I'd just leave it and hope it scabs over.

She sighs again, standing up and grabbing the kit from my hand.

'Just let me do it.'

I can't really argue with her. I honestly have no clue. That and she seems to be a bit brighter when she's bossing me around. Whatever makes her happy.

She takes out a blue looking liquid and sprays it onto my cut. It stings like a motherfucker!

'Aaagh!' I flinch, throwing my leg out of her way before she can inflict more pain. 'What the fuck are you doing?' I blurt out.

'It's just antiseptic,' she tuts. 'Stop being a baby.'

'I'm not being a baby,' I snap, crossing my arms defensively as she starts wiping at my cut. I flinch again.

'Jesus, anyone would think your mother never did this when you were younger.'

My stomach falls out of my knickers, just like it always does whenever she's mentioned.

'She didn't,' I admit sheepishly. She looks up into my eyes, clearly confused. No one knows about my past apart from Samuel. 'I mean, I never cut myself before,' I lie. I want to make her feel better. People hate feeling bad about putting their foot in their mouths.

She applies a plaster over it while I watch, fascinated. The truth is that of course I've had cuts and scrapes before, but the difference with being in a random foster home is that you don't want to be any trouble. These people are already letting you live with them. The last thing you want to do is be a bigger nuisance. So I'd just wash it with water myself and leave it. I never died. All this antiseptic shit is for pansies if you ask me.

She shocks me when she plants a quick kiss over it. 'There,' she smiles. 'All better.'

Why is it I suddenly feel like I may burst into tears? People like Mags were made to be mum's. Why couldn't I have had someone like her? Not the drug addict delinquent I ended up with. I feel my throat start to clog up with emotion.

'Anyway.' I shake my head to try and get back in the room and away from my past. 'Why were you being sick? I thought your chemo was last week?'

'It was,' she nods sadly. 'It seems to get me the worst the week after,' she admits reluctantly.

'Then why the hell did you let Lexi leave? You should have told her.'

'And what?' She smiles sadly. 'Asked her to stay in and look after a pathetic old woman?'

Is that really how she sees herself? My heart breaks.

'Mags, you're not pathetic. Or old,' I quickly add.

'Well, I feel it right now.' She bows her head down, and before I know it she's full on crying.

Shit. I am *not* good with criers. I pat her head, much like I would a dog and make shushing noises. That's what they do in films, right?

'Where are your kids?' I ask lightly. 'Surely they should be checking in on you?'

I know she has four grown children; three boys and a girl.

'I don't want to worry them,' she sniffs. She looks up but quickly avoids my gaze.

Hang on a minute. Something fishy is going on here. If she was my Mum you wouldn't get rid of me.

'Wait a minute. You…have told them you have cancer, right?' I end it with a laugh, feeling ridiculous for even having to ask that question.

She looks down ashamed, tears falling onto her lap. She shakes her head slowly.

'WHAT?' She jumps at my scream. 'Why the hell wouldn't you tell them? I know you don't want to worry them with the money stuff, but this is serious. This is something they should know.'

She straightens herself up, her face suddenly determined. 'They've just lost their father.'

'Mags, that was months ago.' I realise how heartless I sound the minute it comes out of my mouth.

She shakes her head adamantly. 'They'll only want to worry about me. Be here all the time, clucking around me like worried hens. I couldn't handle it. They're busy with their own lives, their own families.'

She's such a good mother. It pains me to even think it. Here she is holding back what could be devastating news to them, potentially making herself sicker in the process, just so she can keep the pain from them. She deserves a medal.

'Well then,' I say, just as determined. 'It looks like *we're* going to look after you.'

She looks up at me, her brows furrowed.

'I'm fine,' she says. 'Honestly.' Her voice breaks on the word. It's pretty clear she isn't.

She really is pig-headed. There's no way I can tell her about Harry investigating me now.

'No arguments, Mags. We'll work out a system or something. You need help.'

'I don't,' she tries to argue.

I put my hand up to halt her. 'No more of this shit, Mags. Go get your arse into bed right now or I'm calling your kids.'

'You wouldn't,' she gasps in horror.

'I would.' I smile devilishly. 'Now march that arse back into bed while I make you some lunch.'

She unwillingly goes along with it. I make her lunch and bring it in. She tries to refuse it, claiming her stomach can't handle anything. Luckily, I know what's light on the stomach. If my mum was ever on a come down she'd be sick as a dog, and crackers with jam were the only thing she could handle. I think the sugar in the jam helps too.

As I feed her the crackers and sips of her tea I realise how fragile she truly is. Has she really been performing so that we think she's better than she is? That must be exhausting. No wonder she's so grey. I take the tray away from her, tuck her in, and carry the tray back downstairs.

After washing up I call Lexi.

'Hey, bitch, what's up?' she answers.

'We need to talk,' I whisper. 'We have two serious problems.'

She tuts. 'God, chill, will you?' she says, short-tempered.

I roll my eyes even though she can't see me. 'There was a detective around snooping around. Apparently they've been given my name.'

'Shit the bed!' she shouts, immediately losing her cool. 'Okay, this *is* bad.'

'That's not the worst though. Mags is seriously ill. We really need to talk.'

Chapter 10

The girls and I have worked out a system. There's to always be someone with Mags at all times. The chemo sessions are easy, as that's when we deliver most of our latest stock. I find it helpful if I refer to it as 'stock'. Makes me feel less like a criminal and more like an entrepreneur.

I've just left Mags with Steph and Ruby, after also telling her that Harry is onto us, and am returning home when I feel that someone is watching me. I first feel it when I go in to get a coffee, but I shrug it off. I mean, loads of people are in there. I'm just being paranoid. Thank God I don't smoke this stuff myself.

As I walk along the road to the tube the feeling of being followed surrounds me. It's like the walls are closing in around me. I look all around, gathering more bewildered stares from passers-by. Why am I so worried? Oh, that's right, because I'm an underground criminal now. I forget sometimes.

I pull my coat collar up around my neck and hurry my pace. I'm totally overreacting. I know I am. But that doesn't stop me from wanting to burst into a sprint screaming HEEEEEELP ME! Instead I choose a strange kind of skip. It brings me more attention. At least people will notice if I get attacked and dragged into an alley.

I'm just turning the corner when I bump into a hard wall of muscle. Ouch. I rub my forehead and look up, sure I'm about to be murdered. Instead it's Harry. Or DC McKenzie as I should really be calling him. Harry sounds too familiar. I must start looking at him as the detective.

'Hi,' he smiles. Well, I say smiles, but it's a tight-lipped smile. Not one of his megawatt ones. Still so gorgeous I want to suck on him though.

'Were you following me?' I accuse, out of breath from panic.

He tips his head back, his face turning serious. 'You're being followed?' He starts looking around me discreetly.

Okay, so it's clearly not him. Calm down, woman. He's a policeman. You're safe now.

'I was hoping I'd bump into you actually.' He does another tight-lipped smile.

What am I saying? He's a policeman! He's clearly looking to arrest me. Could I kick him in the shins and run until I'm in Mexico? Doubtful. His legs look long and muscly. Damn, they really do. I mentally slap myself in the face. Get a hold of yourself, woman. You can't fancy the detective trying to send you to prison.

'Oh?' I ask vaguely, looking around as if I have no idea what he's on about. As if I have no idea I'm going to be in prison clothes soon.

'Yeah.' He looks me dead in the eye, his face more serious than normal. 'I was wondering if you'd like to go to dinner with me tomorrow night?'

My eyebrows furrow as I replay his words in my mind. He's…asking me on a date? I stare back at his rectangular face, searching for answers. Is he trying to set me up?

'But…aren't you investigating me?' My lips have started twitching. I bite down on it to try and stop it.

'Not anymore,' he shrugs dismissively. 'You're innocent, right?'

'Right!' I shout too enthusiastically. My neck feels hot. Why the hell am I suddenly so hot?

'Well then.'

I bite my lip harder as I consider this. I know it's a bad idea. Having dinner with the enemy. What good could come from it? Nothing. He probably just wants to get me drunk so I'll spill all my secrets. But his crystal clear blue eyes are inviting me in. They're how I imagine the water in the Caribbean is. Not that I'll ever know. I'll be lucky if I get to Scunthorpe this year.

'Come on,' he smiles, encouraging me with his cheeky grin.

I allow myself one lazy look over his glorious face. He really is stunning. His cheeks and jawbone are so prominent they could be made of stone. Add to that his perfect nose and luscious pink lips against those eyes and...well, it's a wonder he didn't go down the modelling route. But that doesn't mean I can fancy him.

I shake my head. 'No. I'm sorry, but I'm not free.' I turn and start walking away. It's easier if I don't have to look at him while I'm rejecting him.

He's at my side in one quick stride. 'Well then, what about the following night?'

God, he's persistent. I look down, eager not to meet his eyes. I can feel them on me like laser beams burning through my resistance. What the hell is it with this guy? Why is he affecting me so much? It must be the whole danger of it.

I shake my head to try and clear my thoughts. 'I can't do that night either.' I pretend to look at my watch on my wrist, forgetting that I'm not actually wearing one.

'So…what you mean is…you don't want to go out with me?' he asks in barely concealed disbelief.

I risk a look at him and see the utter shock on it. It makes my mouth twitch with a smile, and before I can help myself I burst out laughing. I quickly cover my mouth to try and stifle it. I must look like a nutter.

'And now you're openly laughing at me?' He tries to make it sound like a joke, but his voice shows he's actually hurt. 'Way to break a guy's self-esteem down.'

As if. I bet this guy has a long list of willing participants.

I force a tight smile. 'See, I'm a bitch. You don't want to take me on a date.'

Jesus, why can't he just leave? The longer I'm walking next to him the longer I want to drag him into the nearest alleyway and rip all his clothes off. I wonder if his muscles are as sharp as those jaw bones. I wonder how his hard dick would feel pressed against me.

'But I'm a *delight*,' he grins. 'I've never had anyone refuse dinner before.'

He's such a cocky bastard. I get a strange thrill knowing I can refuse him and leave him stumped. Teach him a lesson; he's not God's gift to women. Even if he kind of is.

'Look,' he grabs my shoulders and turns me to face him on the busy street. 'Just think about it.' He looks intently into my eyes as if knowing they can shoot out sting rays of persuasion. 'Like I said, I'm a great dinner date.'

I'm sure he is. I'm also sure he has *lots* of experience. The man whore. I'd also guess he'd be a passionate lover. Oh Jesus, this is why I can't be around him. Pull yourself together, Sadie. Just get rid of him.

'Okay, I'll think about it. But only if you promise to stop following me. It's creepy.' At least this way I'll get him off my back.

His features drop in alarm, his brow furrowing. 'I'm not following you.'

He steps closer to me, his fresh scent surrounding me. He smells like citrus. I wonder what aftershave he wears. I want to buy it and spray it all over myself and then go to bed so it's all over my sheets. Is that wrong? If that's wrong then I don't want to be right.

He looks over my shoulder suspiciously. 'But now I'm thinking I should look into this for you. Have you reported it?'

And give the police more excuse to look into me? I don't think so. I follow his stare, but can't see anyone. How on earth do the people who smoke this stuff cope with the paranoia? I can't cope normally, let alone adding fuel to the fire. When I look back I find him staring intently at me. When did he get so close?

'Nah. It's nothing. Just a feeling.' I shrug to let him know it's no big deal.

'So…is that a yes to dinner?' He strokes my cheek with his thumb, sending a line of tingles along with it, zinging all the way down to my toes.

Whoa, someone has no issues with personal space. I'm not used to people touching me like that.

'I'll think about it,' I admit, shuffling from one foot to the other.

I feel bad letting him down. He's had the balls to ask me. And it does help he's drop dead gorgeous. But I can't seem to think clearly around him, and that's far too dangerous to risk mine and the girl's safety.

<u>Thursday 24th September</u>

The next day we've called a business meeting at Mags'. Steph has been dealing with the sums of everything, but it's been so crazy that we haven't worked out how much money we've actually earned and split it up yet. We're all eager for the cash.

'Wow,' Steph gushes as she hits the equal button on her pink calculator.

'What?' Lexi asks, narrowing her eyes on her. 'What's wrong?'

'Nothing,' she smiles, her eyes wide. 'It's actually fantastic.' She writes down a sum on a piece of paper and shows us all.

'That's the total?' Lexi shrieks, her eyes lighting up with pound signs.

'No,' Steph grins, still seeming dazed. 'That's each.'

'What?' Mags and I shout at once.

That's enough to pay back all of my minimum payments on my credit cards and cover the next month's mortgage and bill payments. Shit. Who knew? Crime pays. No wonder the world's gone to shit. Of course it all means fuck all if Harry raids us and sends us all to prison, but I don't want to scare the girls.

I'm still trying to figure it all out on my walk to the tube station. My car finally gave up on me. I keep checking my phone to see if Harry has contacted me, but there's nothing. Not that he took my number, but I assume he could get it if he wanted to. He's a cop. I'm clinging onto the small belief of hope that he'll change his mind about wanting to take me out.

As I walk towards the station, the same uneasy feeling of being watched creeps over me. I look around at the crowd, but don't see anything suspicious. I put my head down against the wind and pick up my pace. I'm almost at the tube when I feel someone grab me around the waist and pull me to the right.

It happens so quickly that I don't have time to register what's happening before I'm slammed up against a brick wall. Ah, my fucking neck! I look up to see I'm in an alley way and a threatening looking man is looking down at me, his fist holding onto my coat. He's got heavy stubble, which on closer inspection is going grey and an ugly looking scar over his lip. Oh my God. I'm getting raped.

'Please don't rape me!' I sob. 'I'll do anything. Take all my money, please!'

'Shut up,' he barks, slamming me hard against the wall again.

Fuck, it hurts, pain shooting down my spine. I silence myself, pure panic racing through my body. I'm going to die. I'm going to *die*.

'I have a message from my boss,' he snarls, his breath smelling of onions and potatoes.

His boss? Is he from our old company? Does he think I'm suing the company or something?

'You mean the CEO?' I blurt out.

He looks so annoyed I actually flinch, scared he'll smack me in the face.

'I'm here for Joaquin. He's well aware of your little *business.*' He smiles as if he finds me pathetic.

Business? Oh my God.

'Do you mean…the drugs?' I whisper, my lips trembling so hard I can barely get out the words.

'Of course I mean the fucking drugs,' he snarls, rolling his eyes. 'Fucking amateurs,' he hisses under his breath.

'Okay.' I tremble. 'What's the message?' I try to sound confident and strong, but I sound like a scared, squeaky mouse.

'Close down,' he spits, a bit of saliva shooting into my eye. Gross. 'You're starting to affect our business. And that makes it our business.'

He's talking in riddles, whether he realises or not.

'Take this message with a warning. The boss doesn't like to be ignored. Some would even say he gets nasty. Am I understood?'

This isn't considered nasty? I nod, my chest physically jumping up and down from fear. And just as fast as he appeared, he's gone.

Holy shit balls.

Chapter 11

I run all the way home from the station. It's the only way to stop myself from thinking. I know the minute I stop every terrifying thought is going to come crashing down around me. I leap up the concrete stairs, my shaking hands barely able to get my keys in the lock. I slam the door behind me and try to get my breath under control. In and out, Sadie. That's it.

Samuel sticks his head out of the sitting room door. 'Where on earth have you been, you dirty scally wag?' he asks jokingly.

Err...just running away from a threatening drug dealer. You know, just the usual Tuesday.

'Nowhere.'

If only he knew. Since when did my life turn into an episode from the Sopranos?

'Nowhere, my arse,' he laughs, cackling like a witch. 'Who were you with? A man?'

I look down so he can't see the fear in my eyes. Just remembering the way he slammed me against that wall makes me shudder with dread. How the hell am I going to sort this out? I just want my normal life back.

'No one you'd know,' I shrug.

I glance up to see his eyes widen. 'Oh my God, who is it?' he asks, clapping his hands, clearly thinking I have something exciting and fun to hide. I wish.

'I told you. No one,' I snap, walking into the sitting room and throwing my coat onto the sofa.

He follows me, smiling sadly. Why does he always look so disappointed that I don't have a boyfriend?

'Well, get dressed. We're going scouting.'

I groan loudly. Scouting means we're going on the streets to help homeless people. I really don't feel like helping anyone right now. What the hell can I offer them now that I'm a jobless drug dealing thug?

Unfortunately, my groan is ignored and I find myself begrudgingly getting dressed into jeans and a bomber jacket. We find it's better to blend in. Samuel still wears his pink hat and does the crazy act.

We're walking down Broad Street half an hour later when we spot a new girl. We can tell she's new immediately, not only because we haven't seen her before, but also because she's out in the elements. She's not under cover, not in a doorway. She clearly has no idea what she's doing. Samuel smiles at me as we approach her.

'Hi,' I smile as brightly as I can. 'Can we join you?'

She looks up at us, her chin trembling with apprehension. Her face is dirty and her eyes red rimmed. She's got such an innocent little face; large eyes and small barely there lips framed by wispy blonde curls. How the hell did she end up here?

She pulls her legs up into her chest, obviously afraid of us. Well, I suppose it doesn't help that Samuel's wearing that crazy pink hat. He really needs to rethink that approach.

'Suppose,' she shrugs, her eyes widening. She's freaking out.

I look at Samuel, trying to communicate to take off the hat. He ignores me, as per bloody usual. We sit down next to her. My bum flinches from the ice cold pavement. Ouch, I've forgotten how cold the ground is in weather like this.

'So what's your story?' Samuel asks, pulling out a jam sandwich and offering it to her.

She takes it from him enthusiastically. She obviously hasn't eaten in a few days.

'My story?' she says, bewildered.

'You're new,' I smile, trying to appear normal. Not that I even know what that is. 'Why are you homeless right now?'

She looks down at the pavement. 'Well...my...' her voice starts to break a little. She shoves the rest of the sandwich into her mouth. 'My stepdad,' she mumbles with a full mouth, the tears streaking down her face.

I nod. We've heard this story all too well. He's obviously abused her or at least tried. I look into her vulnerable eyes. She's too young to know this much sadness.

'Why don't you come back to ours? Have a shower, we'll feed you a dinner,' I offer, surprising myself.

Samuel shoots me a warning look. We don't normally bring them in upon first meeting them. But she's got something about her. She just seems so defenceless and I know we can help her. If we get her early enough she might stand a chance. If it wasn't for Samuel I dread to think what could have happened to me.

'Hey!' someone shouts behind us.

We both swivel round to see Welshie approaching us. Ugh, I still can't believe that twelve years later he's still around. He makes me physically sick. Scum like him just shouldn't exist.

'Are you scaring my girly here?' he asks, crouching down to smile at her. If I didn't know him I'd think he was a friendly guy. She smiles weakly back at him. Shit, he's already made a connection with her.

'We're not the ones scaring her,' Samuel says, rolling his eyes.

I point to him. 'You realise Welshie is a pimp, right?' I blurt out aggressively.

'Sadie,' Samuel whispers. It's true that we don't normally scare them this much straight away, but she needs to know before this shit gets real.

'What?' she asks, leaning away from him, her eyes wide with trepidation.

'That's right,' I continue. 'He doesn't carry a pimp stick like in those Snoop Dog videos, but he's still a pimp.'

Her eyebrows meet each other. 'Who's Snoop Dog?'

Sorry, what? Snoop Dog is still totally relevant, right? Although I do remember hearing he's a grandad now.

'Look, if you want to be selling your body in a few weeks for less than twenty quid go ahead and let him befriend you, but that's what will happen.'

'Sadie!' Samuel shouts. 'Don't scare her.'

'I'm sick of you two,' Welshie growls, his whole face screwed up into an angry snarl. 'Always sticking your nose in where it's not wanted. Why don't you just fuck off?'

My blood boils. How dare he? We're actually trying to help her. Not turn her into a cheap hooker. This guy is a total waste of oxygen. To think good people die of cancer every day and this low life is still breathing.

I walk up to him, my fists clenched at my sides.

'What I'm sick of is you preying on young girls when they're at their most vulnerable.' I'm aware I'm shouting and drawing a small crowd, but I can't help it.

He pulls a sickening smile. 'What's wrong, sweetheart? Upset I didn't want you?'

That's it. I see red. Red everywhere. Before I can talk myself out of it I raise my knee and kick him in the balls with as much force as I can muster. He hisses with pain, doubling over.

'You fucking bitch!' he yelps, almost on the floor. 'You're dead. Both of you.'

Samuel looks at me as if I've flipped the load completely. Maybe I have. 'Anyway, gotta go,' he calls back to them, grabbing my hand and dragging me off.

When we round the corner he pulls me to one side.

'Sadie, what the hell is wrong with you? Where has this feisty bitch come from? You're normally the sensitive one.'

I sigh and clench my fists. Maybe it's being threatened by a scary drug dealer. Maybe it's having my whole life turned upside down. Who knows? Either way, I don't even recognise myself, let alone try to explain it to him.

'I don't know. Maybe I've just stopped being such a fucking walk over. And people like him deserve a lesson being taught to them.'

He raises his eyebrows. 'Okay, whatever you say, queen bitch.'

Monday 28th September
I've decided not to tell the girls about being threatened. At least not yet. Although we've earnt good money so far I'm still nowhere near out of the woods. I still have a whole credit card to pay off and I could really do with the extra time. Plus his threat could be just that; words. For all I know he could be a pussy cat, hoping I run off crying. Which, I mean, okay I *did*, but still. Maybe if I stand my ground he'll back off. I *will* tell them, of course I will. Just not yet.

I hear him before I see him. I'm in my silk nightie trying to tidy up the living room when his soft, silky chuckle fills the air. My body tenses. Shit. What the hell is he doing here again?

I pull up the blinds and look down to find him talking to Ivy in the front garden. He's leaning on her mailbox, his full on charming smile plastered on his face. From the look on Ivy's face I'd say she's fallen for it. What a sucker. What the fuck is he doing here? It's clearly not to ask me out again or he'd be up here. Trying to dig up more dirt on me? The slimy bastard.

As if he can hear my aggressive thoughts he glances up and locks eyes with me. His eyes are such a cool, cold blue they actually make me quiver. With what, I don't know. It should be disgust, but it's more likely lust.

His face lights up in a smile as if I've made his day or something. Then he nods, his eyes glancing down my body. It's then I realise I'm only wearing a nightie. I look down, attempting to smooth it down. And my nipples are hard. Great. Am I turned on by him or something? Well, that's what he's going to think, arrogant prick.

I force the blinds down and lean against it, desperate to be hidden. What is it with this guy and him trying to unnerve me?

Maybe he'll knock on my door to speak to me. Last time we spoke he was pestering me about that date. God, I should get dressed just in case. I bet he'd love to perv over me in next to nothing. I won't give him the satisfaction.

I skid down the hallway and crash into my room. I fling open the wardrobe and start pulling out random clothes while trying to apply deodorant and throw mint chewing gum in my mouth. I mean, I don't want to look and smell horrendous when I let him down again.

I assess my clothes on the bed. What the hell should I wear? What does someone wear to confront a police detective trying to dig up dirt on them? Jeans? God, if I had time I'd google it. I'm sure there's a blog post online somewhere.

I quickly throw on my skinny jeans, black long sleeved t-shirt and red and white striped dolly shoes. I check myself in the mirror. My hair's still wavy from sleep sweat, but I don't have time to tart. I run my hand quickly through my hair. Well, maybe I'll throw on a blazer jacket. And a scarf. And a little lipstick. There, that's better.

Two minutes later I'm tapping my foot impatiently, waiting for him to come up here. I mean, where the hell is he? Is he trying to make me wait? Did he leave? I hate how I feel excited at the thought of seeing him. Now I'm just pissed off.

I open the blinds and find him still talking to Ivy. What the hell are they talking about? What on earth could be so interesting? And what am I doing? Hanging around here hoping he comes up? Like I want to see him or something. No, I need to take some control back. Show him whose boss. I do *not* pine over men.

I open the door, making sure to put the latch on, and bound down the concrete stairs. It's colder out than I thought. I'm glad I brought the blazer. He *must* have heard me coming out, but the bastard's acting like he hasn't noticed me. Like he's genuinely interested in what Ivy has to say.

I walk towards him, my previous simmering anger now at boiling point.

When he still doesn't turn I point my finger and poke him straight in his back. He stumbles forward, clearly taking the piss out of my girl strength. He turns with a mock shocked impression.

'Sadie! How are you?' He grins, pretending to be surprised.

God, he's infuriating.

'Why don't you tell me?' I snarl, my eyes narrowing on him. 'You're the one trying to dig up dirt on me.' I fold my arms across my chest.

Is it not enough that I have a crazed drug dealer threatening me? Now I've got him on my tail.

'Don't be so rude, Sadie,' Ivy snaps, horrified by my outburst. 'Harry here was just telling me all about his work as a police officer. Isn't that exciting?'

I roll my eyes, but smile sweetly at her. 'It sure is, Ivy. But more importantly, have you remembered to eat this morning?'

Harry looks at me questionably. She's obviously having an okay day today. She can seem completely normal and with it sometimes. He obviously has no idea.

'Don't be silly, Sadie,' she tuts. 'I've just had my dinner. It's early evening.' She laughs at me as if I'm being ridiculous.

We both look down at her nightdress. It's nine in the morning. Bless her heart. This dementia is getting worse by the day. She normally just forgets to eat. She doesn't normally get day and night confused. I need to book her a doctor's appointment. She won't be doing it herself.

'Okay,' I say, smiling in mollifying tones. 'But I've heard that eating cereal is the new after dinner treat.'

'Really?' she asks questionably.

'Oh yeah,' Harry joins in, winking at me. 'We'll show you.'

I look at him suspiciously. Why is he playing the nice card? He must still be wanting to get a date so he can ply me with alcohol and get me to spill my secrets. The idiot.

I start to lead Ivy back into her flat.

I turn back to him, annoyed by his presence. And the way he smells so good. 'You don't have to come. We're fine,' I snap.

I lead her into the kitchen and sit her down at the old oak table. I flick the kettle on and search the place for any proof of her eating. There's no dirty dishes, no dirty sauce pans. She's clearly not eaten in hours.

I ignore Harry's footsteps as he follows us in. I have more serious things to attend to right now. I go in search of cereal. I finally find some porridge sachets in the fridge, when I specifically told her not to move anything since the last time I unloaded her shopping. I go about putting it in the microwave and put two slices of bread in the toaster.

'I'm not even hungry,' she smiles. She looks back to Harry. 'She fusses over me all the time like this. I keep telling her there's no need, but she doesn't have a boyfriend you see. I think she gets lonely.'

I try to hide the smile creeping on my face and hope my red hot cheeks simmer down. I know she's like this and funny as hell, but it's still embarrassing in front of him.

He walks over to my side and catches the toast as it pops. Bloody show off.

'I really don't need you here,' I hiss, snatching the toast from him. Fuck, it's hot. I throw it down on the plate. 'Just ask me what you want to know and I'll tell you, but don't drag Ivy into this.'

He gives me a long sideways stare. I ignore him and finish getting her breakfast ready.

Although she protests at first, the way she wolfs it all down tells me she was starving. I'm going to have to visit more. I keep forgetting that she can fool me into thinking she's okay. And maybe I've been too lazy, only choosing to see what I want to. I've been too busy fucking up my own life to have time to worry about others.

Harry is *still* here, just leaning back against the counter like he belongs here or something. It's pissing me off royally. What the hell does he want from me?

'Anyway, I'm sure Harry has to get going,' I announce, hoping he'll get the hint.

He straightens up, clearly shocked to be thrown out so cruelly. I'm seriously starting to think I'm the only woman who's ever been rude to him. It amuses me to no end.

'Walk him out, will you?' Ivy asks, a dreamy look in her eyes.

I roll my eyes at her. She's clearly seeing some Cinderella happy ending here.

I lead him out, opening the front door and leaning against it. He puts his hands in his pockets and looks down at the floor. Oh God, why is he delaying leaving?

'So...you keep surprising me,' he says, smiling shyly. It's weird to see him show any shyness around me. I thought he was one hundred percent arrogant bastard.

I shake my head, trying to focus. 'Surprising you? What are you talking about?'

He stares intently at me. 'You just...I think I have you figured out and then you go and surprise me again. You look after Ivy a lot?'

I shrug, hating that he's asking a reasonable question. 'Not as much as I should. She doesn't have anyone else. I should really be visiting her twice a day.'

I feel guilty just thinking about it. I'm a terrible neighbour. She was so kind to me and Samuel when we first moved in. She cooked us loads of dinners and bought us candles when we couldn't afford the electric meter. I look down, shame rushing over me.

'Hey.' He tips my chin up with his thumb, forcing me to look at him. His touch sends an excited zing down to my knickers. I clench my thighs together. 'You're doing a lot more than most neighbours.'

Why am I suddenly breathless?

'Yeah…well,' I shrug. 'That's still pretty shitty.'

He stares at me for a moment, as if he's considering something. Why was I so eager to leave again?

His cocky smile quickly comes back on his face. 'So have you come to your senses and decided to come to dinner with me?' he asks. His eyes twinkle, as if it's a dare.

He can't seriously have come all the way here to persuade me to go out with him. I know it's to try and trick me. I dread to think what Ivy might have told him. I roll my eyes and lean on one hip, sighing heavily.

'You've got to eat, right?' he presses. He looks over my skinny limbs. 'From what I can see you need to eat more.'

My stomach plummets. Not another one. I *hate* when people insinuate I don't eat.

'I eat like a horse, thank you very much! It's not my fault I have a metabolism that's faster than lightning.'

How I would *die* for some womanly curves. I hate being reminded of how straight up and down I am.

'Prove it,' he challenges with a wink.

His winking is seriously pissing me off. Can't he see he's upset me? That's probably the extent to how hard he's ever had to work. Just winked and got everything handed to him on a plate. Little brat.

'I'm not stupid, you know.' His eyebrows crease in confusion. 'I know you just want to loosen me up with some Pinot so I'll blurt out something you're sure I'm guilty of.'

He purses his lips. 'Sadie, I'm not investigating you anymore. I'd just like the pleasure of your company. And to be honest, the more you refuse, the more of a fun challenge you're becoming.'

'Fine,' I snap, quickly realising he's not going to give up. 'You pay and I'll eat like you've never seen before. Get ready to re-mortgage.'

He grins, finally satisfied. 'Good. I'll call you.'

He leans in closer to me, so close his lips are at the same height as mine. Oh my God, is he going to kiss me? I can almost taste his minty breath.

'And just so you know,' he whispers. My breath catches in my throat. 'I like to eat a shit load too.'

Oh. He's not going to kiss me. But why does that sound so erotic coming from his lips? His perfect plump cherry lips. I wonder if he uses Chapstick. Maybe he even tastes of cherry. I lick my lips before I can stop myself. He grins, as if he knows what I'm thinking. Crap.

He walks away in the opposite direction, his natural swagger making me want to follow him down the road. But he didn't take my number?

'Wait. Don't you need my number?' I shout. A bit too pathetically may I add.

'I'm a copper,' he calls back with a cheeky grin. 'I can find out anything I want about you.' He smiles before saluting me like a soldier.

That's what I'm bloody worried about.

Harry's Diary

I finally got her to agree. You'd think she was signing her life over with the fuss she made. It was hilarious watching her try to resist me though. I knew if I talked loud enough to her neighbour she'd hear me and look out her window. What I wasn't expecting was for her to be wearing some come fuck me now negligee. I nearly passed out when I saw her wearing that pale pink satin and black lace nightie that left barely anything to the imagination. Add that to the messy bed head hair and my dick was twitching, begging for immediate release. Which was weird as I was actually talking to an old lady. That would have been awkward. But the way she was fuming made me chuckle. I've never seen a little thing like that get so mad. It was adorable.

And then the way she got all dressed up just to come down and pretend to ignore me. I mean, is this the first time she's done this?

She keeps pretending she finds me infuriating, but I know the way she looks at me; she wants me. She's just scared. Keeps assuming I'm trying to dig up dirt on her. Which...you know, I am, but still. I'm shocked by how low her self-confidence must be. Surely she would just assume I was after her for the date. I assumed she must have guys chasing after her all of the time.

What Ivy said about her never having boyfriends was shocking. Samuel must be right. She has issues or something. She must. Why on earth else would she be single? She's fucking gorgeous.

She keeps surprising me. Just when I think that she's the sex vixen drug dealer I suspected, she goes and shocks me again by taking care of her elderly neighbour.

It turned out the only way I could get her to agree was to make myself a royal pain in the arse. As long as she doesn't cancel, the deals' basically done. Once she gets to know me over dinner she'll have no choice but to fall for me. Good. I'm getting pressure at work to make some breakthrough in the case, but with no one talking there's not much else to go on. I need her confession. Or at least the promise of her resolve weakening.

Wednesday 30th September

I've decided that after Monday's debacle Ivy needs to be seen by a doctor. I've been ignoring it for too long now and she's only getting worse. I chatted to Samuel about it last night, conveniently leaving out the whole Harry involvement, and he's agreed to come with me. She's like a surrogate mother to both of us. At least she was until she started going do-lally.

We're seated in front of a stern looking doctor with eyebrows so far up his forehead it's almost another hair line. Except he has no hair on his head. What a strange looking fellow. But he's in his fifties, hopefully he's settled with some wife that loves him anyway. If he's single he's in trouble.

I glance at Samuel and he's staring at the eyebrows. I discreetly kick him.

'Ouch!' he screeches. 'Why did you kick me, Sadie?'

I glare back at him to shut up. 'I didn't.'

'You totally did!'

'Shut up, Samuel,' I hiss. 'We're here for Ivy.'

Ivy smiles back at the doctor. I could only get her out of the house today if she was allowed to wear her wedding dress. I know I should be horrified by this, but I'm actually more impressed that it still fits her. I've only ever seen her eat a shit load of carbs. Maybe she has a metabolism like me. I always assumed I'd grow older and get a bit chubbier around the edges. I was looking forward to it actually. No more 'don't you eat?' comments.

I decide to start talking. No one else seems to be willing. I take a deep breath and avoid looking at Ivy. I feel strangely like I'm betraying her.

'Um...I think Ivy might have early stages of dementia.'

He looks over her wedding dress, nodding.

'Or...you know, late stages. She's just getting very confused lately.'

'I can see that,' he says, no humour in his voice. 'Ivy, normally I'd refer you for tests, but I'd like to do a few now.'

'Fine by me,' she nods cheerfully. 'I keep telling these two there's nothing wrong with me.'

He raises his eyebrows at her. Wow, now they actually *are* touching his hairline. 'Okay. Can you tell me what the year is?'

'I can,' she smiles confidently. 'It's 1962.'

Oh my God. I had no idea she was this bad. I thought the whole war thing that day was a one off.

The doctor stares back at her, no emotion on his face. 'And who is the current prime minister?'

'Why, it's that man. Oh, what's his name?' She scratches her head and clicks her fingers, clearly racking her brains. 'That's it! Harold Macmillan.'

Now she's really lost it. I've never even heard of him.

The doctor makes some notes on his pad. 'And why are you wearing a wedding dress?'

Finally he confronts the elephant in the room. That would have been my first bloody question!

She smiles, her eyes lighting up as she strokes it affectionately. 'Because today I'm marrying Ernest. I'm the luckiest girl in the world.'

Samuel just stares at her, horrified. 'Ivy, you're not marrying anyone today,' he tries to calmly explain.

'Yes I am!' she shouts back. 'And there's nothing you can do to stop me.'

'Right,' the doctor says loudly, making us all jump. 'I've seen enough. I'm still going to send you for the tests. They'll be done in her own home, but I'm also going to recommend she gets carers to come in and check on her throughout the day.'

Carers? He means bloody strangers. Big scary women, maybe even men rifling through all of her stuff. What if they steal her money? Or beat her? You hear about cases like this all of the time!

'She doesn't need a carer,' I say adamantly. 'I can look after her.'

'Sadie, you can't,' Samuel protests, looking at me as if I'm crazy.

'I can!' I shout back defiantly. 'I'm not having her looked after by strangers.'

The doctor looks at me seriously. 'This would be a big commitment, do you understand? She'd have to be visited four separate times a day. You'll have to cook all of her meals.'

'Ha!' Samuel exclaims. 'She can't even cook pasta! If it wasn't for me the girl would be living on jam sandwiches.'

I glare at him. He might be right, but...I'll sort out something. Buy some healthy ready meals or some crap like that. If it means Ivy keeps some dignity then it'll be worth it. She's done nothing but look after us since we moved in ten years ago. Now it's payback time.

'I'm afraid that I have to specify how much of an enormous responsibility this will be for you,' the doctor presses.

Four times a day? That is a lot. But hell, she has no children to look after her. We're the next best thing.

'I understand,' I nod.

'Fine,' he relents on a sigh. 'I'm happy for you to try for a month, but after that I want another appointment to check how everything is going. If I'm in any doubt that Ivy is a danger to herself then I'll be forced to report it to social services. They'd insist she be put someone secure.'

Social services? Those bastards!

'Like a looney bin?' Samuel shrieks, standing up and knocking his chair back. 'We're not letting you put her in a bloody asylum!'

'I mean a care home,' the doctor calmly explains. 'You have to realise that Ivy shows signs of late dementia. She could be a danger to herself.'

I stand up, sick of his judging tone.

'That's fine,' I snap too quickly. 'Come on, Ivy, we're going.'

'Where?' she enquires excitedly. 'To the church? Oh, I don't know if I'm ready yet. I still need to do my make up.' She pats her hair. 'How do I look?'

I look into her vulnerable eyes and see that the woman we once knew and loved is dying away slowly. It makes me tear up.

'You look amazing,' I say, a tear trickling down my face.

We walk out, Samuel and I exchanging worried looks whenever Ivy isn't looking. She's chatting away all the way out of the surgery and down the street. Most of it doesn't make any sense, but she seems happy to just talk.

'Samuel!' someone calls in front of us.

We both look over to see Alana and Eric, our old friends from the street. They used to make their living being street performers, and by the looks of things it's still the case.

'Sadie's here too!' Alana shouts back to Eric.

She flips backwards towards us, drawing a small crowd.

'How the hell are you guys?' she says, embracing us separately. 'Oh,' she looks over Ivy. 'Are you on your way to a wedding?'

Samuel looks at me, trying to hide a smile. 'Not exactly. This is our friend, Ivy.'

Ivy looks up to her in confusion. 'Have you seen Ernest?' she asks desperately.

Alana looks back at her baffled. 'Err...no, sorry.'

We walk over to greet Eric who's currently putting a knife down his throat. I still don't understand how he does it, and to be honest, I don't want to know.

The crowd applauds. He turns to us. 'You guys! I haven't seen you in forever!'

He hugs us so tightly it hurts my chest. If I had boobs they'd be completely crushed.

'Ernest?'

We all turn round mid embrace to see Ivy looking up at Eric's face. What the hell is she talking about?

'It is you!' she cheers, jumping up and down on the spot. 'I've been looking for you all day.'

Oh Jesus. She doesn't....she doesn't seriously think that Eric is Ernest? Does she?

'No, this is E-R-I-C,' I say clearly.

'No, it is you!' She flings herself into his arms.

Alana walks over, clearly puzzled. 'Err...everything okay here?' She looks more to me and Samuel.

'Sorry,' I apologise. 'She has dementia.'

'Oh.' She puts her hand on Ivy's shoulder. 'That's Eric, love.'

'Get off me, you whore!' Ivy shouts back, throwing her hand off.

Whoa. Where the fuck did that come from? Alana looks back, stunned.

'Ivy!' Samuel and I shout at the same time.

I walk over and try to prise her hands off Eric. 'Come on, Ivy, it's time to go home.'

'You want him too, don't you?' she accuses, looking at me with serious suspicion.

'No! I just want us to get home.' Haven't we had enough stress for one day?

'She really does,' Samuel agrees, trying to lead her away. 'How about we go home and have a cup of tea? That sound good, hmm?'

She slowly seems to contemplate this. 'Yes. Okay. That sounds like a good idea.'

Thank God. We make our apologies to Alana and Eric and walk towards the car while a sudden exhaustion takes over my body. Four times a day? What the fuck did I just sign up for?

Chapter 12

Friday 2nd October

I'm about to leave for my date with Harry Friday night when I decide to look into the mirror one more time. I know I look hot. My hazel eyes are loaded with mascara and I've got perfect winged eyeliner. All of those Pinterest tutorials are finally paying off. I used a business card to make it perfectly straight. It's not like I'm going to need them anymore. My lips are a dark burgundy and my hair is full volume with barely there waves. I really don't even know why I've put so much effort in. Or why I've got butterflies going hysterical in my stomach at the thought of seeing him again.

My phone rings. It's Lexi. I could do with someone reminding me why I can't like him.

'Hey, hun,' I sing down the phone.

I have to act normal. I obviously haven't told the others my mad cap idea to go on a date with a man who has the potential to bring us all down. I'm sure I'd be carted off to the nearest looney bin.

'Hey, Sadie,' she says sadly. Her voice is barely audible.

My brows furrow together in turmoil. She never sounds melancholy. Angry, yes, but never just plain sad. Then it slowly dawns on me. Oh my God, has she been threatened too? I knew I should have told them about it. What if I've put them in danger when I could have warned them? Here I am worrying if I've got enough lipstick on and she's being threatened with no pre-warning from me. She could have been attending self-defence lessons in that time. What is wrong with me?

'What's wrong?' I ask, my stomach filling rapidly with dread

She sighs heavily down the phone. 'Jason's been sending me loads of abusive messages.' She sighs again. 'I'm just sick of it.'

Oh, thank God. She's not been threatened by thug drug dealers. Although her ex-boyfriend threatening her is hardly cause for celebration.

She's thankfully settled into Mags' house well. I think she secretly loves how Mags dotes on her and is always on hand to cook her eggs on toast. I'm thinking I might move in there myself.

'Just try to ignore him, hun. He's bound to get bored eventually. Have you thought about changing your number?'

'Yeah, I should I suppose. It's just that everyone knows me on this one. Plus I don't want to have to be the one to change, you know? I've done fuck all wrong.'

There's my girl. The fight in her voice is coming back.

'Preach, sister. The good news is that he doesn't know where you are so you're safe.'

'Well...,' she says hesitantly. I hear her inhale on a cigarette.

'What?' I know her well enough to know when she's got something to say. I remember when she broke the photo copier by smashing the screen in a moment of rage. She tiptoed around telling me for two hours.

'Well…he's saying he knows where I am,' she finally admits. 'He's saying he's gonna turn up here.'

'What?' I shriek, my mouth going dry. How could he have known that? 'There's no way he'd know…right?'

'Of course not. I mean, he doesn't even know Mags. But I don't know. I'm still kind of freaked by it.' I can sense the fear in how quickly she's puffing on her cigarette. I hope she's not smoking in the house.

'Have you told Mags?'

The last thing we need right now is Mags getting stressed out and worried over it. She's already taking on too much.

'God no!' she snorts. 'She'd piss her pants. There's no need to put that kind of worry on the old lady.'

At least we're on the same page where she's concerned.

'Don't let her hear you calling her an old lady.' I smile at the thought of Mags' face.

'She's already smacked me on the head twice for it. I keep telling her I moved in to get away from violence.' She laughs, and I can hear in it that she adores Mags.

It's funny how we've worked together for years, but only now are we drawn together by these weird circumstances, and all suddenly so close. I mean Lexi never called me. Not even when she was sick and she was *supposed* to let me know. At least something good is coming out of this.

I look at the clock on the wall. I should have left by now.

'Okay, well keep safe. And if anything happens call me, okay?'

'On speed dial, bitch. Peace out.' She hangs up before I get a chance to respond. She's such a fruit loop.

I put the phone back in my purse and take the chance to survey myself one last time in the mirror. I swear it's the last time. Okay, time to double check the outfit. I think I've gone for the right mix of sexy but classy. God knows I don't want to give him the wrong idea. It's just this one date to get him off my back. That's it. Calm the fuck down, butterflies! I wish they'd get the memo.

I'm wearing my black satin dress. Its lace scalloped edging on the shoulder and neckline shows off my slim shoulders. It's tight, showing off my slim waist, and then falls into a pencil skirt with a small slit at the back. My legs, waist and shoulders are really my only redeeming features. I have no ass or bust to speak of, so I've got to work with what I have.

Not that I care what he thinks. Oh God, why the hell do I care? It's so dangerous to be even considering meeting this man. Nothing good can come from it. Well, maybe a good shag, but I've never done that before so doubt I'll start now. No, nothing can come from it. I take out my phone and scroll down to his number. He of course rang me yesterday to confirm, stalker that he is.

A knock on the door stops me. Damn Samuel forgetting his keys again! I'm going to have to attach them to a chain around his neck. It's the only way he won't forget it. I stomp over to the door and swing it open, ready to take my frustration out on him.

'How many fucking times-' I stop when I'm met with an alarmed Harry.

'Err…I'm sorry?' he offers, his eyes smiling mischievously. God, he's hot.

'Sorry, I thought you were Samuel. And I thought we were meeting at the restaurant?' I could have sworn that's what he said.

'You didn't think I'd really meet you there, did you? What kind of gentleman would I be if I let that happen?'

I raise my eyebrows. I have a feeling he's anything but a gentleman.

'Plus, this way you can't stand me up,' he admits, looking shy for half a second. Only half a second though. It's quickly replaced by his calm, cool exterior, but not quickly enough for me to wonder where the hesitation came from.

'Touché,' I grin. 'By all means, lead the way.'

He drives us to a fancy French restaurant in town and he manages to keep it from being awkward by talking idle chit chat. He leads me towards the restaurant, pushing me on my lower back. It tingles from his touch, making me grin like an idiot. That's exactly what I am. A bloody idiot. What am I doing? And why don't I want to stop?

I notice a homeless couple sitting a couple of doorways down. They look cold. I can remember that cold only too clearly. The way it seeps into your bones until they ache, crying out for you to find warmth. The pain it eventually turns into, while you count down the minutes until morning. Until you can find a warm open coffee shop to sit in or find a centre serving a hot meal. You seriously consider stabbing people just so that you can take their muffin. Harry doesn't even notice them. Typical rich boy.

'Table for two in the name of McKenzie,' he says to the hostess once he's ushered me quickly inside.

I recognise her. It's Samuel's friend Hayley. The last time I saw her I was vomiting in the street during gay pride last year. I hope she doesn't remember.

'Hey, Sadie!' she beams.

Damn, she remembers. She walks round the table and takes me into an over friendly hug. 'How are you doing?'

'Yeah, good thanks.' I smile towards Harry, smug that I know someone. He might think I'm a regular socialite. Not someone that prefers to frequent burger bars and gay clubs in Soho

She looks over Harry admirably, totally eye fucking him. *'Damn girl, it looks like you did more than good.'* She raises her eyebrows cheekily at me.

He clears his throat, obviously feeling awkward. Or loving it. Man whore that he is I'm sure he does.

'Oh right.' She grins, grabbing two menus. 'Back to hostess mode. Follow me to your table.'

She seats us in a far back table with lots of privacy. It makes me wonder whether he asked for this table specifically. I'd rather be well within eye level of everyone so he can't try to seduce me for information.

'How do you know her?' he asks as soon as she walks away to get our drinks.

'She's a friend of Samuels.'

'Oh,' he grins. 'I did wonder.' He looks down at the menu.

Sorry...is he insinuating that I'm not posh enough to be a frequent diner here? I've been here loads of times! Well, once for a friend's birthday and we had twenty percent off vouchers. But still! He's so pompous and full of himself.

'What the hell is that supposed to mean?' I glare at him, expecting an apology.

'Oh, nothing,' he shrugs, like it's no big deal. Like he's not a major douche.

'Are you making out I don't dine in posh places? Because I'll have you know that I'm a frequent diner at places like this!' My voice is higher than expected, totally betraying how I want to come across. This is not making me look classy, not that I should even care what he thinks.

'I didn't mean that,' he says, clearly shocked. 'Jesus, overreact much?'

I look down at the menu, trying and failing to calm myself down. Why do I always have such an inferiority complex with snobby people like him? I should rise above it and not give a shit, but I know why. He's some little rich boy who grew up with a loving family and probably went to a posh boarding school. Of course he's used to frequenting these types of snobby places. Whereas I worked my arse off to be able to come to even feed myself. You didn't see me being handed everything on a silver plate. Some of us have had to fight for it. Or beg, borrow and steal in my case.

The waiter comes over with our drinks.

'Are you ready to order?' he asks in a French accent.

I decide to shock Harry a little bit. Knock him off his pompous pedestal.

'Puis-je se il vous plaît avoir le breton de poulet. Je aimerais aussi deux portions à emporter de demi poulet amenés en même temps . Merci.'

Harry looks back at me flummoxed, his eyes as wide as saucers. I look back at him smugly.

'Err…I'll have the eight ounce sirloin, please,' he says sheepishly. As soon as the waiter walks away he leans over to me, clearly intrigued. 'I didn't know you spoke fluent French.'

'There's a lot you can't find out about me from a police report,' I say smugly, pursing my lips together to stop myself from smiling.

He smiles. 'How did you learn?' he asks, intrigued.

I could really have some fun with him.

'I studied in Paris for my last year of university,' I lie, trying to keep a straight face.

'No way! That's so cool,' he gushes, clearly thinking I'm now impressive enough to introduce to his posh friends. What a dick.

I almost hate to burst his bubble.

'Actually, I'm taking the piss. I did a night course at my local college. I never went to uni and I've never left this country.'

His mouth falls open in shock and his forehead creases. 'Then why did you…'

'Because I just proved my point,' I snap. 'You wouldn't be impressed with the real version of me. I'm really very boring.'

The sooner I cut to the chase of this whole pretend date thing the better.

'I completely disagree,' he beams, his eyes twinkling with amusement. 'I find you fascinating.'

I roll my eyes. He must be trying to be sarcastic. Surely?

'Like how you find a chimp fascinating at a zoo?' I offer, smiling despite myself.

He frowns. 'No. Stop being so self-depreciating,' he admonishes.

I pucker my bottom lip out in anger. I hate being told off. Who the hell does he think he is? Typical policeman, used to being in control. He needs to stop talking to me like he's already arrested me.

My phone bings with a text. I know its terrible date protocol, but I check it anyway. It's not like this is a real date.

It's Lexi.

He's left me three screaming voicemails. I'm freaking out here!

Shit, he's really not giving up on her. I'd tell her to call the police, but I'm not even sure what they can do. Plus the less the police are aware of us the better. What if they wanted to search the place and found something?

It gives me an idea. I can try to find out some things from Harry that might help her get that loser off her back. I put the phone back in my bag.

'Anyway, I was wondering. What if...someone was leaving threatening messages on your phone? Can you report that to the police?'

His face flashes a glimpse of anger, before concern replaces it.

'Are you still getting followed?'

Wow. He still remembers that. Any normal person would have written me off as a paranoid nutcase.

'No!' I laugh shrilly, only managing to draw more attention to myself from some other posh knobs. 'I'm asking for a friend.'

'Okay.' He seems to relax slightly at this. 'To be honest there's pretty weak stalking laws in place. You can report it, even get a restraining order, but until they cause physical bodily harm it will probably be ignored.'

What? What kind of bloody sense does that make? I shake my head in disbelief.

'So someone has to wait until their head is kicked in before they get any help?'

How fucking ridiculous.

He leans forward and surprises me by taking my hand in his. It's cold and his grip is strong. 'Sadie, you can confide in me.'

His thumb starts to stroke my knuckles, sending zings of passion up my arm, into my veins and straight to my heart. Jesus, calm down love. Pull yourself together.

'If you've got yourself involved with the wrong kind of people I might be able to help. You just need to tell me everything.'

Wait...he still thinks I'm talking to him about myself? About the drugs. My God, even in this romantic atmosphere, with his charismatic charm, he's still trying to get me to confess to him. Why the hell did I agree to go along with this again?

'Stop with the trying to get me to confess to something,' I snap, clawing my hand back. 'I haven't done anything.'

He sighs heavily, his eyebrows furrowed. 'Sadie, I can help.' His tone is supposed to be reassuring, but it just gets my back up. 'Please let me help you.' He looks at me pleadingly like I'm just going to relent and tell him everything.

This guy is a total arsehole, but I'm the bigger arsehole for letting him take me out. This was such a dumb idea. He's never going to leave me alone. Not until he has me safely locked up in prison.

My phone starts ringing, saving me from his probing stare. It's Lexi. Thank God. I can just pretend it's some big emergency and get the hell out of here.

'Hey, babe,' I say, not caring that I look even ruder answering a phone.

'He's here!' she shrieks down the phone so loud I have to pull it away from my ear for a second. 'The bastard is here.'

'What?' I'm on my feet straight away. 'How the hell did he find you?' I ask, already gathering my purse and coat.

This really isn't good. What if he wants to kill her? What if he hurts Mags?

'I don't know, but he's trying to kick the door in while Mags is trying to reason with him through the letter box. She keeps offering him fucking tea!'

Oh my Jesus.

'Okay. Call the police. I'm coming straight over.'

Harry's concerned eyes meet mine. I look away. I can't stand his questions right now.

'I can't call the cops. There's weed growing all over this house. If they search it we'll all go to prison,' she hisses.

I cup the phone, hoping to God Harry hasn't heard her.

'Fuck.' I look up to a worried Harry. I suppose I could always bring him with me. He's not ideal, but he's the only thing I have right now. 'Don't worry. I'm bringing reinforcements.' I snap the phone shut before turning to him. 'I don't have time to explain, just get your coat and take me to 28 Sheepcot Avenue.'

He jumps up, fannying around with his wallet, leaving some money down.

'Immediately,' I add, grabbing his arm and pulling him out of the booth.

The waiter runs over. 'Miss! At least take this,' he insists, handing over the two doggy bags I ordered for the homeless couple outside.

'Thanks,' I mumble back, snatching it from him.

Harry grabs hold of my upper arm and all but sprints back to his car. Then I remember the reason I got the food to go; the couple. I push him off me. It's the only way to stop him from dragging me away. I don't think he knows his own strength. He stares back angrily, completely confused.

'Wait one minute,' I shout, sprinting back across the road.

'I thought you said immediately?' he shouts back, clearly pissed off at my erratic behaviour.

I run over to the homeless couple and hand over the bags of food. 'Here, take this. I hope you like.' I wink before running back over to him.

He shoves me into the car, straps a seat belt around me, as if I'm incapable of doing that myself, and then gets in and speeds off.

'Talk,' he demands gruffly, holding onto the steering wheel so tight his knuckles are turning white. 'First of all do you know those people?'

Of course he wants to ask about the homeless first. Bloody snob.

'No,' I shrug. 'But they looked cold and hungry.'

He takes his eyes off the road to stare at me in agitation

'You have to be careful with the homeless,' he stresses, as if speaking to a child. 'Most of them are druggies.'

My chest expands as I intake a sharp breath, my blood boiling. That's exactly what some little rich boy like him *would* think. I bet he's never given them more than a second glance, let alone twenty pence.

I'm about to rant my tirade of abuse when he interrupts me.

'What am I walking into? And has your friend called the police?'

I shake my head and try not to get turned on by how in control and powerful he appears right now, but it's hard to calm my tingly bits. They don't seem to link up with my brain which is furious with him for being such a snob. I cross my legs as tight as I can, willing my lady parts to calm down.

'She doesn't want the police involved. It's her crazy ex that used to beat her. He's found her and is trying to break the door down.' I don't have time to sugar coat it.

'Okay.' He nods, a steely determination on his face.

God, he's hot. No, stop it. You have Lexi to worry about right now. What if Jason manages to get in? I dread to think of the damage he'd cause. Poor Mags. She was just trying to help out and she's ended up with a psychopath on her doorstep.

Within minutes we screech into Mags' drive. There's another car there which I can only assume is the arseholes.

Harry turns to me, unclicking his seat belt. 'Stay here.'

Yeah, *right*. I decide to humour him, nodding in understanding, but as soon as he's walking towards the front door I open the car door and follow him. He doesn't notice until it's too late. Jason is banging his fist against the door so hard his knuckles are bloody. His face is contorted with rage. How can this be the same guy I accidently made out with? He was so charming then.

'Calm down, fella,' Harry says sternly. 'I'm DC McKenzie, and if you don't calm the fuck down I'll be forced to arrest you.'

Is it wrong that him saying that makes me wanton for him? Oh God, the feels!

'Who the fuck are you?' Jason snarls at him like a crazed wolf. It's now I realise he's drunk. He stinks of whiskey and he's missing two buttons from his shirt.

'DC McKenzie,' Harry repeats calmly.

The arsehole slowly seems to realise I'm there and stares at me, his face scrunched up, perplexed. 'Esmerelda? What are you doing here?' he slurs.

Oops. This is confusing. Harry looks at me puzzled. This is going to be hard to explain.

'I'm Lexi's friend. Please just leave her alone,' I plead.

'Where's your accent gone?'

Oh yeah, I forgot I was French.

'She loves me,' he states firmly, as if it's a fact.

He wasn't worried when he was snogging my face off.

'Why don't we all just have a cup of tea?' I follow the voice to find Mags speaking out of the letter box. Bless her.

'Alright,' Jason says, flexing his shoulders, as if to calm himself down. 'I'll go.'

Really? Well that was unbelievably easy. He turns to leave, but within a split second he swings round and punches Harry square in the chin. Harry, being completely caught off guard, falls against the wall.

Well fuck, that escalated quickly. Harry's face twists to murderous.

'You fucked with the wrong cop,' he smiles evilly. He lunges for him, grabbing him around the waist and pulling him to the floor.

He gets in a few punches before Jason overpowers him and is on top. He drags him to standing and starts to pummel him in the stomach. I react, every punch Harry receives feeling like a punch in my own stomach. Not that he's not putting up a good fight. He's acting as if it's not even hurting him, when I know it must be. Harry's tall and strong, but this guy's built like a brick shit house. He could end up killing him. The thought of that happening tears my chest into two.

I take my stiletto heel off, grasp the shoe in my hand, and walk towards him.

'Jason!' I yell as loud as I can.

He swings round, more from curiosity I'm sure. It's all I need. Those two seconds of being caught off guard. I wallop the stiletto heel into his eye with as much force as I can muster. He drops to the floor immediately, clutching at his face and wailing like a baby. Ha! Got you, dickhead!

'Bitch, what did you do? What did you do?' he wails, his eye bleeding.

Harry looks back at me in a mix of disbelief, horror and amazement. 'Fuck,' he utters, running his hands through his hair.

He takes the time to pull out a pair of handcuffs and cuff him while reading him his rights. I wipe my shoe on my dress and put it back on.

'You can open the door now,' he shouts through to Mags.

Mags tentatively opens the door in her flannel night dress.

'Don't worry,' Harry beams at her proudly. 'I've got him cuffed.'

She swoons on her feet. It's embarrassing. I don't know why he's acting so pleased with himself. I'm the one that took him down. Talk about stealing my thunder.

We follow her into the kitchen where Harry throws him onto a chair and stands over him. Mags goes to put the kettle on. What is with this woman and tea? Harry takes out his phone and places a phone call.

'Hi, it's me. Yeah, I need you to pick someone up for me…yeah…long story, but we'll do him for drunk and disorderly. Okay, thanks.'

'What did you just do?' I ask confused.

'I'll explain later,' he shrugs, running his hand through his ruffled black hair.

God, he's hot. I realise I'm drooling.

'Okay.' I smile at him suspiciously before going to find Lexi.

I find her locked in the upstairs bathroom sobbing her little heart out.

'Oh, Lex,' I say as soon as she opens the door. 'Come here.' I've never seen her so upset. Actually upset, period.

She slumps back down to the floor and I follow her, hugging her close to me. Sometimes you just need to be held by someone at times like this.

'He's always going to find me,' she sobs into my dress. 'No matter where I try and hide, he won't give up.'

It must be horrendous to feel so helpless. I can't believe the police can't help more.

'Harry is on the case now. It's going to be sorted,' I say reassuringly. I actually have no idea. This really could escalate for all I know. Maybe we should move her again.

'Harry? Who…' Her face starts to register the name. 'The cop that's been looking into you? Detective Mckenzie? Why is he here?'

Uh-oh. This is awkward.

'Um…I was with him. I...bumped into him in a restaurant.'

I can't tell her the truth right now. She's stressed out as it is the poor thing.

She nods her head in understanding, but keeps her suspicious eyes on me. They rake over my outfit.

'Why are you dressed like that?' she grumbles, frowning.

I suppose I can't get away with saying I was just going for a walk when I bumped into him. I avoid her gaze, pretending to tidy up the toothbrushes on the sink.

'Err...I was just...out,' I croak. Even my voice is going against me.

She narrows her eyes at me. 'Out with who?' she taunts, clearly enjoying my discomfort.

'No one,' I protest far too loudly.

She smiles cruelly. 'So you just decided to go out, to a restaurant, dressed like that, on your *own?*'

'Yep.' I nod, attempting to smile confidently.

'Oh fuck off, Sades!' she yells. 'You were totally on a date with him. With the enemy!'

'No, I wasn't,' I protest as convincingly as I can.

'Fuck off! Yes you were.'

 I hear the doorbell go and some men's voices. Perfect excuse to get out of this.

'I'm just going to check what's going on. Back soon.' I smile as confidently and reassuringly as I can.

I run downstairs to see two uniformed police officers taking Jason out of the door.

'Will Lexi have to make a statement?' I ask Harry as I follow him back into the kitchen. She's traumatized as it is.

'Nah,' he says, shaking his head. 'They're buddies of mine. They're going to call it in as a drunk and disorderly. Someone they caught on the street. He'll probably just get cautioned.'

Just a caution?!

'That's good,' Lexi says from the doorway, making us both jump.

He turns to her, his face grave. 'But you should seriously consider getting a restraining order in place.'

She jumps when he looks directly at her. Not enough for him to notice, but I do.

'Maybe,' she smiles weakly, avoiding his gaze.

'Tea for everyone,' Mags says, ushering everyone to the breakfast bar.

'Thanks,' Harry smiles, his pearly whites mesmerising her momentarily. He'd probably be a real catch to bring home to the parents. Shame I don't have any.

'It's my pleasure, love. Saving the day like that. You did a marvellous job.'

He waves a hand dismissively. 'All part of the job.'

When is he going to admit that it was actually me? The arse hat.

'Oh?' she enquires, clearly intrigued. 'You're a policeman?'

'Yep,' he nods, looking around the kitchen.

Shit. With all the drama I forgot about the possibility of him seeing something incriminating.

Mags shoots me a *what the fuck* look. Not that she'd ever use those exact words.

I ignore her and turn back to him. His eyes are zoning in on something behind Mags. I follow his gaze to see a batch of Mags's brownies. Her dope brownies. Holy fuck.

'Mind if I take a brownie?' he asks, putting on a sweet innocent face.

'Um…' she stalls, looking over at me for help.

'You shouldn't have chocolate,' I laugh unnaturally. 'It'll ruin your figure.'

He stands and lifts up his shirt to reveal perfect abs, with a V leading down to his happy place. Yum-my! Lexi's jaw falls open unashamedly. What was I saying?

'I'll take my chances,' he grins, grabbing one before any of us can stop him.

His damn fucking abs distracted us!

Lexi looks at me in desperation. Shit. He's going to eat it and get stoned and know. Of course he'll know, if he doesn't already. He raises it to his lips, my own upper lip starting to sweat. This is it. We're done for. Only he stops just before it reaches his mouth.

'Do you need a lift home, Sadie?'

'No, I'm fine. I'll crash here.' He raises the brownie to his lips again. 'I really don't think you'll even like it. Mags's brownies are terribly rich and stodgy.'

Mags looks briefly offended before catching on. 'Oh yes, some people say I'm the worst brownie maker in town!' She forces a laugh.

He looks at all of us confused. 'Well then maybe I'll take it to go.' He grabs a napkin, folds it over it and places it in his pocket.

'Thanks for a lovely evening, ladies,' he grins. 'Very eventful.' Then he takes the brownie and leaves.

Fuck a duck. We're screwed.

Lexi turns to me. 'Well done, Sadie. It looks like Detective Mcrugged is gonna land us all in jail just because you couldn't resist his cock.'

Chapter 13

Saturday 3rd October

I try to reassure myself that he might have not fancied the brownie on the way home, maybe even threw it in a bin. But a terrified little part of me knows that he's eaten it. Or at least had it tested in some lab. That he *knows*.

Lexi and Mags have agreed to keep it all a secret from Steph. She'll just worry and she's in no state for that. She's stressed out enough with Ruby, who's still insisting on waking three times a night. Plus, whenever she even sees a kebab shop, she's reduced to a blubbering mess.

I've had five missed calls from him, but I've ignored them. At least send me a text with a 'run' or something. I just hope I don't go home to a cordoned off house and Samuel with his big disappointed eyes, demanding to know why I've put his career in jeopardy.

As soon as I get home from food shopping I decide that I have to speak to the girls. We need to end this now. Burn all of the product. Flush everything down the toilet and hope to God we don't go to prison.

I dump my bag down in the hallway and throw my keys on the small table. I pick up the phone and dial. I don't even want to leave this hallway before getting it under some sort of control.

They put me on speaker and I try my best to be calm.

'I've been thinking, girls,' I announce, twiddling my thumbs nervously, 'that we should quit while we're ahead.'

'Huh?' Steph says. 'What are you talking about, Sadie?'

Oh shit, when the hell did she turn up?

'I...I just think, you know, now that we've made some money, we should cut our losses and go before we get caught.' I start picking at the peeling wallpaper on the walls.

'He might not even have eaten it,' Lexi pipes up.

I cringe. What the hell did she say that for? Now Steph is going to find out.

'Who might not have eaten what?' Steph asks, her high pitched voice showing how bewildered she is.

I can just imagine her confused face, looking to Lexi and Mags for clarification. Mags is a shit liar, Lexi might not have enough tact to keep it from her.

'Should I make us all a cuppa?' I hear Mags ask in the background. She's obviously trying to duck out into the kitchen.

'I don't want a fucking cup of tea,' Lexi snaps. 'I want you to stop pissing yourself like a scared little girl and just hang on for a while, okay?'

'Don't swear, Lexi,' Steph berates. 'Ruby can hear you.'

'Ruby's a fucking baby, Steph,' she barks. 'Chill the fuck out.'

'Well, there's really no need for that,' Steph says, her voice wobbly.

Oh Jesus, she's on the verge of tears. I know that wobble. I once had to tell her off for filing incorrectly. She thought V was before T. I got this same reaction.

'Look, it's no big deal,' Lexi says. I can imagine her rolling her eyes and kicking her feet up onto the dining room table. 'That Detective McKenzie just came round and took a dope brownie home with him.'

I hear Mags walk back into the room clanging tea cups down.

'What?!' I hear Steph shriek.

'Look, Sadie, we'll call you back,' Mags says before hanging up.

Oh shit, well this is a nightmare. The only other option would be to tell them about the scary guy in the alley, but there's just no way I can do that. That would really scare the shit out of them and there's been enough drama. I already know they're being careful because of Jason, so I'm not too worried.

I lean back against the wall, bumping my head repeatedly against it. Why is my life so ridiculous? I catch a glimpse of myself in the mirror. Panicked eyes meet mine. Calm down, Sadie. Your life may be a shambles, but there's always a way out, right?

A knock at the door startles me. I hold onto the wall as fear washes over me. My heart thumps hard in my chest, willing me to run away. I already know its Harry. He's here to arrest me. Of course he is.

Unless...could it be the drug dealer from the alley? Has he found out where I live? Is he here to kill me? Jesus, this whole time I've been worried about prison. What if I end up in a body bag at the bottom of the Thames? My stomach curdles at the thought.

Or, my rational voice reminds me, it could just be Ivy checking that I've got her bits from the shop.

I swallow, trying to force down the panic as I drag my jelly legs over to the door. I lean up to look into the peep hole, but barely look through before I jump to the side. What if he has a gun there and he shoots me through the eye? Oh my God. How did my life come to this?

'I can hear you moving around in there,' a deep voice calls.

It's Harry. Relief washes over me, bringing some life back into my body. I try to ignore the stupid thrill of hearing his voice. It's obviously just relief that it's not that scary guy. I shouldn't be relieved its Harry at all. I'm going down.

I take a deep breath, straighten myself up and open the door an inch with my clammy hands.

'Hi,' I smile weakly, keeping the chain on.

'Hi,' he says, his eyes seeming bemused at the chain. 'Can I come in?'

Could I just say no? Or would he break the door down? Samuel's already going to be pissed off that I've put his job in jeopardy when I go down. The least I could do is save him from also having to replace a door.

I sigh, my limbs suddenly heavy in defeat. 'Okay, fine.'

He's here to arrest me. I just know it. I've even started to accept it. But then...he could have just knocked the door down. Why didn't he do that? That's weird.

I unlock the chain and let him follow me into the sitting room. I stand by the window, trying to remember the feeling of sunlight on my face. It might be a while before I feel it again. Unless there's a sun trap in the exercise yard.

I ignore him, hearing him as he settles himself on the sofa. Make yourself comfortable why don't you? I try to focus on what's happening on the street, waiting for him to say something. He doesn't, which just irritates me further.

'Go on then,' I demand, swinging round to face him, my arms crossed over my chest. 'Arrest me.'

His eyebrows shoot up, his eyes puzzled. 'Are you confessing to something?'

'Huh?' I look at him, trying to work out if he's trying to trick me. 'I thought…'

He nods in understanding. 'You thought I was here to arrest you for the weed brownie.' His face is impassive making it impossible to read.

'Err…what weed brownie?' I shriek. Sweat is forming on my upper lip.

'Don't bullshit me,' he says kindly. 'I know it was a dope brownie.' He's dead serious.

A sudden defiance fills my veins. It must be his cock sure attitude pissing me off again. I decide to style it out.

'So what?' I challenge, my hand on my hip.

'So nothing,' he shrugs.

Sorry, what now?

'It's not like I can do anything about it. Mags could just be making them for her own consumption.'

I stare at him. Is he…letting me off? I sit down next to him on the sofa.

His gaze swings to me, his eyes serious and full of unspoken words.

'I'm here as a friend as well as a police officer. You've been avoiding my calls and our night was cut short last night. We need to have a proper chat. I don't want you replaying history.' He looks at me with sympathetic eyes.

'Replaying history?' Why does he look like he feels sorry for me?

Dread hits my stomach with a thud. Does he…does he know about my mum? Has he found out about my mum and her drug addiction?

He obviously did a background check on me, but I didn't know it would flash up about my time in foster care. Or the reason I was there. I just assumed it would tell him of any illegal activity. Of course he'd make it his mission to find out if not. How could I have been so stupid?

'You looked into my past?' I accuse, still so shocked I can't move.

'I did,' he nods sadly. I hate the sympathy. Thinking he's better than me. 'It can't have been easy for you growing up in foster homes.'

With a sudden rage over powering me, I jump to standing and leer over him.

'How fucking *dare* you feel sorry for me!' I scream, trembling, any fragment of self-control letting loose.

'Sadie,' he says, standing, trying to find my eyes. 'You had a rough start in life. It's nothing to be ashamed off.'

'Too right it's nothing to be ashamed off!' I shout, poking him in the chest. 'How dare you insinuate that I'm *anything* like my mother! You think you know me because you read a few bits of information on a fucking piece of paper. Well fuck you, Harry. You have no idea who I am and what I'm capable of.'

'It's what you're capable of that I'm worried about,' he snaps.

A surge of red hot hatred rises through me so fast the only thing I can really see is red.

'Get out! Get the fuck out!' I scream, my voice erupting into an angry growl. My face feels boiling hot with rage.

'I'm trying to help you,' he says, trying to approach me with open arms.

'Are you fucking kidding me?' I shriek. 'I said get out! Now go!'

He stays standing, his eyes sad. Like he's disappointed in me or something. How fucking dare he act like he even gives a shit about me.

Well if he won't go, I will. I storm out of the room and into my bedroom, slamming the door shut behind me. I sit on my bed and let the first tear fall. How can he think I'm like my mother? The crack whore who abandoned her daughter? Is that what he really thinks of me? I'd almost rather he'd arrested me than compare me to that heartless bitch. What a prick.

Shortly after, I hear the door click shut. I'm more confused than ever. I throw my head under a pillow and close my eyes, wishing it all away.

Chapter 14

I still can't believe he said that. *End up like my mother.* What an absolute bastard. I'm nothing like her. But I know deep down that the reason I'm so pissed off is because that's my own fear. Of course it is. You read everywhere how an addictive personality is hereditary. I mean look how obsessed I get with shoes. That's why I've refused to try it myself.

What if I did it once and it was so good I couldn't stop? And then after a while I'd want a better buzz? Before you know it I'm giving blow jobs in a nightclub bathroom just so I can afford my next hit of heroin.

That's why I'm glad we're only selling to cancer patients and not kids. Kids are dumb and could easily get messed up on it. I honestly don't see the attraction anyway. I like to be in control of my own emotions. And if I want to let loose I'll do some flaming Sambuca shots. Although I really need to remember to blow it out first. It burnt all of my tash off last time and it hasn't even grown back properly. Not that it's a bad thing. It's actually a pretty good hair removal. I considered doing something similar with my legs, but reasoned that I'd probably just set my legs alight. And nobody wants third degree burns.

Anyway, I've gone off on a tangent. Where was I? Oh, that's right, Harry being a dickhead. How could I forget? But what I really don't get is why he even felt the need to warn me. Surely a normal policeman wouldn't be offering advice like that? He'd just take me in for questioning, trying to get some information out of me. Or stay quiet and slowly build up a solid case against me. But to warn me...well, it's weird.

I'm positive that the only reason he asked me out on that date in the first place was to try and get information out of me. But warning me makes me think he actually cares about whether I go to prison or not. Which is crazy. That's his job. Unless...my stomach curdles at the thought. Unless this is all part of a grand plan. He wants me to trust him and what better way than to think he's looking out for me? Oh, he's good. The sneaky little bastard. Luckily for me I'm better. He must be crazy if he thinks I'm gonna fall for that.

Sunday 4th October

I decide to go over to Mags' house the next morning to check on how her plants are growing. Lexi and Steph are there too. This place is quickly turning into some sort of youth club. Not that Mags seems to mind. She's already in the kitchen baking an apple pie. I think she must be one of those women who enjoy having a chaotic house. I suppose having four kids would get you used to it, only for the little bastards to grow up and leave you.

Steph slumps down onto the sofa opposite me.

'I'm never going to find love again,' she says quietly, barely loud enough for me to hear. She's just staring into space.

'Yes you will,' I say encouragingly.

Probably not encouraging enough. How are you supposed to tell someone to believe in the fairy tale when you don't?

'Will I?' she asks hopefully, her eyes begging me to lie to her.

'Probably not,' Lexi says coldly, not an ounce of compassion in her voice.

'Lexi,' I snap, glaring at her in warning.

'No,' Steph says, waving her arms in the air, 'She's right. Who's going to want to go out with some single mother with stretch marks all over their arse?'

She has them on her *arse?*

Lexi looks just as confused. 'I thought you carried Ruby in your stomach,' she laughs hysterically, 'not your arse.'

Steph doesn't even react. 'Oh, I have them there too.' She grimaces to herself. 'I'm basically just a very pale tiger.'

Lexi bursts out laughing, unable to even look at us anymore.

'Hey! You earned those stripes,' I say confidently. 'All you have to do is look into Ruby's eyes to see how worth it she is.'

'I don't know,' she mumbles, her head dropped down. 'Sometimes I feel like I resent her.'

'Resent her?' I echo in shock. 'Why on earth would you resent her?'

She sighs heavily. 'Because if she hadn't come along maybe me and Darius would still be together.'

She can't seriously think that, can she?

'That's fucked up,' Lexi states, narrowing her eyebrows down at her judgingly.

'Yeah, where has this even come from?' I ask, still in shock.

Steph's always been crazy for babies. The minute anyone at work announced they were pregnant it was like some strange chemical reaction started in her brain. She'd just go absolutely gaga over the scan pictures and constantly ask all of those annoying questions like *'how are you feeling? Do you want a boy or a girl?'* Then when the baby was born she'd coo and say weird shit like *'my womb is aching.'* I mean, who says that, right?

'I just...' she looks down, ashamed. 'I just feel so trapped a lot of the time and I can't see a future with any kind of romance in it. It makes me sad.'

Lexi looks at me with pity in her eyes. We're probably the two least romantic people in the world, but even we feel sorry for her.

Mags walks in placing a tray of tea and freshly baked biscuits on the table.

'You need to go on some dates then,' Mags says, clearly having eavesdropped.

'Mags!' Steph says, turning the colour of beetroot. 'What did you hear?'

I can see why she'd be embarrassed in front of Mags Mother Earth.

'I heard everything.' She smiles warmly, squeezing Steph's shoulder. 'And there really is nothing to be ashamed of. If me and Bill didn't have our date nights I'd have lost my mind.'

'But you had four kids. I've only got one.'

'The first is the hardest,' she smiles. 'It gets easier after that.'

'Jesus,' Lexi says under her breath. 'Your poor vagina, Mags. It must look like a battered old cabbage.'

'Lex!'

'What?' she shrieks back, as if that wasn't offensive.

'Even if I wanted to meet someone, where the hell am I gonna bump into someone? Not many eligible bachelors around the children's centre.'

'Well,' Mags claps excitedly, 'there's a cancer charity event that's happening Friday.' She hands out our tea. 'I was thinking we should all go.'

'Huh?' Lexi grunts from the arm chair in the corner. 'That sounds dull as fuck.'

'Language, Alexia,' Mags berates with a smile.

How did this woman ever keep four kids in order? She's too bloody soft.

'And it won't be boring. They've got a band!' She seems really excited about this.

'Case in point,' Lexi snorts under her breath. 'Anywhere with a band is lame. I bet it's an old tribute band or something.'

Mags looks down at her hands. 'Well…I…I do know that they do covers,' she admits sheepishly.

'See? Lame,' she laughs with absolutely no worry of hurting her feelings. 'I'm not going.'

I glare at her. She can be such an insensitive bitch sometimes. Mags has done nothing but be there for her and take her in.

Steph picks up the purple invitation Mags left on the table, her face lighting up. 'Ooh, free bar.'

Lexi jumps up and runs to the table, snatching it out of Steph's hand and inspecting it closely.

'I'm there,' she nods, still no smile on her face.

Is she for real? 'Oh, I wouldn't want it to ruin any cool points,' I say sarcastically with a laugh.

'Oh, shut up,' she snaps. 'I just want to help Steph get some. And you know, the cancer people.'

I roll my eyes.

'Anyway, it'll be good advertising for us.'

'Advertising?' Steph snorts. 'We're not exactly going to be giving out business cards. I keep telling you, Lexi, this has to be low key.'

'I know that, dummy,' she snaps.

'But Lexi may be right,' Mags tries to reason. 'I've heard a lot of women say they're still scared of the unknown. Maybe meeting you in person would calm their minds.'

'Women can be such pussies,' Lexi sighs dramatically, falling back into her chair.

It might be a good idea. Plus I could really do with a night out. I've been absolutely exhausted since looking after Ivy. She might only live downstairs, but she's getting so confused with everything. I might as well be looking after a toddler. I have to explain everything and constantly try to calm her down to reassure her that its 2015. It's frustrating, but also so hard to watch. It's so strange to have someone alive in front of you, but still feel like you're losing them.

Plus I had a lot of explaining to do last night when she managed to escape in her nightdress and wander the street. Mr Hendricks found her hammering on his door, demanding to be let in. Apparently she thought it was her flat. In her defence the front doors are identical.

I take the invite from Lexi and inspect it. Ooh, the dress code is cocktail attire. I picked up an amazing dress from the local charity shop a couple of months ago and I've been looking for an excuse to wear it. It's not the kind of thing you can sling a jacket over and buy milk in. Fuck it, we could all do with a night out. What have we got to lose?

Chapter 15

'I totally need to sign Steph up for online dating,' I tell Samuel that night. 'If she doesn't get another boyfriend soon I think she's gonna go weird.'

He looks back seriously, his forehead creased. 'What, like a serial masturbator?'

I burst out laughing. He's deadly serious.

'Samuel, you crack me up!'

He just shrugs. 'Okay, so let's do it. Let's get the mumma some action. But I'll have to help you. If you were that good at it you'd have someone already.'

'I don't want someone, remember?' I remind him.

'Yeah, yeah, whatever,' he laughs. 'Right...' He starts opening up websites on his laptop.

He bites his thumbnail. 'What websites do you straight people use?'

'What? Don't tell me there are actually separate dating sites for gay men?'

'Oh yeah, totally,' he nods. 'There's even ones designed specifically just for meeting up and shagging, no strings attached.'

'No way!' I squeal, snorting out wine from my nose. 'That's horrible!'

'Is it?' he asks, completely shocked. 'Everyone gets what they want. No one gets hurt. Look.'

He shows me an app on his phone. Most of the guy's pictures are of naked chests. Gross.

'You gays can really be stereotypical sometimes. Wait, what's your picture?' He looks away. 'Samuel?'

'Whatever.' He grins devilishly. 'Okay, so I've got up More Rabbits in the Hutch.'

'More Rabbits in the Hutch? Jesus, who came up with that name?'

'Who cares?' he laughs, downing his drink. 'Right, let's set her up. I've used a photo from her Facebook. How would you describe her?'

'Err...single mum looking for love?' I attempt lamely.

He glares at me. 'We are *trying* to get her a date, right? I'll put her down as single mother of one looking to have some fun.'

'Samuel! You can't say that. That sounds like she wants a quick shag.'

'That's what she wants, no?' he giggles, raising his eyebrows up and down comically.

'No! Move over.' I push him out of the way and settle myself in front of his laptop. Let me think. I decide to make him giggle. He's always telling me how serious I am.

Single mum of one looking for some romance/companionship. Must not mention anything Greek. No anal.

I laugh hysterically to myself. Just imagine if I was serious! Samuel cracks up too when he sees it.

'Perfect,' he smiles, clicking a button.

I look at the screen and realise to my horror that he's clicked submit. Shit.

'Samuel! What the fuck did you do?'

'What? That's what you wanted, right?'

'Of course not, you idiot!'

I start clicking back and edit, but it keeps saying *'unable to edit. Please try again in twenty four hours.'*

What the fuck have I done?

Friday 9th October

So, like it or not, Friday night we're on our way to this stupid cancer charity event. Well, it's obviously not stupid. It's raising money for charity and apparently tonight is actually a celebration that they've raised enough money to build another chemo wing at the hospital. Which of course is great, but I actually find it terrifying that we need to build more. Is cancer getting more frequent or are we just curing more of it?

I've left Samuel looking after Ivy so I can relax a little. I look at Mags, dressed in a floor length black lace dress with three quarter length sleeves. It does a good job of covering up how much weight she's lost, but still her collarbones stick out from the neckline. I hope to God she survives it. I mean all we've ever told her is how she's going to fight this and kick its arse, but the truth is that we have no idea. I mean, what if it's too late and it's already spread around her body?

'You okay, hun?' Steph asks, adjusting her boobs in her sexy slinky one shouldered maxi dress. If you still have pregnancy boobs you really shouldn't try and go for a one shouldered bra. She looks seriously uncomfortable, and I swear her tits are on the tilt.

I snap myself out of it when she follows my gaze down to her boobs.

'Yeah, sorry. Just thinking.'

'Well snap the fuck out of it,' Lexi snaps, stepping forward to take her black coat off. 'We're here for business. Get your game faces on.'

Never one to follow the black tie dress code, she's wearing a short crimson velvet dress with cut out sides by her stomach and a see through mesh material starting from her sweetheart neckline and ending around her neck. She's teamed it with matching thigh high boots and tights that have little black bow ties all over the place. I'd say she looks like a tart, only she doesn't. The truth is she looks fucking fantastic. Only a nineteen year old who truly doesn't give a shit what people think of her could pull this look off. She looks sexy as hell and every man in the place seems to notice the minute the coat is off. She smiles smugly, her winged black eyeliner making her look like the kitten who got the cream.

'I see a few of my ladies.' Mags smiles, waving over at a group of women. I know from seeing them at the hospital that they're wearing wigs, but it's only noticeable on one of the women. 'That's Darcy,' she whispers in my ear. 'Refused the NHS wig and insisted she got a privately made one. And it looks far cheaper than ours.'

I grin to myself. I've never heard Mags gossip so much before. It's strangely thrilling. She walks off waving and chatting animatedly.

'Let's get a drink,' Steph grins. 'I can't believe I'm out without the baby. I'm so blummin excited!' she gushes, heading towards the bar.

Lexi rolls her eyes at me and I giggle quietly. Steph takes out her purse and grabs the attention of the bartender. I think it had something to do with the fact one of her boobs has nearly fallen out of her dress.

'How much is a glass of champagne?' she asks, counting out her change on the bar. How embarrassing.

His face lights up and I realise he's quite the fitty. All dark bronzed skin, amber eyes and a killer grin. Steph seems to notice too, because she blushes beetroot.

'You're in luck tonight,' he purrs.

I blush. What the fuck is he propositioning her with?

'R...Really?' she stammers back, raising a confused eyebrow.

'Yep.' He leans over the bar, almost in her face. 'It's a free bar.'

'Fuck yeah!' Lexi yelps. 'How could you forget?'

'Great,' Steph coos, practically drooling. 'Well then, we'll have three glasses of champagne.'

God, I love champagne.

'Not for me,' Lexi says. 'I'll have a whiskey and coke.'

He looks at her in shock, but quickly gets on with it when she shoots a daring glace back.

We get our drinks and each take a large gulp of them. Bartender boy ignores me. Obviously my dress is too tame for him. It's high necked and falls just below the knee. The only flirty detail is the cream mesh inserts on the skirt that flare out every time I move. It makes me feel like a princess. Not that I'd ever admit that.

'Right, I say we separate,' Lexi announces. 'We can cover more ground like that.'

'Lexi, why is it I never saw this ambitious attitude when you were at work? You're like a different person.'

'Oh yeah, because you can really get excited about photo copying. What exactly could I dream of? Being promoted to scanning? Come on, Sade.'

'I started at office junior,' I snap. 'If you work hard enough-'

'What?' she interrupts, raising her eyebrows. 'I could end up like you? We're both in the same situation here, Sadie. All of those years of you slugging away have still resulted in nothing. We're just a number to the man in charge at the end of the day.'

I roll my eyes. 'Oh spare me another speech on how 'the man' is trying to get us all to conform.' She's just exhausting.

'Fine. I'm out,' she snaps, flicking her hair in my lipstick before stalking off.

God, she's frustrating. I look to Steph, who just shrugs.

'Actually I think I'm gonna stay at the bar,' she announces. She looks back towards the barman, who raises his eyebrows in challenge. 'You know. I bet a lot of people will come to the free bar.'

God, she's transparent. I'm surrounded by idiots.

'Okay, sure,' I say sarcastically. 'You do that.'

I down my glass of champagne and grab another from a walking waiter with a tray. I straighten myself up and take a deep breath. I survey the crowd and wonder what it is I'm actually supposed to be doing. It's not like I can just walk straight up to people and offer them drugs. They could be police for all I know.

Really, I suppose the only reason I agreed to come was to give Mags a night out. I haven't seen her this excited for a long time. I find her in the crowd laughing and joking with her friends as if she doesn't have a care in the world. It makes me so happy to see her like this. Not worrying about everyone else for a change.

I walk towards the other side of the huge ballroom. I don't want her to see me looking glum and subsequently worrying about me. I glance up at the enormous raised ceiling, the exposed wooden beams covered in twinkling fairy lights. Anywhere else it would risk the chance of looking tacky, but in this venue, with its traditional barn like design, it actually adds to the relaxed ambiance.

A jazz quartet is playing an instrumental of *Fly me to the Moon* on stage. They're pretty good, and I find myself swaying along to it while I take a handful of mini toad in the holes from a passing waiter. Jeez, it's hard holding three of these with my champagne in the other and my clutch bag under my arm. But I persevere. I'm starving. Champagne always makes me hungry. I don't know why I even like it. I think it's the idea of it more than anything. When I was younger the idea of people drinking champagne was like a fairy tale to me. Some girls dreamt of growing up and becoming a princess and marrying prince charming. I dreamt of growing up and working hard at a job and being able to afford to drink champagne in a big bubble bath. I still haven't gotten around to doing that. I only ever drink it when it's free at events. I just can't part with the money. You know what they say; once you're poor, you're always poor at heart.

As I shovel the last bit of my toad in the hole in my mouth I somehow manage to drop the other two on the floor. Damn it. I bend down as ladylike as I can to pick them up. I almost get trodden on a few times, but I hate to see good food go to waste. I stand up, blowing on them to make sure they don't have any dirt on. Two second rule and all that. I'm just about to bite one when I notice a firm chest in front of me. I look up into Harry's face, his expression a mix between amused and disgusted.

Shit. What the hell is he doing here?

'You're not really going to eat that, are you?' he asks, raising his eyebrows sceptically.

I'm so shocked and embarrassed that I drop it on the floor. Again. Like a fucking moron.

I bend down to pick it up, but manage to crack my skull against something. Aah! I look up to see him also clutching his head. He must have tried to pick it up too. Idiot.

'Jesus, what is your head made of?' I snap. 'Bricks?'

He smiles. 'I have a pretty strong skull. You know, to hold my really big brain?'

'Really?' I drool sarcastically.

'Yep. In fact I'd say everything about me is pretty big and strong.' He wiggles his eyebrows suggestively.

I roll my eyes. My head throbs. 'If it's that hard your women must have battered vaginas,' I blurt out without thinking.

Oh my God, why did I say that out loud? I really need to work on my brain to mouth filter around him. I feel my cheeks redden and then my eyes are drawn to his crotch. He does seem to have an impressive bulge in his trousers. They're pretty tight actually. Who does he think he is? Olly Murs?

'Hello?' He waves, snapping me out of it. 'My face is up here.'

I look back up into his amused blue eyes, mortification flooding my body. What the hell is wrong with me?

'Err…sorry.'

I can't look at him right now. I decide to take the opportunity to pick up the toad in the hole. I don't want anyone slipping on it.

'I meant what I said you know,' he warns while looking at me suspiciously.

God he's a dickhead. Bringing up my mother again.

'And I meant what I said!' I snap. 'You can go fuck yourself if you think you can go about accusing me of things and talking about my mother. It's none of your business. *I'm* none of your business.'

'Actually,' he snaps cuttingly, 'I was talking about you not eating those appetisers.'

'Oh.' Well I feel dumb. I bite my lip, trying to decide what to do. Should I just walk off?

'But if you want to talk about it, let's talk about it.' He folds his arms and leans back, clearly waiting for me to say something. What exactly, I don't fucking know.

I sigh, exasperated. 'There's nothing to talk about. You think you know me from what you read on a piece of paper and I know better.'

I go to turn around, but he grabs my arm. I look down at it in shock. How dare he touch me! He quickly loosens his grip to make sure he's not hurting me. But he's still holding me, making my skin tingle, and keeping me in place.

'I think I already know you a lot better than you think,' he declares, his blue eyes steely.

'Really?' I snarl, throwing his hand off me.

'Really,' he nods, smiling cockily.

I look down at my toad in the holes and grin mischievously.

'Would the girl you think you know do this?' I raise one of the toad in the holes and stuff it into my mouth, chewing slowly.
'Mmmm,' I moan. It tastes gross, like dust, but I won't give him the satisfaction.

He looks back at me horrified, his mouth ajar. 'I…I can't believe you just did that.'

'I've eaten far worse in my life.' With that I turn and stride across the room before he can comment.

I want to leave him shocked and disgusted. Hopefully he'll leave me the fuck alone now.

The music comes to a halt and chatter slows down as a woman stands on the stage, tapping the microphone.

'And now, ladies and gentlemen, I'd like to introduce to you a man that has made this whole evening possible. A man that has helped raise the majority of the money needed for us to build the new chemotherapy wing at St Francis hospital. Local businessman, Joaquin Khoner.'

Everyone applauds as a tall slim man in his early fifties wearing what looks to be a handmade suit takes the stage. He's got olive skin and black hair which is greying slightly at the front. He's got thick black round spectacles which finish off his look superbly. He's like the ultimate good looking older guy. Distinguished, well read, and now I know he's charitable. Swoon.

'Thanks everyone for coming here tonight to celebrate the opening of the new ward. We couldn't have done this without the support from all of our local business partners. I thank every one of you.'

God, his voice is so smooth it's practically honey. And he's so humble. I look around me to see every other woman in the room clearly as taken as me.

'I'd also like to thank my wife for helping put on this amazing party.'

Well, shit. There goes my older man fantasies. Alanis Morissette's *Isn't it Ironic* starts playing in my head. Yeah, yeah, Alanis. I don't want you telling me I told you so right now.

'Now there's nothing more to say than enjoy the party.' He raises his glass of champagne. Everyone copies him, shouting out cheers.

Everyone applauds raucously while he walks off the stage. What a bloody beauty. Waiting for him is a man that's seriously built. I can only see his shoulders and the way he's whispering something in Joaquin's ear. I really can't stop looking at this beautiful man Joaquin. I wonder if he really loves his wife. Whether he could be persuaded to take me to Paris for the weekend. Jesus, I must be sipping this champagne a bit too quickly. I grab another one just in case I need more to forget.

I look back at my older man fantasy, but this time his built friend turns round and locks eyes with me. I feel the colour drain from my face as I take in his cold recognition. That scar on his lip. It's him. It's the drug dealer that threatened me in the alley. He's here. He's fucking here, in a suit, chatting to this Joaquin dude. How does he even know him? Wait…could Joaquin be the boss he was talking about. Could Joaquin be the leader of the drug gang? This good citizen Joaquin that everyone seems to love?

You wanna be in my gang, my gang, you wanna be in my gang, oh yeah.

Dammit, not now, Garry Glitter. Why is my brain singing when this guy is looking at me as if he wants me dead? I've had too much champagne. And now this guy wants to come after me. He starts to walk just as the lights go off and we're plunged into darkness. The six piece band on stage begins pelting out *Celebration*.

It's enough to snap me out of it. I can't see him in the dark anymore and I'm sure he can't see me either. This is my chance to get the girls and get the fuck out of here. Quickly. I turn and start walking, excusing myself as I push past people. The hairs on the back of my neck are up and I feel a sickly taste rise in my throat. The panic of knowing he's looking for me but not having any idea where he is makes me feel the two things I hate the most; helpless and scared.

I spot Steph first. She's sat on a stool at the bar, one leg up on it, pointing to the butterfly tattoo on her ankle. The barman's taking her shoe off, clearly playing the 'I want a closer look at it' card. By the time I get to her he's stroking her instep. What a creep.

'Steph,' I shout in her ear, the music now so loud it's hard to hear each other. 'We need to get out of here. We're in trouble.'

'Oh lighten up, Sadie,' she laughs. 'This is my fwirst night out in forever! I'm twying to forget about that twat in Cyprus.'

It's only then I stand back to look at her and realise she's shit-faced. She's got a bit of spit in the corner of her mouth, her mascara is smudged and her dress is dangerously close to exposing a boob on one side. Jesus, what is it with these excitable women?

'Yeah, stay,' the barman shouts. 'I saw your profile online. Let's just say I like what I saw.'

She creases her eyebrows in confusion. Crap. No wonder he's all over her.

'What?' she slurs.

'No.' I put my hand up to show I mean business. 'We're leaving.'

'But I don't wanna,' she whines, jutting out her bottom lip like a toddler. She's been hanging around with Ruby too long.

I pull her arm and whisper harshly in her ear, 'If we don't leave this very second we're going to get murdered. Now hurry the fuck up or I'm leaving you here.'

She seems to realise the severity of my words, her eyes doubling in size. She waves goodbye to the barman. Not serious enough not to blow him a kiss though.

I pull her along after me, weaving through the crowd of strangers, careful not to step into the drug dealer's path. Not that I'd have any idea until it was too late.

I can't see *anything.* I can't find Lexi anywhere. It's far easier to spot her with the pink hair. But I find Mags still with her crowd of friends. She also seems a bit tipsy, but nowhere near as bad as Steph. If I don't hold her up she's swaying all over the place, trying to dance to the music.

'Mags,' I breathe, relieved as I tap her on the shoulder.

She looks up at me and immediately knows something's wrong. 'What is it, dear?'

'We're in trouble. There's a dangerous guy here who's after us. I don't have time to explain. But he's here and we need to get out of here, now.'

'Understood,' she nods, rushing to say her goodbyes to her friends. I turn back to Steph to find her gone.

Oh fuck. Has he got her already? Then I notice her. On the stage. The motherfucking *stage* dancing and singing along to *I Will Survive.* Oh. My. God.

I look back at Mags in astonishment. She doesn't even seem that phased.

'He knows you, correct?' she asks quickly. I nod. 'Well then I'll go get her. You meet us in the toilets in five minutes.'

'But he might know you too. We have no idea how much they know about us.' I'm starting to get hysterical.

She furrows her brow, obviously dying to find out what the hell I'm going on about.

'I said go!' Mags shouts. 'The longer you're standing next to me the less safe you're making me right now.'

Wow. She's right. I need to pull myself together. I start walking towards the ladies, every few steps glancing back to the stage. Mags got to her in time and is guiding her off the stage when Steph's boob falls out. A few men in the crowd cheer. Oh my God, way to draw attention to ourselves. I run into the toilets and lean against the sinks. I look into the mirror and realise I look a bit dishevelled myself. I try to smooth down my hair and take deep breaths. This is all going to be okay.

What the hell is taking them so long? And where the hell is Lexi? I get my phone out and call her. It just rings and rings. She probably can't hear it. I text her.

We need to leave. Emergency. Get out of here as soon as you can.
I get a ding almost immediately.
Met someone. I'll be fine. Peace out x
Is she fucking serious?
Get your arse out of her right now! Life in danger!

The door finally swings open and Mags comes in practically dragging a drunk Steph.

'Thank God,' I gush, releasing the breath I didn't realise I was holding.

'It's okay,' Mags soothes. 'Time to come out ladies,' she calls towards the toilet stalls.

Four doors open at once and her friends come out.

'We need your help,' Mags declares. I've never seen her so full of authority. It's awesome. 'We need to get out of here sharpish and we're worried we're being watched. We need to look different.'

The women look towards each other, a silent conversation happening before us. Then they reach for their heads and take off their wigs. Mags swaps her blonde wig for a short black one and takes one of their red shrugs, wrapping it around her shoulders. Steph is taken out of her dress, which let me tell you is easy it's so flimsy, and swapped with a lady called Eleanor's blue ball gown. It doesn't look cheap either.

'Now you,' Mags says, looking at me. 'I don't think the girls' clothes will fit you.' They all look over my skinny limbs disapprovingly. 'You'll have to wear a wig.'

'Here,' the lady with the terrible wig offers, stepping forward and giving me the offending red wig. It looks so ridiculously unrealistic. 'I don't mind,' she smiles. 'I still have some hair under here.'

I look closer to see that she's just cut her hair really short and has only lost small patches of hair. You probably wouldn't notice unless you looked closely.

'Thank God,' the other friend says. 'I'm as bald as a baby's backside,' she laughs, jamming her wig back onto her head.

I grab it and put it on, struggling to make it look natural in the mirror. If anything this is just going to draw attention to me.

I turn back to Mags and Steph. 'You two should go out first. I'll hang back and go in a minute.'

'You think I'm going to get out with Steph being this drunk and noticeable?' Mags asks, clearly looking for help.

Shit. 'You're right.' I grab Steph's arm and place her in front of the sink. 'Now, Steph,' I warn, biting my lip and trying to get the nerve. 'This is going to hurt.'

'Huh?' she slurs, almost asleep standing up.

I slap her hard across the face. Her whole body whips round in a circle and she falls into the sink.

'What the fuck?' she shouts, lifting herself up, clutching her face.

'I'm not finished,' I snap, grabbing her head and turning the cold water on. I splash it onto her face so harshly she gurgles and sounds like she's choking. I finally let her go. 'Now I'm finished.'

She straightens herself up, completely out of breath. Maybe I did go a *tad* overboard.

'What the fuck, Sadie?' she blurts out, water still running down her face.

'Look, there's no time for apologies. You're sobered up enough to walk. Now go get out of here.'

She looks seriously livid, but I don't have time for it.

'Now, Steph! Unless you want to be murdered.'

Mags grabs her, wiping the water off her face and leading her out. She looks back at me and nods, her face grave. I nod back, swallowing down the lump of panic in my throat. The ladies walk out with them, probably aiming to cause as much confusion as possible.

I look at my phone again. No reply from Lexi. What the fuck is she playing at? Does she have no regard for her personal safety?

Typical nineteen year old, thinking she has nine lives. Thinking she's untouchable. Or maybe she's already left. Maybe she saw my text and ran and she's already back at Mags' house. Yes, for now, to keep me going, I choose to believe that.

I look back into the mirror at my stupid red hair. It makes me look like a devil. Hell, maybe it's a representation of what I've turned into these last few months. Maybe that's who I am now. The kind of girl that has to sneak out of a charity event for fear of getting beaten up.

I take a big deep breath, letting the oxygen fill my lungs completely before letting it go. Show time.

I open the door and head straight towards the only exit. It brings me into the small brightly lit foyer. I unclench my buttocks, my escape finally looking possible. I stride towards it when I feel strong hands on my hips pulling me back. I yelp and attempt to fight the bastard. Only it's Harry instead.

'Harry? What the fuck are you doing?' I go to stand back, but realise he has me in a corner.

'No, what the fuck are *you* doing wearing a strange wig? I saw your friends leave here too. What's happening?'

Why is he so fucking nosy?

'Nothing. I just need to go.' I try to push past him, but he blocks me.

'I agree,' he nods, looking serious. 'You're not safe here.'

'How do *you* know?' I blurt out. I never told him I got threatened. 'Are you following me? Is that why you're here tonight?'

'No, I'm here following Joaquin. I've been trying to take him down for years, but he has half of the station in his pocket. Anyway, he doesn't like competition.'

'What?' I don't have time for his stories right now.

At that exact moment the big guy comes barrelling out of the door, speaking gruffly into his phone.

'I'm gonna check out here,' he says into it.

Shit. He's only about a metre away from me. Harry hasn't spotted him yet, he's still too busy looking at me. All he'd have to do is look this way and he'd know it was me. I look to Harry, pleading with my eyes for his help. He just looks confused.

Before I have time to reason with myself I grab the collars of his suit jacket and yank him towards me. I crush my lips to his in an attempt to hide myself. At first he freezes, his lips doing nothing. Then he wakes up. His hands hold my cheeks as he deepens the kiss, turning his head so that his tongue has better access. My God, he's a bloody good kisser. It's almost as if he's sucking the life out of me, my nerves and terror slowly slipping away. In its place is a nice warm, fuzzy feeling. A feeling of content mixed with knowing someone wants me.

I know this is only to hide myself, but my God, the longer I suck face the longer I can pretend this is a normal guy I met in a normal bar and we have the opportunity to live happily ever after. Not this train wreck of a situation.

He's the first one to pull back and release me. I struggle to open my eyes, feeling dozy. I could easily face plant into a bed right now and sleep for a million years. When I drag them open I see him biting down on his lip. God, how I'd love to suck on it sometime. No. Pull yourself together, Sadie.

I mentally slap myself in the face, much like I did to Steph, and try to concentrate. He looks regretful. Shit. Not that I should care. I only did it to hide myself. I shouldn't give a crap, right? Then how come I do care? So *so* bad.

I look around him to see that the scary guy is nowhere to be seen. I'm safe. For now.

'Sadie…' he starts regretfully, running his hand through his hair.

This is awkward. Ugh, I could really do without the whole *'why did you kiss me'* conversation.

'Err…I have to go.'

And just like that I run the fuck out of there.

Harry's Diary

Fuck! Where the fuck did that kiss come from? This chick is seriously confusing. And what the hell was she doing showing up at Joaquin's event like that? She'd have to be pretty bloody stupid not to know he's the biggest drug dealer on the scene. Only...well I'm starting to think she might be that stupid. The way they were all suddenly trying to get out of there in a hurry. It was like they'd just realised.

God, that girl's a head fuck. But that kiss...well it was pretty fucking great. She has the softest little lips. It was adorable how she tried to take control. Yeah, I wasn't having that shit. I took over, but as soon as it started getting good and I had wood in my pants hard enough to bust a door down, I pulled away and she ran for the hills.

Total. Bloody. Head fuck.

Chapter 16

<u>**Saturday 10th October**</u>

I didn't sleep all night. I couldn't. That stupid bloody kiss kept invading my mind. Then I'd imagine what it would feel like for him to truly hold me before I fell asleep at night, which is not like me *AT ALL!* I don't know what's wrong with me. The guy is trying to send me to prison. I should be disgusted that I kissed him. But then I don't understand why he was warning me I wasn't safe last night. It's almost like he's trying to help me get away with things. I don't get it.

Anyway, by nine the next morning I've already fed Ivy her breakfast and I'm at Mags' house to try and find out what the fuck happened to Lexi. I tried calling her all night, but it just kept going to voicemail. I considered calling the police, but Mags texted me to say she heard her come in at about two in the morning. She added that she didn't think she was alone either. Imagine being that disrespectful to Mags. Bringing some strange man into her house. It's beyond rude.

But I have to appear happy in front of Mags. Her nerves must be shredded after last night. So I plaster on a smile as she opens the door.

She looks tired; really bloody tired. Dark purple bags have taken up residency under her eyes and she seems paler than normal. She quickly throws a forced smile on too.

'Morning, sweetheart. How are you feeling?'

Me? How am *I* feeling? She's the one with cancer. She looks terrible. To think I caused her that anguish makes me sick to the stomach.

'Forget me, you nutcase! How are *you?* How did you even sleep knowing there was a strange man in your house?'

She's already dressed in navy trousers and a plain white long sleeved t-shirt. I follow her into the kitchen. She gets some mugs out of the cupboard and fills up the kettle.

'Cup of tea, sweetheart?'

How the hell can she be so calm right now? I'm about to chew my own hand off.

'So…are you not worried about what went down last night?' I can't believe she can be so calm.

She shrugs while flicking the kettle on.

'I mean, you don't want to bombard me with questions?' I persist. 'Ask why I freaked out last night and said a guy was coming after us all? We need to sort this out now before we all end up dead.'

She looks back at me with an amused smile on her lips.

'I'm going to give you a decaf,' she smirks.

Is she *mental?* How can she be so calm? I'm starting to think we all are, ever thinking this was a good idea.

'How the hell can you be so calm?' I fall back onto the small sofa in the corner, exasperated.

'There's no point worrying about it,' she dismisses with a wave of her hand. 'We'll all talk about it when Steph gets here and Alexis wakes up.'

I raise my eyebrows at the mention of Lexi. 'Did she have a late night?' I can't help but smile at the ridiculousness of it. What I really want to ask is was she loud when she shagged this unknown man.

'I may have heard a few bumps in the night.' She smiles devilishly.

'Mags! You make it sound like you were listening!'

The dirty bitch. It's true what they say; it's always the quiet ones.

'Of course I wasn't,' she laughs, her cheeks going red. 'I just think she deserves a bit of fun after what she went through with that Jason.'

She deserves a bit of fun? What about her right to sleep peacefully in her own house?

But I suppose she's right. She has been through the mill. But it's only because she has such terrible taste in men. She's proving that by bringing back some randomer who could rob Mags' house. I quickly check around that nothing's missing. The TV's still here, so I think we're okay.

Anyway, I must try and remember not to shout at her. She won't react well to that. I need to just chat with her. Make it appear like a conversation.

At that moment, we hear movements on the stairs. We stop to stare at each other nervously. Two seconds later Lexi walks in dressed in ripped black jeans and a white t-shirt. Her skin is glowing, her cheeks flushed and her hair is messier than usual. The little whore. I want to smack that smile off her face. And it's not because I'm jealous. Not at *all*.

Mags and I share an amused grin over our tea cups. Behind her is a hugely built man. I notice his muscles before anything else. They bulge through his tight white shirt.

'Guys, this is Gabriel,' Lexi smiles, proudly presenting him to us.

My stomach turns to lead and the motion of keeping myself on my feet is suddenly the hardest thing in the world. I feel dizzy as if I might pass out from shock and terror.

It's the guy from the alley. The guy from last night. I do a double take and it's definitely him. The same scar on his lip. The maniac that threatened to kill me.

'What the hell are you doing here?' I blurt out in surprise. I meant to sound strong and annoyed, but instead my voice betrays me, quivering on the last word.

Mags and Lexi stare at me in befuddlement. Lexi looks between me and him.

'You guys know each other?' she asks innocently.

Oh Jesus. How the hell do I tell her the guy she just slept with is the guy out to ruin our business or worse.

'We're old acquaintances,' he answers quickly, seeming completely not shocked to see me. 'But you probably don't remember me.' He stands up and strides over to me. I flinch, terror screaming in my veins for me to run away. 'I'm Gabriel. I escorted Lexi home last night.'

'He did more than escort me, let me tell you,' Lexi chuckles under her breath.

I'm sure I feel my mouth touch the carpet, its gaping open so wide. She's slept with the very guy we were running from last night? Our fucking enemy? She's not only slept with him, but she's invited him into Mags' house and unwillingly exposed all of us to his danger. What a stupid little bitch. I could kill her myself.

'I was just leaving.' He smiles down sweetly at Lexi, who gazes up at him adoringly.

Jesus, how long has this been going on? She looks like she's got it bad. They did just meet last night, right?

'Sadie.' He locks eyes with mine sending a chill down my spine. 'Walk me to the door and we can have a quick catch up.' It's not a request. I can almost feel his presence pushing me towards the hallway.

Mags raises her eyebrows at me but I ignore her, quickly scuttling off to follow him. I want to get him out of here as soon as possible and bolt the door. And maybe book a one way ticket to Mexico.

The minute we're out of ear shot I start my questions. 'What the hell are you doing? Is it a coincidence you came home with my friend?'

'I don't believe in coincidences,' he grins devilishly. 'I did it to let you know.'

Oh my God. It was totally deliberate. My heart clenches with fear, as if someone has its hands clamped tightly around it.

'Let me know what?' I ask, my bottom lip trembling.

He leans in close to my face; so close I can smell his mint chewing gum. 'That you guys are easy to infiltrate. Amateurs. You might have managed to run last night, but I know more about the four of you than you can even imagine.'

He lets that settle in for a second. He knows about all four of us? Crap. He knows Mags is weak from fighting cancer. He knows Steph has a baby. I gulp down the bile.

'I see you still haven't given up your new little business venture. Shame if you ask me. It's a dangerous business, and I'd hate for something to happen to Lexi. She really is a great piece of ass.'

Is he threatening me? Is he threatening Lexi? My mouth falls open in astonishment. I might actually be sick all over him.

'Is that a threat?' I mumble, my voice shaking and showing no control of my emotions.

'Of course not,' he smiles smugly, leaning back. 'Just a warning. Have a good day.' He opens the door and strides out like he didn't just threaten all of our lives.

I bolt the door and lean against the wall, trying to compose myself. My heart is beating twice as hard as normal, the blood pumping through my veins so quickly I feel light headed. How the hell has this happened? Lexi's only just come out of a relationship with that psycho Jason. How on earth could she be ready to date again? I suppose that's the benefit of being nineteen. You get over things mighty quick. But still...to sleep with him straight away without any regard for her own safety. It's just irresponsible.

The door knocks again so loud I almost jump out of my skin. Shit, has he come back? Decided he might as well pop a bullet in our arse now…or whatever it is that they say in those American films. I take a steadying breath and open it. It's Steph, thank God.

'Oh. Hey.'

'Who the hell was that piece of man candy I just walked past? Yummy.'

I ignore her and step out of the way so she can find her way into the sitting room with her enormous buggy. They all start chatting animatedly, but I can't listen. I'm in too much shock. How the hell can this be my life right now?

I'm about to ask Lexi all about it when I see that the girls are surrounding a crying Steph. How did she even become upset? That was quick.

'Steph, what's wrong?' I ask, rushing over to her.

What if he's threatened her too?

'I'm just being stupid,' she says, waving her hand as if to dismiss her feelings.

'No, you're not,' Mags says kindly. 'You can tell us.'

'It's just Ruby.' She looks over to the pram where she's fast asleep and looks angelic. 'I know she looks like butter wouldn't melt, but she's hard fucking work. She's had me up every two hours since two am and I'm just so tired. And I'm not eating right and I just…I don't know. It's just so much harder without someone to lean on, you know?'

Poor Steph. She didn't ask her boyfriend to bugger off.

'Oh, sweetheart,' Mags sympathizes. 'I remember all too well how difficult it can be.'

'If I ever see that dickhead again I'll rip his balls off,' Lexi mutters under her breath.

It's surprisingly affectionate for Lexi.

I don't really know what to say so I decide to keep quiet.

'And I feel so embarrassed after last night. Why the hell did I have to get so drunk?'

It's pretty clear that the reason she's so emotional is because she's also hungover. Hungover with a baby does not go well.

'You could always move in here, sweetheart,' Mags says with kind eyes.

She really is the bionic woman. She never fails to surprise me with her selflessness.

'No,' she shakes her head adamantly. 'I think it's just the whole stress of last night that's not helping.'

'I know what you mean,' Lexi adds. 'I didn't sleep last night. I mean, not that I could, if you know what I mean.' She raises her eyebrows suggestively to let us know why she was awake. Yeah, yeah, we get it. 'But I'm sure it will all be fine,' she adds when she sees Steph's anxious expression.

Oh crap. I can hardly tell them that Lexi's one night stand is a drug dealer now, can I? They'll all be admitted to a mental hospital for stress.

'The only thing that drifted me off was having another quick session with Gabriel,' she grins.

Mags shakes her head. That statement is enough to make me realise I need to lay it all on the table. I can't have her falling in love with this guy or worse, actually getting hurt by him.

'I'm calling an emergency crisis meeting,' I announce with as much authority as I can muster. I can't let this go on any longer. 'Come to the dining room table.'

They look at each other, bemused. I practically run there, desperate to get this all sorted out. I tap my foot impatiently. Deep breaths. I need deep breaths.

'What's the deal?' Lexi asks, begrudgingly dragging herself over to the table.

'Okay, this is hard to say,' I attempt, my pulse racing. I take another deep breath.

'Jesus, just spit it out,' Lexi snaps. 'You're totally ruining my after sex buzz.'

'It should be ruined,' I roar. 'That guy you slept with is a drug dealer.'

Steph and Mags stare at me aghast, silence descending on the room.

'I know,' she shrugs, avoiding my gaze.

My jaw falls open again and my head starts spinning. She knew? How could she know?

'What the hell do you mean?' I demand.

'I mean I know he is a drug dealer. He told me.'

'What?'

Why the hell was he so honest with her?

'And that doesn't bother you? You don't care that you just slept with a drug dealer?'

She stares at me for a long time. 'So? So are we. Doesn't mean he's a bad guy.'

What the hell? She knew? She knew she was going out with a drug dealer and didn't think this was a massive deal? What is it with her picking terrible men? She must have serious Daddy issues.

'Yes it does!' I snap. 'He threatened me!'

Lexi's forehead creases, completely bewildered.

'What on earth are you talking about?' Mags asks looking between us.

'Yeah,' Steph agrees. 'What the hell?'

I take a deep breath. 'Look, I didn't want to tell you at the time, because I didn't want to worry you all.'

'But what?' Steph shrieks. 'Someone's threatened you and you didn't tell us! Do you owe money or something?'

'No, dummy,' Lexi snaps. She turns to look at me. 'Does he know about our business?'

At least one of them is quick to catch on.

I nod my head. 'He told us to stop. Or…things would happen.'

'And you didn't think to tell us?' Steph shrieks. 'He wasn't only threatening you. He was threatening all of us and you've let us just carry on without a clue. Jesus, I thought you were just drunk and over-reacting last night. What if they would have hurt one of us?'

'Well, I admit I didn't think it through properly, but I did try to get you to stop.'

Mags tuts. 'You really should have told us, love.' I hate the disappointment in her voice. I wish she'd have shouted. It wouldn't hurt so much.

'I know.' I hang my head in shame. 'I'm sorry.' I look to Lexi. 'But in my defence I didn't think that while we were all running away from him last night you were running into him, fanny first.'

'Hey, that's not nice,' Steph says, patting Lexi kindly on the shoulder.

Lexi shrugs it off cruelly. 'You know I have a penchant for bad boys!' she snaps. 'You should have foreseen this!'

Is she seriously trying to blame this on me? *Hello!* The minute a guy tells you he's a drug dealer it's normally a red flag to get the fuck out of there.

'There's no way she could have,' Mags tries to reason. 'Look, there's no point crying over spilt milk. We need to figure out what to do.'

'Well dump him for starters,' I snort. 'That is if you planned on seeing him again.'

Lexi shoots daggers with me with her eyes. 'So now you're calling me a slut too? Maybe I really like him.'

'I don't care if you really like him!' I scream, starting to lose it. 'Dump him. And then we're gonna have to stop the business.'

'It's so unfair,' Steph whinges, twirling her hair anxiously. 'Just when we were starting to make some good money.'

'I call bullshit. I say we carry on,' Lexi says determinedly.

Is she *serious?*

'And what, risk our lives?' Steph shrieks in disbelief. 'What if they were to hurt Ruby?'

'You're being dramatic,' Lexi huffs. 'Just like always,' she says under her breath.

'I think she's right, Lexi,' Mags agrees, her face contorted with worry.

God, I hate that I've put that worry on her face. This is the last thing she needs. How did we even get here? We just wanted to make some cash and help cancer patients along the way. It's turned into a monster.

'Actually...' Lexi says, as if remembering something.

'What?' I snap, my small thread of patience disappearing by the second.

'Well...he did kind of choke me while we were having sex.'

My eyes nearly pop out of my head. 'He did what?' Steph shrieks in horror.

'Don't judge,' she snaps back. 'I've done it before. Only...well he did seem a bit shocked when I regained consciousness.'

Is she serious? I throw my hands to my temples, a migraine coming on.

'Look,' Lexi says loudly, getting our attention. 'They've followed and manipulated us. I say it's our turn.'

'Are you seriously suggesting we start stalking these drug dealers?' I ask in disbelief. She must be high herself. I wonder if Mags is keeping count of the brownies.

'Discreetly,' she rolls her eyes. 'I mean *obviously.* We need to work out what their weak spots are.'

'They don't have any,' I shriek. 'This guy is brutal.'

'He's not the boss. He mentioned his boss last night. We need to find him and go straight to him. Forget the monkey and go to the maker.'

'I've already worked that out. It's Joaquin something. The guy that donated all that money. You know, the party was in his honour last night? I hardly think he's going to be easy to infiltrate.'

'Well, I say we at least try,' she says, defiantly crossing her arms over her chest.

'This is a bad idea,' I say, standing up.

'Let's vote,' Lexi says, gesturing towards Steph and Mags. 'All those in favour of trying this *first,* raise your hand.'

They both look back at me, obviously ashamed, as they raise their hands.

'I can't believe you two! I thought you were the sensible ones.'

'I'm sorry,' Steph says, 'but I really need the cash. I just think we should see where we are first before we throw away such a good business opportunity. You could have misunderstood all of this. I could send Ruby to stay with my mum for a while.'

Ambitious bastards; that's what I've turned them into. They're my own Frankenstein's, only they have marijuana and spreadsheets.

'I have to agree,' Mags chimes in. 'Plus, I've met the lad. He doesn't seem vicious to me.'

They have no idea what they're talking about! I grab my bag in a huff and make for the door.

'Let's hope for all of our sakes that you're right.'

Chapter 17

<u>Sunday 11th October</u>

I still can't believe they're all being so bloody oblivious to the danger we're facing here. These are clearly middle class twits that have never dealt with this kind of guy before. I have and I know first-hand that they can be nasty. If it wasn't for Samuel protecting me on the streets I dread to think where I'd be right now. I physically shiver and try to push the thoughts of forced prostitution out of my mind.

I've decided I'm going to speak to Lexi and suggest we follow Gabriel without Mags and Steph. He'll lead us to Joaquin. Only as I walk out of the coffee house I notice a flash of pink hair. She's here. Well that makes things easier. I'll go over it with her now. I watch her walk excitedly down the street and am just about to call out to her when I see her jump into someone's arms. Could that be? No. She wouldn't seriously be dumb enough to still be seeing Gabriel, the maniac drug dealer? They turn and start walking towards me. She is. She's a fucking nutcase!

They walk arm in arm down the street, chatting and laughing as if it's no big deal. I *cannot* believe her. Before I have time to reason with myself, I'm following them down the road. I stay as far back as I can without totally losing them. Every now and again I have to duck behind a tree. People look at me strangely, but I just jerk my neck a few times like I have a nervous tick. They seem to write me off immediately as a nutter. No one wants to interact with a nutter.

They go for lunch at a posh Italian restaurant. I watch them from a bench on the other side of the road, feeding each other bits off their own plates. It's disgusting and highly annoying as I'm so bloody starving myself. I subject myself to it for two hours, when it in fact feels like days. They walk out of the restaurant arm in arm before giving each other a long and grope-filled kiss. They look like any normal new couple, all smitten with each other, but only I know his true intentions. How can Lexi want to be with someone that tried to strangle her? I don't understand her at all.

They separate with a sickening sort of wave. It's as if she's waving him off to war. How pathetic. She looks like she's got it bad. I shudder when I consider what she might have been telling him. What if he's manipulated her and now she's working for them? He might have offered her money to trade secrets. I mean, can I really trust her? Before we started this she was just a friend from work. We've never truly had a heart to heart or anything. I've never met her parents. Never been invited out with her before. She's a bloody mystery to me.

I try to block it out as I follow him along the high street. He finally stops and goes into a coffee shop where he meets a tall olive skinned man with thick black framed glasses and a broad nose. It's Joaquin. He looks far more like the type of man who wears Armani suits than leather jackets. I always assumed drug dealers were Russian or Italian thugs. I probably watch too many films.

I watch them; enthralled by how good looking he is for an older man. I really need to get some. Harry pops into my head and I shudder, pushing it back out. Why the hell am I thinking about him? I'm still mortified that I kissed him. But, God, when I think of those perfect lips my lady parts can't help but tingle.

They have a quick coffee and finally exit onto the street. I hide behind a lamppost, which is foolish. I know I'm skinny, but even I'm not *that* skinny. A black shiny Mercedes pulls up and Joaquin goes towards it. This guy has a driver with a Mercedes. What on earth is going on?

Either way I know I need to follow him. I try desperately to hail down a taxi, but they're all just regular cars with people looking at me strangely. Where have all the good Samaritans gone? Can't they see when a damsel is in distress?

Joaquin's in the car now and its indicating to pull out into traffic. I need to follow him. This is my only chance. I look around me in desperation. Just then I spot an elderly lady get off her disability scooter and go into the co-op. I bet those things can reach a good speed. But obviously I *couldn't*. The poor woman wouldn't be able to get home.

But then… If I don't do this we could all be without a home. Hell, we could be murdered. I'm sure this would be nothing when compared to that. It's pretty evident I'm going to hell now anyway. May as well have some fun if I'm going to be burning for all eternity.

Before I have time to talk myself out of it, I run over and jump on it. I look down at the dials and realise I have no idea how to work it. I rev the handle and it jolts forward so quickly my head flies back. I quickly steer it left before I take out a toddler. Don't these mothers look after their children? I watch as the Mercedes pulls off and I speed along the pavement trying to keep up with it.

'Move!' I shriek at pedestrians, waving my hands frantically. 'Move out the way!'

Can't they see when there's an emergency? Bloody idiots.

Thanks to the traffic I manage to keep up with the car. We're barely around the corner when it pulls up outside a white Victorian town house. I look up at it to see its five stories high. Jesus! I look back down just in time to see I'm headed straight for a brick wall. Aaaagh!

I spin the wheel, veering off just in time. Well, just in time to crash into a pile of over flowing dustbins. I fling my arms up to protect myself, but it doesn't stop the carrier bags of rubbish exploding into the air and crashing back down on top of me. Ew!

I take the shredded lettuce from my hair and wipe the sticky chips from my lap. I wrestle myself out from it just in time to see him go into the house. Phew. At least I know what house he lives in. I squint my eyes to see its number 206. Well, he's clearly not aware of his surroundings. I'm pretty sure I'd notice some nutty girl driving into the dustbins on a nanny disability scooter.

Just then a small van pulls up next to it. It's got a giant picture of a dog on the side. A lady jumps out and lets a black poodle out of the side door. It flounces towards the same front door. 206. It can't be. A drug lord *cannot* have a ridiculously prissy dog like that. Surely?

The lady knocks on the door and a woman answers it. She's stunning with long glossy brunette hair and caramel skin. I recognise her as the woman standing near him last night. She must be his wife.

She's dressed casual in jeans, boots and a t-shirt, but I can tell they're designer just in the way they're cut, hugging every curve.

Her eyes light up when she sees the poodle. She bends down with her arms open and embraces the dog like you would a long lost relative. The poodle licks her face. Ew. But she seems to be loving it. Cooing all over the poodle.

How can someone love a dog that much? It's weird. And then it hits me. That's how we're going to get to this guy. Behind every strong man is an even stronger woman. And if that woman loves a dog that was to mysteriously go missing…well, it could get pretty messy.

###

As I'm driving the scooter back towards the co-op, I notice a police car outside of it. I hope they haven't been robbed. God, nowhere is safe nowadays. It's a sad society we live in.

I park it up as best I can and reach into my handbag for a scrap of paper and a pen so I can leave a note.

Thanks for lending me it. Sorry about the smell, I crashed into some bins x

'There she is!' someone behind me shrieks.

I turn to see the old lady. She's pointing her wrinkly finger towards me and hitting a police officer on the shoulder with the other hand.

'That's the girl! Arrest her! Arrest her now!'

I roll my eyes. These old people these days are so bloody dramatic. He's not going to arrest me for stealing a scooter. He walks over with a typical policeman stance, like he has a stick up his arse. Thank God Harry doesn't walk like that. If he did maybe I could stop thinking about the kiss and how he hasn't tried to contact me since. Not that I'm bothered. Hell, I'm relieved. It means he's no longer trying to put me in jail.

'Excuse me, Miss, but did you steal this lady's disability scooter?'

'Err….no?' I say unconvincingly.

'Then what is this note?' He takes it off the seat and starts reading it. Oh shit, well this doesn't look good.

'What I mean is…I didn't steal it. I borrowed it.'

'You stole it, you filthy tramp!' the old lady shouts, her face puce with rage.

'Hey! Who are you calling a tramp?' A bit of lettuce falls from my hair. Damn, that's bad timing.

'Mrs. Fanthon is clearly unaware that you borrowed it,' the policeman continues. 'This makes it stealing.'

Nothing left for it. I'll have to lie. Her word against mine and all that.

'No…but…I totally asked her if it was alright. She said yes.' I lower my voice to a whisper. 'It's not my fault she's obviously senile.'

'How dare you!' she gasps. Well she's obviously got no problems with her hearing. 'In my day I'd take you over my knee and spank the living lights out of you. No discipline with kids today.'

She's really starting to piss me off.

'I'm not a kid. I'm twenty eight years old.'

'Old enough to know better,' she says, getting up in my face.

If this bitch was forty years younger I'd totally pull her hair.

The policeman frowns. 'I'm afraid I'm arresting you on suspicion of theft. You do not have to say anything…'

'You have to be joking! She just threatened to spank me. Arrest *her!*'

He starts the usual little speech while she looks on smugly. What a bitch. If only she knew the real reason I took it. We've got a bloody drug lord living down the road from us. Isn't that a hell of a lot more concerning?

Yes, so in hindsight, stealing the old ladies disability scooter wasn't the smartest idea, but I mean, I really didn't think it would end like this. Being arrested by an overzealous police officer. I mean, I returned the bloody thing, didn't I? What harm's done? There are far bigger crimes going on. Actually, what if they look into me further and see that I'm already being investigated by Harry? They might have enough on me to lock me up for a while. *Shizza.*

'This is a mistake.' I try to laugh, as my head is pushed down and I'm thrown into the back of a police car. 'I honestly just used it.'

'Stealing is a criminal offence, miss,' the policeman says with no hint of amusement in his voice, tutting at his female partner. I see her look at my stilettos approvingly.

'This is rubbish,' I shriek, starting to lose it. 'Don't you have anything better to do?'

'Like we haven't heard that one before,' he laughs, rolling his eyes at the female officer.

'Whatever,' I snort under my breath, deciding to stare out of the window like a moody teenager. I won't give them the satisfaction of a bigger response.

How the hell could this have happened? I have seriously bigger fish to fry right now. Not that I can tell them that.

When I get to the station they book me in and allow my one phone call. *One* phone call. It's so pathetic. It's the one time in my life that I need to call everyone and tell them what's happened. And what if it goes to voicemail? Do I just rot in here forever?

I go through my options. I don't want to call Samuel. He's suspicious enough as it is. If I tell him I'm calling from a police station he's bound to demand what the fuck is going on with me.

I could call Mags. She'd help for sure, get me a solicitor and all that. But I know that she has a chemo session today and Lexi's going with her. Obviously the only reason why she rushed off from her romantic date with Gabriel.

Steph would panic and probably start blabbing down the phone. I'd probably end up having to reassure her. But then she is my only option. Ivy wouldn't even remember the telephone conversation.

I'm about to dial Steph's number when I remember she has a doctor's appointment for Ruby. Trying to work out if she has some tropical baby disease that makes her cry all the time. Crap. I only have one person left and I really, really don't want to have to call him. But I don't have many options. Harry it is.

'Sadie?' he answers after two rings. 'Are you okay?'

'I'm fine,' I snap. Why am I snapping? I called him. For help, you ungrateful woman. 'Well, *actually,* I'm at the police station. They've arrested me over something ridiculous.' I try to laugh to make it sound as if I'm really not worried, when in fact I'm shitting myself.

'Really? What?' he asks, clearly intrigued. Do I sense a hint of humour in his voice too?

'For…' I gulp down the bile. I don't think I can say it over the phone. It sounds too humiliating. 'Look, it doesn't matter, just come and help me okay? I need to go and check on Ivy.'

I really need a lesson in charming people, but I don't know how much time I have.

'I'll see what I can do,' he answers, sounding far more amused than he should. The bastard.

Twenty minutes later, as I sit in my rectangle grey cell, I start to wonder where it all went wrong. Was I doomed from the minute I was born? Born into that crack addicts excuse for a mother's life. I probably shouldn't have even survived the pregnancy, let alone gone on to try and build myself a life. And just when I'd built myself a respectable life it all gets torn away from me again.

I hate to think of myself as a victim, but I'm allowing myself today to wallow. There's not much else you can do when you're alone in a police cell. It's pretty hard to see the sunny side of life in here, shivering from the cold with only a manky blue blanket for comfort.

I've let myself fall into a bad world full of drugs, well-dressed drug lords and threatening men just so I can earn enough money to keep a roof over my head. I could actually go to prison because of all of this. I could end up spending my days in a small cell just like this because of a few bad decisions. Well, when I'm not being attacked in the toilets or raped by my butch mumma.

A key rattles in the cell door and it opens to reveal a normal clothed police officer, and next to him is Harry. I sigh, massively relieved to see him.

'Come on, trouble,' he smirks, his eyes dancing playfully. 'I'm busting you out of this place.'

'Really?' I grin, already running out of the room before he can shout 'gotcha' and slam it again.

'Really.'

He places his hand at the curve of my back and guides me out. It makes goose pimples dance along my skin. It must just be that he's saved me and I'm feeling emotional right now. Not that I'm remembering the way his lips grazed passionately against mine.

He leans in so I can feel his breath on my ear. 'Stealing a disability scooter?' he asks. I can hear the smile in his voice.

'I was just borrowing it,' I whisper back. I can't help the smile from creeping onto my face at the way he looks at me.

'Only you,' he snorts. 'Come on. I'm taking you home. I don't want you to have to resort to stealing any children's bicycles.'

I glare at him, but allow him to show me to his car.

Chapter 18

We travel back in silence. It should be an awkward one, especially as our kiss was the last time we saw each other, but it's not. I steal a glance at him every now and again, studying his profile. He really is beautiful in a rugged cop who could send me to prison kind of way.

He parks outside my flat and turns to me, his expression grave. 'So...are you going to tell me what happened?' he asks, his lips twitching, as if he wants to smile.

I sigh loudly, letting him know I'm in no mood for this. 'All you have to know is it was an innocent mistake.'

He pouts. 'And I'm sure you're glad I helped you. Right?'

'Obviously,' I snarl. I can't help feeling hostile around him when I know it's not his fault. 'But I do think the police should be spending their time arresting real criminals like that pimp Welshie, rather than me, who only borrowed a scooter.'

'Welshie?' he repeats in confusion.

'Forget it,' I snap, realising I shouldn't have said anything.

I take a deep breath to calm myself. This is all my own doing. I called him. I should play nice. I sigh loudly, too tired for any of this. 'Do you want to come in for a cup of tea?' Mags would be proud of me.

'Is that safe?' he asks with concerned eyes.

Is he asking if I still have weed in the house? Thank God the girls have moved it to Mags'. It made more sense with her having the bigger house.

'You're not going to attack me with your lips again are you?' he smirks.

Oh my God. He brought up the kiss. I feel my cheeks burn, my whole body turning beetroot. And *me* attack *him*? I'd hardly say I attacked him. I kissed him. Were my lips massively chapped or something?

'As safe as any house,' I shrug, rolling my eyes.

I get out of the car, acting as unbothered as I can. Fine, stick my polite tea offer up your arse, you arrogant prick. But I'm secretly glad when I hear him following me in.

He makes himself comfortable at my kitchen table, running his hands through his wayward hair. In this close kitchen I can't help but inhale his fresh citrusy scent. Yummy. He smells like a sexy fruit salad. I wonder what his *banana* looks like. No! Focus Sadie. Since when did you become such a filthy bitch? Since Detective Mcrugged came into my life.

'Seriously, thank you though,' I offer with a polite smile. Wait, what if he thinks I'm thanking him for the kiss? Arrogant arse like him, it's possible. 'For *today*,' I clarify.

He looks up at me, his beautiful face impassive, but his eyes searching for something in me.

'I'm thinking you don't like the whole damsel in distress thing like most birds?'

God, he's a pig. I hate how he talks. I hate everything about him. Well, I would if he wasn't so bloody sexy and enticing. He's such a contradiction.

'Birds? I'm a woman, not a bird, thanks very much,' I snap snarkily. 'And yes, I don't like relying on people to save me. I like to save myself.'

I think back to all the times in my life when I could have taken comfort in someone looking after me, but I've always refused. I'm a fighter. Maybe not in the punch someone in the face way, but in the spirited, I can save myself kind of way. I only ever rely on myself. I don't even rely on Samuel, especially as he's so unreliable with things. I always have a back-up plan. That's what happens when your mother doesn't give a shit. You grow up quick.

His intense ice cold eyes meet mine. They look all the bluer next to those jet black eyebrows. 'That's pretty rare these days.'

He has a few stray strands of hair over his forehead. He never looks properly put together; always like he's just gotten out of bed from a night of wild sex. Maybe he has. The idea has me feeling irrationally jealous. The temptation to reach across and push the strands back is overwhelming. I feel like I want to take care of him, which I realise is pathetic. I'm a strong, independent woman, not some wife wannabe. And he's trying to get me arrested. Although he did bust me out today when he could have left me to rot and dig myself out. He's so confusing.

He's still staring at me intently, obviously waiting for some kind of reaction.

'Maybe that's because all of the women you're meeting are nit-wit bimbos.' I can't help it. My default with him is to be snarky.

'Maybe,' he shrugs, completely unoffended. 'I do love a bimbo.' He grins widely, exposing his perfect white teeth.

He gets these adorable laugh lines around his cheeks and at the sides of his eyes when he does it. It's enough to light up my dull kitchen, and before I know it I'm grinning back. Why on earth am I smiling when he's admitting to liking bimbos?

'Well, I'm no bimbo,' I say confidently, leaning on one hip.

'No,' he sighs, looking down and leaning into the table further. His eyes shoot up, meeting mine. 'You're not. And maybe I like that.'

Tingles spread across my neck. Did he just say he likes me? I look down, suddenly feeling ashamed. I always loved that I could hold down a great job and make money by myself, but right now I'm not proud of myself. I may as well be a bimbo.

'I used to feel like I had a career. Now I guess I'm just drifting. It's making me realise how much of my identity was based around it. I kind of feel lost without it.'

I have no idea why I'm telling him this stuff, but it feels nice to say it out loud.

'I know what you mean.' He smiles kindly. 'The only reason I went into the police is to make my dad proud. He's retired now, but my brother also went into it. He's already on the anti-terrorism squad.' His hands ball into fists, his knuckles turning white. He looks bitter and pissed off. I'm sensing some sibling rivalry here.

'Do you not get on?' I ask carefully.

He sighs heavily. 'We do. We're just really different. I'm different to all of them.'

I have an overwhelming urge to cuddle him. Tell him everything will be okay. But obviously I can't. I'd look insane.

'Black sheep, are you?' I grin playfully, trying to lighten the mood.

'Exactly that, actually,' he smiles back, but it doesn't meet his eyes.

'What do you mean?' I push, frowning at him. He keeps on intriguing me.

'I'm adopted.' He throws it out there like it's no big deal, but the way his eyes are suddenly down on the table tells me he's not as comfortable with it as he makes out.

My mouth drops open and my eyes double in size. I can't help but react. I mean, he just doesn't seem the type to be adopted. He seems completely perfect.

'*You're* adopted?'

I know a normal person would fuss all over him, telling him that he can trust me. That he can tell me his story, but I just can't force myself to do it. I've heard way too many stories over the years from people on the street, and let me tell you, getting adopted is a happy ending. Something kids like me dreamt of. Being invited into a loving family that want you. Instead of sharing a bunk bed with another reject and never knowing when you're going to be passed on to the next family. Yeah, I'd have grabbed at it.

How is it that someone like him can be so lucky? Get adopted by a loving rich family that showers him with love? And then there's me, getting passed around from foster home to foster home. It actually makes me irrationally angry when I know a normal person would be feeling sorry for him right now. As far as he's concerned he's baring his soul and all I want to do is stomp my foot and shout how unfair my life is. What the hell is wrong with me?

He nods. 'My parents died in an accident when I was two.'

So he wasn't even properly abandoned. His parents wanted him. Were probably married and actively tried to get pregnant with him.

Then a tragic accident took them away, not an uncaring mother who hardly noticed.

I stand up abruptly, the chair scratching against the wooden floor. I can't look at him right now. I can't let him see the bitterness in my eyes. It's not normal. *I'm* not normal. I'm a freak and that's exactly what he'll think.

I look out of the window, down at the over grown garden feeling completely hopeless. I just want him to leave now so I can go to bed and sulk. I can be positive tomorrow. Right now I feel completely drained and I want to eat *a lot* of ice cream.

I hear him stand up behind me. Good. He's got the hint and he's going.

I jump when I feel a hand on my shoulder. What is he doing? I shrug him off and swivel round to face him. Instead of finding him expecting sympathy he seems to be sympathetic towards me. A tear escapes from my eye and I quickly wipe it away, ashamed that I'm showing any emotion around him. I hate sympathy.

I look away, back out of the window, but he grabs my chin and forces me to look at him.

'I know you had a rough start in life,' he states matter-of-factly.

I keep forgetting that he has my life on paper. Not that it can touch the reality.

My chest tightens. 'You know I was in care?' I ask, more to myself. I know he made that comment about my mother, but I didn't think how he'd know I was in the social care system. How embarrassing.

He nods, his eyes drooped in sympathy. His forehead wrinkles underneath his wayward messy hair. I can't bear the pity. It's suffocating.

'Don't feel fucking sorry for me,' I spit, peeling his fingers from my face.

He frowns. 'I don't.' I look into his eyes and see that he's sincere. 'I just know how it feels.'

I snort snarkily. Did he honestly just say that? Is he really trying to compare my childhood with his? He has no idea.

'Yeah, I'm sure you do,' I snarl sarcastically. 'Growing up with a posh little family that doted on you. I'm sure it's exactly the same as being passed around foster homes.'

I wonder if he knows about my time on the streets. I hope to God he doesn't. It would be *too* humiliating.

'I don't mean that.' He takes the tops of my arms and holds me still, clearly sensing that I want to run away from him. 'I get that I was lucky. But I still get it. I get not feeling like you belong anywhere.'

My eyes meet his in an instant. No one's ever got it before. Got that real sense of being lost in a world with no one tied to you by blood. Don't get me wrong, Samuel is the closest thing I have to family and he's not blood, but he doesn't get it. He wasn't abandoned as such but thrown out by his parents when he was eighteen and came out to them. He still grew up knowing who his family was. There's so much to that.

But this is the first time someone has truly understood the feeling of loneliness. Of feeling like you don't belong anywhere. I always thought it was just because of my shit position, but here's Harry, living with a proper family and still feeling like that. Maybe it is inevitable.

'So…you don't feel sorry for me?' I can't help but try to suppress a smile that is playing on my lips, which I know is ridiculous.

'Far from it,' he grins back, instantly changing the atmosphere to playful. 'Frankly, you annoy the hell out of me.'

I burst out laughing so hard I'm worried I've spat on him. It seems to break the tension. He joins in and we laugh until we've both got tears running down our faces. He throws his head back, still in barely concealed hysterics, his eyes pressed shut. I stop to watch him, to take in all of the small details of his face. His stubbled neck and chin. That messy black hair falling over his eyes. He looks like an adorable six year old when he laughs this much. I get an image of what he must have looked like as a boy. All messy hair and big blue eyes. He must have been gorgeous.

He stops to take a breath and obviously trying to compose himself. He catches me watching him and his eyes become inquiring, his breath heavy. The atmosphere in the room changes in a second to electric. My fingerprints tingle with the need to touch him.

I gaze up into his crystal clear blue eyes, now clouding over with dark, sexy thoughts.

He steps closer so he's now towering over me. My God, he smells amazing this close. I look up to him, my eyes the same level as his chin.

'You annoy the fuck out of me,' he repeats slowly, his eyes almost completely black with clear carnal desire.

It's suddenly agony to not be touching him. My clothes feel restricting and my skin is burning, screaming for contact.

'Well then,' I say, breathless, my chest rising and falling noticeably. 'Maybe you should fuck some sense into me.'

My mouth falls open as I just realise what I've said. I've never said *anything* filthy like that in my entire life! And I think it shows. It sounds so unnatural coming from me. How could I be so bold? How utterly cringe worthy.

He seems equally shocked, his chiselled jaw hanging open, his red lips begging for me to kiss him again. I would give a million pounds right now just to suck on that bottom lip. Then he grins.

I'm thrown against the wall and his lips crush mine before I have time to comprehend what's happening. One of his hands is holding my cheek and the other is holding my hip, pressing me up against him. He's already hard. Holy moly.

I place my shaking hands against his chest, not to push him away, but to feel the hot strength beneath his shirt. My fingers find the buttons on their own accord, randomly undoing them. He shrugs off his jacket and lets it fall to the floor. My God, my lady bits are so excited I'm worried I'm going to take off any minute, spinning round the room like a let off balloon.

He grabs my thigh and wraps them around his waist so I can feel *fully* what his intentions are. And fuck if I'm not completely too weak to refuse him. It's hard with this tight pencil dress on, but it soon rides up.

I rip his shirt open, hoping the remaining buttons will shatter spectacularly onto the floor like in the movies. Instead I just damage his shirt, but get nowhere. Oh, that's embarrassing. I break from his lips and grimace, leaning down to concentrate on the last few buttons. I pull the shirt off his shoulders, grinning triumphantly like a Goddamn fool. Only the shirt gets stuck around his wrists. Why can't I catch a break?!

'Cufflinks,' he breathes onto my lips, his breathing unsteady.

I stomp my foot in aggravation. This is beginning to get humiliating.

He smiles down at me, pushing a lock of my hair behind my ear before undoing the cufflinks himself. I place my hands awkwardly over my chest. Where do I go from here? This is awkward. Isn't sex supposed to run smoothly? Not that it ever has before.

'You haven't changed your mind, have you?' he asks, amused, as if I'd be ridiculous to refuse him.

He pulls off his shirt, showing off why he's so cocky. His chest looks like it was made by love Gods. His chiselled six pack...wait, is that an eight pack? It leads down to that magic V leading below his trousers. My mouth is actually watering.

His arrogance annoys me. Annoys me and turns me the fuck on.

'No,' I practically spit, grabbing the back of his hair in anger and pulling him back into me.

I kiss him slowly and deeply, savouring the taste of him on my lips. Now I'm setting the pace, *I'm* in control. His hands go around my waist, slowly travelling up my spine, tickling every nerve receptor on my skin. I shiver and try to drink in every last drop of pleasure. His hands reach the back of my neck where he draws tiny circles with his thumbs. Oh my God, that feels *good*. It feels like he's cherishing me. Touching me like no one else ever has. It's making me want to cry pathetically on the floor. What is happening to me?

Tingles dance around in my knickers like never before. Calm down, vajayjay! You are *not* having sex with him. You're just...oh, God only knows what you're doing.

He moves his hand back down to squeeze my arse cheek. I moan into his mouth like a wanton whore.

Oh, who am I kidding? He's got me good.

One hand goes to the zipper of my dress and it's tugged down incredibly slowly. Too slowly. He's teasing me and he knows it. I want him to ravish me quickly, not leave me hanging and desperate for him like this. At this rate I'm going to be on my knees, begging him to fuck me.

He slips the straps off my shoulders and pushes it over my hips to the floor. Standing in just my bra and knickers I feel completely exposed and vulnerable. I mean, I do have on a great matching sexy pair of pale pink satin bra and knickers. I always like to wear pretty underwear. Not that anyone normally sees it, but it still makes me feel nice. Now I'm glad for my rule. The saying shouldn't be 'what if you get hit by a bus?' It should be 'what if you get lucky?'

But still, I'm basically naked and he's not, still in his trousers. He steps back to fully take me in, his eyes scanning slowly over my body. It makes me squirm uncontrollably. He licks his lips just as I raise my hands over my chest, feeling self-conscious. I've never had big boobs, and having them on display like this feels humiliating.

He takes my arms and pulls them down, a cheeky smile on his face.

'Nothing to be embarrassed about here,' he grins, wrapping my arms around his waist. The heat from his skin almost burns my fingertips.

'Whatever,' I mumble, looking at the ground. 'Just get naked quickly.'

I look up to see him grinning. God, he looks delicious when he's grinning like that.

He grips my hands and places them onto his belt. I gasp, my hands shaking, knowing I'm only a few fabrics away from his dick. It'll be the first time I see it.

'Go on then,' he grins, feigning bossiness. 'Quickly.'

I undo his belt with trembling hands, then the buttons and his zipper. I can see his erection straining through the fabric. Crap, he must be massive. I'm scared to even touch it. But then his hand travels up my back and unhooks my bra. It falls down my arms. I almost want to grab it and put it back up. My boobs are nothing to write home about. Barely there B cups. And I know from the photo of his ex that he's normally a busty blonde type of guy.

He senses my hesitancy and furrows his eyebrows in confusion. 'You okay?'

I nod shyly, letting the bra finally drop to the floor. 'They're small. Sorry.'

Why the hell am I apologising for my small boobs? God, this is majorly cringe worthy. Why didn't I just keep quiet? My own insecurities are ruining this moment. This is why I normally stick with guys that I know are uglier than me. That way I can feel they're grateful for anything I give them.

He looks back at me, confused. 'No.' He shakes his head, raising one nipple with his finger and thumb. I shiver from the touch. 'They're perfect.' He kisses the nipple softly before putting it in his mouth, licking and sucking until my head is thrown back and I'm making noises like a jungle cat.

Suddenly his dick isn't so scary. I grab hold of it through the material. I need him inside me. Now.

I yank his trousers down as he moves his attention to my other boob. My God, his mouth! If he carries on like this I'm going to come on the spot. Past boyfriends have never gone near them. I always knew it was because they weren't interested in them. I attract arse or leg men. But I suppose them ignoring my boobs has only added to my insecurities. Who knew they'd be so sensitive and that this would feel…amazing?

I grab hold of his dick again, my fingers unable to go around the width of him, and start stroking him. He feels as smooth as velvet. My hands go along it and I realise I wasn't wrong. He's big. The biggest I've had. Not that I've had a lot.

He stops sucking abruptly to squat down in front of me. I look down at him with raised eyebrows. What's he doing? He grins back at me while his hands find the sides of my knickers and pull them down. He looks back up me again briefly before going….well…down there.

Holy mother fucking hell! I've never had a boyfriend do this to me before. Holy shit. I'm fucking dripping wet. I start throbbing with pleasure, my legs shaking so much there could be an earthquake and I'd never know.

He stops and slowly trails his nose back up my body. Watching him rise up like that is beyond hot. I can't do anything but pant. He finally finds my mouth. It's still wet from my arousal, which grosses me out, but I push the thought to the back of my head. As if sensing my hesitation, he leans back and looks down at me. I'm panting heavily now. Completely and utterly a wanton whore. But I still can't help but feel vulnerable. I'm completely in his hands.

His grin disappears as he turns serious for a second. Has he changed his mind? It's quickly replaced by a reassuring smile.

'Turn around,' he demands in a gruff voice.

Huh? I'm still in a weird kind of dream world. I don't feel like I'm in control of my own body right now. He owns it all.

I let him guide me and turn me around. Then I'm leant over the worktop, the side of my face pressing into the drainer of the sink. He picks up one of my legs and spreads it so they're further apart. Then he's nudging towards me.

Oh my God. I'm really doing this. What the hell am I doing?

Shit. He has to wear a condom.

'Condom!' I shriek.

'Shit,' I hear him mutter. He steps back a minute and I hear him rustle around in his trouser pocket. I'm left leaning over the worktop, feeling like a wally. Did I just totally ruin the moment? But I want to be safe, and if he gives any kind of shit about me he'll want to make me feel comfortable, right?

I look straight ahead and realise that if anyone looks carefully enough from a passing train they'll see me completely naked and bent over.

After what feels like an eternity he's back where he just was. But I've tensed up again. Why am I such a bundle of nerves?

He leans over me again, his dick at my entrance, his lips grazing my shoulder.

'Trust me,' he whispers into my ear, setting off an explosion in every nerve ending in my body.

I take a calming breath and try to relax myself, because against all of my better instincts I do trust him. Even though he's currently investigating me for a crime and has me bent over my kitchen sink. Oh God, what am I doing?

I don't get a chance to doubt myself further because he thrusts into me, slamming me hard against the worktop. Fuck! His dick is *huge*. I swear he just touched my ovaries. It stings like a mother fucker.

He doesn't leave a second before he thrusts relentlessly into me again, keeping hold of my hips. It's hard and rough. And fucking amazing. I've never been fucked like this before in my life. My *entire* life. God, the way he's slamming into me, the sound of his balls slapping against my skin. It's all so erotic. So…not like my life. And he's *so* deep. I cry out with each thrust, from pain or pleasure I'm not sure.

One hand leaves my hip to stroke slowly along my spine. I tingle against his touch. The mix of roughness and this gentleness leaves me feeling like I'm hanging off a cliff. I need him to stop. Or carry on. Or stop. Oh fuck, I'm sweating and I'm sure my eyes are at the back of my head. Why do I feel so….oh God, why? I can't even unscramble my thoughts.

Then his hand is massaging my clit. Fuck, it's too much. All of the sensations spiralling around down there. This must be unnatural. Is this what everyone feels during sex? Why do people even go to work?

Then his hand moves to my breast, grabbing at it roughly. He clasps a nipple between his finger and thumb and rolls it back and forth. Not the boob. Oh shit, I'm going to explode. Actually explode into smithereens! There will just be a big pile of ashes by my clothes.

Before I have time to question what the fuck is happening, my mind spins and my eyes go hazy. I fall off the cliff, or the planet, or wherever the fuck I am right now. All I feel are the sensations racing through my body from my ears to my toes. Bliss. Pure fucking ecstasy.

He stills for a second with a grunt. He must have come too. His thrusts turn into long, slow, deliberate movements. I savour every one, already sad for it to be ending so soon. Dear God, his penis is magnificent! He should get an award or something. Prized Penis.

He plants a quick soft kiss on my shoulder before pulling gently out. I realise now how much he was actually holding me up. I desperately try to steady my jelly legs and hold onto the sink for support.

His belt jingles behind me. What's he getting out of his pocket now? He can't want to go again so quickly? I use the last bit of remaining energy to turn round to face him. I'm shocked to see he's already taken the condom off and is putting his trousers back on. Well that was quick.

'You're going?' I ask, raising my eyebrows in disbelief.

'Yeah,' he says, still out of breath, his expression cold. 'I'm supposed to be on duty.'

'Oh,' I gasp.

Oh my God, this is humiliating. He's getting dressed quickly because this was, in fact, a quickie. This didn't mean anything. Why on earth did I think for a second that it would? I mean, the man fucked me from behind. He didn't even want to look me in the eyes. But I can't help the hurt growing in my chest. I quickly grab my dress off the floor and cover myself with it.

'I'll call you,' he says, his face impassive. His eyes are vacant, his body language dismissive.

He won't call me. I'm never going to see him again. Unless he wants to arrest me.

'Just get out,' I snap, my voice shaky, a telling of how upset I am.

He looks back at me with apologetic eyes. But not long enough to care. He bolts, slamming the door behind him.

Chapter 19

Harry's Diary

How could I do that? How could I fuck her in her kitchen and then just leave like a total arsehole? Because I am an arsehole. I must be. Well, it's probably better if she thinks of me like that. This all started out as me trying to get her to trust me so she'd confess and it was fun at first. Especially when she seemed like a total smart ass, sassy bitch. But seeing her emotional about her upbringing... it tugged at something in my chest.

Then I couldn't believe when she asked me to fuck some sense into her. But I relished the challenge. Only she seemed more shocked than me. I couldn't help but grin. I had her.

I threw her up against the wall, my dick springing to life. I expected her to take control, but she was nervous. She fumbled with my buttons and seemed embarrassed when I stripped her down to her bra and knickers. I have no idea why. She had a banging body. Small pert tits, long legs and an ass I could spend all day biting.

Then when she apologised for her boobs. What the fuck was that? They're the most perfect little titties I've ever had the pleasure of holding in my hands. Small and pert with bright pink nipples against her creamy white skin. I was always taught any more than a handful was a waste anyway. I prefer them to massive tits that are paraded around like a trophy on a bird's chest. I showed her just how much I liked them when I sucked them to my heart's content. They fit in my mouth perfectly, and I couldn't help but think they were made for me. Which is crazy.

She seemed shocked when I went down on her, and it made me wonder how many ex-boyfriends have been shitty, greedy lovers to her. I imagined her demanding what she wanted in the bedroom, but here she was panting and groaning like she'd never been properly touched before.

As I looked into her eyes I saw a vulnerability I never expected. Guilt swept through me. Did she think this meant more to her than it did? I couldn't look in those massive doe like eyes anymore. They were asking too many questions. Asking for promises I couldn't keep. But God help me, I was selfish and still wanted to fuck her. So I made her turn round and I fucked her hard over the counter. She was so tight and perfect. Slapping against that perfect arse of hers, well, it's a miracle I lasted more than two minutes!

I felt better when I couldn't see her. It made me feel better about what I was doing. But the truth is that by the time I came I couldn't remember any other reason than she was sexy as fuck and I liked her. I liked her. It freaked me the fuck out. What the hell was I doing? Sleeping with a suspect and starting to like her? What the fuck is wrong with me? But then I've always been able to fuck women without liking them before. Hell, I could despise them, but give me a pussy and I'll fuck it. But this felt different. I felt like we shared something. God, when did I grow a vagina?

I couldn't concentrate or think about what a huge mistake I'd made. I quickly got dressed, wanting to get the hell out of there as quickly as possible. She looked devastated when she asked me if I was going. It hurt. I knew I was being a prick, but it only made me want to move quicker. I wasn't good for her. I was bad news. I was trying to get her to confess so that I could stick her arse in prison. Stick this beautiful, intelligent woman in a prison where she probably wouldn't last two minutes.

I mumbled something about calling her, but I saw her put her guard up again. She told me to get out. I could only gladly run. Except from the minute I left I felt a tug back towards her. Like I want to go back and take her in my arms, rub her back in calming circles and tell her everything is going to be okay. What the fuck happened to me? Her pussy must have hypnotised me or something.

# # #

I can't believe I let him do that to me. I gave myself to him on a fucking plate only for him to pull out and act like I was rubbish. I am *not* rubbish. Hell, I may have slept amongst it when I was on the streets, but I know I'm worth more than that.

I've worked fucking hard to educate myself, dress well and have a proper job. I'm a well-respected woman. Well, I was when I had a job. Now I don't know anymore. Now I'm selling drugs and I'm sleeping with detectives that are trying to send me to prison. Maybe I am a dickhead.

I slump myself down onto the kitchen floor and let the raw feeling of being used wash over me. I've worked my whole adult life not to go through this feeling, and now that I've let it happen I feel disgusting. I've only ever slept with three guys. And one of them was Samuel. I know, my gay best friend Samuel.

The story goes that I ran away from my foster home because my 'foster brother' was making advances towards me. I wanted to protect my virginity and give it to someone worthy. Obviously when I ran away that night I didn't think I'd end up on the streets. I suppose I was young and dumb, but it was my only alternative. That or wait until I turned sixteen and had what my 'foster brother' called a ripe cherry ready for picking. God, he was creepy. I'm still waiting to see his face in the paper as some kind of sex pest or serial rapist.

That first night sleeping outside a shop, a big welsh man, who I'd later known as Welshie, approached me asking all kinds of weird questions about my age and stuff. When he asked if I was a virgin I nearly threw up from fear. I was on the street. There was no one to protect me. Not even a shitty foster mother this time.

That's when I saw him. Samuel Matthews striding towards us wearing a ridiculous pink woolly hat, a navy poncho and tartan trousers too short for him. He looked like a nutcase. I was sure when he started shouting to the Welsh guy to fuck off that his unicorn would attack him. He had no unicorn. Only as he got closer I saw that he *was* carrying a child's pink fluffy wand. He started waving it around frantically.

'Don't make me bippety boppety boom your arse, mother FUCKER!' he screamed like a mad man.

Welshie looked terrified. 'No, Samuel. I'm leaving, okay? Fuck!' I've never seen anyone run so fast in all my life.

I looked to Samuel in horror, expecting him to murder me. Who was this insane man? And what the hell did he want? But as he approached me his body language started to calm down. The tick I'd noticed disappeared and he seemed sympathetic.

'Hey, babe. First night sleeping rough?' I nodded, still too stunned to speak. 'So what's your story?'

It turned out that Samuel was normal. Well, as normal as Samuel is. He told me that his parents had kicked him out eighteen months ago when he told them he was gay. From there he decided to act like a nutcase so that people wouldn't mess with him. It was a great strategy.

Over the years I saw him do some real crazy shit, but always for the better good. He used to look out for girls like me. Vulnerable newbies. He'd keep them away from pimps like Welshie. I didn't realise the gravity of him saving me that night until years later. Until I watched girls be taken in by him and how they ended up; addicted to drugs or dead.

Anyway, once we finally got housed, after a year and a half, I asked Samuel to take my virginity. I guess I was always scared that something horrible was going to happen to me and it be taken from me in a horrifying way. First the creepy foster brother, then Welshie. I was scared. I wanted to do it with someone I trusted, and who better than my gay best friend?

Only…well it wasn't as special or as straight forward as I thought. Straight being the word. Samuel couldn't get it up without putting a poster of Jared Leto over my face. Plus I couldn't get turned on by him so we had to squirt KY Jelly all over my downstairs department. By the time he did actually get inside me he was slipping in and out constantly. It took a good few minutes for me to even feel pain and be 'broken through'.

He couldn't come and kept going soft, so we agreed that since I'd bled the deed had been done and we could finish. Then with all the jelly the condom slipped off and he ran around the house screaming 'I just conceived spawn with a woman! A fucking woman!' It's safe to say it wasn't the beautiful experience you dream of as a teenager.

The only other guys I've ever slept with were my boyfriend's Eric and Aaron. I chose them carefully. I knew I was prettier than them. I know that sounds big-headed and totally terrible, but I felt like I needed someone who liked me more than I liked them. And they were both lovely. They treated me like a princess, making me feel adored. The sex was…mediocre at best. Same thing each time; one finger, then two, then penis, hump for thirty seconds and finish. I guess I just assumed that sex wasn't that great. Why the hell did Harry have to show me that it could be mind-blowing? Arsehole.

The door slams, breaking me from my self-destructive thoughts. My hope rises for a second, when I hope that it's him back to apologise. And to fuck me again, only this time letting me look him in the eye.

Instead Samuel comes walking into the kitchen looking shattered. I know he must have just come off a twelve hour shift. He looks me up and down, slumped pathetically on the floor, tears running down my face, holding my dress to my body.

'Sade? What the fuck's happened?' he asks, his eye wide with dread.

He bends down onto his knees so he can force me into a cuddle. I remain stiff. I hate showing weak girly emotion, even in front of him. It's pathetic.

'Who did this to you? Were you raped?'

I look down at myself. My dress is still only held in my hand. I suppose it could look worse than it is.

'N…no,' I croak. 'I had sex. Willingly.'

'No way!' he grins, seeming more surprised than if I'd told him I was raped. 'So why are you upset? Was he shit? Small penis? Big spotty one? Try to do you up the arse? What?' he asks impatiently.

'Nothing like that,' I snap. 'I just…I shouldn't have done it is all.'

'Who did you have sex with anyway?' he asks, puzzled. 'I didn't know you were seeing anyone.'

I shake my head, feeling like an enormous slag. 'I'm not.'

His jaw drops dramatically onto the floor. 'No fucking way! You little slut, Sadie,' he smiles affectionately. 'I'm proud of you.'

I glare at him. 'Do I look like a happy woman?'

'You look thoroughly fucked, which is how you should look. Don't tell me you were filling your head with happy ever afters? The big white horse, marriage and babies?' He laughs.

'I'm not a thick twat, Samuel! I know I don't belong to a life like that.'

His face drops and his eyes droop with sadness. 'Sadie, don't say things like that. You deserve anything you want.'

I sigh heavily, looking down at the tiled floor. 'I just didn't expect him to run the minute his dick was out of me. I feel dirty.'

He raises his eyebrows. 'And not in a good down and dirty kind of way?' he giggles.

'No. Like I need a good scrub!' I shout, quickly losing my patience.

'Well then, that's what we'll do. Come on.' He drags me up to standing and pushes me up the stairs towards the bathroom. He turns the shower on, flicks me with some water and tells me to get in. Then I remember Ivy.

'Wait. I need to go check on Ivy. Make sure she eats.' Although it truly is the last thing on my mind.

He holds his hand up to stop my nonsense. '*I'll* check on her.'

He walks out of the room as I strip, going under the waters stream, closing the glass door behind me. There's nothing like a steaming hot shower to remind you that life isn't so bad. Years ago the thought of a hot shower would have me trying to sell my soul. I have a home, great friends, and…well, no career as such. But…I'll be okay. I always am. I nod to myself, pleased with my stern talking to.

The shower door abruptly opens. I try to cover myself best I can as Samuel shrieks, 'You wash that dirty fanny good, you hear!' in a Southern American accent.

Sometimes having a nutty best friend is all you need.

# # #

I don't know how it happens, but somehow later that night I'm at a roller skating disco. Samuel talked me into it, as per bloody usual. We asked Mr. Hendricks to tell us if he sees Ivy again. I still feel terrible for leaving her. Only...well, it's actually brilliant fun. I thought I'd hate it, but here I am in some smelly roller skates that over a hundred people must have worn and I'm skating around this club like a carefree teenager. Which I never actually was.

Samuel skids to a stop in front of me. He's so good at skating it's sickening. He tried to pretend that he'd never skated before, but the way everyone greeted him by name told me otherwise. Who would have known it; Samuel, a skating queen

He grins, looking like the cat that got the cream. 'I told you, *right?*'

Uh, I hate it when he's right.

I shrug. 'Yeah, yeah, I'm having a blast. Now get me another cocktail, bitch.'

We skate and dance around to all of the cheesy tunes. S Club Seven, Steps, Britney, all the classics. Samuel and I know dances to most of them. I don't know if we should be proud that we learnt them, but either way it's gotten us attention. Everyone's been buying us drinks all night, and by the time the lights go up, blinding me, I realise I'm quite drunk. It's just like at the end of a school disco when they want you to leave.

'My face!' I mock shout to Samuel, in a wicked witch of the west impression. 'People can see my face! I'm melting!'

By the end of the night I normally have sweaty hair stuck to my head, lipstick on my teeth and smudged mascara under my eyes. With all of this skating I must look ten times worse. The thought that people can actually see that is horrific.

'You look fwine,' he slurs, tipping the rest of his cocktail back. 'Let's get a cab.'

'Okay,' I smile, feeling a little woozy. 'But I'm totally keeping these skates.'

'Don't you want your shoes back?' he asks in disbelief.

'Nah, fuck em. Let em have em, the fuckers!'

Okay, so I'm *pretty* drunk right now. Samuel rolls his eyes and drags me over to the shoe people. He gets me to stand aside while he changes his shoes. Never would he leave his special edition converse.

'You're sure?' he asks again before we leave.

'As sure as the day is gay!' I sing, stumbling over the perfectly straight floor.

He rolls his eyes. 'Jesus, Sades, I can't take you anywhere.' Then he burps. Yep, he's just as pissed as me.

We manage to escape without being stopped by the shoe police. Samuel quickly gets us a cab back home. It's only when he's trying to persuade me out of it that exhaustion takes over.

'I don't wanna,' I pout. 'I'm sure Mr. Taxi Man wouldn't mind me sleeping here.'

I curl up into the fetal position. This is the comfiest cab in the whole wide world. I can't believe it hasn't got its own TV show. Ha, that makes me giggle. A car with a TV show. Mind you, I suppose Kit in Knight Rider totally stole the attention in that show. It's possible. First thing tomorrow I'm writing to the prime minister, or you know, whoever gets TV made and telling them of my brilliant idea. I'm gonna be *so* rich. I can buy all the roller skates in the world if I want.

'I mean it, Sadie. Get your arse out of that car right now,' he exclaims, standing with his hand on his hip.

He's such a drama queen. And he *literally* is. A queen who loves drama. I giggle at my own joke. I'm *so* funny.

I force my legs out onto the concrete, trying to find my balance so I don't go over in the skates.

'Okay, Mr. Bossy Pants.' I slam the door shut behind me.

Samuel still looks so pissy. He's such a spoil sport. It was his idea to take me out and get me drunk in the first place. Anything to stop thinking about that heartless shit Harry and how he's probably high fiving his mates right now. All *'yeah, so I fucked her and left, man.'* What a fucking douche. I hope he trips on some bird shit.

But Samuel is so funny when he's trying to act sober and responsible when I know he's not. He's stumbling just as much as me, but he has the gift of fooling everyone into thinking he's fine. He would be a great alcoholic. Whereas I just want to cuddle everyone, dance like a lunatic and then pass out in a cosy corner.

I smile mischievously over at him as he gets the keys from my bag.

'Race you to the top!' I bellow, racing up there.

I hear him following, his chuckle the happiest sound in the world. I'd do anything to hear that chuckle.

It's kind of hard in the skates, but I'm managing. Anything to beat him. Ooh, I wonder if he'll make me cheese on toast if I win. I should have totally stated that as the prize, duh.

I reach the platform outside our door, already fist pumping my win when I feel one of the skates slipping forward. I try to pull my leg back, but it only makes the other skate wobble. Shit. I flail my arms around, attempting to grab onto the railing. I don't reach it in time and feel myself falling backwards.

My last thought is that this is going to hurt like a bitch. Totally should have had more cocktails.

Chapter 20

<u>Monday 12th October</u>

I wake up, my head throbbing so bad I don't even attempt to open my eyes. I'm dying. I'm actually dying from this hangover. Why oh why do I ever think it's okay to drink that much? I'm a moron. I'm going to bitch slap myself if I ever get that idea again.

'Samuel,' I call, my own voice causing my head to rattle. 'Put the kettle on. I'm dying.'

'Thank God, Sades.' His voice comes far too close to my ears.

I flick my eyes open, ready and willing to shove him off my bed. I need that tea STAT. My eyes are insulted by bright fluorescent lighting. Ugh, God. Where the fuck did we end up? I take a deep breath before opening them wider and attempting to take in my surroundings. My head hurts so badly.

I see that I'm in a bed and Samuel is almost right in my face, grinning like an idiot.

'Jesus, Samuel, where are we?'

Once I woke up and we were on a train that had finished its line and was being cleaned. Those poor cleaners got the shock of their lives. Especially as I vomited all over them. Not my best moment.

'Fuck, Sades, you don't remember?'

I try to concentrate on his face. He seems concerned. I didn't get that trashed, did I?

'You're in the hospital. You fell down the stairs to our flat last night. You cracked your fucking skull open. You've had to have stitches. I've been waiting for you to come around properly.'

Shit. Stitches? I reach my hand back to my head, feeling around for some stitches. I come across a prickly part of my hair. Wait, I feel around some more...is that a...bald spot?

'Samuel, why the fuck do I have a bald spot?'

As I move my hand over it I can feel stitches. My stomach tightens at the thought. Gross.

'They had to shave it so they could stitch it properly, babe.' His eyes are sympathetic.

'Are you fucking kidding me?' I scream, causing my head to explode. 'I have a partly shaved head?'

He rolls his eyes. 'It's really not so bad. You're lucky you're bloody alive.'

Yeah, yeah. Tell that to my shaved head.

Tuesday 13th October

The next day I'm better. Far better. Turns out it's not the biggest bald patch in the world, and if I style my hair properly it's barely even noticeable. I feel better about the whole Harry thing. Turns out all I needed was a day with my bestie, Samuel. Obviously I could have done without the head injury, but still.

Samuel and I spent the whole day yesterday eating lots of ice cream and watching rom coms. Well, while occasionally checking on Ivy in our pyjamas. My story isn't something that happens in rom coms. Not in any of those films were they fucked over their kitchen sink and then left like a piece of shit on the side of the road. But like I said, I'm *totally* over it.

I've decided to focus all of my energy on Lexi and what an idiot she is for seeing Gabriel again. I know I'm hardly one to advise on wise men choices, but the anger I'm feeling towards her is currently covering my own self-hatred. So for now I'm pretending that the whole sex thing didn't happen yesterday.

I'm on Lexi the minute I walk into Mags' house.

'I can't believe you're still seeing him!' I shout at her across the kitchen table where she's sitting in her dressing gown, barely awake. 'He threatened to kill you. What more do you need?'

At first she seems shocked, but she quickly replaces it with a mischievous smile. 'What can I say? I love the danger.'

'What?' Steph shrieks, appearing from nowhere with Ruby. I didn't even know she was here. 'How could you do that, Lexi?' she asks in disbelief. 'It's *really* irresponsible.'

Lexi snorts and takes a slow sip of her tea. 'Oh please! Like you can lecture me on being responsible. It was only a few days ago that you had your boob hanging out on stage while you mimed to *I Will Survive*! Hardly one to lecture me.'

Steph turns beetroot and covers Ruby's ears. 'Don't say stuff like that in front of Ruby. Her ears are innocent.'

'She's a fucking baby! She can't understand anything.'

'Language, Alexis,' Mags says with a warning smile.

Steph smiles back at Mags before turning back to her.

'All I'm saying is that we just got you out of a violent relationship,' she tries to stress. 'Why on earth would you walk straight into another one?'

She took the words right out of my mouth.

She juts out her jaw defiantly. 'Look, he hasn't laid one finger on me yet. Well…' she grins devilishly, 'he has, but let's just say he's put them in the right places.'

Images of Lexi getting fingered and potentially fucked up the arse invade my mind. Yuck! I wince and scrub at my eyes desperately trying to get the image away. Agh, it won't go away!

'Too much information, thanks, Alexis.' Mags smiles tightly.

'And you said he'd strangled you!' I shout. 'Surely that counts as laying a finger on you?'

'That was just a misunderstanding. So he's into rough, kinky sex. I don't have sex *without* the kink. It just means we're compatible.'

She is beyond reasoning. I stand up and walk away from the table, unable to look at her while she licks her lips, clearly daydreaming about their last sex session.

Why is everybody into kinky sex these days? Whatever happened to a man just sticking it in a lady's parts and making it enjoyable? Nowadays it has to come with so many accessories. Not that Harry had any and he still had me coming like a freight train. Oh God, stop thinking about him. I force my anger onto Lexi.

'I forbid you to see him,' I state, standing firm with my arms crossed.

I frown down at her, trying my best to look full of authority, pulling all of my training from the management course work paid for me to attend. Radiate authority. No one will respect you unless you respect your own authority. That's what I need to do.

'Sorry,' she laughs, although it's a laugh that tells me she finds nothing funny. 'Did you honestly say you just forbid me to see him? Who do you think you are, Sadie?' She crosses her arms and leans back arrogantly in her chair, challenging me.

I suddenly feel like her mother and it's her fault she's making me feel like this.

'I'm your manager,' I snap back quickly. 'And I'm telling you this isn't good for business.'

'Manager,' she snorts. 'You couldn't run a bath.'

I gasp. That hurts more than it should. I must just still be feeling fragile from yesterday.

'To be fair, Lexi,' Steph interrupts, 'Sadie has tried to get us to quit and we've refused. She's obviously just trying to cut our risk.' She turns to face me. 'Right?'

'Right,' I nod, glad someone gets it.

'I'm sure I can get him to change his mind,' she grins.

I roll my eyes. 'Lexi, you're not getting this. The guy is a professional drug dealer! He's not to be reasoned with. Right now we're interrupting his business and he's not going to stand for that. And can I just reiterate, the guy wants to kill you and your friends!'

'Always with the drama,' she huffs, leaning back on her chair as if she doesn't give a shit.

Mags leans forward and takes Lexi's hand. 'Maybe she's right, love,' she tries to reason.

Bless Mags. Always the calm and loving one. If I had a daughter like Lexi I'd want to string her neck, but although it kills me to say it, she reminds me of myself at her age. Headstrong and stubborn; angry at the world.

'You have to at least consider Mags,' I plead, hoping her soft spot for the older woman may persuade her. 'You can't have him here in her home. You're endangering her, as well as everyone else.'

'Oh, I'm sorry,' she snarls bitchily, 'have you forgotten your date with Harry? The cop trying to bring us all down? You know, send us to prison?'

Just hearing his name hurts my chest. It brings back the other day in an instant and all the self-loathing. I'm such a slut. She's right. I'm a terrible person, only thinking with my lady parts, not caring about the danger I'm putting us all in. But I don't want to admit that. Especially right now when I'm trying to get her to change *her* mind.

'That was completely different,' I retort, tucking a bit of hair behind my ear self-consciously. 'I was just trying to find out what he knew about us.'

She raises her eyebrows and pouts. 'Yeah, well he knew an awful lot more about us after he took a weed brownie home! Real smart bringing him here.'

Smart arse little bitch. I'd happily pummel her in the face right now. And I'm not even the violent type.

'He was only here because your nutter ex was trying to break the door down,' I snap back.

She pokes her finger in my chest. 'That wouldn't have happened if you and Mags would have just minded your own business and left me there.'

Is she *serious*? She'd rather still be with Jason who beats her to a pulp like some psychopath? She can't mean that.

'You'd rather have been beaten up?' Steph asks in disbelief. 'You're actually having a go at them for trying to help you?'

'I don't need anybody's help,' she snaps, crossing her arms defiantly over her chest and trying to turn away from us.

Why is she so bloody infuriating? And why is it every nineteen year old these days thinks they know everything? I could just throttle her. I take a deep breath and try to dissipate some anger and try to calm myself. I need to just get this sorted.

'Look, we need to just come up with a plan to try and reason with the dealers. And I think I have it.'

Steph looks at me expectantly. The poor thing looks terrified, her eyes wide with fright. How I ever thought involving her in this would be a good idea I don't know. Lexi looks as if she couldn't give a shit about what I have to say, when I know her inquiring mind can't help but listen. Mags gets up and boils the kettle.

'I followed Joaquin yesterday. After I found you on a date with his guy.' I stop to give her another quick accusing stare. 'Anyway, I think I've found his weakness. I saw his wife letting in their dog.'

'His wife,' Steph claps excitedly. 'Of course! We kill his wife.'

'What?' I shriek in disbelief. Is she seriously excited at the idea of killing his wife? I've created monsters.

'I don't think killing is ever a good idea, love,' Mags chimes in, her voice still kind.

'We are *not* going to kill his wife,' Lexi snaps. 'Stop being so stupid, Steph. Sadie's talking about the dog, right?'

At least *she's* on the same wave length as me. Even if she is a stubborn little bitch.

'Exactly,' I agree, shaking my head at Steph. I can't believe her. 'We need to work out a way of getting the dog.'

'We're dog nappers now?' Steph asks, horrified. As if she didn't just suggest killing his wife two minutes ago.

'Sorry, but a minute ago you were excited about killing his wife,' I remind her. 'We're just going to hold the dog hostage until we can talk.'

Mags tuts. 'You say that as if it's a normal thing. I'm not sure about this. I'm against cruelty to animals. I check all of my shampoos for the bunny sign and everything.'

Bunny sign? What the hell is she talking about?

'Whatever. This is our only option. For once let's all just agree and get on with it, okay?'

'Sadie?' Mags says, standing behind me. 'Why do you have part of your head shaved and with stitches? Have you been in an accident?'

Oh God, this is *so* not the time for this.

'Yes, okay!' I exclaim. 'I fell down the stairs. It's no big deal.'

'No big deal!' Steph screams, horrified. She runs straight over to me, parting my well placed hair to take a better look.

'I take it you were pissed?' Lexi sniggers.

'No,' I lie, avoiding looking at her. I bat Steph's fussing hand away. 'I'm really self-conscious about it and I'd really appreciate if you didn't keep drawing attention to it.'

Mags looks down sadly. Oh God, I've said something insensitive, haven't I?

'I know how you feel, love. Mine's started to come out in my hair brush.'

Oh God, now I feel bloody awful. Here I am bitching about a bald spot when this poor cow is going through chemo, soon to lose all of her hair.

'Mags, I'm so sorry. I didn't think.'

She smiles kindly. 'It's okay, love. I've been considering shaving it, but I just don't have the guts.'

'I'll do it for you,' Steph offers. 'I used to do Darius's before...before...' she sniffs.

Oh God, here we go again.

'Before he left you,' Lexi finishes, rolling her eyes impatiently. 'We *know*.'

Mags twiddles with the ends of her cardigan. 'I don't know. I mean, I haven't lost *that* much yet. Maybe I've overreacting.'

I can imagine how she feels. Without my hair I'd look like an ugly egg. Jessie J is officially the only person to rock that look.

'I say bite the bullet,' Lexi says, sitting down next to her. 'Hell, I'll shave half my head with you. For solidarity and all that.'

She'd shave half her head? Wowza. She really does care. Don't get me wrong, I love Mags to bits, but I just couldn't shave my head. I just *couldn't*.

Mags smiles back at her with appreciation. 'That's a very kind gesture, love, but there's no need for us both to be baldies.'

Lexi snorts. 'Don't sweat it, Mags. I've been wanting to try this hairstyle out anyway.' Then she turns and winks at me. Wow, she really is doing this to help Mags.

'Well...okay,' she finally agrees. 'I think I can find my husband's old shaver around here somewhere.'

Half an hour later, Lexi's shaving half of her head. She keeps it so that the back and side part still falls naturally. It shows off the million piercings in her ear. How on earth does she sleep with those things?

When she's finished I'm actually shocked by how much it suits her. She totally rocks it. Only someone like her, who gives zero fucks about what people think, can pull of a look like that. God, sometimes I wish I was that cool.

'Done,' she announces proudly.

Mags starts twiddling with her necklace and swallowing hard. Poor thing is scared to death.

'Your turn,' Lexi says, handing the shaver to Steph.

The buzzing starts again and Step smiles, creeping closer to Mags on the sofa. 'Here we go.' She touches her head with it starting at the front. She's just taken a strip from the top when Mags jumps up.

'STOP! Just stop! I changed my mind. I've changed my mind, okay!' she screams, covering her head with her hands.

We all stare back at each other in shock. She can't be serious. Can she?

'Talk about an overreaction, Mags,' Lexi sneers.

'You should have just said if you didn't want it done,' Steph says, clearly feeling terrible.

'Either way you can't just leave it like that,' I say, pointing to what now looks like a weird balding spot.

Mags runs in front of her mirror. She grimaces, desperately trying to pull hair over it. She turns back to me, a new determination on her face.

'Who says I can't? I think it looks fine.'

We all look at each other before collapsing in laughter. We laugh so hard tears fall from our eyes. At least she gave us a laugh before we go kidnap a drug dealer's dog. I miss this. Just us messing around in the office, chatting about the latest episode of Mad Men. These days our lives are so serious. It's kind of exhausting. Oh well. We've gotten ourselves into this mess. Time to get ourselves out.

Wednesday 14th October

So the next afternoon we're all in our places. Lexi's our getaway driver. She's the one that would probably raise the most suspicion with her bright pink hair. Steph is already positioned near his house and Mags is watching him at his office. Turns out he has a proper work place. He's the CEO of some plastics company. God knows if that's just some big drugs cover or the real deal.

I signal for Lexi to drop me off across the street from his house, just like I played out with Oreos this morning.

'Thanks.' I force a confident smile. 'Stay close.'

I get out, slam the door behind me and go to cross the street. Only I fall down onto one knee in the middle of the frigging street. Ah, that stings. The only thing that stops me going all the way face down is the thing that is strangling me. I reach up to it to see it's my scarf. I look back and see that it's stuck in the car door. A motorbike swerves past me, sticking up his middle finger while another car beeps. I should really get out of the road.

I spring myself up as best I can. In hindsight I shouldn't have worn stilettos. I turn around to face the car and tug on the door handle, but it's locked. I try to signal to Lexi to open it, but I can already hear that the music is ridiculously high. I said to be inconspicuous. Not blast Anaconda by Nikki Minaj out of the speakers.

I bang on the window, but still she doesn't react. She's too busy indicating and trying to pull out. Shit. I'm still attached.

I try to untangle the scarf from around my neck, but I'm dragged along before I get a chance. Shit! I run, trying to keep up with her, all the time holding onto the handle for leverage and trying to bang my fist on it.

'Lexi! You fucking idiot! My scarf is stuck. Stop the car!'

People on the street are staring now as I shout, sweat dripping from my forehead. The scarf is getting tighter around my neck with every pull of the car. Way for us to stay inconspicuous!

It's only when she stops at the traffic light that I get the chance to full on body slam the door. She jumps out of her skin, turning to stare at me as if *I'm* the mental one. She rolls down the window slightly and leans over.

'I told you to call me when you were finished. I have Bluetooth,' she says calmly, looking at me as if I'm an idiot.

'My fucking scarf is stuck,' I hiss through gritted teeth. 'Open the door and release me.'

'Oh,' she laughs, taking in my full red and puffy face. 'I lock my doors. You can never be too careful, right?' She opens the door and swings it out to me.

I try my hardest to reason with myself. This isn't her fault. It's just bad luck. So what if the whole street is now looking at me with interest? It's not her fault. But it doesn't stop me from flipping her the bird before I slam the door shut, this time with my scarf safely out of the way.

I try desperately to ignore the stares of the blatant nosy people trying to laugh in my face. Yes, I fell people! Well done for noticing. Now go back to your pathetic lives and leave my embarrassment alone!

I walk closer to Joaquin's house. Steph puts her hands up in the air, as if to say 'what the hell?' I shake my head. I don't want to talk about it. I take out my phone to look busy and notice that my hand is shaking. Calm down, Sadie. This is going to be done and dusted in a few minutes. Once we have the dog we have the power.

The dog van rounds the corner, causing me to jump in fright. I look to Steph and nod. This is it. We're stealing a drug dealer's dog.

Dear God, why the hell do I keep coming up with all of these dopey ideas?

It stops in front of the red traffic lights. I use the pause to try and collect myself. Deep breath in, deep breath out. Positivity in, negativity out. This is going to be fine. I'm an independent woman who is capable of doing anything I put my mind to.

My phone rattles in my hand, suddenly blaring out Beyoncé's Halo. It's Mags. Shit, is she okay?

'Mags?' I answer breathlessly.

The van starts coming up the road towards us.

'He's leaving. I think he's going home,' she whispers frantically.

'What?' I shriek in alarm. 'Why the fuck is he leaving? Doesn't he normally do a full day?'

The van is indicating to pull in outside the house.

'I don't know,' she cries. 'I just know he's left and he'll be there in a few minutes if you don't move right now. Maybe this is a sign to abandon it all?'

The van pulls onto the curb. Too late to stop this now. I hang up the phone and dart out in front of the van doors. The lady jumps out of the front and goes to open it up the side door.

'Hi,' I smile broadly. 'I'm Pam, Mrs. Khoner's PA. I'll take the dog for you.' I go to reach for the lead of the ridiculous looking poodle, but she pulls it back.

'You're collecting Chardonnay?' she asks in confusion.

They named a dog Chardonnay? I'm doing this dog a bloody favour. Rescuing it from people that clearly relish dressing it up as a drag queen.

'Yes.' I reach for the lead again, just as I hear the front door open and a loud pitched voice squeal.

'Chardonnay, baby!'

Shit. My heart stars thumping in my chest like its playing the bongos. I look for Steph, but the troopers already on it. She pretends to walk past her house when she suddenly starts screaming.

'My baby! She's stopped breathing,' she shrieks. 'Oh my God, help me! Somebody please help me.'

She was right. Those drama lessons in year eleven paid off. I'd believe her if I didn't know better.

'Oh my goodness,' the wife cries, running straight to her. 'Are you okay?' she asks Steph. 'Let me call an ambulance.' She gets out her phone and starts calling.

I look back at the dog woman, holding my hand out again for the lead. I'm starting to sweat on my forehead. I can feel the beads forming, starting to trickle down onto my upper lip.

She looks back suspiciously at me before turning to the wife. 'I'm okay leaving Chardonnay with her?' she shouts.

Jesus, this woman is too bloody good at her job. She's a dog walker, not an MI5 agent. What is her problem? Then I look at her camouflage trousers and butch walking boots. Maybe she *was* in the army. Shit.

Luckily the wife waves over dismissively. She's too busy on the phone to an ambulance. I have no idea why. Ruby's fully awake now, crying hysterically. It's pretty clear she isn't unconscious, but that doesn't stop what's her name from worrying hysterically.

Dog woman finally hands over the lead to me. I smile as graciously as I can, hoping she hasn't taken in too many of my features to tell to the police sketch artist. I grab my phone out of my pocket and speed dial Lexi while Chardonnay tries to sniff my arse crack. I'm a human, you stupid dog!

'Got ya,' she says into the phone before pulling up behind me.

The van pulls away as I stuff Chardonnay and myself into the back. Lexi screeches away from the curb as quick as lightening. I look back in time to see an ambulance pulling up. Shit, how's Steph going to get out of this one? I force myself to look forward, realising too late it's a mistake.

Passing us just that minute is Joaquin in a Porsche. He looks right through me, clearly worried about the flashing lights outside of his house. Thank God. Any closer and he would have spotted Chardonnay trying to hump my leg.

Chapter 21

Its three hours later and Steph's still not back. I seem to be the only one shitting a brick over this. Lexi keeps telling me to calm the fuck down, but even she's chewing her nails rather rabidly. Mags is too busy practically making love to the dog, while attempting to pull off a purple woolly hat to hide her partly shaved head.

'She's just the cutest little thing,' Mags coos, rubbing Chardonnay's belly while she lies on the floor next to her. 'They must be beside themselves by now.' She actually sounds sympathetic towards them.

It's not like the dog is in any distress; she's getting spoiled rotten. Mags went out and bought some gourmet dog food.

'Try to remember these are the drug dealers threatening our lives,' I say shortly.

'Of course,' she says, as if she's only just remembered.

I've just texted Samuel, asking him to check in on Ivy, when Mags's front door suddenly swings open. The three of us look at each other alarmed. Shit, have they got Steph and come back to get us too? Steph stumbles into the room with Ruby in her pouch, looking harassed. She dumps her heaving baby bag on the floor.

'What the hell happened?' I ask, running over to take the delicious Ruby from her arms. She grins up at me. She's going to be trouble, I can just tell. I look back at Steph for an answer.

'Let her sit down first,' Mags says, helping her down into a chair. 'Do you want a tea dear?'

Mags and her bloody tea.

'Love one, Mags,' she smiles affectionately.

She looks absolutely shattered, dark circles around her eyes. Did they question her?

'Cut the shit,' Lexi snaps. 'What the fuck happened? Why have you taken three hours to get home?'

She looks like she might burst into tears.

'An ambulance arrived and I couldn't just tell them to piss off, could I?'

Oh my God. Don't tell me they took it seriously? Surely one look over at Ruby would tell them she was fine.

'I tried to tell them it was a false alarm, but they insisted on bringing us in and getting Ruby thoroughly checked over.' Tears begin welling in her eyes. 'My poor Ruby had to be poked and prodded all afternoon. I am a *terrible* mum!' Her voice breaks on her last word and soon she's full on sobbing.

'No you're not,' I say, trying to look sympathetic when all I can really think about is the time ticking away. We really need to call Joaquin. 'I hate to be insensitive, but...now we know you're safe we need to call Joaquin and tell him we have his dog.'

'But first, tea,' Mags smiles.

This bloody woman and her tea obsession is getting ridiculous.

Within minutes we're all sitting down eating custard creams and drinking tea. I decide not to fight it. I even give some biscuits to Chardonnay. I look around at us all calmly drinking tea. One stupid idea and now we're all drug dealers. Why didn't I just keep my stupid mouth shut?

'Can we just call him now?' I ask anxiously, glancing nervously at the clock on the wall.

'The more time that's passing by, the more nervous I'm getting. What if they've spoken to the dog walker and already worked out it was me from the in-depth description?

'Here, I've got the number,' Lexi says, handing over her phone. 'I took it from Gabriel's phone.'

They all look at me expectantly. 'Oh, so I suppose I'm the one making the call, right?' I say sarcastically.

'It was your bright idea,' Steph says, still seeming exhausted. I hand over Ruby and press dial with shaking fingers.

I'm suddenly so sick with fright I fear I might vomit on the carpet. I just can't stand this niggling panic at the pit of my stomach any longer. It rings twice before it picks up.

'Joaquin,' he answers briskly.

I instantly lose my breath. The girls look at me expectantly.

'Err…hi,' I mumble, suddenly needing a wee. It must be the panic. 'This is…' I look back to the others for support. They raise their eyebrows, obviously assuming I had this all planned. What a support system. 'I mean…It doesn't matter who I am.' I swallow hard. 'I have your dog.'

There's silence on the other end. A long pause of *terrifying* silence.

'I know exactly who you are, Sadie Taylor,' he says coolly.

He knows it's me already? Shit.

'You're one of the dopey women that thought they could start selling drugs on my patch without anyone noticing.'

I can hear my own heart thumping hard in my chest, the overwhelming wish to run away and escape not possible.

'I would have thought the police would have arrested you by now. Surely you're not smart enough to cover your tracks.' His voice is like melting honey. It's terrifying how he's so calm when he's talking about my life hanging in the balance.

How does he know the police are onto us? Unless...

'Wait…did you tell on us to the police?' I blurt out accusingly. It would make sense.

'Please don't make it sound like we're in a playground, Sadie,' he snaps harshly, causing my stomach to squirm. 'Yes, I informed the police of your illegal activity.'

Of course he did, the slimy git.

'You bastard! You could have sent us to prison,' I blurt out hysterically.

Oops. Probably best not to call the scary drug dealer a bastard. But the thought of prison makes me want to vomit. Should I apologise? But then I'll look weak. The tensions of the day are starting to throb unbearably in my head.

'I hope to send you to prison,' he informs me. 'It seems to be the only way to stop you.'

His words hit me like whiplash. Shit. This guy's going to ruin our life.

'Yeah, well…we have your dog,' I utter pathetically, trying to play my last card. Why am I just repeating myself? I sound like a bloody idiot. 'We want to renegotiate.'

He chuckles darkly. 'And how do I know that you even have my dog?'

I look to the others for an idea. Lexi writes down 'send a picture'.

'We'll send a picture,' I offer in my most confident voice. My insides are churning so hard I worry he'll hear me.

'No,' he snaps irritably. 'I want to speak to her.'

I look into the phone in disbelief. He wants to talk to the fucking dog? Have we unwillingly kidnapped a magical talking dog?

'You…you want to talk to the dog?' I ask carefully.

'Yes. Put her on.'

Something tells me I can't question him again so easy.

I hold the phone away from my ear and cover the earpiece. 'He wants to speak to the fucking dog,' I hiss. 'Quickly.' I direct Mags to pull Chardonnay closer.

She prances forward and looks at the phone, confused when it's placed by her ear.

'Chardonnay?' his voice says over the loud speaker. 'Chardonnay darling, it's daddy. Let me know you're okay.'

He calls himself daddy? I stifle a giggle, clasping my hand over my mouth. What kind of weirdo am I dealing with?

The dog looks at the phone, completely bewildered.

'Err…she's not talking. Don't you just want a photo?'

'No,' he barks. 'I want to hear her.'

What the fuck are we going to do? I look at Lexi and she nods in understanding.

'Okay. Wait a sec.'

I pass the phone to her. She starts breathing heavily, panting as an excited dog would.

'That's right,' he says excited. 'Are they treating you okay, sweetheart?'

Lexi looks like she might piss herself laughing. She covers her mouth to stop the giggles and forces a little woof. I take the phone away and hold it back to my ear before she can blow our cover.

'Happy?'

There's an edgy silence. Please God, let him not murder me.

'What is it you want?' he finally asks.

Oh, thank God. He at least wants to hear us out. He could have just sent his men here.

'We want to be able to continue our business. We won't take on anymore clients, but we want to keep the ones we have. It shouldn't be affecting you guys in anyway. We're only getting new clients, not your existing ones.'

Another long silence. This dude hasn't gotten to where he is today by being a friendly guy. More silence. I can't breathe. This is torture.

'Fine, but I want the dog returned unharmed within the hour.'

'So…you want me to take this dog to the door and just ring the bell and leave?'

We've called a pizza place for delivery and are now trying to convince the fifteen year old spotty kid to bring the dog back. The little shit head seems reluctant, even though we've promised him fifty pounds. What I would have done for fifty quid when I was his age!

'It's not rocket science,' I growl. 'Just deliver the dog and we'll pay you.'

He looks between us all sceptically. 'Nah, fuck this. I'm out.'

What an ungrateful little fuck.

Crap. What the hell are we going to do now?

Mags lets him out while Lexi throws herself back onto the sofa. 'Well what the fuck are we going to do now?'

Steph looks terrified. Poor thing. She's already had too much drama today to consider it. Mags is too old and fragile, and Lexi…well, Lexi's just too bloody unpredictable.

I take a shaky deep breath. 'I'll do it,' I announce, my voice wavering. Way to sound confident and sure.

'Really?' Steph gushes, looking at me admirably as if I'm her hero.

I nod adamantly. 'This was my stupid idea. I got us into this. It's only right I get us out.'

My phone rings making us all jump. We're all so on edge. We all stare at it with alarm. Fear grips my insides. I slowly walk towards it and see that it's Harry. Crap. I don't know whether to be relieved or more anxious. I don't want to speak to him. Right now or ever.

'Is it him?' Steph asks, scratching her arm. It looks like she's coming up in hives.

'No, it's Harry.' My voice sounds void of emption.

'What the hell does Detective Mcrugged want?' Lexi asks.

I shrug vaguely.

'Well…answer it!' she demands, thrusting the phone into my hands.

I sigh and press answer. I have no idea what to say. The last time I saw this man he was fucking me from behind over my kitchen counter. Not that I can tell the girls that.

'Err…' I clear my throat. 'Hello?' I bite my lip, already dreading this conversation.

'Sadie, thank God.' He sounds panicky, his breathing loud and erratic.

'What's wrong?' He may be the world's biggest arsehole, but the thought of him hurt makes me want to immediately run to him. I don't want to think about what that means right now.

'I need to talk to you.' His voice is grave.

Oh God, he wants to talk to me about the other night? He must be feeling guilty. Or wanting a re-run. Either way I'm not interested. Especially in front of the girls.

'Yeah…' I look around at the others. 'I can't really talk right now and I think maybe that should be a private conversation.' If they overheard him I'd die of shame.

'That's not what I'm calling about.'

My heart sinks. 'Oh.'

So he's not calling to apologise about his disgusting behaviour. Well he bloody well should be. The pompous arse.

'I've just found out Joaquin is the one who tipped us off about you.'

He *just* found out? Jesus, he must be a shit detective. I've known for almost an hour.

'Yeah, I know.'

'What do you mean, you know?' he asks, clearly intrigued.

Ah, I can't really tell him we're holding the dog hostage.

'Err…it doesn't matter.'

I just want to get off the phone now. Hearing his voice is physically hurting my heart. It must just be from shame.

'Listen, Sadie,' his voice turns grave. 'You need to be careful. This guy is nasty. The last time someone tried to set up on his patch they ended up in the canal.'

A quick stab of fear hits my chest. I gulp. 'The…the canal?'

'Sadie…what have you done?' I can hear the concern in his voice.

'Err…nothing?'

# # #

So ten minutes later Lexi drops me and Chardonnay off outside Joaquin's house. There was no point trying to hide myself with a baseball cap. The scary thing is that these people know exactly who we are. They probably know where we live. Everything about us. It scares the shit out of me, especially after hearing the last idiots that tried to do this ended up dead. But I try to reason with myself that I'm putting an end to this. This was the only way to keep some control over our business. Our fucking lives are at stake.

As I look up at the Edwardian town house I reason that they've probably never had to worry about money their whole lives. We've only turned to this because we're desperate. Not because we're greedy fuckers who want to sell drugs to kids.

I pull Chardonnay up the stairs to the front door and knock. My hands are shaking, my face sweaty. I must look like I've got a fever. I hop impatiently from foot to foot waiting for any kind of sound from inside.

Finally I hear the quick clicking of heels and the door is flung open. His wife looks at me blankly. She seems inconvenienced and probably disgusted by the working class vibe I'm setting off. That is until she looks down and spots an excited, panting Chardonnay.

'My baby!' she shrieks, dropping to her knees and cuddling her. Chardonnay's pants become so loud I can barely hear her cooing, 'You came back! My baby came back! Where did you find her?'

Find her? Oh God…does she seriously have no idea she was dog-napped?

'Err…'

Joaquin suddenly appears from behind her, his tall stature towering over me. He's far more intimidating when he's leaning over you up close.

'Oh,' he says smiling insincerely at me, 'a good Samaritan. Where ever did you find her?' His eyes glow amber as if in warning that I should play along. I still can't believe he didn't tell his wife. Does she even know he's a drug dealer?

'Err…she was just…wandering around the park.'

He nods behind her, pleased with my lying capabilities.

'We're so lucky, Jo,' she gushes. 'Now aren't you glad I got that pink diamante collar tag?' She looks back at him smugly.

Jo? She calls him Jo? I can't help but find that strangely hilarious. He seems less threatening as a Jo. Joey boy. Jo Jo on the farm. A smile starts to spread on my lips, but I quickly bite it down.

'Yes,' he nods solemnly, 'very lucky.'

'We must give you something for your troubles.' She gushes, patting her pockets, looking for some cash.

Huh? Is she insane? Way to anger him!

He looks at his wife with barely concealed rage. 'Darling, I'm sure she did it from the kindness of her heart.' He nods warningly at me. 'Right?'

'Of-of course,' I stutter, just wanting to get the hell away from them. 'I should really go.'

'No,' she says, grabbing my arm. 'We simply must! Jo, get your cheque book out. I'd say this lovely girl deserves at least one hundred for her troubles.'

Is she *serious*? Joaquin is seething behind her. You're going to get me killed, bitch!

'Honestly, I'm fine. I have to get back. Really.' I try to release my arm, but she's bloody strong for a little woman. She must survive on protein shakes.

'Nonsense,' she insists, shaking her head. 'Joaquin?'

His jaw tenses, before he goes to a console table and removes his cheque book from the drawer.

This is horrendous. As if he's going to want to give me any money after what I've just pulled. But it clearly shows who wears the trousers at home.

'Of course,' he says sarcastically. 'Can't have the good Samaritan going unrewarded.'

I look down at the floor to try and avoid his accusing gaze. This is awful. I should have just rang the door and bolted, but then what if Chardonnay would have run away? I would *definitely* have been killed. At least now my chances are fifty/fifty.

He hands the folded cheque over. I take it hesitantly, my hands shaking so much that it's hard to grasp onto the thin paper. I mutter my thanks and spin on my heel, practically running down the road searching for Lexi's Peugeot.

I spot the green monstrosity and jump in, thanking God she hasn't locked it this time. My whole body starts convulsing as soon as I'm sat safely inside. She looks at me with alarm. I must look even worse than I feel.

'Are you okay? What the fuck happened? Why did you take so long?'

My head throbs with her questions.

'The wife didn't know.' I look behind me. 'Just drive, will you, drive!' She pulls out into the road and speeds off. 'She wanted me to give me a reward.'

'You *are* joking,' she snorts, driving like a maniac. 'Some bitches are beyond stupid.'

'I know. She made him write a cheque.' I can't help but keep looking back to check we're not being followed.

'No way! For how much? I wouldn't cash that if I were you. He'd probably murder you,' she chuckles, as if my life is something to jest about.

I giggle, the warm vibrations of her car calming me down slightly. Why I have no idea. He's probably planning to murder me anyway. I open the cheque out of intrigue and gasp.

Bother me again and I'll slit your throat

My blood runs cold. Oh my God. A chill runs down my spine and my throat clogs up. I just got a proper threatening note from a drug dealer.

'Yeah, I don't think I'll be cashing this anytime soon.'

Chapter 22

<u>Thursday 15th October</u>

Well, imagine that. Actually getting a threatening note from a drug dealer. Makes it all feel a bit more real and terrifying. Every time I allow myself to think about it my stomach jumps around, crashing into my other organs. But the main thing is that now we're safe. We've negotiated our safety, and let me tell you, I slept a hell of a lot better last night.

I'm just settling down with a latte in my local coffee shop, giving myself a much needed break from Ivy, when I feel him, goose pimples appearing on my arms. It's like my body is on high alert to him being near me. I remain looking down at my coffee, trying to go un noticed. He might just be here for a coffee. His tan leather shoes are suddenly in my vision. What kind of person thinks they can carry off those kind of shoes? I look up. Him; he can *seriously* pull them off. He looks seriously exasperated, his hair messier than usual.

'Really?' he asks sarcastically raising his eyebrows dramatically. 'Holding his dog ransom? You really think that was a good idea?'

How the hell does he even know this stuff? Does Joaquin have a personal line to him so they can both bitch about me?

I want to be defensive and let him know I can look after myself. That he can fuck off and stop pretending to care about me. Only when I open my mouth and look at his face, concern etched into it, and well, I can't help but chuckle out loud. It's just...well it's just too bloody ridiculous. This police officer telling me off for stealing a dog.

'It seemed like a good idea at the time,' I snicker, rolling my eyes at his misplaced concern.

He sits down on the sofa across from me, loosening his tie roughly. God, that's hot. Visions of me loosening it myself invade my mind. The last time I saw this guy we were both naked. He's ruined me.

'How on earth could stealing a drug dealers dog *ever* seem like a good idea?' he asks, rubbing his face wearily.

I can't actually tell him that without explaining that we're guilty of what he's been accusing me of. And I don't really want to be speaking to him at all. The last time I saw him he was leaving me naked in my kitchen. Abandoned, like a cheap little slut he picked up in some club. How can he suddenly play all concerned? He clearly doesn't give a shit about me. Or maybe he just wants to fuck me again so he's putting on the charm.

He glares at me with such intensity I almost fall off my chair. Okay, so he's not going with the charm.

'This is serious, Sadie. You're playing with your life like it's no big deal. I know you aren't ready to confess to anything right now, but if you do we can offer you the right protection. Protection against Joaquin. I assume he's threatening you?'

I knew it! He still wants me to confess.

I shrug. I doubt his kind of protection is the same as mine. His probably includes a cell with iron bars. It doesn't help that everywhere I turn lately there's reminders of prison. Every TV show I turn on, news stories, documentaries. I even walked past Ann Summers earlier and they were having a sale on handcuffs. It's like it's haunting me.

'I mean it, Sadie.' He looks so worried. Normal policemen don't care this much, do they?

Could he hold some real feelings for me? Or did he just want to get his end away the other day? I'm so confused by him and his all over the place moods.

'Don't shrug this off like it's someone calling you names in the playground,' he scolds. A flash of infuriation passes across his face. A fearful thrill shoots through me, sending tingles all the way down...there. Is it wrong that him being this pissed off is seriously turning me on? Maybe I need to see a therapist.

He rubs the nape of his neck. His eyes are doopy, as if this conversation is really taking it out of him. 'You could end up dead. The last one did.'

My stomach feels heavy with trepidation. Why did he have to remind me? Maybe they did something really out of order.

'What did they do to piss him off so much?' I can't help but ask.

He purses his lips together and frowns, a little V forming in between his eyebrows. It makes me want to straddle him and run my fingers over it, smoothing out the line until its flush again. Whoa, where did that come from? I'm supposed to be furious with this guy. He's fucked me over royally. And literally. But my body seriously wants him. How can I get it to engage with my brain?

'I...' he seems torn whether to tell me or not. 'I can't really say,' he admits, running his hands through his hair. No wonder it's so messy.

I hate how he can play the police card when he pleases.

'Can't really say my arse,' I shriek, grabbing the attention of some other coffee patrons. *Whoops.* I lower my voice to a whisper hiss. 'Just fucking tell me!'

'Okay!' He sighs heavily, rubbing his neck again. 'The last time there was a new ring of drug dealers on the scene...'

Is he trying to trick me into confessing?

'We're not drug dealers,' I interrupt, pleading my false innocence.

He puts his hand up to stop me. It's so obvious between us now that I'm lying, but I still don't want to get caught out. For all I know he could be recording this conversation right now. Maybe I should pat him down for a while. *Now there's an idea.*

'They didn't take him seriously.'

I gulp down the bile. Shit. This is real. Scary real.

'Well, that's not going to happen to me,' I snap defiantly. Especially since we're not even drug dealers.'

'Right,' he nods sarcastically. 'Of course you're not.'

I roll my eyes again. I like to think of myself more as an exotic pharmacist. I hate how he's so pompous, assuming he knows everything about me.

'Will you just stop being so fucking high and mighty? Especially with how you behaved the last time I saw you.'

His eyes flick angrily to mine. Why is he so angry? He gazes at me for a long time, his rage slowly slipping away.

'How I behaved?' he asks, shuffling his feet and looking down at them. 'What do you mean?' Well at least he has the grace to look embarrassed. He should. The bloody user.

I look around me, careful there are no young children whose ears will start bleeding. I lean into him, wishing I had boobs I could squeeze together.

'I mean...after you fucked me over my worktop and then ran out of the flat like it was on fire.' I blush despite wanting to look furious. Of course I'm embarrassed. He totally used and abused me. Why did I even say it out loud? I should be acting completely unbothered by him.

'That wasn't...' he starts and then stops. 'I mean I didn't...' He sighs. 'It's complicated, okay?'

Is he *serious?* He's not even going to apologise or give any kind of reasoning? What an arse hat.

There's an eerie silence between us as he tries to look anywhere but at me, and I try to catch his attention. I want him to look me in the eye when he's trying to fob me off. That will tell me so much more than his words ever will.

No, you know what? No! I'm not going to sit here and be avoided by some prat who thinks its okay to fuck me one minute and then try to preach to me how to live my life the next. Who the hell does he think he is?

I stand up and go to down my latte. Only it's hot, FUCK, *so hot*! I dribble some out of my mouth as I involuntarily try to get my burnt tongue out to the air. He raises his eyebrows, looking at me as if I'm insane. Well there goes my triumphant storm off. I slam my mug down on the table and storm out, stomping my heels heavily on the tiles.

Yeah, this is the exit I wanted. The wind in my hair, looking fabulous and in control of my destiny. Well, apart from the burnt tongue. I really wish that wouldn't have happened.

When I reach outside the rain pelts down onto my shoulders. I shiver, wrapping my arms around myself. Shit. I left my coat on the chair. That's my favourite Zara coat. Not that I got it in Zara. I got it for a fiver in my local charity shop. It was such a bargain and basically goes with everything I wear. You know what they say, *you can take the girl off the streets, but you can't take the streets out of the girl.* I'll always be a charity shop whore first and foremost.

But if I go back now I'll look like a bloody bumbling idiot, when I want to look in control. I already humiliated myself with the whole tongue thing. No, I decide I'll just leave it there. I'd rather sacrifice my coat than what's remaining of my dignity.

#

I get home and kick off my boots. Walking home in the rain is not fun. I look into the hallway mirror and see I look like a drowned rat. My hair is completely saturated and stuck to my head, my mascara all over the place. My white shirt is soaked through, making my pale pink bra visible. Ugh. Great.

I walk into the bathroom and turn on the shower, peeling my soaking clothes off. I climb in once it's warm, letting the hot water soothe my tight muscles. It feels *so* good. I want it to wash away the last few weeks. Or at least the last few hours.

I quickly wash my face and lather some shampoo into my hair. I'm impatient tonight. Normally I love my time in the shower or bath, with Samuel whinging that I use all of the hot water, but this evening all I can think about is what a prick Harry is. To not even *try* and give me an explanation. He's such an unbelievably big arsehole. I can't believe I wasted any of my time on him.

I get out and wrap a towel around myself. Samuel's working a late shift tonight, so it looks like I'm going to spend it with a bottle of red and a galaxy bar. I smile to myself; my kind of evening. But I have to check on Ivy first. This caring lark is exhausting.

I'm just about to walk into my room to throw on some comfortable pyjamas when there's a knock at the door. It's probably Ivy. She'll probably be worried about me, bless her. This checking in on her four times a day is really taking it out of me.

I open the door with a warm smile. 'Hey, Ivy –' I stop when I see a soaked Harry holding my coat. He looks *amazing* wet. I want to catch one of the droplets from his hair with my tongue.

Damn it, why am I bloody naked right now? I grip the flimsy towel around myself a little firmer. I have to get rid of him quick. I grab the coat from his hand.

'Thanks,' I nod, quickly trying to close the door.

He stops me with his arm. 'Aren't you going to invite me in?' he asks with a cheeky smile.

How the hell can he be so calm and laid back about this? I'm fucking fuming. This guy thinks he's having another go on me just because he brought my coat back?

'I would,' I smile sarcastically, 'but I'd be scared in case you might think it is an invitation to fuck me and run off again.'

His face drops and he visibly squirms. 'Look, I want to explain.'

I place my hand on my hip and raise my eyebrows. 'Explain away.'

I know it's harsh, but I feel like being harsh right now. He was bloody harsh with what he did to me. I still feel like the world's biggest slut for letting him do it.

My nipples are hardening from the cold. I hope he doesn't think it has anything to do with him.

He sighs loudly and gives me his puppy dog eyes. 'Please let me in.' Damn those bloody baby blues; it's like they hypnotise me!

And it is freezing out. I begrudgingly open the door and let him in. He goes straight into the sitting room as if he knows his way around now. It pisses me off. I grab my dressing gown from my room before joining him. I need some thicker fabric between us.

He's sat on the edge of our corner sofa when I walk back in, even though there is more than enough room on the sofa.

I fold my arms across my chest, choosing to remain standing. 'So go on then, explain.'

He wrings his hands together, clearly awkward. 'You have to understand that I didn't mean to react like that.'

'You mean you didn't mean to fuck me? Or run off?'

'Yes, I mean run off,' he scolds. He takes a deep breath, as if to calm himself down, and runs a hand through his hair. 'If I'm honest I didn't mean to fuck you at all.'

Oh. Well how the hell do I react to that? He didn't want to fuck me? So what, he just fell dick first onto my vagina over and over and over again? Yeah right. I was hardly a seductive vamp.

'This is coming out all wrong.' He laughs awkwardly. 'Look, I got carried away in the moment. We shouldn't have done it. I mean, I could get fired for sleeping with a suspect.'

Oh my God. That's why he's really here. He's scared I'll tell on him.

'Is that what all of this is about? Me being a suspect?' I can't help but sound as furious as I feel.

'No,' he says seriously, penetrating me with his gaze. 'Don't you get it? If you were just a suspect it wouldn't matter, but...well, I could see that you didn't do that a lot. And...well, it freaked me out. I felt bad for taking advantage of you.'

Oh my Jesus. He's telling me I'm bad in bed. I'm bad at the whole sex thing. What else could he bloody mean by that? This is *beyond* humiliating.

'So because you felt bad you decided to make me feel even worse about myself?' My voice is wobbly. Hold it together, Sadie.

He might as well just take my last shred of pride with him when he leaves.

'I realise it sounds like a dick move in hindsight, but Jesus, I can't think that straight when my dick is hard.'

My mouth drops open in disgust. That's all he cared about. Getting his dick wet. It didn't matter it was me there at the time. Well, only when he realised how shitty and inexperienced I was.

'Jeez, you have such a way with words,' I snort.

'Look.' He stands up, his face serious. He walks forward and takes my hands in his. His touch stings like he's just tried to electrocute me.

'I'm really sorry. Can we start again?' That twinkle in his eye is back again. Damn that bloody twinkle, making me weak at the knees. It makes me want to do silly things.

'Start again?' I attempt to laugh cruelly, when all I really want to do is jump on his lap and beg for his touch. 'What do you mean, start again?'

He smiles, his half shy, half lazy smile. Full hot fucker smile.

'I don't know. Maybe you just sit on my lap and we'll see what comes up.' He smirks teasingly.

Oh my God, he's so bloody crude!

'I don't think so,' I snort.

I can hear dripping. I'm not sure if it's his wet state or my last shred of resistance draining away.

He backs towards the couch, pulling me by my hands onto his lap. I gasp, feeling his already erect dick through his trousers. He kisses me slowly and deeply. I savour the taste of him, the feel of him on my mouth. His hands are on my face, delicately cradling my chin. This feels different, intimate even.

This is the guy that said a second ago that I was bad in bed, I remind myself, but it's like his kisses are erasing any logical thoughts.

I force myself to pull back. His eyebrows knit together.

'What's wrong?' he asks, stroking my cheek with his knuckles.

I can't stop myself. I lean into it.

I don't want to ask him anything. I want to just let him take me and enjoy every second, but I can't when my brain is this upset and vulnerable.

'A minute ago you were telling me how bad at sex I am and now you're trying to jump me again?' I whisper, twiddling his shirt button so I don't have to face him.

I chance a glance up to see him staring back at me quizzically, his eyes burning with perplexity.

'Huh? Oh wait...you don't think I meant *that,* do you?'

I look down, too embarrassed to face him. I hate showing any vulnerability in front of him.

He grabs my chin and forces me to look at him. 'I just meant I could see that you're not someone that sleeps around. That's a compliment.'

I freeze in place, everything inside me heating to boiling point. That's all he meant. The massive relief tells me I care too much. This is only going to hurt me further. But I'll be damned if I don't want to do it anyway.

'You know we shouldn't do this, right?' I ask breathlessly. My lady parts are telling my mouth to shut the fuck up.

His eyes skim along the contours of my face. 'I know,' he nods, bringing his lips down to meet mine in a dominant kiss, reminding me of who's in control.

My heart rate accelerates as he deepens the kiss, his tongue massaging mine. Control slips away from me, a distant memory. He pulls back slightly, but only so he can take my dressing gown rope, tugging at it to reveal my nakedness.

I can't help but not believe my own words. Why shouldn't I do this again? He smiles devilishly, his smirk telling me he knows full well how good he has me. Oh fuck.

Chapter 23

I can't believe I slept with him *again*. What the hell am I doing? This is only going to make things harder. I'm not one of those girls that can just sleep with someone and not let feelings get involved. I can't help but like him. I'm falling for him more each day and the man's trying to get me arrested. I must be brain dead.

It doesn't stop me from trailing the dark hair over his belly button, warming when his stomach tenses every now and again as my hand goes lower. I grin up at him and try to push reality away. Right now he's my sex god. Right now he's my hero. I don't want anyone to burst this bubble right now.

My phone ringing breaks my concentration. God, why does reality have to always interrupt?

'Ignore it,' he whispers, kissing my forehead.

Like I said, I'm happy to ignore reality. We have all afternoon. It's night time now, not that I have any idea of the time. I can just tell you how many orgasms I've had. Three! Three bloody orgasms. Only reality has a way of crashing down at the worst time. When the ringing ends and starts up again I know someone really needs to get hold of me. What if it's Mr. Hendricks? I should have fed Ivy dinner by now. I hope she's eaten. I am a terrible, *terrible p*erson.

I smile regretfully up at him, before dragging myself out of bed and reaching for my bag. I look down at the caller ID to see its Steph. What the hell could she be calling me at, I look at the clock, half eleven at night?

'Hey, Steph,' I say, pulling a confused face at Harry. He's just so ruggedly handsome, lying in my bed, his arms outstretched above his head. I could stare at him all day.

'Sadie, I need you,' she cries down the phone, her breathing heavy and unsteady.

I straighten up, a chill spreading down my spine at her tone. 'Steph? What's wrong?'

'I...I think he's dead,' she says, her voice wobbling. 'I need you here.'

I look up at Harry, trying to think quickly and cover my reactions. I'm too late. He looks concerned. I turn to face the wall.

'Who? Who is...?' I gulp, unable to say the word.

Who the fuck has she killed? We're all turning into gangster bitches right before my eyes.

'I don't know. I just know I woke up and he was in the flat and...and...I got him with the baseball bat.'

She's been burgled. Oh my God! The poor cow. That's all she needs now that Dorian's gone, to feel vulnerable in her own home.

'We'll be right there.'

We hammer on Steph's door twenty minutes later. We got a cab straight over. Harry thinks it's just a normal break in, but it's already dawned on me that this could have something to do with Joaquin. But I mean, if he's dead we'll need help anyway.

Lexi opens the door, startled when she sees Harry.

'What the hell is he doing here?' she demands, her face like thunder.

I shoot her a *calm down* look. 'He might be able to help,' I say, my voice sharp with nerves.

I really don't want to tell her right now that we've come from bed.

She grabs us by our wrists and drags us in. 'She's really done it this time,' she says, rolling her eyes. 'I can't wake him at all.'

'Shit,' I mutter, following her into the peach wallpapered sitting room. Apparently she never got around to stripping it.

Steph is in her purple dressing gown sat on the edge of her sofa, chewing her nails. Mags is trying to rock Ruby back to sleep while making tea for everyone. She's still wearing that stupid hat. Oh, and there's an unconscious, possibly dead, man on the rug in the centre of the room. It's so British. Someone might be dead, we might be going to prison, but we'll still have time for a quick tea to calm us down.

'What happened?' I blurt out, kneeling down to look at the face of the man. I don't recognise him, thank God. He must just be a normal burglar.

'I can't talk about it,' Steph sobs, taking a tissue from Mags.

'Has anyone checked for a pulse?' Harry asks calmly, stooping to his knees and feeling his neck.

'I tried,' Lexi shrugs, 'but I don't know what I'm looking for.'

If she'd have paid attention at that first aid course I sent her on maybe she would. I try to push down the aggravation and look to Harry for reassurance.

'It's there, but it's weak.' He looks around at them. 'Have you called an ambulance?'

They all look at each other, their faces creased in unease. They obviously haven't called the police for fear of them searching the flat. I don't know if Steph has any 'stock' here. She shouldn't, but I don't know that for sure.

'They'll put me in jail!' Steph wails hysterically, her chest and neck getting red and patchy.

Fuck, Steph! Shut up, I try to communicate with my face.

'Why?' Harry asks, frowning thoughtfully. 'It was self-defence. He was breaking and entering.'

Steph gets up and starts pacing the room. 'They'll send me to jail. I'll go to jail. Ruby will go into foster care,' she shrieks, her hysterics uncontrollable now.

Jesus, at this rate she'll be confessing and sending us all to jail.

Lexi grabs her by the shoulders and shakes her. 'Get a grip, you dumb bitch!' She follows it with a giant slap across her face.

My mouth pops open in shock at the sound of skin on skin.

'Lexi!' I shriek, jumping up to push her up against the wall, away from Steph. 'Calm the fuck down.'

She glares back at me with a vicious intensity. I look back to see Steph gripping her face in shock. Her cheek is already bright red, matching the hives coming up on her neck.

'I can't believe you did that in front of the baby,' Mags berates, placing our teas on the coffee table. 'That's awful behaviour.'

Ruby looks contented enough, half asleep in her arms, but I agree. Since when did we turn into animals?

'She's a loose cannon,' Lexi shouts back. 'I can't have her bringing us all down with her.'

My eyes meet Harry's and a bolt of fear goes through me. He must be working this all out. If he hasn't already. He's not a dumbass.

'Stop talking,' he snaps, full of authority. Everyone turns to stare at him, our eyes wide, waiting to hear what he says next. 'I'll take care of it.'

We all look at each other bewildered. Take care of it?

Mags looks especially troubled. 'You mean like…you'll kill him?' She takes a large sip of her tea as if to show how much stress she's under.

'No,' he laughs with a frown, obviously wondering why we're all so mental. 'What I mean is that I'll take him to the hospital.'

'Oh, thank God,' Mags sighs, sitting down on the sofa as if she doesn't have an unconscious man at her feet.

He scoops him up, throwing him over his shoulder as if he weighs nothing. I rush to the door to help him through. He pauses halfway out of the door and stares at me, his eyes warning.

'We need to talk later,' he says, seriously. 'I'm guessing it's not a coincidence this guy is a known member of Joaquin's gang.'

The breath leaves my body in one clean whoosh, bringing with it a sense of dread. I freeze, unable to say anything. I can't. What the hell *can* I say? He nods and walks past me.

#

I'm sat on the floor outside Harry's flat when he gets home at four in the morning. I remembered him mentioning that he lived in this building on the first floor. Apart from that I have no idea so I got someone to buzz me in and I'm just crouched in a corner, half asleep. I didn't expect him to take so long. Luckily I thought to pop home quickly to check on Ivy. Turned out she hadn't eaten, even though she was sure she had. The worst thing was that she'd cut her hair herself. It looks bloody awful, like little tufts have been ripped out. Not that she seems bothered by it.

I see him dragging his tired body along the hallway.

'Hey,' I croak, still sleepy.

'Hey,' he smiles weakly, his forehead seeming more creased than normal.

I force myself to stand up as he opens the door. He's being cold towards me. I'm scared he'll slam it in my face. I don't even know why I'm here. Is it to break things off with him for good? Or to beg him to let me explain? I've been sitting here for hours and I still can't work it out.

I follow him in, the eerie silence making my skin prickle.

His flat isn't like I imagined. I expected it to be all ultra-modern, dark grey walls and black furnishings. But it's actually really homely. Rustic even. There's exposed brick behind his tan leather beaten up chesterfield sofa. Black and white photographs of different shapes and sizes hang from it. I make a mental note to try and have a closer look at them later. If he hasn't thrown me out by then.

He walks into the open plan kitchen. More exposed brick against tall dark wood cabinets. There's a small make shift breakfast bar which looks like it's made out of some sort of reclaimed timber boards. It's bloody gorgeous. He must think my place is a soulless shithole.

'Great place,' I say carefully, nervously twirling my hair.

This is so awkward. He looks seriously pissed and he's definitely avoiding looking at me. He takes a bottle of water out of the fridge and offers me one. I shake my head no, leaning my head against the wall.

'So…are we going to talk about what happened, or…?' I say, attempting to break down the awkwardness.

'I don't know,' he counters, leaning back against the breakfast bar. His trousers hang so perfectly from his hips. 'Are we?' He raises his eyebrows, challenging me.

Oh God. I knew it; he wants me to confess. Just like that he wants me to put myself and my mates in it. I still don't trust him. He's a policeman first and foremost. He took an oath. My vagina's not magic. I can't have just erased all of that.

'Maybe I should just go,' I offer, testing the waters. I look towards his front door, wanting nothing more than for him to ask me to stay.

He crosses the distance between us in seconds, towering over me. He lowers his voice to a deadly quiet whisper. 'Or maybe you should tell me what the fuck is going on, Sadie.'

I gulp, my pulse racing. My jaw tightens, begging me to keep my secrets in.

'What do you mean?' I ask, knowing perfectly well. I look around the room, at anything but him.

He sighs and runs his hand through his hair. 'When are you going to let me in, Sadie?'

I feel tears brewing, my throat feeling tight. Let him in? What the hell does he want from me? How can he expect me to trust him when he's a cop?

'Let you in? You mean rat on all of my friends?' I ask, my voice wobbly.

'No. I just…' He unbuttons the top button of his shirt, as if he suddenly feels it's hot in here. 'I mean, do you even want to know if the guy's alive?'

'Of course I do,' I sob, releasing the tears I've been desperately holding back. My throat burns with them. I have no choice but to let them go, even though it feels abhorrent to be crying in front of him. 'What do you want me to say, Harry?'

He rakes his hand through his hair. 'Come here.' He tries to pull me into a hug, but I fight him. I don't want to be comforted right now. I'm sick of him confusing me. Trying to catch me confessing one minute only to comfort me the next.

'Leave me alone,' I yell, going into instant survival mode. I push him away and start for the door.

He grabs my wrist and tries to pull me back. I fight viciously against him, even though he's not even holding me that tight. The tears almost cloud my vision.

'Get off me, you bastard!' I yell so loud it hurts my ear drums. 'What do you want to hear? Huh? Some pathetic little story of why I am the way I am? How I spent years in foster care and ended up homeless because of a creepy step brother? How my own mother hated me? Nobody wants to hear the truth because the truth isn't pretty. It makes you uncomfortable. And I don't want *anyone's* pity.' I try to twist out of his grip so I can make for the door again.

'Just let me comfort you,' he shouts, grabbing me and pulling me into his chest.

'No,' I sob, still fighting with all of my strength. I punch him in the chest repeatedly, but I'm so weak they just come out as little bitch punches. 'I don't need you. I don't need anyone!'

It's like all of my emotions are coming out at once. Fear, confusion, anxiety - all coming out disguised as anger.

'Shush,' he whispers calmly, restraining me against him.

I thrash some more until every muscle in my body screams in protest, aching heavily. 'Shush,' he repeats over and over again rubbing my back.

I give up. I let my body sag against him as I howl. I didn't even know I could howl, but the flood gates have been opened now. I howl so loudly that I actually scare myself. This isn't just the fear of him finding out. This is the whole thing. Being made redundant. Having my security ripped away from me, the threat of homelessness becoming my reality again. I'm dealing drugs. I'm no better than my druggie mother who couldn't even find it in her to love me. I've let everyone down. Hell, I've let myself down. I'm disgusted by myself and what I've become.

I cling onto his shirt as snot runs down my face. This is *not* attractive.

'You don't have to fight me,' he says, rubbing my back in large, soothing motions.

I don't deserve him and his comfort right now.

'I can't tell you anything,' I sob. I would love more than anything to unload everything onto him. To feel some relief from the constant lies, but I can't.

'I know,' he nods, wiping my wet cheek. 'And right now I don't want you to.'

I look up to him, my forehead creased in disbelief. Is this a trick?

He smiles reassuringly, tucking a bit of hair behind my ears. 'Will you just let me look after you?'

Why on earth does this god of a man want to look after me? I'm a bloody mess. He knows this. He's investigating me for God's sakes.

'Why?' I ask, unbelieving.

He locks his blue eyes with mine, his stare intense. 'Because I have a feeling you're so used to looking after other people that not many look after you in return.'

I lose my breath. How can he be this kind? How can he see the good in me? Is he a secret born again Christian or something? What if I go to bed with him and in the morning he tries to convert me to being a Jehovah Witness? I should run.

Instead I nod, unable to speak. I cling on harder to his chest and let him carry to me to his bed where he strips me, pulls back the covers and tucks me in, holding me tightly to his body. Every sensible thought in my head is telling me that this is wrong, that I should be running far from him. But when it feels this good it's easy to ignore them.

Chapter 24

<u>Friday 16th October</u>

I wake up and startle when I realise I'm not at home. The pillow case smells way nicer than mine. I wonder what fabric softener this is. Then I remember the drama that was last night. Steph's flat getting broken into. I can't believe Joaquin didn't call a truce like he promised. You just can't trust drug dealers these days.

Harry's arms are around me, reminding me of the next part of my evening. Me breaking down in front of him. I know I should feel mortified, but with his scorching hot arms around me I'm reminded how he took such great care of me. I still don't understand if he really likes me, apart from sex. Although we didn't have sex last night.

I turn to face him and he doesn't even stir. He's like an angel, his face squashed into the pillow like that. It gives me the chance to study his dark eyelashes. They're so jet black, such a contrast to when those dazzling blue eyes are open. His messy black hair is all over the place. I smile to myself; he looks edible. And for a second he feels like mine. But then my stomach falls as the realisation that this is in fact a fantasy dawns on me. This can't last. He's not mine. Even if we both wanted it.

Yeah, he might have acted like a knight in shining armour last night, but that was then. This is now. The harsh sunlight shines through his blinds, reminding me that in the light of day things look a lot different. He's a cop, I'm a criminal. No matter how hard I try to change anything, that fact remains. Even if we both wanted to we couldn't be together. And I don't even know if he does. He did look after me last night, but I was so obviously a mess. He was just being a gentleman. I'm kind of surprised I didn't wake up in handcuffs.

His eyes half open as he slowly wakes, his lips parted ever so slightly. He's so adorable. I have to stop myself from leaning over and kissing him. He finally comes around fully, craning his head to look up at me. His neck creates these tiny little wrinkles like a bulldog that I want to stroke. It physically hurts to not lean over and touch him. But I can't. It's best like this. I need to start detaching myself.

A loud hiss makes me freeze. Shit, does he have a snake? A fucking *snake?* Why on earth would someone have a snake? I remember a foster brother who had one and used to chase me around the house with its shed skin. I shudder just at the memory of it. But surely he'd have mentioned it? Especially if it is just allowed to roam around his flat. Then I feel a sharp sting in my foot. Oh my God, it's bitten me. The fucker is trying to eat me!

I sit up, ready to attack the anaconda with all of my might, but instead I look into the eyes of the scariest cat I've ever seen. It's blonde apart from its legs, face and ears, which are dark brown. It has the longest whiskers and the clearest blue eyes. They remind me of Harry's. Its claws are digging into the top of my foot. She hisses again, causing me to flinch. Holy fucking hell. This cat is evil!

I jump out of bed, swinging my leg in the air, but this cat is clinging on for dear life.

'Get off me!' I whisper in a hiss, trying to ensure I don't alarm Harry.

The cat sinks her teeth into my foot. F*UUUUUUUUUUCK!*

'Get off me you crazy pussy!' I scream, my lungs burning from trying to hold in the agonizing pain. Really all I want to do is scream the flat down and beat it off with a baseball bat.

Harry bolts upright in bed with alarmed eyes. By now I'm slamming his cat against the wall in a desperate bid to get it to leave me alone. Well, there goes any chance of him thinking I'm sane.

'Sadie, what the fuck?' he asks, his voice hoarse and his eyes barely open.

Err...Isn't it bloody obvious? Cat attacking human!

'Help...cat...' is all I can splutter, feeling the blood trickling down my foot.

He seems to pull himself together, jumping out of bed and running after us, trying to catch the cat. It's hard when I'm kicking my foot around wildly. It's just too bloody painful! My survival instincts are on high alert. I might have to kill this cat.

'Keep still!' he shouts. He throws me back on the bed, causing a huge head rush. He grabs my ankle roughly.

'MEEEEEEOW!' the cat screeches.

All of a sudden its teeth release me. I pant, lifting my head to see him holding the cat before letting my head fall back onto the bed. Thank fuck for that. I can start to breathe again. Thank God he saved me from that crazy cat. I look down at my foot to see it trickling with bright red blood. Instead of finding Harry fussing over me, he's instead cradling the demon cat in his arms like it's a baby. My mouth drops open in shock. He's looking down at it with adoring eyes. What the fuck? This cat just maimed me?

'What the hell are you doing? Aren't you going to call cat services or something?' I bellow, my heart still racing.

He narrows his eyes in bewilderment. 'Cat services? What the hell are you talking about?' he asks, amusement in his tone.

'Surely you're going to have it put down?' I squeal, not able to hide my disgust.

'Put down?' he repeats, pure hilarity on his face.

He finds this *funny?*

'Yes, put down,' I nod. 'If a dog did that to me there'd be no question about it.' I grab his t-shirt from the floor and apply pressure to my foot.

His eyes dance with laughter. 'Sadie, I'm not going to put down Teddy just because he took a dislike to you.'

His cat is called Teddy? Teddy's are supposed to be caring things that children drag around, not things that attack people when they're sleeping. I honestly don't know what to say. And then I remember I'm naked. I really wish I wasn't. I feel so exposed. You think you know someone and then you realise they're as fucking barmy as their cat.

He finally looks down at my foot. 'We should get you cleaned up.'

Duh.

The cat shoots me an evil smirk. Who knew cats could smirk? This cat is the devil incarnate. The sooner I'm cleaned up and out of here the better.

I carefully stand, wincing slightly from the sting, and start looking around for my clothes. Being naked just adds to this whole humiliation. I've put my bra and knickers on before he even puts Prince Teddy down.

'Come on,' he says, offering me his hand.

I begrudgingly take it and let him lead me into his bathroom. It's so small that he's able to sit me on the toilet seat and place my foot in the bath. He rinses away the blood with his hand held shower. It's already stopped bleeding, and now I that I can get a closer look at it I can see that it's not that bad.

'Are you okay?' he asks when the silence becomes painful.

'Uh-huh,' I nod, forcing a fake smile. I need to get out of here. This whole situation is giving me a headache.

He doesn't look convinced, but still helps me back into the bedroom.

'I'm going to go,' I mumble, searching for my skirt. 'I've got to check on Ivy.'

He lies back down on the bed, the side of his face pressed into his pillow. The duvet isn't over him at all, so I get the full vision of his perfect body. His black boxer shorts are on, but hang so low on his hips that his magic V is showing. His body is perfect. It's like someone went into my head and created my perfect vision. Yes, he has a six pack, but his muscles aren't so hard looking that you imagine them made of stone. His shoulders are broad and his biceps big, but again not gross. No over pumped muscles with those creepy looking veins on them. No protein injections for this guy.

He opens his eyes and catches me gawping. 'I thought you were leaving?' he asks, irked.

I jolt from his change of tone. No need for him to be nasty.

He narrows his eyes at me, his eyes cloudy with barely concealed rage. 'I should have expected for you to act like nothing happened last night.'

Whoa, he's going for it. Full on confrontation. It's far too early for this shit.

'What do you mean?' I murmur, my voice small. I carry on looking around for my top so I don't have to look at him.

He sits up, looking at me with such coldness I can feel my veins freezing.

'Don't bullshit me, Sadie. Last night you opened up to me. I finally saw the real you and I just knew you'd shit yourself this morning and go back to being a scared little girl.'

Scared little girl? His words hit my chest like a hammer. I'm hurt.

'Please don't pull the whole dramatic *you let down your walls* speech,' I snap back. 'Last night was a lapse in judgement. That's all.'

He snorts. 'You seem to be having a few of them lately.'

What a bastard. Using how weak I am against me. It's not my fault I turn into a slut around him.

'I don't regret the sex if that's what you mean,' I sass, my hand on my hip.

He shoots another icy stare my way.

Oh wait, did he mean I had lapses in judgement getting involved in the drugs in the first place? Or getting involved with him at all? Oh God, I'm so confused and it's not even nine am. I turn to leave. I need to go home where I can get my head straight.

'Just be careful,' he warns gravely.

I turn round at his tone. What does he mean by that?

'Did you just threaten me?' I ask in disbelief.

He snorts. 'Obviously not. I'm talking about you and your friends. They've already gone for Steph. You could be next. Especially with the whole dopey kidnapping his dog incident.'

'I'll be fine,' I shrug.

I already know I'm in trouble. I need to sort out some sort of plan. Some way out of this. But I can't be anywhere around him.

'Just please promise me you'll be careful?' he asks, his tone softer. Now that I'm looking into his eyes I see that he's just worried, bless him. It makes my chest ache even more.

I swallow down the lump of emotion brewing in my throat.

'I promise.'

Chapter 25

<u>Monday 19th October</u>

I've had all weekend to stew over it. Not just the whole Joaquin thing, wondering why he didn't keep to his word, but now Harry's been thrown into the equation. It's too confusing. A knock at my door interrupts my thoughts. I shrink into the sofa, afraid its Joaquin. But then I suppose he wouldn't knock. He'd just get one of his men to break in during the night. I must have checked our locks three times last night before bed. Samuel thinks I've gone mad.

I begrudgingly drag myself to the door leaving my cup of tea and chocolate digestives. I look through the peep hole to find Harry waiting patiently. What the hell is he here for? I take a calming breath and then open it.

'Hi,' I say sternly.

'We need to talk,' he says seriously.

I stand aside so he can walk into the living room. Does he really want to hash out our whole weird relationship right now? I'll need a hell of a lot more biscuits.

'I've found this Welshie you told me about.'

'Huh?'

When did I mention Welshie? I rack my brains. When I was arrested I mentioned him, but I never gave a surname or location.

'I can take him down,' he declares. 'But I need your help.'

# # #

So somehow I've volunteered to go undercover so that we can bring down Welshie and his prostitution ring. I'm dressed like an absolute ho-bag to get myself into character. I have on a black leather mini skirt, the most padded bra I own with a flimsy crop top over it. I covered myself up a bit with my trench coat and knee high boots. If anyone I know sees me I'll die of shame. I've got so much makeup on my face that if it rains I'm going to end up looking like a striped Oompa loompa.

Hidden low in my non-existent cleavage is a wire that Harry and his team have attached. I just have to catch him in the act of offering money for my services. Apparently as soon as they have proof they'll storm the building. It doesn't stop me from panicking. What if he susses out what I'm up to?

I look up at the industrial building. Its windows are covered in mesh metal screens. There goes my hope of jumping out of a window if things get too heavy. The bricks are crumbling at the corners. Will it even hold people? It's probably a condemned building or something, but I know from Harry that this is where Welshie keeps the hookers. He uses it as a brothel.

I take a last deep breath and force myself towards it. I pull open the boarded metal door and walk inside to a big foyer. Everything is filthy, like it hasn't been touched in fifty years. There's some dust sheet over old furniture. Is this even the right place?

'Who are you?'

I jump and turn towards the voice. A woman, well a bloody girl of about sixteen, stares back at me. It's only when I look closer that I can see beyond the coats of makeup she's wearing. Shit. It's the new girl from the streets that I only saw the other day.

I start to react, but then quickly catch myself. I have to lead everyone to believe that I'm in a desperate situation too. That I need this just as much as she does.

'I need to speak to Welshie,' I demand, leaning on one hip with my arms crossed.

'Wait.' She narrows her eyes at me, as if recognising my face. 'You're that Sadie that was warning me to stay away from him.'

'Yeah, good job I did, clearly,' I scoff.

'Why the hell are you dressed like that? And why do you want to speak to Welshie?'

'It's none of your business.' I look away, trying to act ashamed. I need her to believe I'm only doing this because I'm desperate. 'Just get him, will you?'

'Fine,' she huffs, turning on her heel. She stomps off upstairs, leaving me alone with my panic.

Is he even going to fall for this? What if he just laughs in my face and tells me to piss off? No, I've totally got this. I straighten myself up, pulling my shoulders back. I'm doing a good thing here. For *once* since this started I'm actually trying to do the right thing. Welshie has been picking girls up from the street for too fucking long. Its time someone took him down.

Heavy footsteps begin down the stairs. I stop nervously, scratching my arms and turn to look at him. A big smirk turns up on his face. Who knew Harry would even care?

'Well, well, well. Little Sadie Taylor. I thought you were too good for this life?' he sneers, obviously enjoying my humiliation.

I pout. When really I'm shaking inside. 'Yeah, well. That was back when I had a job. Now I need cash and I need it now.'

He narrows his eyes at me. 'I thought you were into drugs now?'

How the fuck does he know that? Are people talking about me? Oh my God, if it gets back to Samuel I'll die.

I shrug. 'I was. Not anymore.'

'Good,' he nods. 'I take it you wanna try this out instead?'

I nod, unable to actually voice the words.

'I'll give you a trial run.'

My skin crawls with repulsion.

'What do you mean?' I stammer.

'I mean that the next customer through that door gets you as a freebie. And if you're any good you can stay on.'

Shit. He actually wants me to sleep with a customer. And he's said nothing about money. I need them to storm the place before some dirty arsehole gets ahold of me. This is quickly turning into a horror movie.

'Come on.' He grabs hold of my arm and starts dragging me up the stairs.

Fuck, he's strong. Bile starts rising in my throat. What am I doing? It's not like I could leave now if I wanted to. He throws me into a room with nothing but a dirty old mattress in the corner. The floral wallpaper is peeling and there are no curtains, the view is only that of the shutters. I can hear people in the rooms around me grunting, having what I assume is sex.

'So,' I say, my voice wobbly and high pitched. 'After I sleep with this guy then you'll pay me for the next one, right?'

If I get a confession out of him now then I may still have a chance.

'We'll talk properly after,' he snarls, cutting off any further conversation. 'Just wait here.'

Shit. Shit, shit, shit.

I duck my head as low to my chest as possible and try for help.

'I don't know if you guys can hear me right now, but I'm really not okay with sleeping with a guy.'

There's no response. Not like they can respond to me, but I was expecting something. I don't know, maybe people shouting as the place is raided by cops and arrests are made. Jesus, what if the wire is broken and they can't hear me at all? Okay, don't panic. Don't fucking panic!

I stand up and try to open a window, knowing they're wired shut anyway. Fuck my life! What am I going to do? I should have brought a weapon.

Through the grunting of the surrounding rooms I can make out footsteps approaching. Is that Welshie? Wait, two sets of footsteps. Fuck and they sound male. I can't hear any stiletto heels right now. Has he got someone to sleep with me already? Fuck! Does he just have horny men on standby or something?

I back away into the furthest corner of the room. Okay, think of a game plan. What am I going to do when this whole thing blows up in my face? Kick him in the balls? What if he's too big for me to do that? Oh my God, I'm hyperventilating. How on earth did I ever think I'd get away with this?

The door swings open and Welshie leers at me. 'Got yourself your first customer. Meet Derrick.'

I close my eyes as the man next to him enters the room. I take a deep breath and hope to God he's some skinny fuck I can beat the shit out of before running. When I open them I instead find Harry. What the fuck is he doing here?

He rubs his hands together. 'Exactly what I was looking for. She'll do nicely,' Harry says with a creepy sneer.

What the fuck?

His eyes warn me to play along. How the hell did he even get in here?

'Err...hi?'

'I'll leave you two alone,' Welshie grins, slapping Harry on the shoulder.

The door shuts and I release the breath I didn't realise I was holding.

'What the fuck are you doing? How did you get in here?' I demand, only wanting to throw myself into his arms and have him carry me out of here.

'I'm one of his regulars,' he explains calmly.

My jaw hits the floor. I've been sleeping with a guy that fucks hookers? I think I just threw up in my mouth.

'Wha?' is all I can mumble.

He comes closer, so close I can smell his minty breath.

'You really think so little of me?' he whispers, tucking a strand of hair behind my ear. 'I've got a few girls to agree to testify against him as soon as we have him inside.'

'Oh, thank fuck.' It's like a vice gets released from my stomach. And now I actually feel bad. 'I'm sorry.'

'It's okay.' He smiles, cupping my face with his hand. 'But we'll have to position ourselves in case he walks in to check on us.'

Huh?

'Position ourselves?'

He smiles lopsidedly. 'I mean we have to look like we're getting down to it.'

'Oh.'

Oh *fuck*. I hope he doesn't expect me to get naked with him. With the way we left things the other morning I really don't want to be put under his spell again. Which is what I know will happen. It's like he has magical powers or something. Even now, so close I can smell his citrusy aftershave...well, it just makes me want to ravish him for real until that same aftershave is transferred onto my sweaty body.

He rolls his eyes with a kind smile. 'Don't worry Sadie, we're not going to have sex. Just lie on the bed and I'll lie on top of you.' He takes his suit jacket off and folds it before placing it neatly on the floor.

How can he be so neat with crazy hair like that?

'Oh, okay.' I sound breathless and raspy. Totally not what I was going for. My chest is heaving noticeably up and down. I'm getting turned on at the idea.

Get a hold of yourself, Sadie.

He holds out his hand towards the bed, as if to invite me to lay down first. I gulp down the panic and force my jelly legs towards it. I sit down on it and then wiggle until I'm closer to the top. Real sexy, Sadie.

He smiles lazily, a full on sexy grin, before loosening his tie, undoing his shirt and pulling it down his arms. Not the abs. Fuck, why did he have to dazzle me with the abs? He really has the perfect body. Strong broad shoulders, the smallest bit of chest hair leading down to that sexy line of hair to his belly button. It's an outie. Huh. Is it weird that this is the first time I've noticed it. My stomach does a little dip. I've always been a bit grossed out with outie belly buttons. Don't ask me why, because I don't even know. They're totally normal, but I just get the urge to press it back in like a red button you're not supposed to touch. But on him it looks good. It looks bloody perfect. Especially around those ripples of muscle. Maybe he'll help me get over it. No, stop this, Sadie, right now!

He smiles again before climbing onto the bed and slowly lowering himself over my trembling body. I'm being stupid feeling this bloody nervous. This is only pretend.

'Don't worry,' he says softly, freezing me with those crystal eyes. 'We're not actually doing anything.'

Wait, does he think I'm scared he'll try it on? That's not it at all. I'm scared I won't be able to control myself. I bite my lip, stopping my natural instinct to lick them. God, he really is beautiful up close like this and I actually have an excuse to gaze at his face. We're forced to.

He narrows his eyes suddenly. 'Have you always had this freckle?'

I already know he's referring to the brown freckle on my nose. I normally cover it up with foundation and I currently have so much on he shouldn't be able to see anything natural about me at all. But I suppose he is close enough.

I look away, my cheeks burning. I hate that freckle. It makes me look like a little girl.

'Don't be embarrassed,' he chuckles, turning my head back to face him. 'It's adorable.'

God, I hate being called adorable. Is there really anything worse?

Suddenly the door bursts open, slamming against the wall. I pull him closer to me so his chest can protect me. Not that I'm actually naked. Welshie leers over us, grinning like a Cheshire cat.

'Just wanted to see you're getting along well,' he sneers.

'What the hell, Welsh?' Harry shouts, his voice deep and manly. 'Give me some fucking privacy. I wouldn't have taken this freebie if I'd have known you'd end up watching.'

Welshie suddenly looks apologetic. 'Sorry, Derrick. So sorry. I'll leave you now.'

'Good,' he growls, so loud it vibrates from his chest onto mine.

The door slams and I start to relax. Harry looks down at me.

'We should probably stay like this for a little while. You know, just in case he checks again.'

I smile back at him and he smiles shyly. It's too much. I can't handle that shy smile, it's beyond sexy.

I push my head up, offering my lips to him. It could be seen as an innocent gesture to anyone but him. He doesn't hesitate, crushing his lips down on mine aggressively. I smile inside, victorious. It seems I wasn't the only one holding back. When he relaxes his body on top of mine I can feel his erection. Definitely not just me.

'Fuck, Sadie,' he growls in between kisses. 'Why do you do this to me?'

I can't think about what this means right now. All I know is that I can't resist him; it's physically painful to try and so I'm giving in. Yep, I'm letting my body do the talking. And right now she's having a hell of a conversation.

When we're...ahem, finished, we dress hastily. It's seriously awkward. I mean yes, great sex. Bloody amazing sex. The danger of Welshie walking in on us actually added to the excitement. I really don't know what that says about me. I really don't.

Harry stands by the door and bashes it three times.

Welshie appears from nowhere.

'Ah, Derrick. Did your lady please you?'

'Best I've had,' he says, winking back at me. I blush.

'Good, good,' he says, like Harry's some prince. 'Although I can't be offering you a freebie next time.'

'That's right,' he nods. 'I'd pay good money for her. How much for sex with her next time?'

Only I'm aware of the very deliberate use of words. He's trying to trap him. I lean my chest towards them, hoping my wire will pick his response up. Please, please incriminate yourself.

'That'll be an even hundred. But if you book two sessions I'll do it for eighty quid a time.'

We've got him. We've bloody got him. I thank God it's over. I expect to hear gun shots or something. Sounds of them storming the building. Bloody something, but I hear nothing.

'I'll show you out, Derrick.'

'Thanks,' Harry says, giving me a quick, reassuring smile.

How can he be smiling reassuringly when he's just leaving me here? The sadistic bastard!

He goes, and Welshie walks into the room a little while later. Or cell which is more like it. He sits down next to me on the bed. I shift over away from him, already sensing he's going to touch me. I can feel the need emanating from him. My stomach twists, threatening vomit.

'You did good, girlie.' He pats my knee with his big chubby hands. Ew, please stop touching me.

'Th-thanks,' is all I can muster, my nerves frayed.

Why the fuck aren't the police here yet? What on earth are they doing? Don't they realise I'm in direct danger?!

'I think I'm done for the day,' I say bravely, trying to claw back some authority. 'You know, one was probably enough for me to get used to it.'

He grips my leg tighter. So tight I cry out weakly.

'Don't be silly, Sadie. You know I have to try out the goods too.'

His hand slides up my thigh. Oh my fucking God. This is actually happening. No one's coming to save me! I grab his balls though his trousers and yank them in the opposite direction using all of my strength. He yelps and weakens his hold on me. I stand up and run out into the hallway. Harry is already there with a crowd of policemen. They seem to be creeping along the hallway so as not to spook Welshie. So that's why I couldn't hear them.

Harry's face twists into concern when he sees me running towards him. I can't help it. I run into his arms, crushing my teary face against his chest. I don't look up, but I hear him say, 'I've got her. Go get him.'

He wraps his arms around me, pressing me so tightly to him I can barely breathe. They're so warm and protective; the perfect combination. I feel safe in them. Fuck, if I'm honest with myself I feel safe with him. Which I'm aware is stupid. He's investigating me. But for now all I need are his arms around me.

He leads me gently outside. The sunlight attacks my eyes, causing me to wince. I didn't realise how dark it was in there. He pulls me to one side, still in his arms. We watch from the side as Welshie is dragged out in handcuffs.

'And you really have enough to shut him down?' I whisper into his chest.

'Yep,' he smiles down at me sincerely.

A colleague turns around to smirk at me and Harry. 'Hey, you two! Great acting in there. If I didn't know any better I'd have thought I was listening to real sex!' He chuckles darkly.

Oh fuck. I hope he didn't catch on that there was no acting. How mortifying. I snuggle back into his arms, promising myself this is the last time before I grow a pair, detach myself and go home.

'Harry?' a female voice calls from somewhere in the distance.

I look up to see a middle aged couple across the street waving over at us.

'Who is that?' I ask bewildered.

I look at Harry and see that he's grimacing but smiling back. 'They're my parents.'

His *parents?* Fuck, this just got a hell of a lot more awkward. Then I remember I'm dressed like a hooker and I left my coat inside. Oh my God, how embarrassing. I attempt to run away, but he keeps me tight to him. Why does he love humiliating me?

'Harry, darling!' his mum says adoringly, pulling him away from me and into a hug.

She looks about sixty, but must dye her hair dark as there are zero greys on her head. She's dressed very fashionable for an older lady. Tapered trousers, a blouse with one of those scarves around her neck that also has a necklace attached. She opens her eyes and stares at my ensemble. Oh God. I close my eyes and wish I could be swallowed up.

'Son,' his dad says, clapping him on the back awkwardly. 'And who is this...' he clears his throat. 'Lady?'

'Err...' he looks to me. How on earth is he going to introduce me? 'This is Sadie.'

That's an easy way of getting out of describing our fucked up relationship, if you can even call it that.

His mum leans into him and whispers, 'Is she on the game, dear?'

Harry chuckles. Actually chuckles. The fucking cheek of him!

'No, mum. She's just helped us with an undercover operation.'

'Oh,' she says, clearly relieved. She turns to me, her face bright with excitement. 'Well then you must come have lunch with us.'

What, now?

'I agree with your mother,' his dad nods. 'Give us a chance to get to know Sadie.'

Are they seriously suggesting they take me to a restaurant dressed like this?

'I'm sure Sadie's busy,' Harry says, thankfully giving me an out.

A very small part of me feels sad that he doesn't want me there.

'Nonsense,' his mum snaps. 'You wouldn't deny us of your company, would you dear?'

She gives me the biggest, sweetest puppy eyes I've ever seen. Who knew old ladies could do that?

'Err...' I look down at my clothes. 'I should at least go home and get changed, and that will take at least an hour. I'm sure you'll be quicker if you just go on without me.'

This is *so* embarrassing. Harry's made it clear he doesn't even want me to come.

'You look fine as you are,' she smiles. 'Come on.'

'And I should check on Ivy.'

'Who's Ivy?' she asks, not pausing long enough for me to answer. 'I simply won't take no for an answer.'

'Err...okay?'

#

An hour later we're having lunch at a posh little bistro. Everyone, and I mean EVERYONE, is looking at me and wondering why the hell I'm dressed as a hooker. I try to style it out, pretending I'm just very ahead of fashion, but it's just not possible. After a while Mrs. Mckenzie gives me her scarf to wrap around my shoulders. As if it's done much to hide my sluttiness. Plus I just can't look the woman in the eye. An hour ago I was shagging her son. It's too weird.

His dad seems like kind of a hard arse though. Everything Harry said has been cut off by him comparing him to his older brother. If it was me I'd be seriously pissed off, but he seems to just swallow down his pride and take it. How interesting.

'So, Harry,' he starts again, 'when are you going to get this promotion you keep talking about?' He tilts his head towards him, as if expecting a line of excuses.

Jesus, it's at times like this I'm glad I don't have parents. They're total buzz kills.

'It's...in progress,' he says vaguely, looking down at his hands.

'What on earth does that mean?' he demands, getting the bill from the waiter.

His eyes flash to mine before quickly readjusting. 'I've just got to finish a tricky case.'

Shit. Is he talking about us? Are we the tricky case? Is this the case he is planning on getting a promotion for? That would make sense. Why he'd try to seduce me, pretend to like me, so that I'd confess everything. What an absolute bastard. I've been right all along. I knew it.

I stand up abruptly from the table, the chair scraping loudly against the floor. He looks up at me, his face showing a mix of emotions; apologetic, scared, sad. It's all there, but I couldn't give a shit. My shutters are well and truly down

'Sorry, but I have to go,' I announce to his parents. They must think I'm truly loco. 'Good luck with your case, Harry.'

And with that I'm gone.

Chapter 26

Tuesday 20th October

I'm awakened by a banging on my door. I pull the covers over my chin as my heart rate accelerates, threatening to jump out of my chest and run to Scotland. What if it's Joaquin here to take out his revenge? Even if we stopped selling to our regulars now I'm pretty sure they wouldn't leave us alone. Am I going to be a quivering mess every time the door goes?

The banging comes again, harder this time. Shit. What the hell am I going to do? Samuel's at work and I'm here completely alone. It's not like I can call the police either. What would I say? I pissed off a drug dealer by trying to be a drug dealer and now I'm scared and want to be left alone? I don't think so. I could call Harry, but with the way I left things yesterday I'm sure he won't want to speak to me. He must have had a lot of explaining to do to his parents.

I jump out of bed and look for a weapon. The best I can come up with is a hoover handle. Crap. I'm basically dead.

'Sadie, it's me! Let me in.' I know that voice. It's Harry.

I put down the hoover handle I picked up in the hallway and stomp the rest of the way to the door. What the hell is he doing pounding on my door at this time in the morning? If he wants sex I'm slamming it right in his face.

I swing it open in anger. 'Way to give me a fucking heart attack,' I snap, injecting my face with as much anger as possible.

He's leaning his palms on both sides of the door frame, towering over me. God, he's fit. His eyebrows are furrowed so much his forehead has wrinkled permanently. His black shirt is open at the neck showing off his perfect skin covered in what looks like two day stubble. He looks delicious. Beautiful. All the more beautiful for how concerned he looks.

Is he here to apologise? Too right, he should apologise. He humiliated me in front of his parents, has been using me to crack his case and he still hasn't said sorry for his cat almost killing me. The slimy, ambitious, uncaring bastard.

'What did you do?' he demands, his eyes penetrating mine intensely.

Oh shit. What is he talking about?

'Excuse me?' I ask, my voice wobbling.

I haven't done anything stupid since yesterday. Have I?

'Don't pretend, Sadie,' he says crossly. 'Are you going to let me in?'

He's such a cocky bastard. I should just punch him in the face and slam the door. I seriously consider it for a moment.

He looks down for a second, before looking back up with fresh determination.

'We don't have time for this.' He pushes past me into the flat. 'Get away from the door. Pack a bag,' he barks.

Pack a bag? What the hell is he talking about? Is he trying to take me away for a romantic weekend or something? Does he honestly think he can just barge in and expect me to go away for a dirty weekend with him? What an arsehole.

'I'm not going anywhere with you.' I turn to walk back towards the kitchen, but I'm grabbed around the waist and pulled back into his strong chest.

'That wasn't a request,' he argues coldly, looking down at me.

He shoves me into my bedroom so hard my feet barely touch the floor.

'What the fuck are you doing? Don't you dare try to push me around!'

I never would have pegged him for a woman beater.

He sighs, as if to try and calm himself, and then takes a deep breath. He looms over me in one large step. I go to step back, but realise I'm against a wall. I'm forced to look up into his face. His glorious bloody face. Why couldn't he be ugly?

'I'm sorry if I'm coming across as an arsehole, but you need to pack a back now. Joaquin's put a hit on you. I need to get you out of here.'

A swoop of fear takes hold of me, almost knocking me off my feet. My stomach lurches, threatening to release last night's dinner. A hit on me? He…wants me dead? Like, for real?

'Are you sure?'

He walks over to my wardrobe and removes a sports bag I haven't used in forever.

'I'm sure. Now get your shit together. Now.' The fear in his face is enough to get me moving.

I put on some jeans and a t-shirt, throwing random shit into the bag. I'm not even sure what I'm packing, but I'm on auto pilot right now. If he's scared then it's serious.

'Done?'

I nod, my whole body trembling. This is real. No more guessing that he might hurt me. He's made his intentions crystal clear.

His phone rings. 'Mckenzie,' he answers curtly. There's a pregnant pause. 'You're sure? Okay, thanks, I owe you.'

I look up to him for an explanation.

His face looks paler than before. 'We have to go. Now.'

He takes my arm and drags me out of the flat and down the stairs. I go to walk towards the street, but he's pulling me to the bottom of the garden.

'What? What's happening?' I ask, trying and failing to stop him. 'What about Ivy?'

'A known hit man's been seen in the area. And now we know why he's after you.'

'Why?' I'd bloody like to know why he's suddenly gone for me too.

He looks awkward for a second. 'It turns out Welshie worked for him.'

I allow myself a second for that to sink in. Welshie's boss is Joaquin? He's also into prostitution? I don't know why it surprises me. Either way I can see why he'd be pissed with me interfering and getting his business shut down. What the hell is wrong with me? And what if he thinks it was deliberate? He must think I'm crazy.

'We can't take any chances.'

I freeze, blinking rapidly at him. Shit.

He drags my near frozen body to the back of the garden and points to the bottom of the metal fence. There's a small opening at the bottom where the soil doesn't fully meet the fence. I look back at his expectant face. He wants me to crawl underneath onto the train lines?

'Are you serious?'

He runs his hands through his hair in exasperation. 'Sadie, I swear to God if you don't get under there right now I'm dragging you through.'

He's serious. Is this a nightmare? The expression on his face and the queasy feeling in the pit of my stomach tells me this is very real. No need to pinch myself.

I drop to the floor and start commando crawling through it. It's actually pretty easy if you ignore the dirt covering me. For once I'm pleased I'm so lithe. On the other side is the train track. I scramble through as quickly as I can when I check to see there's no train coming.

Next is Harry who doesn't seem to fit so easily. He forces himself through but yelps. Shit, he must have hurt himself.

'Are you okay?'

'Yeah,' he shrugs, his face clearly scrunched up in pain. 'Just caught my back a bit. Come on.' He grabs my hand and starts pulling me behind him alongside the tracks.

This is so surreal. I feel like I'm starring in my own television programme; a mix between The Railway Children and Murder She Wrote.

We run until we get to the station platform at the end of the road. I really wish I'd thought it through more and not worn my stiletto boots.

People look at us strangely as we climb onto the platform, but not for long as thankfully a train pulls up. Harry doesn't look at me the entire time, just straight ahead with a determined steely expression on his face. It's frightening me to no end.

He pushes me onto the train by the small of my back and into the first available seat.

'So where are we going?' I ask, swallowing down the panic.

I mean, am I ever going to see anyone again? Samuel will be so worried.

'I don't know,' he shrugs. 'We'll change in a few stops and figure it out.'

'Oh.' He has no plan. 'Aren't I going into some police protection or something?' I whisper to make sure no one around us hears me.

He purses his lips into a thin line. 'No. You can only get police protection when you've witnessed a crime or have some information for us. You're not confessing to anything. There's no need for them to protect you.'

Oh. But he's still trying to help me. Why?

'So why are you then?' I ask, confused.

He looks at me with mixed emotions playing on his face. Pain, confusion, hurt, affection. It all shows on that beautiful face of his within the span of thirty seconds.

'Because I can't bear for something bad to happen to you.'

Swoon! I know it's ridiculous to go all gooey over a guy in a situation like this, but the urge to shout *my hero* and throw myself at him, fanny first, is overpowering. Instead I try a smile, but I'm so shocked I'm sure it comes out more as a weird kind of grimace.

I stay silent as I'm pulled from train to train. I text Samuel and ask him to check in on Ivy for me. After about an hour of travelling we seem to stop at Stratford upon Avon station. He hails a black cab and asks him to take us to the nearest and most discreet hotel. We pull up ten minutes later outside a shoddy looking building. Its windows are chipped and dirty net curtains hang behind them.

I look to Harry for reassurance, but he's too busy paying the taxi driver. I go to exit, but he holds me back until he's worked out the change. It's such a small gesture, but it ignites something in me. I love how protective he is. Even if my life really is in danger.

He finally lets me out, not letting go of my waist the entire time. He's basically joined to my hip, and I like it so much it scares me. I want him to be attached to me like this all the time, not just when he's trying to protect me from a mobster drug dealer.

He guides me through a red shiny door with a lit up sign saying 'vacancies' above it. The smell of dampness hits me immediately. I scrunch my face up so hard I can hardly see as I'm guided towards the small reception desk. I force them open properly to find a topless, overweight, balding man behind the counter. What the hell?

Harry raises his eyebrows but quickly covers himself to appear polite.

'Hi, we'd like a room for the night please.'

He doesn't even look up from his word search. 'For the whole night?'

Jesus, does it hire by the hour? What kind of shit hole is this? I can't believe the cab driver recommended this place. Or…well I suppose he didn't recommend it. Just said it was the closest, which is what we asked for. Damn Harry for not being specific.

'The whole night,' Harry nods, getting out his wallet from his back pocket.

'Thirty five quid. We only take cash.'

That's bloody cheap at least.

'Excellent.' Harry smiles at me.

I suppose this way they can't electronically trace us. God knows who Joaquin has working for him. He hands over the money and takes the dirty key from fatso.

'Toothbrushes are in the vending machine,' he grunts, again not even looking up.

They have toothbrushes in their vending machine? What kind of hell hole is this? Harry catches my horrified expression and chuckles.

'Come on, snob.'

Snob? Just because I don't like this shit hole? I used to be accustomed to a lot shitter conditions than that. At least this place has a roof. I suppose.

I roll my eyes and stomp up the stairs quickly. I love how he has to chase after me. It's as if he thinks if he leaves my side for a second I'm going to die. But it is cute and gives me a sense of power in this completely fucked up situation.

We get to the first floor and find our room. Harry opens it to reveal a small dark room with a double bed. The sheets are threadbare and there's peeling blue striped wallpaper on the walls. Gross.

Harry dumps the bags on the floor and quickly closes the door behind us. I don't know why. I have no intention of staying here. He locks it, shaking it a little to check how secure it is. Not very from the way it shakes. He goes over to the window and pulls the curtains open. A brick wall greets us. Great. Just fucking great. This place is no better than Welshie's brothel.

He looks back at me as I cross my arms over my chest.

'Don't moan, Sadie,' he berates, reading my mind. 'This is all we have right now, and my only priority is to keep you alive.'

'Yeah, yeah,' I wave dismissively. 'I just don't get why you couldn't keep me alive at a Hilton.'

'Very few chain hotels will book you a room without a credit card in their system. I'm trying not to leave a paper trail.'

Oh, so there is a method to his madness.

'Okay, whatever.' I sit tentatively on the bed, worried I'm catching diseases from it.

I must remember to be grateful. He's risking his job for me. He didn't exactly say that but surely it's implied. Does his boss know he's gone AWOL?

It's hard to seem appreciative when I'm pretty sure this blanket has flees. I suddenly feel itchy all over.

'You're so easy to read sometimes,' he chuckles. 'Stay here.' He walks towards the door.

My pulse quickens immediately at the thought of him leaving me here. Where the hell is he going?

'You're leaving me?' I ask, panicked.

He gives me a stern look. 'Do *not* move. Do you understand? I'll be two minutes.'

I stand to stop him, but he's already run out of the door.

Shit.

I look around me, wrapping my arms around myself in a weird kind of self-hug.

How could he think leaving me is a good idea? He bloody kidnapped me from my own house, made me crawl under a fence and get on a ridiculous amount of trains so that we *weren't* seen. Now he's out God knows where being seen by God knows who.

After ten minutes I'm freaking out. After fifteen I'm chewing my nails in despair. When it hits twenty I'm ready to call Samuel and beg for his help.

Footsteps suddenly stomp up the hallway. Thank God he's back. Unless...Oh my God. What if that's them? Gabriel or Joaquin? They followed us here. They've watched him leave and now they're coming here to get me. This is *just* like Taken!

I look around me in a state of despair. Shit. I run to the window and try to open it, but it must be glued shut or something. Crap. The bed. I drop to the floor and start backing my way under it when the door starts to open.

I'm still only half way under it, fully visible to them when it fully opens. I clasp my eyes shut and cover them with my hands. I know it's childish and pathetic, but I cling onto the idea that if I can't see them they can't see me. But then if I'm taking tips from Taken I should have called someone and be shouting out any weird tattoos or scars to them. Damn it, where the hell is Liam Neeson when you need him?

Chapter 27

'You okay there?' an amused voice asks.

I look up to see Harry standing over me, a mix of concern and hysteria on his face. Oh thank God. I must look a *little* insane.

I release the breath I've been holding in and thank Jesus in heaven and all of those little angel women that I'm safe. Well, for now.

'Jesus, I thought you were Gabriel and Joaquin here to kill me!' I start shuffling back out.

'Yeah, that's pretty clear,' he grins, finding this hilarious.

'Where the hell did you go anyway?' I ask when I stand up. I stumble slightly and he lunges forward to catch me.

Wow, quick reflexes. I straighten myself up, trying to ignore the intense pull from his bright blue eyes. It's like he *wants* me to gaze lovingly into them. I pull away as quickly as I can. That's not happening. He's not getting anywhere near me like that again. It makes things too complicated. Although the double bed in the room is like an elephant. I'm assuming he's going to sleep on the floor. Well, he better be.

I cross my arms over my chest, trying to put some space between us. God knows that when he's around it's like the air is charged with an electric current.

'Where did you go?'

'Just went to ask the naked guy if we could get another room.'

'Oh.' So he wants single beds too. That stings slightly, even though the rational part of my brain tells me I'm crazy. 'And?'

He shakes his head. 'Nope. They're fully booked now. Apparently people are beating down the walls to stay in this palace.' He smiles that breath taking smile of his and I giggle. I don't normally giggle, but he brings out the giggler in me.

'Oh well. I suppose it's fine for now.' I really need to find out how long he intends on us staying here for. 'It's not for long, right?'

He avoids my gaze and instead takes his jacket off and starts loosening his tie. My lady parts start tingling and a dull aching throb starts in the pit of my stomach. What the hell is wrong with me? The guy is an arsehole. I must remember that.

'We'll take it as it comes,' he shrugs.

God, just saying the word 'comes' does strange things to me. I think I'm turning into a pervert. He begins unbuttoning his shirt. He's getting naked?

'I'm gonna take a shower,' he says, opening it to reveal his taut, tanned muscles.

Dear God, I can almost feel myself salivating.

'Err…okay.' I swallow down my lust and look around for somewhere to run to while he pulls his shirt off his shoulders. 'I should give you some privacy…' I look around, but there's bloody nowhere to go.

In a moment of sheer panic I cover my eyes with my hands. I know that if I see him continue to strip I'm going to become a quivering pile of jelly. I won't be able to speak or hear or move. I'll just be a melted puddle of lust on the floor.

Even with my eyes closed I can hear his belt buckle hit the floor. I hear him kicking off his shoes and socks. If anything, not being able to see is making the whole thing even more erotic.

His feet pad over towards me and suddenly warm hands are touching mine. I shiver as if a chill has entered the room, even though he's so warm. So warm I want to wrap my entire body around him and absorb it. He pulls my hands away from my face gently. I open my eyes in trepidation.

He's so close to me all I can see is his eyes. I'm thankful that I can't take anything else in right now. That gaze with his body would kill me. I'd have my knickers off in a second. He looks both confused and amused.

'Sadie, what are you doing? You've seen me naked before.'

I gulp, my mouth dryer by the second. 'I know, but…that was different.'

I look down embarrassed and quickly realise my mistake. He's in nothing but his boxes, his body ripped and strong. I can almost feel the heat emanating off of him and I want to touch him. *So bad.* I want to re-enact the whole scenario from the other day, even if it ends up with him leaving again. That's how low I've sunk. That's how much this man is affecting my self-esteem. I'm willing to get myself trodden over just so that I can feel his hands on me.

'I know it was,' he says, using his index finger to pull my chin up to face him. 'Hey, girl, my eyes are up here,' he jokes.

I smile despite myself. Am I that obvious? I back away with my palms out to him, warning him not to follow.

'Have your shower,' I nod, desperate to get rid of him.

He smiles, a flicker of sadness in his eyes, before he turns and walks towards the bathroom. It's only then that I see he's got four long scrapes on his back. Then I remember him catching it on the fence. It looks terrible, the skin scraped back to reveal angry dark red blood.

'Oh my God, your back,' I shriek in horror.

He glances over his shoulder, trying to get a better look at it. 'Yeah, it stings a little, but I'll live.'

He's so tough and brave. God, I'm turning into a teenage girl. He turns and walks into the bathroom. God, I love watching him leave. Dang, that arse!

I sit down on the bed and try to remind myself of why I'm here. My life is in danger. I should be doing something practical right now. I don't know, making a will or something. Hell, not that I have anything left to give. Harry already warned me not to call the girls in case my phone was being tapped, so I've got nothing but my thoughts. My thoughts and the sounds of him washing himself in the shower. It's too intense.

The door knocks, breaking me from my erotic thoughts. Who the hell could that be? A quick stab of fear hits my chest. Could *this* be them to get me?

'Get that will you?' he shouts from the shower. 'But check the peephole first.'

I should bloody think so. So much for bloody protecting me. He's letting me answer doors to potential killers. I could have just stayed home and looked through the key hole before answering. I'd probably be safer than this shithole. I sigh, frustrated, hoping it's loud enough for him to hear before checking the peephole.

It's the fat reception guy, only now he's wearing a shirt. What could he want? Ooh, maybe he has another room that's just come available with two single beds. That would be amazing. I fling it open with my friendliest smile.

He grunts and hands over a large carrier bag and a pizza box.

'Oh. Err…thanks?'

He turns and walks back down the corridor without saying a single word. What the hell is with that weirdo?

I shut the door and place them on the bed, scared to look inside.

The shower turns off and I hear him getting out. I imagine him drying himself and start to pant like an excitable dog. Pull yourself together, Sadie. I slap myself across the face. Ouch.

The door opens and he comes out with a tiny grey towel wrapped around his waist. His skin is still damp and his black hair is soaked and extra wild. Little beads of water drip off his skin.

'Oh, he got it then.' He takes the pizza box and pulls out a slice, stuffing it straight into his mouth. 'I'm starving,' he adds with a mouthful.

'Huh? You ordered us pizza? When?'

He sits down on the bed, seeming to be savouring the taste. 'When I went downstairs earlier.'

'Oh.' I grab another slice and sit next to him.

I chew absentmindedly while I stare at his abs. How can someone with a body like that eat so badly? Surely he survives on protein shakes and kale?

He finishes his slice and reaches for the bag. 'And I got these.'

He pulls out a newly purchased package of bed sheets. What the hell? He smiles at my bewilderment. 'I could see how grossed out you were earlier. I got him to run to the shops for us so at least we knew we were sleeping on clean stuff.'

Oh my God. My hero.

He stands up and places the pizza box onto the floor, then pulls the duvet off. Within a few seconds he's stripped the bottom sheet and is replacing it with a crisp white one. All the while with just that teeny tiny towel protecting his modesty. How it doesn't fall I don't bloody know, but I can't help but secretly wish it would.

He went to all of this effort just to try and make me happier? This doesn't sound like the same guy that a few weeks ago fucked me from behind before leaving me immediately without even a high five. This is the guy who wanted me to open up to him, who looked after me when I was broken. Unless he wants to get into my knickers again and this is just another act. God, I have trust issues.

'Anyway, get changed,' he orders.

I stare back at him, confused. Surely we're in hiding now?

'I'm taking you to a shooting range. You need to learn how to protect yourself.'

'What the hell?'

He looks out of the window, trying to ignore me.

'Harry,' I say sternly.

'Okay,' he sighs, turning to face me. 'I want you to learn how to shoot.'

'Shoot? As in guns?'

'Obviously as in guns,' he snorts, his eyes twinkling with humour. 'You need to prepare yourself for when Joaquin and his men to come after you. If you have a gun you might stand half a chance.'

'Gee, thanks for the vote of confidence.'

He raises his eyebrows at me. Okay, so he's kind of right. I'm hardly a ninja.

'Just humour me, hmm?' He looks so adorable with his puppy dog eyes. His mother must have taught him that.

'Fine,' I sigh, grabbing my clothes and storming moodily into the bathroom.

We pull up at a large industrial looking building half an hour later. I look up at the old and battered sign. *Bevell's Shooting Range.* I can't believe he thinks this is a good idea. I absolutely hate guns.

Just the thought of them breaks me out in hives. Let alone actually holding one and trying to shoot from it.

I sigh heavily. 'If you're going to insist I do this, let's get it over with.' I open the cab door, slam it behind me, and walk hurriedly to the door.

He follows after me and opens the door of the centre. He greets the built guy behind the counter, flashes his badge and just like that we're in. Then he grabs my hand, catching me completely off guard.

'Aren't you supposed to pay or something?'

'Nah,' he smiles. 'Just a flash of the badge normally gets me in.'

How irresponsible.

I let him drag me along a dark green corridor. I love the feeling of his warm hand on mine far too much. He leads me into a narrow room, lined with people shooting at a piece of paper with a man drawn on it. The cracking sound of shots being fired makes me jump.

Harry strokes my arm with his thumb, as if to reassure me, as he leads me to an empty booth. He reaches for some neon headphones, breaking our contact. Not having him hold my hand anymore makes me ridiculously sad. I really need to get a grip. He places the headphones around my neck, his face so close I can smell his minty breath.

'I'm just going to teach you how to shoot. This is no big deal.'

I nod, frozen in fear.

'Breathe,' he reminds me with a smile.

He produces a gun and shows me how to remove the safety. Then the earphones are placed over my ears. Suddenly all of the noise dulls down. Well, that's a hell of a lot more peaceful.

Harry instructs for me to hold the gun out straight in front of me. I feel him move behind me, his crotch against my arse. He places his hands on my hips, as if to hold me in place. Its ridiculous how turned on I am.

I try to focus on the piece of paper which feels like miles away from me. I'd be grateful if I could just hit the paper at all.

Harry lifts one earphone and shouts, 'When you're ready, shoot.'

I take a deep breath. Concentrate, Sadie. I try to imagine what I'm doing isn't actually holding a gun. The cold metal presses into my skin, reminding me it's very real. Okay, you can totally do this. I place my hand on the trigger, count to three and then press it in as hard as I can.

My body shoots back into Harry's from the sheer force.

'FUCK!' I shout. I turn back to him to apologise, but he looks so concerned at that very moment that I fall harder than I've ever fallen before.

He loves me. It comes to me like an epiphany. He might not even know it yet, but he totally bloody loves me. I can see it there in those tortured blue eyes.

I quickly turn back around, unsure of how to react. He wraps his arms around my waist and kisses me quickly on my neck. My nerve endings shoot adrenaline through my body. My God, he's so beautiful.

I'm buzzing so much I take a few more shots. It's actually exhilarating. I mean, I'm barely hitting the paper, but it's still fun. Right now I couldn't care less that I'm on the run from a drug lord, strangely enough. I'm right where I want to be.

###

We had a great afternoon. He not only taught me to shoot, but he's given me a bloody gun. Made me promise to carry it with me everywhere I go. For some reason that makes me feel excited and protected. Like I can carry around a bit of Harry with me wherever I go. And powerful. *So* fucking powerful. Not that I actually know when we'll be able to leave this hotel room again.

When we get back we finish eating the kebab he got us on the way home. The whole day has felt like a date, not like we're in hiding from a guy that wants me dead. He goes to the bathroom, giving me a minute to compose myself. He hasn't touched me since the shooting range, but I can't help wanting him to. After everything he's done to me I still can't resist. I mean, look at the sweetness of getting the new sheets so I'd be comfortable.

Hang on a minute. I pick up the duvet set and realise it's a double. Did he even ask if there was a room available with two single beds? Was it his plan to seduce me all along so that he could have a couple nights of sex? Is Joaquin even after me or did he just want to get away for a dirty weekend?

He comes out of the bathroom and leans against the doorframe, mischievousness in his eyes. What a cocky arsehole.

'You didn't ask for another room, did you?' I accuse, throwing the packet at him.

He jumps out of the way before it hits him. Damn reflexes of a cop.

'Whoa!' he laughs. 'What's the problem here?'

I can't help but feel the anger bubbling over. Anger at him for just assuming I'd share a bed with him and anger at myself for wanting him so bad it hurts.

'You! You just assumed I'd want to sleep in the same bed as you!' I'm almost screaming. What is wrong with me?

'So?' he shrugs, his face contorted in disgust at my behaviour. 'We *have* done more than that in the past. I just figured sleeping next to each other wouldn't be a big deal.'

'Well you were wrong.' I pick up a pillow and throw it at him.

He lets it hit him on the shoulder. There's an awkward silence as he just stares at me with a blank face. I'm out of breath from my shouting and he doesn't even seem to have flinched. It pisses me off to no end.

'Did you really just hit me with a pillow?' he asks with a smirk.

I cannot *believe* he just said that. Making fun of me at a moment like this? Can't he see that I'm fuming? Can't he see that I'm upset?

'Fuck you, Harry.' I stomp off to the bathroom and lock the door behind me.

I sit down on the toilet seat and let the tears fall silently down my cheeks. Thank God I'm not full on sobbing. He'd hear me then. This way he never has to know. I can just wallow for a moment without his judging, beautiful face. Prick.

I hear him shuffling about, but after ten minutes or so it goes quiet. I look at my watch. Its ten PM. Could he be in bed already? I look at myself in the mirror. What a bloody mess. Smudged mascara under my eyes and my hair all crazy from dragging my hands through it.

I turn the tap on and attempt to wash my face. I look around for a towel, but then reason that my face would probably be dirtier if I dried it in with one of those towels. I pull my shirt up to dry it instead. There, that'll have to do.

I take one last deep breath before opening the door. The bed looks completely different now that it's been fully made in the cream and brown spotty bedspread. It probably looks all the more attractive because Harry is laying in it. He's on his side facing towards the window and doesn't turn at the sound of the door.

Is he pissed at me? Well good, I'm still pissed at him. I go around to what seems like my side of the bed. Unfortunately it's also the way he's looking. He looks up at me with a serious expression.

'So you decided against sleeping in the bathroom?' he asks sarcastically.

I can't help but smile at his dry humour. 'Ha ha bloody ha,' I snap, biting my tongue so I will stop smiling.

'Just stop being stupid and get changed,' he says with an exasperated sigh.

Get naked in front of him? He *has* to be kidding. I can't even remember if I'm freshly shaved. God, it will be mortifying if I have hairy spider legs.

'I will, if you turn around,' I bark.

He sighs heavily once again. 'Fine,' he huffs, before rolling over to face the other side.

I make quick work of taking off my clothes and putting on my pyjamas. I packed a cami top and fleecy trousers with sheep on them. I obviously wasn't thinking sexy when I was stuffing these in my bag. At least they're long. My legs aren't hairy, but they're not freshly shaved either.

I'm just about to get into bed when he rolls back around. I jump, glad I'm covered. He raises one eyebrow before pulling back the covers. It gives me a flash of him, naked apart from his black boxers. Dear God, he's too beautiful for his own good. I hope I'm not flushed.

I jump in immediately, wanting to cover as much of myself as possible, especially in this draughty room. My nipples could cut ice. I face away from him in an attempt to keep some self-control. The sheets feel so much better against my skin than the threadbare stuff that was on it earlier. It makes me want to thank him, but I'm supposed to be mad at him. I sigh and admit defeat, rolling over to face him. He's already waiting for me, as if he knew.

'So I suppose I should say thank you for the sheets.'

'You're welcome,' he smiles lazily. 'And I want to apologise.'

Apologise? He doesn't strike me as the apologising type.

'About what?' I ask shyly, twiddling with a bit of my hair.

'You know what for.' I avoid his gaze, pretending to be fascinated with my hair. 'For the sheets, but also for the whole kitchen episode. I'm sorry I freaked out.'

Why is he talking about that again? I have crushed it down so much in my mind that I could almost pretend it never happened. Or that it ended with him holding me. You know, whichever.

'Freaked out?' He looked pretty calm to me as he was speedily dressing and running out of there. 'You left me there. Naked. You just ran as if the whole thing had meant nothing to you.' Then I realise how I sound. Some pathetic girl. 'I mean…not that it meant anything to me. It was just sex, but…still. It was mean.'

He takes my hand from around the pillow and holds it in his.

'Believe me when I say I'm sorry. So sorry, but yeah, I was freaked out. It started out as just sex, but halfway through I realised that I didn't want to treat you like I have other women. You deserve better than me. And I've tried to show you that since.'

'So what?' I laugh incredulously. 'You think I deserve better, so you make me feel like shit so I hate you?'

He creases his forehead releasing those adorable wrinkles. 'No, it wasn't like that. It's…it's hard to describe. I mean, we hardly have a normal situation going on here.'

He can say that again.

'You mean because you're trying to put me in prison for something I haven't done?'

'That's questionable,' he smirks. 'But yeah. I should have never done that. I could lose my job for sleeping with a suspect.'

I roll my eyes. I hate when he calls me a suspect. 'Couldn't you lose your job for kidnapping me and keeping me holed up here, too?'

'Yep,' he nods with a chuckle. 'I guess I just worked out that it's worth it.'

I grin. 'It's worth it? You mean…*I'm* worth it?'

He smiles shyly, looking down, a lock of his hair covering his eyes. I instinctively push it back. He looks up, shocked at my contact.

'Is it wrong that I want to do the whole 'L'Oréal, I'm worth it' joke?' I giggle.

'Incredibly.' He grins to let me know he's joking. 'Look, it's been a rough few days. I think we should go to sleep.'

Oh. That's bloody disappointing. It shouldn't be. He's trying to respect me.

'Okay.'

His eyebrows rise. 'You sound disappointed,' he says with amused eyes.

'No…no that's fine. You're right.' A shiver of mischief goes running through me. I hold the power right now. And I love it.

I turn around, but manage to snuggle back into him so that my arse is dangerously close to his crotch. I can almost feel the heat from it.

'Are you teasing me, Sadie?' he asks, amusement in his voice.

'I've no idea what you're talking about,' I say innocently.

'Oh, I think you do. I think having your life in danger makes you horny.'

I turn back to face him with a wide grin. 'Or maybe just being in a bed with you makes me horny.'

I cringe inwardly. I'm so cheesy, but it's like he has some magic fog that he releases around me. It means I can only see his beauty, his raw sexiness and charm. Not the whole reality of our horrible situation.

'Well,' he sighs, stroking my arm with his fingertips, 'luckily for you I'm a very nice man. And I don't like letting women down.'

Chapter 28

Wednesday 21st October

I wake up to soft kisses on my chin. I smile and open my eyes to see the beautiful Harry gazing down at me as if I'm the most precious thing in the world. It makes butterflies dance in my tummy. His stubble is even thicker, his blue eyes creased with first thing in the morning sleepiness. He looks delicious enough to eat.

'Morning,' he grins, kissing me gently on my shoulder. 'I bet I know what you want.'

I gasp, then chuckle. 'Let me wake up first, big boy.'

He laughs and looks down at me like I'm cute. 'I was talking about a cup of tea, you filthy girl.'

'Oh.' I feel myself flush beetroot. Way to come across as an eager slut.

'But don't worry, once we've had the tea and crumpets we'll be doing that.'

I grin. My eyes must look like those of a love sick puppy.

'Only if you feel up to it,' he adds with a wink.

I do actually feel a bit battered and bruised, but only in a good way.

He gets out of bed and I sit up with him, already missing his skin on skin contact.

'You really have crumpets?' I ask, my stomach rumbling loud enough for him to hear.

'Yep,' he smiles, tenderly tucking a strand of hair behind my ear. 'And jam.'

'Wow,' I fake gush. 'You're the best—' I stop myself. Whoa, I almost said boyfriend there.

The nagging feeling of wanting me to ask what this is starts again, but I push it back down under the covers.

'Don't be long,' I try to purr seductively.

'I won't.' He leans over and pecks a chaste kiss on my lips before getting the bits out of the carrier bag and walking to the toaster and kettle in the far corner of the room.

I flop myself back down on the bed and push my face into the soft cotton pillow. It smells woody and citrusy; just like him. I smile at the thought. God, I've got it bad. I'd love nothing more than to spend my weekends with him eating jam on crumpets and having lazy afternoons filled with sex, but sadly that's not meant to be.

I root my head further into the pillow, trying to block out the negative thoughts when I notice a lump. I search underneath it with my hands and something drops from it onto the floor.

'Do you want sugar in your tea?' he shouts over.

I look down and see that it's a diary. I pick it up and feel the soft leather casing. He writes a diary? He doesn't seem the type.

'Err…yes, one please,' I shout back, my heart racing.

I see Harry's writing sprawled all over it. An insight into Harry's mind. I already know I'm going to read it. There's no point in wasting time looking at the morality of it. I already know I'm wrong and going to hell.

I flick open a random page and start reading.

I can't believe it's her. The girl I keep spilling drinks on. She's involved in drugs. She just doesn't seem the type.

At first I was disappointed that this meant I'd never be able to date her. It's against the rules to date a suspect, plus it's just a plain bad idea. But then I thought…what if I pretended to date her? She's bound to loosen up around me the more time I spend with her and eventually I'll earn her trust. She'll confide in me and I'll be able to bring her new drug ring down. It's bound to be enough to impress the boss. I've been asking for a promotion for months now.

I'll finally be able to progress in my career and hey, I might get a bit of action out of it too. Win, win. I just have to make sure boss man doesn't find out about my tactics.

I calmly place it down on the bed, my heart draining of all the love I have for this man. This monster. The guy I let in, at his request, who

I started to care for. The man I've felt bad about lying to. Risking my girlfriends' freedom with every minute I spent with him.

Anger takes place, red and fiery burning through my chest. How could I have been so stupid? Was every word he spoke to me a lie?

He walks back over carrying two cups of steaming tea. His happy face drops when he notices his diary.

'Shit,' he mutters under his breath, all colour having left his face.

'Fuck you, Harry,' I say in a low, controlled voice. I sound far calmer than I feel.

I stand up, walk over to him and throw the teas all over him.

He winces as it burns him, probably causing third degree burns. I couldn't care less. He tries to pull his t-shirt away to relieve some of the pain which is blatantly obvious on his face.

'Now *I'm* the one throwing drinks at *you*.'

I grab my clothes, hastily putting them on without bothering with underwear. He doesn't attempt to move or talk at all, the spineless bastard. I take my bag from the sofa and stumble towards the door, leaving behind my heart and hope.

I let myself into the flat and drop my keys on the side table. I sigh loudly, an almighty feeling of complete and utter sadness filling me from my head to the pit of my stomach. He doesn't want me. I was just a game to him. Something to advance his career. My throat burns with the humiliation.

He didn't give a shit about sending me to prison, as long as he was okay. How could he be so heartless? How could he be the same man that's looked after me when I've been at my worst?

'Sades? Is that you?' Samuel calls from the sitting room. It feels so good and reassuring to hear his voice.

'Yeah.' I don't even recognise my own voice. I sound so flat, so deflated.

I walk into the sitting room, ready to throw myself on the sofa, when I see that Samuel is on the floor picking up broken glass. I look around to take in the whole room, realising that the place is trashed. The dining table is knocked over and the chairs strewn around. The TV's smashed in and the bookcase is turned over, books scattered everywhere.

'Jesus, what happened?' I blurt out. I pick up my favourite book and see that the pages have been ripped out. Jesus. This was no accident.

He looks me over, relief clear on his face. 'I came home from my shift at two am and found it like this. Then I saw that you were gone. I've gone out of my fucking mind!' he shouts, distressed.

I sigh heavily, exhaustion plaguing my body.

'I'm sorry. It's a long story.' I take out my phone so I can look away from him and see twenty two missed calls from him. Whoops. 'So have you been cleaning since two am?' It really doesn't look like it's been touched at all.

'Well...no,' he admits looking sheepish. 'I was just so fucking tired. I searched the place to make sure no one was still in here, rang you about a million times and then...well, I just collapsed into bed.'

I chuckle, I can't help it. He glares back at me.

'This is not a funny situation, Sadie! We've been broken into! And from what I can see nothing's actually been taken. It's just been trashed. Who on earth would do this?'

It's so obvious to me that it's one of Joaquin's men, but to Samuel this is clearly a mystery. How the hell am I going to explain this without confessing everything?

'I don't know,' I say as vaguely as I can. 'Probably just kids or something.' I grab the post and look down at it, away from his inquisitive stare.

'Sadie, cut the bullshit. I know something's going on. You've been acting shifty for months now. What the hell have you got yourself involved in?'

I look at him, my best friend. The guy I trust with my life. The guy I'm lying to. Right now Harry the arsehole knows more about me than him. I've really been thinking with my lady parts.

'I can't tell you,' I admit on a sigh.

He glares accusingly at me. 'Can't tell me what?'

'I mean it, Samuel,' I warn. 'The less you know the better. I don't want you to be an accessory to this.'

'Accessory?' He lowers his voice to a whisper, his eyebrows narrowed. 'Sadie, are we talking about illegal shit here?'

I consider my options. I could lie, *again*. Insult his intelligence with some crap made up on the spot story. Or I could tell him the truth, even though I know he's going to be upset and disappointed.

I nod, resigned. He blows out a breath slowly.

'Shit,' he nods. 'Okay, you have to tell me *everything*.'

It takes almost half an hour to fill him in. We clean up the flat while we talk and I'm glad for the distraction. It means I don't have to look him in the eye while I'm confessing these horrible secrets.

'And you did all this just because you wanted to keep up the mortgage repayments?'

I nod. 'It's not your fault, Samuel, and I didn't want us losing the flat because I can't find a job.'

He scratches his head. 'But you know who I work for. If this ever came out I could be sacked. Then where would that leave us? Back on the streets?'

I feel tears brewing and my chest tightening. 'Don't you see, Samuel? That's why I've done all of this.' A sob escapes my lips. 'I would do anything not to end up there again. We've come too far for us to go back to it. I can't. I won't,' I say, determined.

'But by selling drugs?' he says in disbelief. It's hard not to notice the disgust in his eyes. 'You despised your mother for being involved with them.'

I can't believe he brought her up. He's the only person in the world that knows everything about her. He knows how much comparing the two of us would hurt me.

'Don't you dare compare me to her!' I scream, immediately losing it.

'Okay, chill,' he says, his palms held up to me. 'We need to sort this out. You need to get out of this. Leave the girls to it if they won't stop. We'll find you something.'

'Yeah, right.' I smile sadly. 'I've literally applied for every job in London.'

I start opening the post. Bills, bills, bills...oh wait.

Dear Miss Taylor,

We're pleased to offer you the position of Advertising Technician. Please contact us on the below number to arrange a start date.

Yours sincerely,

Beef in My Bun Ltd

'Oh my God! Oh my God!' I shriek, jumping up and down on the spot. 'I have a job! I finally have a job!'

Someone up there must be working to get my life back on track.

'No way!' Samuel cheers, joining me in jumping up and down. 'See, I told you things are starting to look up.'

Maybe he's right. Oh, but it's quite far away.

'It's a hell of a commute though.'

He raises his eyebrow at me, snatching the letter from my hands. 'Don't you know that Kez lives nearby? I'm starting to think I'll be safer if you're not here.'

'But Ivy...'

'I'll sort Ivy out.'

I nod, resigned. Yet as I place the last strewn book onto the shelf I can't stop grinning. Maybe this is where my life changes. My very own next chapter.

# # #

I drive to Mags' house later that day determined to lay down the law. I can't be involved in this anymore and neither should they. Apparently Steph has moved in here since her flat was broken into. It's like Mags is running a halfway house.

I'm met with an angry looking Lexi at the door, her features twisted with contempt.

'Hi,' I attempt with a smile, trying to appear friendly.

'Hi yourself,' she snaps, giving me an evil eye. 'Finally decided to grace us with your presence, did you?' she smirks sarcastically.

I roll my eyes. 'Enough of the third degree, Lexi.'

I push past her into the living room to find Mags and Steph drinking tea while Ruby plays on the floor on a play matt. Steph jumps up to hug me and Mags smiles before going into the kitchen. I assume she's putting the kettle on again.

'How are you?' Steph gushes, checking me over. 'We were so worried about you.'

'I wasn't,' Lexi growls. 'I knew she was in bed with the detective.'

My cheeks burn and I know they'll be turning pink. How can she know that? Am I that much of an obvious slut?

'It doesn't take a rocket scientist,' she says, answering my unspoken question. 'You were with him when Steph called you. He helped us out even though it's breaking the law not to call it in. It's obvious you're shagging him.'

For once could she not be the kind, supportive friend?

'So what if I was?' I snap. How the hell can she be so high and mighty anyway? This is the same girl currently dating a drug dealer out to get us.

'So you're risking all of our lives here,' she exclaims, throwing her hands in the air dramatically.

'Pot calling kettle!' I shriek.

'Hey! Gabriel's been up front about everything. For all you know your detective could just be trying to get information.'

Jeez, where was she a few weeks ago? I needed someone to beat away my inner slut.

'Well...he was,' I admit sheepishly. I don't have the energy to lie anymore. 'I just found out this morning that he's a total arsehole.'

'I could have told you that! He's the police. They breed them like that.'

'That's not fair,' Steph chimes in, raising her voice. It shocks me. 'Are you okay, Sadie? Did he hurt you?' She looks so concerned. Just her interest is enough for me to start choking on tears.

'N...no, not...physically,' I stammer, desperately trying to push down my feelings.

'But emotionally?' she asks, her eyes sad and sympathetic. I keep forgetting she's been through hell and back with Dorian. I mean, here I am complaining and Steph was abandoned with a bloody baby.

'I'm fine,' I say, choking on my words. The snot's coming now. I can feel my nose filling up.

The truth is that I feel broken. Truly broken beyond repair. That's the only way to describe it. And the fact that it's my own fault burns.

Mags walks in with a cuppa for me. She really is an earth bound angel.

'Oh, love, what's wrong?' she asks, tucking a bit of my hair behind my ear. Even that reminds me of him.

I take it from her and force a smile, trying to appear bright. 'Nothing.' I decide to swiftly change the subject. 'I actually came here to tell you guys that we need to completely shut down Project Unicorn.'

'I agree,' Steph nods. 'It's not safe anymore.'

'No way!' Lexi shouts. 'Just when we're starting to make some real money. I don't think so.'

'Lexi, money's no good if you're dead!' I remind her.

She looks towards Mags. I look between both of them. What are they up to?

'Myself and Lexi have been talking,' Mags starts, twirling her necklace in her hands, 'and we think we can come up with some deal for Joaquin. We have Gabriel willing to help us, after all.'

Is she serious? We tried to call a truce before and look where that got us.

'Mags, you have to be mad. This isn't a guy to reason with.'

'It's not like we have any other choice,' Lexi snaps. She turns to Steph, 'Have you had any job offers in the meantime?'

'Well...no,' she admits, looking over guiltily at Ruby.

Lexi turns back to me, her face suspicious. I hate how she's looking at me right now, prying into my thoughts.

'What?' I ask defensively.

'You've had a job offer,' she nods, as if she can read my mind.

'What?'

How the hell does she know this? Has she been going through my mail or something?

'I can see it on your face. You look all happy and snobby again. Just because *you've* got a job offer doesn't mean *we* should give up the money.'

'Your lives are in danger you idiot!' I bark. 'How much clearer can I be about this?'

'Our lives are in danger every single day,' she says, shrugging and rolling her eyes. 'Each day is a day closer to death. I could get hit by a truck tomorrow, my body splattered all over the M25.'

'Why would you be walking on the M25?' Steph asks, clearly confused.

'It's a fucking analogy, Steph!' she barks.

I need to try and reason with her. She can't be this blind to the danger.

'Be honest with yourself, Lexi. You need to ask yourself if what you're doing today is getting you closer to where you want to be tomorrow.'

'It is. Rich,' she deadpans.

She's so bloody infuriating.

I glare at her. 'I'm serious, Lexi. Money means nothing if you're six feet under.'

'Oh, don't go off on your high and mighty with me. We're not all management material. I've got no good grades to fall back on. This could be it for me.'

Is she serious? Then I remember that she has no idea of my background. No idea of what I've managed to achieve from nothing,

'Lexi, you're nineteen. Don't be ridiculous.'

'You're the ridiculous one,' she snarls. 'And if you don't like what we're doing then you know where the door is.' She looks at it.

I look back to Steph and Mags for encouragement, but they look down at the floor. Hurt radiates through my chest. I can't believe they're dissing me like this. After everything I've done for them. The ungrateful fuckers.

'Fine, I'll go,' I snap, my voice wobbly with emotion. 'But don't come crying to me when it all blows up in your face.'

Chapter 29

<u>Wednesday 28th October</u>

As I walk up and down the high street I wonder what I may have done in a previous life to deserve this. Maybe poisoned Mother Theresa? Killed some famous king or something? Turns out that when I started I quickly learned that Marketing Technician actually meant wearing a sandwich board written with *Put Your Beef in my Bun* up and down the high street.

Yeah, I could have walked away and told them to stick the job, but I'd already quit the drugs. Lexi would revel in telling me to get lost, and I don't do grovelling. I'm too proud. Plus at least this way I'm making honest money. But…if I get one more arsehole coming up to me and telling me he's got some beef in his trousers and that I look like the perfect kind of bread for him to put it in, God help me.

Plus at least this way I'm away from Samuel, hopefully keeping him safe. I've moved in temporarily with my old foster friend Kez, who I'm pretty sure is putting vodka over her coco pops.

Yet, when I see Sally Spencer walking down the street towards me I wish to *God* I'd done some grovelling. Sally fucking Spencer. She was head bitch at one of the schools I attended. She made sure to make my life hell. You see, being the newbie, I was always a walking victim. Add to that my shitty hand me down clothes and not having a good support system behind me and you've got one self-conscious teenager. The minute I started at Mellmont High she made it her mission to humiliate me in front of everyone.

Looking back now I can see that she was only jealous of all of the attention I was getting. Everyone was being really nice to me and I even got invited to a pool party at some rich kid's house. I went along, eager to make new friends, but she had other ideas. Her and her friends cornered me in the swimming pool, and although I tried to kick and scream, they still managed to drag my swimming costume off me.

I was left naked in the pool with everyone laughing, pointing and jeering at me. I've never felt humiliation like that since.

No one came to save me. I was left with no choice but to get out of the pool stark naked and run into the house. The guys mum was apologetic and gave me my clothes to change into, but the damage was already done. I had to face everyone on Monday morning knowing they'd seen me as naked as the day I was born. And my boobs were *completely* non-existent back then. They almost went *in* instead of out. God, just thinking about it makes me shudder with shame.

My foster parents heard a convoluted version of the events and somehow I ended up as the trouble making slut. Shortly after that they moved me to another house in another area. The one with the creepy step brother. All because of that bitch Sally Spencer. And now she's walking towards me and I'm wearing a sandwich board. I need to hide.

I jump behind a tree, but it's hard to hide when you're wearing a sandwich board. I end up bumping into someone.

'Hey, watch it,' they shout, pushing me backwards.

I fall back so hard I end up completely flat on my back. Ah, my bloody back! It aches like a mother fucker. Why is it when you reach twenty eight you suddenly have a fragile back?

I open my eyes to find Sally Spencer looking over me. Oh fuck a duck.

'Oh my goodness, are you okay?' she asks, offering me her hand.

That's weird. I was expecting her to just laugh in my face. She must not recognise me, thank God.

'I'm okay,' I try to say as she helps me up. I shrug her off, eager to escape before she recognises me.

'Wait a minute...' she looks into my face questionably, as if trying to put a puzzle together in her mind.

Too late.

'Sadie? Sadie Taylor? Is that you?'

She remembers my whole name? What am I saying? I must have been the talk of the school for years.

I feel my face turn crimson. This is the worst. I should want to punch her, but all I feel is the same humiliation like it's happening all over again.

'Do I know you?' I ask, trying to act nonchalant. Well, as nonchalant as I can while wearing a sandwich board.

'Yes,' she smiles sadly. 'Well, you did. It's me, Sally Spencer. We went to high school together. Well, only for a short while.'

'Yes, I remember,' I roar, my chest tight with hurt. 'All too easily.'

At least she looks a bit embarrassed, her cheeks reddening up.

'And what are you doing now?' She stands back to read my board. 'Oh...in...promotions? That's cool.'

I'm dying inside. Actually dying. I bet she has some really cool job, like a pilot or something.

'Only at the moment. I'm...well, I'm between jobs right now.' I stand strong, refusing to let her know how humiliated I am.

'Oh, Sadie,' she looks like she might tear up. 'I'm so sorry for what I did to you back then.'

Sorry...what? She's apologising? Well I didn't see this coming.

'Huh?' I blurt out, sharing that I can't even speak as well as her.

'For that whole swimming thing. When I look back I'm just horrified at what I did to you. I've done so many things I'm not proud of.'

Have I fallen into an alternative universe? Is this really happening? She's taking responsibility for what she did?

'Why did you do it?' A question I've wanted to know the real answer to for years.

She looks down to the floor, ashamed. 'I was jealous of you. You turned up and everyone instantly loved you and wanted to get to know the exciting new girl with the huge eyes. I was a different person back then. But I had no idea it would lead to you getting sent to another foster home.'

'Well it did,' I snap, fury building behind my lungs.

How can I feel sympathy towards this girl? She ruined my life. I hate her.

'And that foster home had a creepy brother that I had to run away from. Do you know I lived on the street rather than risk being housed back with him?'

It suddenly occurs to me that I must blame her for a lot. Who knew I had this kind of resentment locked inside of me?

She smiles apologetically. 'I don't expect you to forgive me, but I just want you to know that now I've found Jesus.'

What the frig? Did she just say Jesus?

She smiles back at me, practically beaming. 'That's right. I know you might think it laughable, but it's helped me turn my life around.'

'That's great,' I say sarcastically.

I really hope she doesn't start preaching to me. I don't have the patience for that right now. I might end up having to beat her with her own bible. It would be no more than she deserved.

'Its fine if you don't get it, but I just wanted to say that I'm sorry, and I'm sorry if it ever affected your self-esteem.'

Damn, this bitch is so reasonable. It's seriously pissing me off.

'No, what's affecting my self-esteem right now is having to wear this sandwich board,' I admit with a sigh.

There's no point ignoring my humiliation.

'Why do you do it then?' she asks, seeming completely baffled.

Spoiled little princess. She clearly has no idea about needing money. Even back then she was from a well-respected, loaded family.

'I need the money,' I snarl. 'You probably wouldn't understand.'

She smiles sadly. 'I know you think I'm some spoiled brat, but you have to follow your heart. If this isn't where you want to be right now you should change it. You need to ask yourself if what you're doing today is bringing you closer to what you want to be doing tomorrow.'

Wow. My own words repeated back to me. And she's right. I don't want to be doing this today, let alone tomorrow. I'm a bloody hypocrite. Where I want to be is with the girls. Not selling drugs, but I miss them terribly. Yeah, I know that what we were doing was wrong, but the time I spent with those women was the best of my life. I now realise it's why I was so upset about being made redundant. Not the job, but the people.

What the hell am I doing? Living while looking over my shoulder. It's not how I want to live my life. Making myself look like an absolute plonker in public just so I don't have to admit I was wrong... I need to help my girls. God knows what mess they've been getting themselves into while I've been away. They're probably already in prison.

'You know what, Sally, I actually think you're right,' I admit.

'Of course I am,' she smiles gleefully. 'Now how about we say a prayer together?'

'Err...I think I'll pass this time.'

Chapter 30

Thursday 29th October

As I put the keys in the door the next morning I can't help but feel relieved. I've definitely made the right decision.

'Samuel?' I call, unsure if he's working or not.

'In here,' he calls from the kitchen.

Perfect, he can make me a cuppa. I sit down at the table and let myself start to relax.

'So how have things been?' I ask, while the kettle boils.

'Oh, you know.' He busies himself with opening and shutting cupboards, as if he doesn't know where we keep the tea bags.

'No more sign of Joaquin causing trouble?'

'Nope.' He pours the tea and milk into the mugs and brings it over.

'How's Ivy been?'

His face falls, as if he was waiting for me to ask him this. Shit, what the hell happened?

'Tell me Samuel,' I warn in a stern voice.

'She...I...it wasn't my fault.'

'What the fuck happened? Tell me or I'll just go down and ask her myself.'

'You can't. She's not there.'

A chill spreads down my spine. Is he saying what I think he's saying?

'She's...dead?'

'No! Jesus, not dead. But,' he sighs heavily, resigned to having to tell me. 'Well, the doctor turned up completely unannounced to check on her. And I was at work. By the time I got back he had her in an ambulance. Apparently she had fallen.'

'Oh my God.' This is all my fault for leaving her. 'So, she's still in hospital?'

'No. He said that she was a danger to herself. He's had her put into a care home for dementia patients.'

My stomach falls. She's in a care home? What the hell?

'I tried, Sadie. I honestly did, but the doc was adamant. Plus I've been there, got her settled. It's actually a really lovely place. All of the staff have been trained up on dementia so they know completely how to treat her without her getting distressed. I hate to say it, but I think it's the best place for her.'

'With strangers though, Samuel? Strangers looking after her. It just doesn't feel right.'

He reaches forward and takes my hand. 'Sades, we're almost strangers to her. She's getting bad quickly. She seems really happy there.'

I sigh, attempting to let out all of my self-loathing. This is all my fault. If I'd have been here I could have helped her. But I suppose I was struggling with looking after her. It just seems so sad to think that she's in one of those places. Could she really be happy there?

'We'll go this afternoon,' he insists with a reassuring smile. 'So you can see for yourself how much she loves it there.'

'Okay.'

It turned out to be a lovely care home. Some old building converted, but still has bags of character. Samuel was right, she was happy. I actually felt bad for fighting it for so long. The staff is lovely, she gets three hot meals a day, and she's with other residents who also like talking about the war.

I knock on Mags' door the next morning, nerves tingling down my spine. Now that Ivy's being looked after I need to check that my girls are okay. I mean, what if they laugh in my face? Or more specifically, what if Lexi laughs in my face? I know that Steph and Mags wouldn't be that cruel. But I know she would.

I hear some shuffling around inside before someone speaks.

'Who is it?' someone shouts aggressively. It sounds like Lexi, but her voice doesn't carry its normal snarky tone.

'Um...it's me.' I clear my throat, trying to summon some strength. 'It's Sadie.'

The door swings open. 'I know your voice, idiot,' she says rolling her eyes. She grabs my arm while looking around, on edge. 'Get in.' She throws me inside and slams the door behind me, double locking it.

'Who is it?' a scared Steph asks, peering around from the kitchen holding a giant kitchen knife. Jesus, what's happening here? She spots me and visibly relaxes, her shoulders drooping back to normal. 'Oh, Sadie!' She starts running towards me with her arms spread wide. 'Thank God it's you!'

'Put down the knife first,' I shriek.

What the hell has her so spooked? She places it on the table and squeezes me so tight I worry I'll never get oxygen into my lungs again. When she pulls back Mags takes me in her arms and hugs me too. Well this is going different then how I expected.

'What's going on?' I ask, looking from face to face. They look at each other guiltily.

'Nothing,' Lexi shrugs, crossing her arms across her chest. 'We're fine.'

Steph bursts into tears, a blotchy rash appearing on her neck. Mags pulls her into her chest, making sweet shushing noises.

'Yeah,' I roll my eyes. 'It *really* looks like it.'

'Oh, Sadie,' Mags says with a weak smile, 'I'm so glad you're back.'

'Why? What's happened? I take it you've not taken my advice and stopped?'

Steph nods before bursting into more angry sobs. It's like a dam has broken.

'Joaquin?' I ask.

'He's gone mad now,' Mags explains. 'That detective boyfriend of yours came around to warn us that our lives are in danger.'

He still tried to warn them? To save them even when he knew I hated him? Wow.

'He's not my boyfriend.' I haven't even heard from him since I moved away.

'He could just be trying to scare us,' Lexi interjects sharply. 'Only...' She sighs.

'Only what?' I search from face to face.

Lexi looks at the floor, tracing her foot along it. 'Only someone tried to run me off the road yesterday.'

What?

'Jesus! And you think that's a bloody coincidence, do you? Joaquin has men all over the place! You'd be lucky if this house isn't set alight while you sleep!'

Mags' chin wobbles. Okay, so maybe screaming isn't helping anyone. I need to think clearly. Try to sort this mess out. The first thing I need to worry about is Ruby.

'Right, Steph, first things first. Where is Ruby?'

'She's with my mum in Cornwall. It was all getting too scary. I couldn't risk her being hurt.'

Thank God. The last thing we need is Ruby getting harmed.

I turn to Lexi. 'When was the last time you saw Gabriel?'

She attempts to look confused. I'm no dummy. She's obviously still seeing him. That's if he hasn't tried to kill her himself.

'Gabriel? I haven't seen him since—'

'Cut the bullshit,' I snap, glaring at her. 'We don't have time for this. What did he say?'

She sighs and rolls her eyes. 'Okay, he told me to get out of the country.'

Shit. This really is as bad as I thought.

'You're still seeing him?' Steph shrieks in disbelief, breaking away from Mags' arms. 'Are you bloody insane?'

She looks down to the floor. 'I like him, okay? If it were any other situation we'd be together. It's just because of bloody Joaquin.'

'Spare me the whole Romeo and Juliet crap,' I snap, knowing full well how she feels. Well, how I *felt* before I found out Harry is an evil dickhead. 'I don't have time for it. The main thing is that he's worried. He told you to run, so why are you still here?'

She looks to Mags.

Mags' face contorts in confusion. 'No,' she whispers in disbelief. 'You didn't stay because of me?'

'Mags, your last chemo session is next week. You need to have it. We can't go leaving the country right now.'

'*I* can't,' she corrects her sternly, 'but *you* can. I'm a grown woman, Alexis. I can look after myself.'

'No you can't!' Lexi snaps. 'You pretend you can, but I need to look after you until this whole thing is over. All you do is give and give to everyone else, but you need someone to look after you.'

Ah, who knew, Lexi, the team player.

'So what?' I question. 'You're all just waiting here like sitting ducks?'

They look at each other with clueless faces. Jesus, thank God I'm back. These idiots are unbelievable.

'Okay,' I announce confidently, 'I don't know what we're going to do yet, but we're coming up with an action plan.'

'You and your bloody action plans,' Steph smiles through a teary sniff. 'I've never been so glad to hear you planning one.'

'There is just one other thing,' Mags says, pulling me to one side.

Oh God, what is it? Has her cancer turned more aggressive? I pray to God she's okay.

'Come with me.'

I follow her into the kitchen and watch as she goes rummaging in her draw. She smiles kindly before placing down Harry's diary onto the table.

'Harry dropped this off for you the other day.'

Is he trying to screw me up?

'Why the hell would he have done that?'

'He said there's a note in the front.' I pick it up and trace my fingers over the leather. 'Why don't you go up to my room to read it, hmm?'

I nod my head, unable to speak. I can already feel the tears sitting in my throat, getting ready to release. I run up to her bedroom and get comfy on her double bed. It's so cosy in here, it actually smells like Mags. Flowery and calming.

I open the diary and a small handwritten note falls out.

Sadie,

I'm so sorry for what you think of me at the moment. The truth is that I was that arsehole, but if you read my whole diary you'll see how my feelings for you have changed. I'm still not even sure what it is, but if you read this you might have a better idea that I'd rather die than hurt you.

Harry

I read his diary and all of its pathetic drivel. Yeah, his feelings for me have changed and I'm pretty sure I'm in love with him, but it doesn't change anything. He still set out to deceive me. How could I ever trust him again? Without trust what does a relationship last on? Besides, it's not like me finding out is the only thing stopping us from being together. We're from completely different worlds and I couldn't bear to put his career in jeopardy because he's associated with a criminal.

I did however text him and ask if Joaquin had a warehouse. He tried to call me immediately, but I ignored it. I had to. If I heard his voice I'd probably break and I really don't have time to concentrate on him right now. My girls are in danger. He finally texts back with an address.

So two hours later we've got it all planned out. I've drank about twelve coffees from Mags' super-duper coffee machine and the buzz has kept my mind whirling with ideas. We need to surprise them, catch them unaware.

So, that evening we're waiting outside Joaquin's drug warehouse. It's an old brick building in an area which looks completely abandoned. Several other warehouses are scattered around, all seemingly deserted. I'm shocked that he'd have anything that wasn't brand spanking new. But I suppose this is less conspicuous.

We've watched people come and go, but no Joaquin yet. We asked him to meet us here. Well, we sent a text message. We were too afraid to speak to him.

Finally a black BMW X5 pulls in and a crowd of men in black suits crowd Joaquin as he walks into the warehouse.

'Okay,' I smile, turning to Lexi, and attempting to appear confident. 'It's show time.'

She takes a deep breath. I've never actually seen her so scared. I rub her back reassuringly.

'Don't worry, Lex, we've got this,' I say as reassuringly as I can.

The truth is I have no idea. They could shoot us the minute we walk in for all I know. I'm just hoping that by having Lexi with me it will delay Gabriel from shooting us in the head *immediately*. But I mean, he could be playing Lexi this whole time, only telling her what he wants to. Just like someone else, who will remain nameless. We really have no idea.

'You're right,' she says, straightening up, a new steely determination in her eyes. 'We've got this. Come on.'

We walk with trembling legs to the old wooden door and let ourselves in, it creaking loudly. *Way to sneak in.* We walk through the small porch like area and into the main warehouse. It's more modern in here at least. Heater lamps hang from the high arched ceilings onto rows and rows of marijuana plants.

I don't have time to take much in as we're immediately greeted by a wall of men, Joaquin and Gabriel at the centre. My insides clench, my stomach lurching violently. I go to open my mouth, but guns are suddenly pointed at us from all directions.

Shit. They *are* going to kill us straight away.

I grab Lexi and throw her in front of me.

'Don't kill me,' I shriek like a baby. 'Kill her.'

Wow, who knew I'd sacrifice my friend? The prospect of death does funny things to you. Turns out I'm a total coward.

I hear the safety being removed from their guns. This is it. I'm going to die. And I never saw the last episode of Lost.

'Stop!' Gabriel shouts, his voice booming around the warehouse with authority.

I look around Lexi to see him standing in front of both of us.

'Not her.' He grabs Lexi roughly and pulls her to one side. The other men look on, completely befuddled.

He turns back to her, exasperation all over his face. 'I thought I told you to get going. Why the fuck are you still here?' he shouts angrily.

'I couldn't leave my friends,' she says sadly. She looks over to me. 'Please don't hurt, Sadie. We have a proposition for you.'

'Enough!' Joaquin snaps loudly, silencing the room. 'Enough with the propositions. We've warned you repeatedly. There are no second chances.'

'But if you'd just listen to my idea,' I try, my hands trembling as I plead with them.

His icy stare stops me. Shit. He's really not going to hear me out. Thank God I have a plan B.

'Or we could just set your warehouse on fire,' I say as calmly as I can.

There's an eerie silence where everyone looks to Joaquin. This is it. His reaction will tell us a lot. He finally erupts into loud laughter, rocking back and forth on his heels. 'You threaten me? *You are threatening me?*'

I hold his stare, desperately trying not to blink. 'It's not a threat. It's a promise.'

At just that minute the faint sound of shuffling comes from the back of the warehouse. Standing where we planned are Steph and Mags holding a lit match in each hand, while their other one pours out petrol from containers. Thank God we found that back entrance.

Joaquin's mouth drops open in complete and utter shock. He quickly recovers and points to his men.

'What makes you think I wouldn't shoot them first?' He smirks.

I smirk back just as confidently, when inside I'm a quivering wreck.

'I think you're mistaking us for women with something to lose. Without this we have no home, no money, and no life. We'd move heaven and earth to ruin it for you.' I smile cruelly to try and show I'm not bricking it in my knickers. Which I am.

'Shoot them,' Joaquin says, clicking his fingers at his men.

Shit!

I look towards them as the men focus their guns. It's as if time slows down. I try to scream to warn them, but gun shots are already being sounded. Thank God we didn't use the real Steph and Mags. My friends Alana and Eric, the very talented street performers, leap across the back of the warehouse, somersaulting and twisting their bodies in the air. The men keep firing, the noise deafening, but with them jumping every which way it seems impossible for them to be hit. Thank God. I really didn't need their deaths on my hands.

I grab Lexi and try to run, but Gabriel pulls her back towards him.

'I can't let you both go,' he shouts over the mayhem. 'Joaquin would kill me.'

Lexi looks back at him, completely devastated. 'But...But I thought you loved me?' she says, her voice small.

'I do, babe,' he says sadly, the gun fire dying down. 'But I have to do what's right.'

'For who?' she screams. 'You fucking arsehole!'

Within seconds she's bitch slapped him so hard I swear I actually felt it. He's dazed for a second which is long enough for us to run. But of course, Lexi being Lexi, she has other ideas. She flings herself onto his back like a chimpanzee and starts strangling him. Shit!

I look around me to try and access any help. Everyone is reloading guns and shooting at Alana and Eric when suddenly orange flames dance off the floor towards us. Shit! Someone lit the match. The flames shoot down, following the trail of spilt petrol.

'Fire!' someone shouts.

Duh!

A loud bang almost breaks my ear drums and carries me off my feet. I'm flipped in the air and land on my front. Shit. What the hell just happened?

I look up to see that something exploded and the small fire is now an inferno. Half of the ceiling has fallen down, and Joaquin's men are kicking me out of the way so they can get out. Well, that escalated quickly. I push myself up with my hands, wincing when glass cuts into them. I look around for Lexi. Where the hell is she? Could she have left without me? Maybe she's outside.

I stand up, wincing when my ankle gives way. I must have twisted it somehow. I start to walk out, when the slightest bit of pink hair grabs my attention. Debris is in my way. I run towards her as fast as I can with a bad ankle, throwing the debris away, and using all of the raw strength that I had no idea I could possess. I can feel the glass in my hands cutting deeper, but I ignore it, gritting my teeth against the pain.

When enough is removed I see that her and Gabriel are both unconscious, with him passed out on top of her. Crap. He's going to be a hard guy to move.

I jump on his chest, slapping his face repeatedly. Ouch, my hands sting.

'Gabriel! Gabriel! Wake the fuck up. Please!' I scream desperately, the smoke already clogging my lungs.

He starts to stir slightly, frowning his forehead as if in pain, but still doesn't open his eyes.

'Just get off her, you big bastard. You're going to kill her!'

It's enough for his eyes to snap open.

'Thank God! Gabriel, you need to get up! Lexi is underneath you and this place is going down.' I don't dare look behind me at the devastation. It will freak me out too much. I'm already hanging on by a thread. I can feel the heat on my back like I'm in a sauna. That can't be a good sign.

He tries to move, but struggles. 'I...I can't,' he says confused. 'Wait.' He manages to lean to one side so that I can get to Lexi.

Something else falls from the ceiling and narrowly misses us. I look around at the flames licking against the walls. Lexi's still out cold. I don't have time for pleasantries. This smoke is slowly suffocating me, leaving next to no space in my lungs to breathe. And it's just so unbelievably hot. I slap her as hard as I can across the face.

She wakes up, her face woozy and confused.

'Get the fuck up, Lexi! We need to get out of here!'

If this fire keeps building we'll quickly be goners. That's if I haven't passed out from smoke inhalation.

She slowly rises up to sitting. 'Shit,' she mutters, looking around bewildered. She jumps up quickly and grabs me, dragging me along and weaving around the fires and destruction. It's hard with what I suspect to be a sprained ankle. Anytime I put any weight on it I want to scream in agony. Not that anyone would hear me. The fire roars so loud I can barely think straight enough to keep placing one foot in front of the other.

We're almost at the door when she stops.

'Shit, Gabriel,' she says her eyes wide with panic. 'We have to go back for him.'

I narrow my eyes on her in disbelief. 'Are you fucking crazy?' I point around to the fire spreading wider by the second. I cough, the smoke feeling heavier on my chest.

'I can't leave him there,' she shrieks. She throws off my arm and runs back towards him.

Shit! I can't leave her to try and move him on her own, can I? He's too big for that. She'll end up dying here. Damn you, Lexi! I hobble back with her and try to assess the situation.

She's already with him. Things are still randomly falling from the ceiling. I cough again so roughly I nearly vomit.

'I can't move my legs,' he shouts over the fire. 'I must have fallen funny and they're playing dead or something.'

Shit, he could be paralysed for all we know. I look into Lexi's face and see it right there in the pain that's blatantly showing. She's in love with this guy. She's not leaving him anywhere. Well, that doesn't bode well for me.

'Come on,' I shout at her. 'An arm each.'

We both grab an arm and try to pull. I use all of my strength, but fuck, this guy's built. He must weigh at least fifteen stone. It doesn't help with my ankle, sore hand and lessened lung capacity.

'Again,' I shout. I'm starting to feel light headed and woozy. I shake my head, desperately trying to un-clog it.

The roars of the flames are getting louder by the second. The smoke is compressing on my chest like I've got a double decker bus on top of me. It's hard to even breathe, let alone talk.

We quickly get into a routine of counting to three and then pulling with all of our might, but it's still only getting us so far. I collapse over in a coughing fit. We're going to die in this warehouse.

'Sadie!' someone shouts.

I look up to see Harry running towards me. What the hell is he doing here?

'Help us,' I shout back, having no time for chit chat. Tears start falling down my cheeks. This is it for me. I just know it.

He takes in Gabriel and immediately helps to tug him. Within seconds we almost have him completely out of the door. Thank God, this nightmare is nearly over. The overwhelming urge to get to fresh air is so strong I'm tempted to just dump them all and run.

Only then I hear it. A whimpered, 'Help!'

I look around completely puzzled. Maybe I have a concussion. It's possible.

'Help! Somebody help me!'

There it is again.

'Wait! I can hear someone.'

I collapse over in another coughing fit. I decide to crawl and look for them. I'm sure I heard something about smoke rising. Or is that heat? I look around the bright flames and find Joaquin with his leg trapped underneath some timber. The fire is creeping closer towards him. Crap, he'll slowly burn to death if left like that. Hell, *I* might burn to death if I waste my time trying to help him.

He may not be worth it, he may have just tried to kill me and my friends, but I cannot watch another human being slowly burn to death in front of me when I know I could have done something. It doesn't matter who they are.

'I have to help him,' I shout to Harry, already trying to get to me. It doesn't help that the fire is spreading by the second.

'Sadie, don't!' he shouts back. 'He's not worth it.'

I ignore him. He might be able to watch someone die, but I can't. I crawl to Joaquin and try to pull the heavy plank of wood off his leg. I try with all of my strength to move it, but his shrieks of agony stop me. He's going to have to brace himself.

'This is going to hurt, okay?'

'Please!' he shrieks, desperation bleeding from his eyes. 'Please help me.'

Seeing him like this makes me realise he is still just a man. He's someone's son. Someone's husband. Chardonnay the poodle's dad.

I manage to grab it, again using all of my strength that I had no idea I even possessed and throw it off his leg. He screams in agony. I've never heard anyone scream like that before. It makes me want to giggle. Wow, I'm definitely high from this smoke.

I grab his arm and wrap it around my neck, forcing him to standing. I start to hobble towards the door when Harry appears. He came back to help me. He finally grew a conscience. We're all getting out of here alive, thank God. Although from the sound of my own wheezing I'd say we need to leave pretty sharpish.

Suddenly Joaquin pulls his arm tightly around my neck so he's now strangling me. What the fuck?

I look up dazed to see Harry looking terrified, holding his gun towards us.

'Let her go,' Harry shouts over the loud flames.

'I don't think so,' he snarls next to my ear. It's only then I realise he has a gun pressed to my head. Shit.

He's...holding me hostage? After I just tried to help this arsehole! *Unbelievable.*

'You let me out of here or the girl gets it.'

'Jesus, Harry, let him go!' I shout.

Harry doesn't even flinch. At this moment in time I'm not sure what is right. Does he love me or does he not really give a shit about me? He might just take the shot and blow my head to smithereens by accident. Who cares if a criminal survives? I want to live! And either way if he keeps deliberating I'm going to die from suffocation.

'I have the shot!' he shouts back, not taking his attention away from Joaquin.

What the fuck? He is! He's going to try, the heartless fuck!

'But will I have shot her first?' Joaquin says. I hear the cruel smile in his voice.

'For God's sakes, Harry. Put it down. I don't want to die,' I plead. I don't care about being brave right now. I just want to live.

A bang rings out so loud it feels like my head is exploding. I scrunch my eyes shut, the most intense fear I've ever felt shooting through my veins, freezing me completely in place.

Am I dead?

I dare to open one eye first, then the other to find I'm on the floor. My knees burn. I feel my head and I can't feel anything wet. Haven't I been shot in the head?

Harry's suddenly at my side, checking me all over. I look up to him, completely dazed.

'Am I dead?' I ask stupidly.

He looks at me with raised eyebrows. 'No. He is.' He points behind me.

Joaquin is on the floor, his head a bloody mess. Ugh. That's going to haunt my nightmares.

'We need to get out of here,' he shouts, coughing and beginning to drag me outside. God knows I can't walk right now. I'm still in shock.

The fresh air burns my lungs. I inhale it far too quickly, causing me to cough even harder. Harry keeps dragging me until we're a safe distance away from the burning building.

'You risked the shot?' I ask in disbelief after nearly coughing up a lung. 'You could have shot me, you bloody idiot!' I hit him in the chest.

He has the audacity to chuckle. I mean, really. Is this a time for chuckling?

'That was never going to happen, babe. I'm the best shot around.'

'I'm not your babe!' I scream, shoving him in the chest. But I'm so weak he doesn't even move.

I cannot believe him.

He stands behind me and holds my hair back while I continue coughing so hard I think I might cough up my stomach.

'Anyway, we need to come up with a story.'

'Oh, God, give me a bloody chance. I'm still recovering from my near death experience!'

He grabs hold of my arm, turning me to face him. 'No, Sadie, you don't understand. Backup is on their way. You have to come up with a story as to why you're here. Say he kidnapped you or something.' He seems desperate, his eyes imploring me.

I look back into his scared eyes. Scared due to wanting to protect me. I look over at the girls. They're all fine, still out of breath from the drama and fussing over Gabriel. I need to come up with something. I *cannot* let them get into trouble for this. This was all my stupid idea.

And poor Harry. I look back into his trusting blue eyes. He's willing to put his job on the line and lie for me. I don't deserve that. None of them deserve any of this.

'No, Harry,' I say sadly. 'I'm handing myself in.'

His face drops, his eyebrows narrowing down on me. 'You can't be serious,' he barks, furious.

'I am,' I nod, touching his arm to try to reassure him.

Don't ask me why, but even after everything he's done I still want to placate him.

He shrugs me off. 'You don't fucking realise what you're saying.' He takes my shoulders and shakes me slightly. 'You'll go to prison, Sadie. Fucking *prison*. We're not messing around here.'

It's funny, but I don't feel scared. Maybe it's the smoke. Maybe it's a concussion.

'I know what I have to do.'

Police and fire fighters start swooping in, beginning to tackle the blaze.

He grabs my face in his hands and looks intensely into my eyes, desperation pouring from them.

'I can't lose you.' He seems genuinely distraught.

My chest aches to think of me hurting him. I don't want to lose him either. When you take away all of the bullshit I'm pretty sure I love him. Of course I don't want to go to prison, but I can't let him do this for me. I need to be punished for what I've done. I can't risk the girls getting in any trouble for this and I can't risk him losing his job. I love him too much to have him lose everything.

But I know he won't let me do this. Which means I have to hurt him. It's the only way. I take a deep breath and tell myself it's for the best.

'I don't want to lose you either, but we can never be together. We're from different worlds.'

'That's bullshit,' he shouts loudly, so loud it makes me jump. 'You're just coming up with excuses.'

'Mckenzie,' one of his colleagues says to him, grabbing both of our attentions. 'What happened here?'

He opens his mouth to talk. I know it's to lie. I can't let him.

'I'm a drug dealer,' I blurt out. 'This is all of my fault. Please arrest me.' I place my hands out in front of me.

Their mouths drop open. Harry shakes his head, anger radiating off him. He backs away slowly from both of us.

'Harry...' It tears my heart up inside to hurt him like this.

'Don't,' he snaps, shaking his head as he looks away, hurt pouring from his face. He turns and walks away from me while the officer cuffs me and reads me my rights.

Knowing this might be the last time I ever see him slices my heart in two. Not even the thought of saving my girls is enough to make me feel better. Tears well up in my eyes. I want to run to him and collapse into his arms. I want to ask him to hold me, tell me everything is going to be okay and stroke my hair. But this is the real world. Things don't happen like that in my world.

Chapter 31

<u>Six Months Later - Friday 30th April</u>

So, prison is not so bad. I thought it would be *way* worse than this. I had my whole crazy act down. The minute I arrived I started walking with a limp, blinking rapidly, shouting out at nothing to shut up and threatening people with forks for no good reason. It turns out I didn't need to.

On my second day here, I was told the woman that basically runs this place, a prisoner that's been here for years, wanted to see me. I thought I was about to get shanked. I got the shock of my life when my mum smiled back at me. She'd aged terribly, her skin grey and her bones protruding, but that didn't stop everyone in here from being scared of her. We had a talk, and although I explained that I could never believe a word out of her mouth again and had no interest in any kind of relationship with her, she promised my safety. And for once she stayed true to her word.

I found a few old friends in here too. It's sad that a lot of the girls from the streets ended up here, but hey, who am I to judge? I'm here too. Carly, Tasmin and Rebecca. They were new to the streets once, and Samuel and I took them under our wing. We tried to help them, tried to keep them away from trouble. Only it didn't work for them. Welshie became Carly's pimp. She's in for soliciting. Tasmin got mixed up in drugs and ended up selling them for her dealer to try and pay back a debt. Rebecca was caught robbing a bank with her boyfriend.

Thankfully they remembered me. They may have changed in the years since I've seen them, their faces gaunt, their eyes desperate, but deep down they're still the same girls I met once. They took me under their wing and have protected me. Sometimes when we're all giggling together I can almost forget it's not a normal sleepover, until someone shouts to get back to our cells for lights out.

So aside from the crap food, it's actually alright. Yeah, I have way too much time on my hands to think about everything, but I quickly got into a routine. I was lucky to get the sentence I did. They took into account my mitigating circumstances and decided to give me three years, with a two year suspended sentence. With good behaviour I should be out of here in a few weeks! I can't wait!

Harry's written to me every week since I got here asking for a visitors pass. I haven't replied to any of them. It's better this way. He needs to move on and go get himself a normal bird. Someone without a criminal record. It's not like I have much of a future. If I couldn't get a job before I sure as hell won't be getting one now.

My only solace is that Samuel has stuck by me throughout all of this. He visits me every two weeks and fills me in on all of the gossip. Lexi visits with him occasionally. Mags and Steph write. I've told them I don't want them to visit. Mags is in remission and I couldn't risk her picking up some kind of prison plague, and Steph's got Ruby. Prison is no place for a baby.

Steph is now a childminder, meaning she can stay at home and look after Ruby. Mags is now a foster mother to two teenage girls. It's the perfect job for someone like her. She gets paid to do what she does best; look after and love people. I only wish I'd been lucky enough to get a foster mum like her. God knows where I would have been by now. But then I would have never met Samuel. For all of my mistakes I can't regret anything. It's all made me who I am today and despite being in prison I'm strangely proud of myself. I stood up and took responsibility for what I did. I took the flack for my girls. I did the right thing. I might be in prison and I might be ignoring the man I'm pretty sure I'm in love with, but I'm doing it for the right reason.

'Hey, Sadie, it's visiting time,' Tasmin reminds me with a smile.

I grin back. I can't wait to see Samuel today. With only a month until my release the idea of coming home is suddenly becoming real. I haven't wanted to think about home for a long time. Not that I even really have a room to sleep in. Lexi's renting my old room from Samuel to help him pay the mortgage. But I don't care. He's already said I can share his bed until we figure something out. It will still be like heaven compared to these hard beds.

Lexi's temping at the moment, still not sure what she wants to do with her life. Apart from being with Gabriel. That's right, they're still together. Apparently he's taken to running Joaquin's legitimate business. *Apparently.* But she seems happy.

I make my way down to the visiting room, waving to girls I know on the way. Rebecca told everyone I killed someone so everyone's pretty friendly. They all think I'm a psychopath.

I walk into the room smiling, but stop when I notice someone sat next to Samuel. Is that...Oliver James? Samuel's famous chef boss? Am I hallucinating? Have I lost it in here? Maybe I'm in a psych ward right now being treated after I stabbed someone with a fork in the eye. Perhaps this whole thing is a hallucination. I pinch myself but flinch from the pain. It's real.

I walk over, shyly assessing the situation. Samuel is smiling widely, unnaturally. His eyes are trying to communicate with me to play nice. Not that I wouldn't. Oliver James looks impassive. What the hell is he doing here? He shouldn't be seen anywhere near a prison. Then it dawns on me, he's here to tell me off. I know he got some negative publicity after I went inside; his top chef living with a drug dealer. But that was ages ago. Surely he's over it now?

'Hi,' I say timidly, slumping into my seat. I look down at the table, ashamed. I'd never considered he want to have a go.

'Sadie, good to see you,' he says cheerfully.

I look up, completely perplexed. He's practically beaming at me. I look to Samuel and he's smiling too. What the hell is going on here?

'Err...you too,' I croak. I clear my throat, trying to appear brave. 'So...what are you doing here?'

He looks to Samuel and smiles, as if they're sharing a secret. 'I'm here with good news.'

Oh God, has he won another cooking award or something? Why on earth would he come in here to just rub that in my face? It's very rude and insensitive of him.

'Oh...right?'

'Samuel tells me you're out in a month and I have a proposition for you.'

Proposition? What the hell could he mean? Shit, does he want me to have one wild night with him in order to make it up to him? He's always seemed like a really nice guy, but maybe it's just all a front.

'Don't look so worried,' he laughs. 'Do you remember last year's summer barbecue?'

I think back. Oh yeah, that was the barbecue he held in a large field with free champagne. I was so drunk I ended up trying to walk home, getting lost and vomiting on a cow which then kicked me in the leg. It wasn't my best moment.

I cringe. 'If I'm honest...not really. I was pretty drunk.'

He chuckles. 'I know and it was great.'

How on earth is me getting shit faced great? Is this guy mental?

'Sadie, not many people tell me the truth anymore. I'm surrounded by yes people and people that just want to advance my career or theirs. That night, although you were very drunk, you told me how I should be giving back more to the community in which I grew up in.'

My stomach drops as if I just went down a rollercoaster. Oh my God. I can just imagine myself leering over him, reading him the riot act. What an imbecile.

I wring my hands together awkwardly, looking down at them. 'I'm sorry if I was rude.'

He chuckles. 'No, you were just honest. You told me about your idea.'

Huh? I literally have no recollection of even speaking to him, let alone getting some great idea.

'Idea?'

He nods. 'Yes, your idea. You...don't remember it?'

'I don't think you realise how drunk she was,' Samuel giggles. 'She vomited on a cow.'

Shut the fuck up, Samuel! I glare at him.

'Oh,' he says, trying to hide a smile. 'Well, let me remind you. You told me that I should open up a restaurant for the homeless. You told me that any food that was going to be wasted could be sent there and it could be run alongside counselling and advice so that people can find a way out.'

I said all that while I was pissed? I should drink more.

'That does sound like a good idea,' I smile. 'So you're setting this up? That will be so fantastic for so many homeless people.'

And it doesn't escape my notice that it'll give him great publicity.

'It'll also be fantastic for you. You're going to be managing it.'

My mouth drops open. Did I mishear him? 'Sorry...what?'

'That's right,' he smiles. 'I need someone who can work with both me, my restaurants and the homeless. You're the perfect person. Don't get me wrong, they'll be a lot of work involved. We've got a lot to organise before the opening.'

Oh my God. He's making me the manager. The bloody *manager!* I'm going to be able to work with the homeless. I'm going to be able to help people, not just do some soulless job. This is unbelievable!

'I...I don't know what to say,' I mumble, my skin breaking out in goose pimples. 'I mean, are you sure you want me? I mean, look at me right now.'

He smiles confidently. 'Just say yes.'

'YES!'

Chapter 32

Saturday 29th May

So a month later I'm opening up The Street Cafe. All of the local press have come along to support us, although after talking to them I'm sure the headlines will read something like 'Ex Offender Opens Homeless Cafe.' But I really don't care. The main thing is that people are going to hear of it. We're encouraging members of the public to donate their time by volunteering. Hopefully some will help out. Not that we haven't got it covered.

Lexi is my assistant manager and so far has been truly amazing. I watch her interacting with some guys from the street, laughing and joking. That's what the main thing is; I want the homeless to feel comfortable here.

Then I look at Carly serving tea. People like me and Carly have been there. We've felt that intense loneliness. Sometimes all it takes is for someone to understand and listen.

As well as serving hot drinks and leftover cakes, pastries, danishes and basically anything else from Oliver's restaurant, we're also offering some services. A lady from The Citizen Advice Bureau will be here twice a week so that people can ask questions. We've also got leaflets advising people on how they can get onto the council housing list, find their nearest shelter, help beat addiction, get out of bad relationships and keep as warm as possible on the street. I've studied them and asked every question available so I feel like I can speak to people about them. Sometimes people have not learned to read properly.

But this is only the beginning. I have ideas that we can roll out as time goes on like packed lunches for them. That way we can ensure that they have a lunch or dinner for later in the day. Plus I've suggested to Oliver the idea of opening up another shelter locally or supporting Jenny, who runs the current one with extension plans. There's just not enough room for everyone.

I'm going to be busy for the next couple of months. *Really* busy. Hell, the next year if Oliver was honest about me setting up other cafe's like this around the country. It's not the best timing for me, but I'm finally doing something I believe in. I'm helping people so that they don't make the same mistakes that I did. Even if I only save one person then it'll all be worth it.

I'm just cleaning behind the counter when I feel someone behind me.

'Hi stranger.' I know it's him before I've even turned around. I gulp down the anxiety before turning.

He looks incredible, probably all the more for not having seen him in months. He's wearing a grey V-neck t-shirt with dark denim jeans. His hair is slightly longer than before. Memories of me running my fingers through it flash through my mind. Apart from his hair he's the same delicious guy I fell in love with.

How the hell is he here after how I've treated him? His face is stoic. Could he be here just to shout at me? He'd have every right. It's at times like this that I'm glad Oliver James insisted on such a high counter. He was keen for us to have as much security available to us as possible.

'Err...h-hi,' I stammer. Even my tongue is trembling with nerves.

Where's the confident woman who a minute ago was getting ready to save the homeless? It seems one quick look at Harry and I'm a quivering wreck. What a *girl*.

He puts his hands into the pockets of his jeans and starts rocking slowly onto his heels.

'So...I don't want to sound like the Notebook, but...I wrote you.' A small smile plays on his lips.

I can't hide my own smile. He's the same Harry. I can't believe how happy I feel just being in his presence.

'I know,' I nod, smiling apologetically. 'I figured I was doing you a favour. You deserve better than me, Harry.'

He nods. 'I agree.'

'Huh?' I'm gobsmacked. Has he seriously just come here to tell me he's better than me? What a dick head.

'But that doesn't stop me from wanting you.' His eyes burn with intensity.

Holy fucking hell. My knickers just got set on fire.

But I have to let him go. He does truly deserve better than an ex-con. Even if it does break my heart to do it. I'm not right for him. He doesn't want or need to take on my baggage.

'Not everything we want is what we really need,' I say with a sad smile.

He steps into my personal space and his scent takes over me, making me light-headed from want. I already feel stupidly giddy.

'Why don't you just shut up and kiss me?' he says, his voice deep and husky.

My breathing accelerates and I can feel my chest rising and falling ridiculously. He leans in and places his lips on mine. I pull away.

'Harry, listen...'

'No, you listen,' he snaps. 'Stop this *I'm better than you* shit and just be with me.'

'But I'm a criminal. You're a policeman. Surely it would ruin your career even being associated with me, let alone your girlfriend.'

'I don't give a fuck. You've served your time. And anyway, I'm not asking you to be my girlfriend.'

'Oh,' I gasp. Is he seriously here to ask for a quick shag? What an absolute bastard.

'I'm asking you to be my wife.'

The room starts spinning. His what now? Did he seriously just say that?

'You want...what? I think I misheard you.'

'You didn't,' he smiles. 'I'd be on one knee right now, but I really don't want to humiliate myself if you're going to say no.'

Can this seriously be happening? He wants me to be his wife? Wouldn't he be ashamed of me?

'I thought you were wrong all those months ago when you basically called me a cave man who wanted a barefoot and pregnant wife. But with you you're spot on. You make me into an over-protective cave man who wants to bang you over the head and carry you back to my cave. Especially since you're so fucking stubborn.'

Jesus. I'm still reeling.

'I've tried living without you, Sadie. I can't do it and I refuse to do it when I know you love me too.'

Has he even said he loved me before? I don't know, but if I'm honest I already knew deep down.

'But, Harry...even if I want to, I'm not wife material. But...you say you want kids? If I'm as shit as my mum the kid stands no chance.'

'I'm not saying we have kids straight away. But we will,' he smiles confidently. 'Because when two people love each other as much as us it's only natural for us to want to create a little person together.'

I look down at my swollen belly hidden by the counter. With Harry by my side suddenly the idea isn't as terrifying.

'And as for wife material? There's no job description. You're already everything I want in a person and that's enough for me. Even if you don't say yes now I'm not giving up on us. You're stuck with me I'm afraid.'

I can't help but beam from ear to ear. He places his hands on my face as he looks down at me with nothing but unconditional love. It's the first time I've ever truly seen it from a person.

'You're it for me, babe.'

'Okay,' I say, a big fat tear trickling down my face.

He pulls back in confusion. 'Huh? Do you mean...'

'Yep,' I interrupt. 'I'll marry you, but only if you accept two things.' He nods. 'First, realise that my first priority is getting this cafe up and running successfully. This is really important to me.'

He smiles encouragingly.

'And the second...'

Hmm, how do I broach the whole pregnant with his baby thing? Maybe I should have told him straight away, but the selfish part of me wanted to know if he really wanted me, not just the idea of a family.

I take a deep breath and go to the hatch. I unlock it and quickly, well as quickly as an inflated penguin can go, walk towards him.

At first it's like he doesn't notice, he so busy staring into my eyes. Slowly, painfully slowly, his gaze travels down my body. I see the realisation in his eyes as his mouth pops open.

I need to say something. *Anything* to fill this awkward silence.

'Yes, it's yours. I'm seven months, and if you want to take that all back I completely understand. I'll still let you see him. I'd never be unfair like that. I *was* going to tell you...eventually.'

Maybe when he turned twenty one.

He nods but doesn't say anything. He just smiles the brightest smile I've ever seen in my life before leaning down and kissing me with so much love and hunger that my legs almost collapse from under me.

'So, soon to be Mrs. Mckenzie...we're having a son?'

He still wants me. The relief and safety I feel in that moment is enough to make me float. Well, it would if I didn't weight the same as a hippo right now.

'Yep,' I grin.

He pulls me into a bear hug and I realise it's all I've ever wanted. To be held by someone who loves me unconditionally. With him beside me I'll never be a bad mother.

I guess I never thought girls like me got their happy ever after. Turns out I was wrong.

THE END

Acknowledgements

Firstly a massive thank you for buying my book – you keep my toddler in shoes! Thanks to all of my supporters; you guys have helped my dreams come true. Still feel like I'm going to wake up any moment!

Thanks to my family and friends for putting up with me. It can't be easy having a sleep deprived, day dreaming nutcase around. Special smoochy kisses to my husband Simon who makes me endless cups of tea and cooks continuous dinners so I can keep typing into the early hours. Also my two cheerleaders Mum and Mad; what would I do without your unconditional love and belief in me?!

Big hugs to my friends Clare Pinkstone, Julie Wills and Nikki Chamberlain who are my trusted ladies to read the first draft and tell me all of the holes and inconsistencies in the plot. Without you nothing would make sense!

Thanks to my Dad for answering all of my police/prison questions. You being an ex-copper came in very handy!

Major shout out to all of the many blogs that have helped spread the word about me. There are SO many, but a few I feel I'd like to mention are Loving the Books, Two Ordinary Girls & their Books, A Reader's Review…my God, there's so many! If you're not mentioned please don't feel I don't love you any less. Without each and every one of you taking time out from your day to help spread the word of us Indie authors, we'd be nowhere!

Thanks to KMS Freelance Editing and finally all of my new author friends. Thanks for accepting me into the family ☺